Inked Destiny

JORY STRONG

HEAT | NEW YORK

THE BERKLEY PUBLISHING GROUP
Published by the Penguin Group
Penguin Group (USA) Inc.
375 Hudson Street, New York, New York 10014, USA

USA I Canada I UK I Ireland I Australia I New Zealand I India I South Africa I China

Penguin Books Ltd., Registered Offices: 80 Strand, London WC2R 0RL, England
For more information about the Penguin Group, visit penguin.com.

This book is an original publication of The Berkley Publishing Group.

HEAT and the HEAT design are trademarks of Penguin Group (USA) Inc.

Library of Congress Cataloging-in-Publication Data

Strong, Jory.
Inked Destiny / Jory Strong. — Heat trade paperback edition.
pages cm
ISBN 978-0-425-25361-8
1. Elves—Fiction. 2. Women tattoo artists—Fiction. 3. Psychic ability—Fiction.
4. Fantasy fiction. 5. Erotic fiction. I. Title.
PS3619.T777I49 2013
813'.6—dc23
2012046050

PUBLISHING HISTORY
Berkley trade paperback edition / July 2013

PRINTED IN THE UNITED STATES OF AMERICA

10 9 8 7 6 5 4 3 2 1

Cover art direction by Rita Frangie.
Cover design by Sarah Oberrender.
Cover photograph by Tony Mauro.
Text design by Tiffany Estreicher.

For my cousin, Jamie. May you find a Quinn of your own.
And for my cousin, Venesa, who is also a fan. Enjoy!

One

Etaín stood naked in the shower, hot water and the heat of the men on either side of her eradicating most of the chill that lingered following her rescue from the Harlequin Rapist. "I could get used to this," she said, eyes closed to savor the sensation of masculine hands gliding over slick flesh.

The truth of their feelings was a hum against her senses. They might have ensnared her equally but their call differed. With Cathal it was raw sensuality and fierce imperative, while Eamon was the attraction of like to like.

Had she once truly believed she was okay with casual sex and lack of permanence? Before Cathal and Eamon had come into her life, true intimacy had been impossible.

Skin didn't lie to her. It was her gift, her curse, to be able to touch the eyes inked into her palms to skin and not only see another's memories, but take them. She shivered, because now that gift was changing and her control of it failing.

Cathal and Eamon were safe where others weren't. She shivered again, harder, at thinking about how close she'd come to having to use her gift on the Harlequin Rapist to save herself.

"It's over," Eamon murmured, his hard cock pressed to her ass and lower back while Cathal's was a heated announcement of need against her belly.

"Thanks to the two of you."

If not for the tattoos—infused with Eamon's magic—that she'd put on Cathal's arms, creating a bond that allowed them to find her, even now her existence would be marked by cycles of torture and rape.

"Parker won't be able to put off taking a report." They were lucky no one of superior rank had been among the first responders. As an FBI taskforce member, her brother's permission to leave had allowed them to escape.

"We'll find a safe truth when the time comes," Eamon said.

She opened her eyes, taking in Cathal's good looks, short dark hair and the ever-present stubble that came with being Black Irish. Opposite to Eamon's long blond hair and smooth chest.

Until they'd come into her life, sex had been a safety valve, a way to release some hidden buildup of pressure from too much touch, too many bodies inked. And now . . .

It was so much more. Looking back, she was torn between amusement, for thinking it would be easy to enjoy them and walk away afterward, and fear when it came to what the future held.

Because of Cathal she'd been made an accessory to four murders. There would be a fifth when his father and his uncle caught up with the last boy who'd been involved in the drugging and rape of two sixteen-year-old girls. This wasn't behind them. Not yet. Maybe not ever.

She slid her hands down Cathal's naked back, pressed kisses along his throat. His eyes remained closed and she knew the cause. He didn't want to see Eamon on the other side of her.

I'm not a man to share when I'm serious about a woman.

Then don't get serious about me.

She'd warned him, but still a fist formed around her heart, squeezing at the threat he might come to regret his involvement with her, that in the end, he might walk away, unable to handle sharing her.

Her hand brushed over his hip on its way to curl around his hardened length. "I want you. I want you both. Let's go to bed."

They left the shower.

Cathal took the towel from her, sliding it over her body, lingering over breasts capped with dark pink nipples. Within days of meeting her she'd become the beat of his heart, the relentless, molten pour of lust pumped directly into his bloodstream so that time away from her had become the crawl of eons.

Her lips curved with knowing. "Like what you see?" she asked, echoing the question he'd issued when first joining her in the shower.

"Definitely." He'd like it even more when sight was accompanied by taste and scent and the touch of skin to skin.

A murmured command from Eamon and a warm, unnatural breeze swirled to life around them, smelling of tropical winds, drying shower-wet hair, though raising chill bumps on Cathal's flesh. Magic again. Eamon's again. So casually and easily summoned it made Cathal's heart race with something other than need for Etaín, with a hard-wired fear accompanied by a sense of foreboding.

"Show-off," he said, hearing the growl beneath the joking tone he'd tried for.

Eamon's smile was the white flash of shark's teeth, his amusement a deadly thing. "Feeling threatened?"

Cathal bared his teeth in response, a reaction he'd been fighting from the first instant Eamon had made his interest in Etaín known.

"Boys, boys," Etaín said, the label turning the tide of hostility and unintentionally uniting them in common purpose.

"Is that how you think of us?" Eamon asked, hands going around to cup breasts capped with nipples that hardened instantly, the sight of them sending a throbbing pulse through Cathal's cock. "As boys and not men?"

Her laugh was a hot, fisted squeeze around Cathal's dick. "Less flattering to call you junkyard dogs fighting over a hunk of meat, even if you're gorgeous enough to be paraded around a show ring."

Eamon's thumbs brushed across her nipples, causing a hitch in her breath, and her back to arch in an offering Cathal could no more resist than had it been a summons. The towel in his hands fell to the floor.

They'd shared her once before. On that night, too, Eamon had stood behind her, hands on her bare breasts. Daring him to join the two of them, inviting him, and he'd crossed the distance like a man drunk on lust, a man compelled . . .

By magic. He sensed it now, but it didn't fog his head this time any more than being alone with a naked Etaín did.

Cathal bent, capturing a nipple between his lips and laving it with his tongue. Satisfaction was a hot surge through his cock at her soft moan of pleasure, at the way her hands speared into his hair, holding him against her breast as she pulled away from Eamon in an effort to give herself more fully to him.

It made him harder, hungrier, touching on primal, competitive instincts she'd no doubt claim reached back to the caveman days when strength and prowess and victory determined who fathered the next generation. He wanted it all with her. He'd agreed to come here, tonight, and he wouldn't lie to himself—Eamon's presence didn't diminish the desire. But tomorrow was another day.

It'd grate on his nerves, those nights she spent with Eamon, but he'd welcome those he had alone with her. And he intended to have them.

Etaín could feel the hum of Cathal's resistance even as she felt the heat of his lust joined to hers. She could know his exact thoughts if she desired it.

Don't think, just feel, she wanted to tell him. *This can work. I need it to work.*

Desire burned her from the inside out, a hunger for both men that transcended the physical. She moaned as pleasure moved through her, a coiling turbulent wave going from breasts to clit.

Cathal's sucks, the pull of his mouth on her nipple, were echoed by the tug and twist and tightening of Eamon's fingers on the other areola as he kissed upward along her neck, pausing to nuzzle her earlobe.

More. Everything. That's what she wanted. What she craved.

She reached backward and grasped the long strands of Eamon's hair as Cathal kissed downward, his tongue tracing the rim of her belly button, dipping in then moving lower. If she had more will-power when it came to him, she would protest, telling him to wait until they were stretched out on the bed. Instead she parted her thighs in invitation, whispered *yes* the instant his lips captured her clit.

His hands settled against her hips, holding her firmly against Eamon, preventing movement and making her prisoner to sensation. Not just the coil of her own desire or the scorching heat of it, but theirs as well.

She wanted to watch Cathal. She wanted to eat him with her eyes, devour him, but with the first stroke and swirl of his tongue to her clit, he made her helpless. The truth was, she'd been unable to resist the allure of either man though she'd known both would bring trouble.

On a moan she surrendered, closing her eyes and giving herself over to their care. Eamon's hands were like molten fire on her breasts, but then fire was one of the elements he was most strongly linked to, *the essence of who I am*, he'd told her as they looked into a mirror taking up a great expanse of wall, the spells woven into it allowing a glimpse into things hidden by skin and physical form.

She'd seen and experienced more evidence of magic, but this, being alive, being with them both at the same time, was the purest of magic, the most addicting of it, better than anything.

Pleasure whipped through her, turning her breath into fast, shallow pants. Her blood pooled between her thighs, and her heartbeat thundered there as if it lived in swollen, wet folds and engorged clit.

She strained, trying to drive her clit deeper into Cathal's mouth, begging him to suck harder as orgasm shimmered just out of reach. Now! The scream built inside her only to have him abandon her clit.

He slid his tongue through puffy cunt lips and wet channel, teasing her with shallow thrusts so her opening clenched and un-clenched. She struggled against implacable male hands, held stationary by firm grips.

Eamon's tongue mimicked Cathal's, fucking into her ear canal, hot torment to an area that had turned into an erogenous zone since meeting him. Their twin assault while imprisoning her was very nearly a punishment, sensual torment for coming so close to dying and leaving them behind to wonder at what she suffered before breath ceased and she went still and cold.

She tried to cant her hips, her inner thighs wet with arousal instead of water. "Do it," she ordered Cathal, channel rippling, trying to grasp and hold his tongue, to pull it deeper into her body and make it a substitute for the thick, hardened cock that rose to press against his belly while Eamon's felt like satin against her buttocks and back.

Eamon's husky laugh was all that came of her command, followed by a silky threat. "We're not the ones at your mercy this time, Etaín. You're at ours."

They proved it to her, holding her on the edge of release as she writhed and strained, the vines tattooed on her arms like live things absorbing the lust and heightening it to the point where her heart beat too fast, burned like a small sun trapped in her chest and about to explode. And then it did, consciousness disappearing in a sundering pulse of ecstasy, pleasure sweeping outward and leaving deep, infinite peace.

Magic slammed into Eamon with Etaín's surrender to pleasure. He nearly came, his cock pressed hard and hot to her flesh, his testicles swollen, tight sacks pulled upward in near agony.

Victory and satisfaction surged through him, along with a sense of camaraderie as Cathal rose from his crouch, features flushed but eyes filled with the same emotions. She was theirs. Safe and whole because of them. Wordlessly Eamon lifted Etaín into his arms, Cathal reaching the bed first, jerking luxurious sheet and comforter downward.

Etaín's eyelashes fluttered as Eamon lay her on the bed, her lids opening as he stretched out on his side next to her, Cathal doing the same opposite of him.

Her dark, dark eyes were pools of sultry seduction, languid still from orgasm, though sparks of amusement shimmered like the flash of silvery minnows in ocean shallows. "Well, that was a first for me. Not that either of you need a boost to your egos when it comes to sex."

She took possession of hardened cocks, Cathal moaning, breath seizing in a quick, sharp inhalation where Eamon refused to cede control. "Take him while I watch," he said, issuing a command, his hand replacing hers, fingers wrapped tightly around his cock when she obeyed, releasing him to roll into Cathal, onto him as Cathal went willingly to his back.

Like a pagan goddess rising from the sea of deep blue sheets, and created of flame, she straddled Cathal. The sun streaming through the window caressed her, the gold of her aura almost that of a pure Elf, the sheen of magic reminding Eamon of water lapping a pristine shore as he wanted to lap her, to probe her wet core with his tongue and taste her essence.

From the very first, Eamon found the sight of Etaín with Cathal arousing. It was more so now as he watched her guide Cathal's cock to her opening, teasing him by allowing him to experience the satin heat of her channel only inches at a time.

Cathal's hands palmed her breasts, fingers clamped on nipples as intoxicating as the finest of wines. His hips lifted from the mattress in hard jabs meant to press him deeper into her body, his cock glistening, darkened in his need for Etaín.

"Tease," Cathal panted, the growl in his voice a warning he wouldn't let her torment him for long.

"And you're not? The two of you aren't?" she said, including Eamon with the slight turn of her head. Her gaze swept over him, the liquid hunger her expression delivered making his hand tighten in a near-painful fist on his shaft.

Dark satisfaction settled in her eyes. In centuries of being alive, he'd never ceded as much to any woman as he had to this one in just days.

Her attention returned to Cathal, her body lifting and lowering, drawing out the pleasure until finally Cathal put her beneath him. He pounded into her, hands held to the mattress, his mouth on hers, swallowing her moans and finally her cry of release before pistoning furiously, muscles cording, his breathing ragged and rough as he yielded to ecstasy.

Eamon had just enough control to allow Cathal to relinquish Etaín by rolling to the side. Cathal's features were flushed, his eyelids at half-mast. His expression held possessiveness as well as lingering jealousy, yet he didn't look away as Eamon covered Etaín's body with his.

A thrust took him home, into a storm of sensation. Magic and woman. A welcome echoed by arms around him and feminine hands on his back. *His*, though he could share her with Cathal.

Desperation seized him, at how close he'd come to losing her to death. His mouth fused to hers, tongues battling, twining, tangling in a wild, hungry joining that had only one goal, only one end. Ecstasy came with the ripple of her sheath, with her surrender, then his in a shuddering, jagged rush of semen.

But pleasure shattered with the alien grasping of his power. The pull of it through him and into her was like a fiery tornado, a hungry wrenching.

He reacted instinctively, defensively, uttering a knock-out spell as he jerked away from her. Rolling from the bed entirely rather than risk continued contact.

The shock and suddenness of what had happened left him shaken. Only slowly did calm return. But it was calm possessed of wariness. The *seidic* bound their mates to them, were said to *possess* them, the boundaries stripped away. *Mind thief. Gift thief.* They were epithets applied to the *seidic*.

Here, in his home, untrained and only barely aware of her own power while remaining completely ignorant of what she was, what she would be, she was helpless against his will made manifest or she wouldn't have succumbed so quickly to the spell. But she wouldn't remain so for much longer. Intimacy had lowered his guard. He wouldn't give up the first, but needed to shore up the second.

Cathal lay insensate next to her, his proximity making him a victim to a spell aimed but not limited to a specific person. Just as well, Eamon thought, rubbing his chest where his heart still pounded, a hammer beat of fear, not only of her, but *for* her.

She was changeling, not yet able to control magic and gift. And he was lord, whose duty it would be to kill her if she couldn't.

"Sleep," he said, expanding the defensive action in the lilting tones of a language born in another realm, one created to harness magic and feed it into spells either written or spoken.

It would hold them, at least for a little while, and when they woke, it would be to a new reality. The time for ignorance had passed.

He crossed to the dresser, calling a fine mist to wash away the scent of sex, and then air warmed by fire to dry his skin before opening a sigil carved box and retrieving a small silver dagger. Returning to the bed, he cut a length of Etaín's hair where its loss wouldn't be noticed.

He didn't intend for her to leave the estate, but from the very beginning she'd managed to evade his vision of what the future held, and she still had far too many dangerous ties to the human world. His gaze dropped to the exposed eye on one of her palms, a weapon now to be wielded against Elf or human if she felt threatened.

"You may come to hate me, for a time, because of it. But I will do what I must to keep you safe, from others as well as yourself."

Two

⌾∼⚬∼⌾

Etaín burned but there was no escaping the heat. It consumed her, traveling through the ink she wore, radiating inward like fire turned against itself, flame reaching into her very core.

She struggled against it but there was no respite until finally she dreamed, aware she was dreaming. *Magic* she thought and heard its voice say *yesss*, sibilant like a snake's hiss as coils encased her, pulling her downward into an ocean of blackness where images from the last week, both real and imagined, played across the screen of her mind.

That first glimpse of Cathal as he stood outside Stylin' Ink.

Passing through the wards at Aesirs. Recognizing the symbols carved into the doorway without understanding their meaning.

Eamon's approach, the tattoos on her forearms writhing and rippling as if soaking in his presence, raging fire and stormy seas, the call of like to like.

A hospital room with her brother Parker and his partner Trent at her back. Stealing memories from a victim of the Harlequin Rapist.

Then stealing additional memories, this time from Cathal's cousin Brianna.

Cathal's father and uncle, envisioned, imagined as they delivered vengeance, the deadly justice of men whose code and livelihood were bordered by violence—aiming, firing, the recoil from their weapons pulsing through Etaín like a shockwave, plummeting her stomach as the all-too-real repercussions of their actions made her chest tighten.

The police arriving at her apartment and taking her to the floor. Cuffing her. Incarcerating her in a windowless interrogation room. Photographs of four murdered boys. The barriers falling, sending her into the loop of Brianna's relived memories. The pain slashing, clawing through her heart as the suspicion that Cathal's campaign of seduction had been about getting her to use her gift firmed, and then was confirmed with the touch of her palms to his skin.

Images fast-forwarded to those moments of peace and connection after her reconciliation with Cathal. A day of lovemaking interspersed with working ink into his arms.

I ssseee, the voice said, coils tightening mercilessly as she fought to wake, panicked in a blackness that was the absence of color, the roar in her head getting louder and louder as fire returned, burning in her chest, hotter and hotter, pressure building, building until reality became a hundred thin highways writ in gold.

Slowly they winked out, all but one of them. Then it too faded, becoming a dream where she sat in a moving car.

Through the window she recognized an Oakland street she'd driven the Harley down only days ago. She turned, heartbeat ratcheting up when she saw her companions wearing ski masks, then felt the same against her face and glanced down to find black gloves on her hands.

The coiled constriction was no longer present. She renewed her struggles, trying to surface from what she knew was the beginning of a nightmare, but against the backs of her eyelids she could see sigils writ in red twined with blue and understood they were Eamon's, a magical command like a wave holding her beneath it, making escape impossible.

The bar where the Curs hung out came into sight. She counted seven motorcycles and feared what would come next in the dream, this splintered reality, the aftereffects of the last couple of days when the barriers she'd erected against all the memories she'd stolen from those who'd survived horrendous, brutal crimes, had begun tumbling down.

Days ago she'd come to this bar in an effort to help the police identify the Harlequin Rapist. She'd been hunting . . . and in turn was being hunted.

For an instant the interior of the car blurred, becoming the metal cell of a shipping container filled with terror. Her own. That of other victims of rape and torture.

She shivered and whimpered, once again trying to escape the dream, once again failing. This time looking down to find a gun in her hand, made longer and more terrifying by the silencer attached to it.

The car stopped a few feet away from where she'd parked the Harley when she went there to talk to Anton, a few feet from where she and Eamon had fought a little while later.

She was first out of the car. Her companions followed, four others, all of them moving with purpose toward the bar.

Lifting the gun, she waved the barrel in a silent order. Two of the four peeled away, hurrying down the sides of the building toward the back.

She and the remaining two took up positions on either side of the front door. A moment later the phone in her back pocket vibrated.

She gave a thumbs-up, going in first.

Aiming.

Firing.

Curs. Their women. Their hangers-on. The trigger pulls fast, the weight of a second gun there at the center of her back, jammed beneath the waistband of jeans.

The club wannabe who'd tried to claim her when she went to

see Anton fell from a bullet she fired. Movement, and she locked onto the guy who'd racked the pool balls when she and Anton played.

He went down, somebody else's bullet adding to the carnage. Everywhere there were bodies. Most were still but a few moved, bleeding and crying, though there was only silence in her head as another bullet ensured their deaths.

She took care of one section of the room as her companions handled others. Swapped out guns when she'd emptied the weapon she came in with, everything methodical, planned, as though it were a military exercise, timed so that an internal clock went off and she motioned toward the door.

The two black-masked figures went ahead of her. She followed.

Steps away from the entrance she felt the burn at her wrists, a tight circle of it that climbed upward into the vines on her arms, searing heat and an awareness that someone nearby wore her ink. Spinning, she saw a hand reaching for a gun that one of those already dead had never drawn. A face lifted, and she renewed her struggle to wake at recognizing Vontae.

No! A silent scream and there was hesitation in her nightmare self. Then the gun in her hand barked, jerked, the pull of the trigger and the horror of seeing blood coat Vontae's face in an explosion of red finally enough to free her from the dream.

She woke gasping, trembling, her heart rabbiting in her chest and her skin coated with sweat.

"Fuck, Etaín, fuck!" Cathal said, sitting up, arms like bands of steel as he pulled her onto his lap. "What the hell was that?"

"You saw?" Shock added to the frantic, trapped wildness in her chest.

"Hell yeah, I saw."

Against her back his heart pounded as furiously as hers.

"Jesus. Stolen memories? Something you got from someone your father or brother asked you to touch?"

"No. Just a bad dream." But uncertainty shivered through her because her gift was changing, turning into something that felt alien. "Where did the dream start for you?"

"Outside of a club." She felt the skittering of his heartbeat when he added, "I guess this is a side effect of the . . . magic, the connection that let me find you."

"Yes." What other explanation was there? But his physical reaction to it had her turning in his lap to—

"Don't go there," he said, covering her lips with his, silencing her concerns with the thrust of his tongue against hers.

E amon felt the early dissolution of the sleep spell like a boomerang crashing into his personal shield. He quickened his steps, entering the room where his second and third in command played backgammon.

Rhys glanced up from his study of the board. The red sun dangling from his ear caught in room light. Its brilliance was no less than the rounded, polished rubies he'd chosen as game pawns.

Across from him Liam had chosen onyx pawns, their color as black as an assassin's heart was said to be. But where Rhys couched his greeting and question in silence and the lift of eyebrows, Eamon's third did him no such favor. A wicked smile slashed across dark features. The braided mane of Liam's hair left the impression of a lion in a night lit by only the barest of moons.

"Tired already of sharing your intended?" Liam asked, laughter in his voice. "Had you but asked, I would have tendered my services." *His deadly, very fatal services.* "You know I live to make your life easier."

Eamon refrained from challenging the statement, directing his comment to Rhys. "Call Myk and Heath home, then take what humans you deem necessary and go to Etaín's apartment. Settle her lease and move her things here."

The red sun of Rhys's earring shimmered in a hint of movement, suppressed amusement or unspoken objection, it could have been either, though neither was present in his voice when he said, "You do live dangerously, Lord."

"An understatement," Liam said. "Lucky for us, we've got front rows seats to this grand courtship. I can hardly wait to witness the next act given how interesting the first one was."

Liam's comment coaxed a laugh from Rhys. He stood, the backgammon game abandoned for the moment. "I'll see to my task and hope you're not banished by the time I return."

"Hardly a likelihood considering the humans our Lord must now be concerned about thanks to his intended's choices."

"True. You might yet get to kill someone who offers a bit of a challenge."

Liam snorted. "Among humans? You come very close to insulting me." But all lightheartedness fell away when their attention landed on Eamon's ears, and the additional protections he now wore above the sigil-inscribed studs that served as focal points and magical draws.

"She grows stronger," Rhys said.

"Her gift changes." In the garden, in the sacred circle where he'd worked Etaín's hair into a charm and activated the earrings he typically didn't wear unless summoned to the queen's court or traveling into another's territory, he had come to view the grab and pull of magic through him as a positive sign that her magic now tasted his more deeply in preparation for a bond between them, though he would not leave himself unprotected again.

Eamon placed the thin twine of honey-gold hair on the table next to Liam. "I won't require this of you."

But his third was already lifting the charm and touching it to his wrist, the contact all that was necessary for the ends to seek and find each other, to lock tight, creating a magical leash between his intended and his assassin, in case she should manage to escape the estate.

A nod of thanks and Eamon returned to the bedroom, cock filling and rising again despite what had happened with the last hot rush of semen when he was buried in her depths. He hardened further at entering the room to see Etaín on Cathal's lap, at feeling her magic slide against his flesh as if freed by lovemaking, coiling around him as if checking his defenses and finding them solid. This time, the element of danger only filled his testicles and shaft with the scorching heat of desire.

He joined them on the bed, leaning in to kiss her shoulder, expecting welcome but stilling when Etaín's lips left Cathal's and her head turned to send a glare in his direction. "Don't ever do that to Cathal or me again, Eamon."

"It was necessary."

Her confusion made it plain that she had not felt the grab and pull of magic, yet given the crash of a broken spell against his shield and her greeting, she must have been aware that he'd put her, them, to sleep.

"What's going on here, Etaín?" There was an edge to Cathal's voice, hostility, and Eamon read in her expression the desire to avoid conflict though she couldn't take back what had already been said.

"Etaín's gift is changing," Eamon answered, hoping to ease the tension. "You are safe from it, but I have been careless."

Fear tightened her features. "I nearly stripped your mind." Said on a whisper and he wondered if she would attempt to distance herself from him. "That's why you did the sleep spell."

"I'm not sure what might have happened. I reacted defensively and Cathal fell to my spell as well."

"Don't do it again." Cathal's words were a low growl, his anger embodying the natural fear at losing control, and a human's reaction to the use of magic.

Eamon tilted his head, acknowledging Cathal's edict without agreeing to it. He could not offer Cathal the reassurance he sought, not when he wore Etaín's ink and now was bound by magic to her.

Etaín flinched away when Eamon reached out, fear pulsing through her. "Maybe it would be better if Cathal and I left. Safer for you."

"I believe I am safe now. The time you slept was put to good use."

He traced the rim of her ear, halting at the tip, his delicate circling strokes sending shivers of erotic pleasure through her. He followed it with the brush of his mouth against hers, the slide of his tongue between parted lips in a shallow foray hinting at a much deeper, much fuller penetration.

"There is no way to test it, not without this," he murmured, and her body clenched in anticipation then in protest with a knock on the bedroom door.

From the other side of the door, Liam said, "There is a matter requiring your attention, Lord."

Eamon's groan held the same frustration she felt. "I'll return as quickly as I can."

He left, the door closing behind him before Cathal broke his silence again. "Lord of what? Assholes?"

The truth of his emotions pierced her skin and poured into her bloodstream. Anger resurfacing, at having to share her. But that anger was trumped by fear, by the sense of a life spinning out of control.

She attempted to slide off his lap, to break the physical contact and gain some breathing room. His arms tightened, preventing it, allowing only enough movement for her to change position on his lap.

She straddled him so she could see his expression and he could see hers. "Sorry now?" she asked, encompassing all of it—magic,

Eamon, their relationship, though Cathal had sought *her* out, and by his actions, brought her to Eamon's attention in the first place.

"No." He touched his mouth to lips still glistening from the press of Eamon's mouth to them. "Never."

"Never say never."

"So you told me once before and now I'm wearing your ink. When it comes to you, I seem to be a slow learner." His tongue teased the seam of her lips and desire coiled hot and tight in her belly, spilling downward to her cunt.

"A slow learner, are you sure about that?" She opened for him, enticing him to enter her mouth so her lips could clamp down on his tongue and with a suck, gain the instant reward of feeling him harden against her stomach.

Hands speared into her hair on a moan, his fingers tangling there as her own combed through the luxurious dark mat on his chest and found a tiny male nipple. A brush of fingertips against it, the tug and twist of possession had his mouth leaving hers to say, "We'll make this work, Etaín. No regrets."

No regrets. She wanted it to always be that way, but she feared . . .

"Say it, Etaín," he demanded.

"No regrets." How could she have them? She'd needed him in her life all along, though she rarely admitted to feelings of loneliness.

Love, it swelled inside her, fierce and tender at the same time, and she wanted to give him pleasure, to express it in a way that would have him crying out in ecstasy.

He moaned in protest when she took her mouth from his, fingers tightening in her hair in a demand that she return.

"Let me," she murmured against his ear, detouring there for the quick brush of lips and dart of tongue.

His hips lifted off the mattress, hard cock driving against mound and clit and abdomen, distracting her from her intentions.

"Maybe I should make you come on my belly," she said, rubbing her clit against his length, fiery sensation streaking to her toes so they curled against soft sheets. "Isn't that a popular male fantasy? To come on a woman's pussy and breasts?"

His hands left her hair to grip her ass as she continued to rub and grind against his cock. "Have you been watching porn?"

She laughed. "I don't need to now that I have you and Eamon."

He gave a low growl at the mention of Eamon, tried to lift and settle her onto his cock. She resisted, feminine satisfaction a hot spread through her chest when she felt the spasm of his cock against her belly, the tip wet now with arousal, the musky, intoxicating scent of desire making her fight herself as well as him.

He shifted their positions so penetration became impossible, turning her into the one with the fierce need to come instead of the siren who'd wanted him to.

She moved, breath catching with each strike, each press and rub of her clit to his cock.

"Put your mouth on me," she pleaded, hands leaving his hair to cup her breasts, to squeeze and twist and tug nipples tightened into knots of ache.

His nostrils flared. His hunger intensifying the desire. "Say please."

"Please." It was whispered feminine submission.

His smile was a flash of victory. "Another night I'm going to make you beg even prettier."

"And another still, I'll make you do the same."

He laughed, a man anticipating rather than one afraid. "You can try."

His mouth replaced her fingers to suck, each pull making her channel clamp and release, clamp and release.

Her head went back, eyes closing as her movements quickened, her clit swollen, erect, a throbbing center of pleasure between her thighs.

Her breath came in short pants. Arousal streamed from her slit, wetting him, wetting her inner thighs.

His breath was equally ragged, his mouth savage, inflicting heated torment with tugs and bites to her nipple, with the swirl of his tongue and hungry sucking.

The hands gripping her pulled her lower body more tightly to his. Hers was not the only frantic movement.

He thrust against her, freed her nipple to say, "Fuck, Etaín. Fuck, you make me crazy."

"Good." She didn't want to be alone in her addiction, didn't want to be the only one made helpless by a craving that intensified rather than abated.

Good. That single word echoed through Cathal like a challenge, like a red flag waved in front of a bull.

From the very first she'd had him by the cock, and now she held him with her ink, by magic. *No regrets.* It was the absolute truth, but he'd show her just what type of man she'd bound to her.

"Come for me," he growled, his balls hard and tight with the need to do the same, his hands changing the angle where their bodies touched. Her clit a hot firm knob he worked against his cock, exulting in each of her whimpers, in the way she touched herself, fingers reclaiming nipples.

She was totally uninhibited. A goddess dedicated to pleasure. So sensuous he fought against lifting her, filling her and pounding into her until release took him.

"Come for me," he said, grinding against her, watching her face flush as orgasm claimed her, giving her those moments before he lifted and positioned her onto hands and knees.

She went immediately to her elbows, canting her hips and spreading her thighs to reveal a glistening pink slit and plump folds, an offer so primal and carnal he gripped his cock to keep from immediately covering and thrusting inside her.

He was in control here. Not her.

Reaching out, he traced the seam between her buttocks, gave a husky laugh when her ass cheeks clamped in instinctive denial. He hadn't taken her there, *yet*. But he wanted to, he would. The driving urge to claim and dominate lying just below the surface was a lesson he'd learned about himself thanks to her.

He traced the seam again, fingers slick with arousal coating the puckered rosette of her back entrance. "Maybe next time I'll fuck you here. Are you going to say no?"

She shivered, erotic fear, anticipation, he didn't know which, but it had fire streaking through his cock, everything inside him screaming for him to join his body to hers.

"Maybe I'll say yes because I want you both inside me at the same time."

It was his turn to react with instinctive denial, an automatic response to any allusion to Eamon. He did it with the thrust of his cock through parted cunt lips and into wet, tight heat. With pounding movement, a furious beat meant to eradicate her need for anyone but him.

She rocked backward, meeting his thrusts, driving him deeper. She took him as he took her, the sound of flesh against flesh accenting his low grunts. The feel of his balls hanging heavy and full between his thighs, striking her clit and making her cry out, filled him with savage possessiveness and feelings of power.

He staved off orgasm until hers was done, one last masculine victory before pleasure rendered him helpless, before semen jetted through his cock to fill her and the two of them collapsed to the mattress, bodies still joined.

Three

E amon stood as Liam escorted Etaín's brother and father into the room. He'd expected the one but not the other. He had reservations about both, given the way they'd used Etaín's gift over the years, exposing her to danger and seemingly unaware and unconcerned about what the use of it cost her.

Both men were dressed casually, expensively. He would have preferred to delay this particular meeting but the contact was as inevitable as the impending confrontation.

"Parker," Eamon said, acknowledging the FBI agent who remained alive only because he couldn't be certain Etaín's brother had meant to make her the Harlequin Rapist's target. "Captain Chevenier."

The men claimed side-by-side chairs. Eamon sat across from them while Liam lounged in the doorway, interested audience and lethal bodyguard.

"Where's my daughter?" the captain said, not bothering with pleasantries, his voice edged with tension, the fierce concern of a parent.

Eamon was willing to believe this man loved Etaín as his own, despite it not being the truth. He was willing to accept that one day he might have to add these two humans and those related to them to his clan, but currently he had only one concern with respect to them. "She and Cathal will join us once certain matters have been settled."

Twin expressions of dislike and disapproval appeared on his visitors' faces. Eamon very nearly smiled over the reaction. If their hostility alienated them further from Etaín, and with it, human concerns, then it served him.

"Why is Niall Dunne's son still with her?" the captain demanded.

"Surely you know she's seeing Cathal."

"You find that acceptable?" Disbelief, condescension, a hint of moral outrage, the question making it obvious Parker had correctly interpreted the relationship and passed the information on to his father.

Eamon shrugged. "Some battles are best avoided. I mean to keep Etaín safe and one of the things I will protect her from is the harm that comes of using her gift at your behest. You will not be allowed access to her if the purpose of your visit is to ask her to touch crime victims and relive the horror of their memories. In fact, you will be escorted out of my home immediately without seeing her if you are unable or unwilling to swear an oath you did not come here with such a request."

The captain leaned forward, enough menace and aggression in the gesture to have Liam straightening out of his laconic pose. "If my daughter refuses to use her unique abilities, and I hear it directly from her, I'll accept Etaín's wishes. I don't know who you are. Until today, I'd never heard of you or seen you in all the times I've been to Aesirs. I don't know what your connection to the Dunnes is, but be assured I'll be looking now that you've come onto my radar screen. I demand to see my daughter. Get her in here or I'll—"

"Dad, let's calm down here. Please. I need to get my paperwork wrapped up and you wanted to make sure Etaín was really okay. Eamon knows this meeting with Etaín has to happen. I let her leave the crime scene without giving a statement. I let them all leave. Let's shelve this discussion for now. All Eamon has asked is that we promise we're not here to ask for her help on another case. I know I'm not. Are you?"

"No." The answer was glared, delivered with open hostility.

"Good enough?" Parker asked, meeting and holding Eamon's gaze.

It would have to be. Eamon had vowed to himself that this night would not pass without Etaín knowing the truth of what she was, *and would be.* The sooner this was done, the sooner more important matters could be addressed.

"Neither of you will mention this discussion to her."

He hadn't intended to set the men at ease, but his words had that effect. "Fine by me," Parker said, placing a folder on the coffee table and flipping it open. A glance at the elder Chevenier gained his acceptance of the terms, a sharp nod and an easily read expression of confidence rather than defeat.

Eamon hid his smile. Neither of them thought him capable of persuading Etaín to give up their cause of justice. They were mistaken. His word was law in the world Etaín would soon learn existed.

"I'll return momentarily with Etaín and Cathal."

In the presence of Etaín's family members, his third refrained from issuing a mocking comment, though Liam's eyes glistened with suppressed amusement and unholy anticipation.

"He who laughs last, laughs best, and that will be me," Eamon murmured a step away from Liam. "The day will come when you fall in love."

"You're mistaken. That particular nightmare is not for me."

"I think otherwise and will enjoy every moment of your discomfort."

"And here I didn't think you cared, Lord."

Eamon allowed himself the smile he'd held back. There was

hardly any point in suppressing it, given that its absence wouldn't curb Liam's tongue.

He passed through the doorway, moving without haste to the bedroom to find Etaín on her side with Cathal against her back, his arm across her belly and his thigh over hers in possessiveness.

He joined them, Etaín's lambent gaze making him wish he could resume where they'd left off. She rose onto her elbow, tempting him with the thrust of pink-capped breasts.

Eamon leaned in, claiming them with light sucks, lingering until her soft sigh expressed her desire for him. He moved to her mouth then, a long kiss followed by a feathering of them to her ear, his tongue flicking into the canal before licking the rounded tip in both reminder and promise of pleasure.

"Mmmm, back for more," she said, hand going to the front of his pants, sending a jolt of lightning-white heat up his spine with the grasp of his cloth-covered erection.

"I wish it were so."

"What's up? Besides the obvious?"

"Your father and brother are here."

Her hand left him and he felt its loss as a howling, twisting, storm wind. His mouth returned to hers in a spill and mix of magic, his controlled and hers a wild buffeting, though there was no threat, no grappling for control other than what came of being in her presence and wanting nothing more than to join his body to hers.

He drank her down, aware of Cathal's hand sliding up her side to cover her breast, intensifying the eroticism of being with her, though he didn't need to share her to find utter satisfaction. She'd enthralled him from the very first and remained a dangerous fascination. He'd given her more leeway than he once would have imagined possible.

The kiss ended with a moan of protest on her part, sending

satisfaction purring through him. "It's the work of moments to satisfy the reason for their visit. The sooner we attend to them, the sooner we can return to this much more interesting pursuit."

"True," Etaín said, nervous at the prospect of being in the captain's company, and then immediately irritated at feeling that way. She was self-aware enough to know what lay beneath the nervousness—hope, an often bitter emotion when it came to her relationship with the man she'd once called "Dad." She hadn't seen him in months, and that last encounter had ended in an argument the same as many of the previous ones had.

She played with a length of Eamon's hair, letting the silky strands of it distract her. It made her think of gentle waves lapping over pristine beaches.

"Do you have a bathrobe I can borrow?" She'd arrived at Eamon's estate in nothing but his shirt, the clothes she'd been wearing when she was abducted no doubt bagged as evidence in the Harlequin Rapist case by now.

"I can do better than a bathrobe." One last lingering kiss and he left the bed. He crossed to folding closet doors, the wood polished and expensive, the swirling designs carved into it turning the functional into elegant artwork.

He pulled them back, revealing several feet worth of woman's clothing, grouped by occasion, from casual shirts through elegant eveningwear. "I arranged for the beginnings of a wardrobe."

Her heartbeat sped up, dismay crowding in. Everything in that closet would be far more expensive than what she would have chosen to buy or wear. *Now it begins.* The changes she'd known would come, the expectations she wasn't sure she'd be able to accept or tolerate or accomplish.

She glanced at Cathal, who grimaced and said, "Lucky you. Clean clothes. Now I'm sorry we didn't swing by my place on the way here."

"Mine too."

Surrendering the warmth and comfort she gained with the touch of her skin to Cathal's, she left the bed, and he did the same, heading for the bathroom.

At the closet she liberated the most casual of the shirts, though the rich texture of the fabric confirmed her suspicion about cost. Hiding her discomfort in humor, she said, "For a second there, when I saw the clothes, I thought maybe you were a cross-dresser like Derrick."

"That's a show you won't see here."

She laughed, but uneasiness about the future had her suddenly craving a return to normal, where normal held no worries about magic, where it was defined by days spent at Stylin' Ink, sharing insults with Derrick and Jamaal and Bryce, easy camaraderie mixed with teasing as they created art that would last only for the lifetime of its human canvas.

Eamon tugged a pair of designer jeans from a hanger. "Let's get this over with, Etaín."

She took them from him. For a different occasion, she'd enjoy wearing nothing beneath the clothing and knowing he and Cathal were aware of it. But to meet with Parker and the captain, she needed all the armor she could get. "Panties? Bras?"

"In the dresser. Top left-hand drawer. I've got craftsmen working on additional furniture."

Her footsteps faltered. But with Cathal's emergence from the bathroom wearing dark pants and a slightly wrinkled shirt, she left discussion about living arrangements for later. She continued to the dresser, hastily choosing silky strips of blue lingerie before getting dressed.

"Let's do this," she said, though her heart gave a stuttering, skipping beat at seeing Parker.

She balled her hands into fists, shoving them into her pockets.

Eamon had told her he believed it was the nature of her gift to want to see everything, to know everything, and she'd lost control of it. She would have stripped her brother's mind if Eamon hadn't used a spell to stop her as Parker embraced her, glad she'd been saved from the Harlequin Rapist.

Disapproval cemented the captain and Parker in place. Neither offered a smile or a hug. She hadn't expected otherwise, yet that traitorous emotion of hope left her vulnerable.

An ache spread through her chest in a slow, treacherous wave. Cathal's hand settled at the base of her spine, driving the pain behind a wall of resolve.

No regrets. There was nothing about the way she lived her life that she had to apologize for . . . and yet, in the same room with the man she still thought of as Dad, a part of her still craved love unconditioned on conforming to his expectations.

She let Cathal guide her to the couch, didn't protest when he encircled her wrist, tugging her hand free of the pocket and clasping it as he sat.

Anxious to get this over with, she said, "I can guess what brings you here, Parker. What about you, Captain?"

There was censure in his expression. Hard intolerance in the presence of a man he'd convicted based solely on what his father and uncle were. Killers. No doubts there, though without her, the authorities had nothing.

"I wanted to make sure you are okay, even if the company you keep remains a concern."

"I'm good." She didn't have the stomach to launch an accusation at him, that he'd had something to do with her being scooped up and confined in a small, windowless interrogation room. That he'd suggested it might break her so she'd become the prosecution's golden witness in a case against the Dunnes.

She focused on Parker. "I won't sign off on a lie. How do you want to spin this?" They could hardly include the terms *psychic-bond* or *magic-infused tattoos* in the official report.

"There's enough evidence to get a death sentence anyway, so let's keep your statement simple. Tell me everything that happened prior to your rescue."

She did, adding her signature to the end of Parker's written account. "Now for the tricky part."

Cathal's hand tightened on hers, an apology sliding into her through the contact or through the connection created by the ink on his forearms, she didn't know which. "Not necessarily. For purposes of the report, I'll sign a statement saying I had a tracker on you."

A truth, though a misleading one. With the inked eye touched to his palm she saw a memory and knew the tracker was actually on the Harley.

Cathal's determination poured into her like molten steel. It was all the warning she got before he said, "Given my father and uncle, you'll understand why calling the police wasn't a first choice when I discovered the woman I'm going to marry had been abducted."

Silence exploded through the room like a bomb, sending shockwaves through her as well. She turned toward Eamon to gauge his reaction but his expression was the calm of a glassy sea.

Parker was the first to speak, a furious, "No fucking way, Etaín." But she didn't refute Cathal's statement. Didn't argue he was nothing like his father and uncle.

Cathal's hand left hers to take up the pen she'd placed on the coffee table after signing her statement. He made quick work of writing his own and placing his signature on it.

"I'd like to speak with you, Etaín," the captain said. "Alone."

Eamon took Etaín's hand in his. "That won't be possible this evening. I believe we've concluded the necessary police business. Liam will show you out."

With the mention of Liam's name, Eamon glanced toward the

doorway, drawing Etaín's attention there as well, to see eyes dancing with suppressed laughter, and more.

Shhhadow walker. Assassin. The words came hissed in the same
sibilant voice she'd heard in her nightmare, as if her gift now had
a voice and didn't always require the press of her palms to skin. The
label given to Liam tightened her chest as shards of ice slid into her
bloodstream with the question, *Why would Eamon need a killer in
his employ?*

"Do you intend to let this man dictate what you can and can't
do, Etaín?" the captain asked, demand in his voice, but concern
too, worry for her future. And at the moment she was a little concerned about it too.

Dragging her gaze from Liam she said, "No," and was cut off
from elaborating by the ring of the captain's cellphone.

He removed it from his pocket, checking the incoming number
before answering it. The caller did most of the talking. When the
captain spoke again he said, "I'm with her now. Let me get back
to you."

Lowering the phone he said, "That was Oakland PD, there was
an armed invasion at a biker bar. Twenty-seven dead, one survivor.
He's not expected to either regain consciousness or live. They've
requested your help."

"No," Eamon answered. "I won't allow you to put her in danger
again."

Imagined coils tightened around her chest, suffocating her.
Cathal reclaimed her hand, his shock nearly overriding the fear
drenching her, numbing her lips as she felt the phantom pull of a
gun's trigger. Not a bad dream, but something else. "When did it
happen?"

"A little over an hour ago."

Icy cold invaded her limbs, coming with the sense that she'd
lived it real-time, not as some premonition of impending events.
"Was it the bar where the Curs hang out?"

A cop face met her question. Answer enough. "Why do you ask?"

She squeezed Cathal's hand in an unnecessary message not to mention the dream, now nightmare reality. "I was there a few days ago, doing what Parker asked me to do."

"Then you'll know some of the victims." He stood, Parker doing so as well. "I'll escort you to the hospital unless you intend to let Eamon dictate what you will or won't do."

"I'll go."

"You won't," Eamon said. "*Think*, Etaín, just how dangerous touching the dying might be *to you*."

But she wasn't worried about herself. Not as she flashed back to the scene of the slaughter and felt the phantom burn at her wrists, a tight circle of it that climbed upward into the vines on her arms. Searing heat coming with an awareness that someone nearby wore her ink—coming with the sickening dread that they all wore it, her, the killer, and Vontae—and worse, because of it, the killer she'd been in the dream had sensed Vontae.

Guilt sank gut-twisting roots inside her. *Magic both attracts and repels*, Eamon had told her once, and this seemed horrifying proof of it. "It doesn't matter. I have to do this."

Preempting further argument, she told the captain, "I'll touch the remaining survivor. I'll get the memories and draw them. I swear it." The words brought with them her mother's warning. *Never make an oath you aren't willing to pay dearly for if you break it.*

"Let's go," the captain said.

Eamon's hand settled around her upper arm in an unwavering restraint. "Etaín will follow shortly. I will ensure she keeps her pledge but there are matters we need to discuss first. What hospital?"

"Highland General."

The captain's expression when he met her eyes conveyed the message he wasn't leaving until he heard what she wanted. It would have warmed her heart except this had everything to do with solving a crime, and had the additional benefit of getting her out of *both* Eamon's and Cathal's company.

He never contacted her just to find out how she was doing. It was *always* because he needed her to touch a victim. And it wasn't any different with Parker.

Cathal ended the tense moment, siding with Eamon. "A few minutes won't matter, Etaín." His hand tightened on hers and she could feel his fear *for* her. "It might be better if you don't walk into the hospital with your father and brother. Not after all the hype about your involvement with the Harlequin Rapist taskforce."

He had a point there. News media speculation had her as psychic artist or bait, but so far they didn't have her face or know she'd nearly been a victim.

"We'll follow you," she told the captain.

"Soon or there won't be any point in coming to the hospital."

"I've made you a promise," Eamon said. "I'll see that it's kept."

Both the captain and Parker stiffened, as if hearing more in Eamon's words than she did. And then she stiffened too, wondering what he'd said to them before returning to the bedroom to tell her they were waiting.

The moment they left the room Eamon said, "I mean to keep you safe, from yourself if necessary and by whatever means are required. Ignorance is deadly, Etaín. You cannot remain so any longer."

More words followed, spoken in what must be the language of magic, what water and fire would sound like if they had a voice. She felt as if some barrier was being brought down, saw it in a sudden luminescence, not surrounding Eamon but emanating from him, making him otherworldly, breathtaking in a way that was more than heart-stopping gorgeous or beautifully handsome, in a way that was beyond compelling, reminding her of tales of the shining folk, the stories her mother used to whisper to her at bedtime, or sometimes as they traveled by bus, leaving old names behind and taking up new ones.

Four

～⟶

"W hat the fuck," Cathal murmured, but there was reluctant awe there, unwilling appreciation.

Eamon took her unresisting hand and carried it to his face, using the back of her knuckles to push the golden waves of hair aside to reveal a pointed ear tip. Her heart skipped a beat then raced wildly, denial swelling in anticipation of what came next, though it didn't prevent him from saying, "You're on the cusp of change, Etaín. This is what you'll be, if you survive."

Somehow she spoke through the throbbing pulse at the base of her throat, the words miraculously not sticking to a suddenly dry tongue in an equally dry mouth. "Guess I'd better learn the Vulcan salute then."

"Elf, Etaín." Said with just enough edge to dare her to face and accept the truth, to warn against denial or deflection.

And oh yeah, the temptation was there to do both of those. But she was no fool to think she could either run or escape from herself, not with all that had happened to her since meeting Eamon.

"Lord," she said, as if tentatively picking up a pebble in a streambed lined with them.

The gesture relaxed Eamon. His expression softened. "Yes, this is my territory. Among supernaturals, you hold what you claim, or you lose it."

"And I'm one of those things you claim? I think I already warned you I wouldn't become one of your possessions."

"Not a possession, Etaín. You'll be my wife-consort."

"Will I?"

"Don't pick a fight you can't win. And ultimately won't want to."

"And Cathal?"

Eamon shrugged. "A complication, in many, many ways. But if you mean, what about your human lover's bold declaration he intends to marry you? I have no objection to it."

"Big of you," Cathal said, the distinct growl in his voice warning things were about to escalate.

She squeezed Cathal's hand in a request to remain calm though her own vanished when Eamon said, "Everything changes as of now, Etaín."

The edict scraped over nerve-endings made raw at having just experienced her father and brother's disapproval. "We'll see."

"The outcome is a foregone conclusion."

"Says *Lord* Eamon."

"Yes."

"We don't have time for this. We need to get to the hospital."

Liam stepped into the room as if her comment had summoned him. Seeing Eamon, his appearance changed too in a shimmer of magic. Sheer human beauty slipped away to leave him radiant and shining, breathtaking even without the pointed ear tips visible through the long braids of hair.

Eye candy. That's what she'd thought each time she'd stepped into Aesirs and seen the men working there. Now she knew differently.

Demonstration apparently completed, Eamon reworked whatever spell he'd brought down. In a blink he looked human again. An instant later, so did Liam.

She could feel Cathal's fierce need to escape, to step back into some semblance of normalcy. Fear trickled in, her own worry he'd change his mind and take back the *no regrets*. She couldn't blame him, not with tight panic swelling inside her, this on top of the nightmare reality of the slaughter. She needed breathing room too, a chance to process this new twist despite having dealt with supernatural stuff since the call to ink at thirteen.

"Let's go," she said.

Eamon's grip prevented her from standing. "Liam, my third, will accompany you without making his presence known unless it's necessary. He's capable of keeping you safe from threats you wouldn't recognize."

"From other . . . ?" She couldn't quite bring herself to say Elves.

"Elves are not the only supernatural beings in existence."

It gave her pause, but she forced herself to focus on the most urgent. "What makes you think I'm in danger? I've lived in San Francisco since I was eight and as far as I can tell, you're the only . . . person . . . who's noticed me."

Eamon's smile made her think of the thin blade of a knife. "Because of your ill-advised promise, those answers will have to wait. Liam will accompany you to the hospital. When you have finished there, he will bring you back to the estate, where you will remain, for your own safety, until you have transitioned from changeling to full Elf and have learned what you need to know of our culture."

"And if I refuse?"

"Refusal is not an option."

"Fuck that, Lord Asshole," Cathal said. "We're out of here."

Cathal's fury burned hot while she wrestled with what to make of a lover turned icy dictator, though she was equally resistant to Eamon's casual assumption of total control. She stood, Cathal rising at the same time, her eyes meeting Eamon's, heated with an unspoken promise of absolute resistance to taking orders. "We're leaving now."

"Have you considered what might happen to him if you die? Or worse, and let me assure you, there are far worse things than being killed outright."

No other emotion could be sustained in the icy encasement of fear. "Why should anything happen to him if I die?" But she had only to glance down at the arms now encircling her waist, to see the tattoos she'd placed on Cathal and feel the ever-present hum of connection to know how Eamon would answer the question.

He moved in, expression tender rather than arrogant, and because of it she didn't try to evade his touch, or resent the possessive, assured way he once again cupped her cheek, his thumb feathering across her lips.

"I am not accustomed to explaining myself," he said in the same soft tone he'd used earlier, in explaining his use of a spell against her.

"Get used to it, Eamon." Rough against his soft.

"Perhaps it will be necessary to some extent."

Not exactly a whole-hearted embracement, but then she probably couldn't expect one from *Lord* Eamon at the moment, and she couldn't let the lack sidetrack her. "What does my dying have to do with Cathal?"

"His fate is linked to yours, Etaín. With enough study, I could *possibly* find a way to break that bond through a means other than his death. But it wouldn't be easily done, nor would it be without a cost. If you perish, there is a good chance you will take him with you.

"The magic chose him. I accept the choice though I wouldn't have made the same one. It arouses me to share you. Others would not feel as I do. Most would eliminate him immediately. Many would slaughter any human who wore your ink, with or without cause."

"You say that as if there could be cause." The words came out as a whisper, accompanied by the desperate desire to hear Eamon say there was no justifiable cause, but even thinking it, she relived that instant of getting out of the car and with the wave of a silenced gun, directing four masked men in an assault on the bar where the Curs hung out.

Eamon shrugged. "If that's not cause enough for concern, by royal decree those who are like you, *seidic*, soul seer, are supposed to be turned over to the queen. It is luxurious captivity, though a completely isolated one. It's a prison there is no escape from, Etaín, and one Cathal would in all likelihood be permitted to share with you, until it ended in assassination."

By someone like Liam? Perhaps even by *Liam if Eamon couldn't have her.* Eamon's attempt to stop her from helping the police after twenty-seven people had been slaughtered was a glimpse at how ruthless he could be.

"You didn't turn me over to your queen."

"No. Go to the hospital, Etaín. I won't have you foresworn by further delay. When you get back, I'll share more of what you need to know."

"And will she be free to leave again?" Cathal asked, bringing the conversation full circle.

"Etaín needs to get control of her gift. She needs to start disassociating herself from the human world. Our lifespans are measured in centuries, not decades. Yours will be too if she survives the transition. Something for you to consider, I'll allow you some say as to whether or not your family members are brought into my household. But they will fall under my rule, a fate your father and uncle might come to view as worse than death."

Etaín couldn't begin to get her head around the kind of lifespan Eamon was talking about, and didn't have time to. She concentrated on the simple, an edict in close proximity to words like *allow* and *my*, all just another way of saying "no," which was an answer she didn't find acceptable.

Cutting to the chase, she said, "I'm willing to accept you're trying to keep me safe, Eamon, but I won't be made a prisoner. Either you give your word I can come and go as I please, or I won't come back here after I'm finished at the hospital."

"Have you already forgotten what nearly happened the last time you touched Parker?" *Have you already forgotten what you nearly did to me?* Though pride probably kept him from saying that in front of Liam.

She shivered. "I haven't forgotten. I understand there are things I need to know. I understand I'm a danger to others. I get that, Eamon. I'm trying to be reasonable here, to find a middle ground where we can all be happy, and happy is not going to be me locked away from my friends with Cathal popping in for conjugal visits. I need space. My own apartment. Time spent with just Cathal at his house and club. Time spent with you here and at Aesirs. You get the picture. I'm not going to let you become my jailor."

"Nor do I wish to become your jailor, Etaín. But what I said earlier stands, I will keep you safe, from your own choices if necessary."

"Then we're at an impasse because I'm not coming back here until you drop the attitude." It made her heart ache to say it. "My being in a relationship with you doesn't give you the right to lay down rules where I'm concerned."

"Perhaps not, but being Lord of this territory does."

"Then we'll leave your territory as soon as Etaín is finished at the hospital," Cathal said. "She's promised me a week, destination undefined, remember?"

The air around them became the frigid of Arctic waters, Eamon's silent reminder that he was a being of power and magic. "Do you really have so little regard for her life and your own?"

"I'm willing to take my chances if Etaín is. Better that than the scenario you're laying out."

"I'm willing," Etaín said. Cathal was absolutely safe from her touch, that much she was positive of. And maybe distance would help bridge the seeming impasse caused by Eamon's concern.

Eamon's hand tightened where it still rested against her cheek. Externally everything about him might be reminiscent of ice, but there was heat in his expression, not roaring flame but enough fire to promise all the barriers to what he wanted could and would be burned away. "One week, Etaín, starting now because you gave the oath while ignorant of what you are and will become. As I remember it, your promise to Cathal allowed for my presence, and I will be present where I can safely do so without drawing attention to you. At the end of seven days, if you're still alive, it'll be my will that prevails."

"Don't count on it."

He shrugged, sparking her temper with the gesture. His hand left her face. "Longevity and the ability to wield magic are the reasons Elves value oaths so highly. This evening you and Cathal have used that to your own advantage, but you'll find such a weapon is a two-edged sword. Ask Cathal what promise he gave in exchange for my use of magic to create the bond that allowed us to rescue you from the Harlequin Rapist."

"Fuck," Cathal said. "I didn't—"

"Know?" Eamon's smile was as sharp as a blade. "Ignorance is dangerous, if not often deadly."

"What did you promise?" Etaín asked, the race of Cathal's heart beating against her back marking the deepening of his anger and resistance, though not his regret, considering what the alternative would have been.

"I promised you'd tattoo him, putting ink on him with the same meaning as what I wear."

Oh yeah. No escaping that one.

"A bond with you whether I want one or not?"

"Do you dislike the idea so much, Etaín? I told you from the very beginning I wanted more than just sex."

Was there a hint of pain in the words? A chord of it strummed through her chest. If he'd warned her in the beginning, then she'd also warned herself, known as she lay in his bed, looking at paintings by Cezanne and Van Gogh and Cross and Lemmen that being involved with him would ultimately lead to heartache. Into expectations she wouldn't be able to meet—and that was *before* things supernatural added weight to the equation.

And yet, even now, she couldn't hate him. Couldn't forget the tenderness, the gift of knowledge he'd given her so she was able to touch Cathal's cousin and take away Brianna's memories without suffering as she had on the first visit.

What they needed was space, breathing room. "We're leaving," she said, not driving the point home she and Cathal wouldn't be back tonight, though she shivered at having Liam follow them out of the house, a dark assassin there and then gone.

Five

Frederico Perera stood at the head of the casket, his wife at his side, the two of them accepting condolences while their daughters moved among Jordão's friends, eyes wet and puffy from so many tears.

His eyes too were wet. There was no shame in crying at the loss of a child.

The room was awash in the scent of flowers mixed with expensive perfumes and colognes. The smell of it choked him, a man already struggling to breathe through the tight constriction of his throat.

If not for the hand on Margarita's back, the oft-spoken words of encouragement, his wife would have collapsed beneath the weight of her grief, and he with her, not to pray, but to rail against God in the pain of his loss. Their firstborn was dead, killed in America by a sniper's bullet.

"Courage," Frederico murmured to Margarita. "We will get through this."

The words he spoke were for himself as well as his wife. And he repeated them many times as the number of those gathered swelled and receded like a cold tide emphasizing the desolation he felt, the guilt at having accepted the post in San Francisco.

It was a minor position, not a stepping stone to a more important one. He was little more than a paper pusher for his government, and almost equally insignificant to the man who'd gotten him the position, one that came with diplomatic immunity and pouches that could not be searched by the American authorities.

He was nothing but a glorified mule, better paid than those who carried bundles of drugs on their backs, but a mule all the same. He accepted the label without shame, taking pride instead in the fact that what he did meant greater wealth for his family.

When the last of those who'd come to view, to grieve, to offer what comfort they could, trickled away, only a single visitor was left in the room.

"Go home," Frederico said to his wife, pulling her into a hug along with their two daughters. "I will join you later."

They left, giving the man no more than a fleeting acknowledgment as they passed him, even in their pain sensing the stranger was not someone to become known to.

"He will see you now," the man said.

Frederico nodded, turning toward the casket to look down on the face of his son. A sob welled inside him, threatening to split open his chest and spill his heart onto the floor.

He leaned down and kissed Jordão's forehead. "You will be avenged," he whispered against cool skin before straightening and following the stranger to a dark sedan.

They drove in silence on streets high above the *favelas*. The lights visible in those violence-infested areas the police themselves were afraid to enter, became one of many facets, part of the glittering jewel that was Rio de Janeiro.

A wall surrounded the sprawling home that was their destination. But it merely served as a warning against entry and the men patrolling it with machineguns.

The sedan parked amid a collection of exotic automobiles. He followed the stranger into a room of opulent luxury.

His guide stopped just inside the doorway while Frederico continued, approaching the man sitting across from another with a chessboard on the table between them.

Eduardo Faioli rose from the couch, offering a hand, clasping Frederico's when he took that hand. "I am sorry for the loss of your son."

Frederico calmed as he met the steady gaze of the man who had lifted him from the ranks of the common, though it had been done through others in Eduardo's employ. He had not been sure he would gain the audience he'd requested. And he feared what had happened in San Francisco might lead to torture and death, and not his own first, but his daughters, his wife, his sisters, and aging parents.

"Thank you for seeing me."

"Sit," Eduardo said, indicating a nearby chair as he settled into the one he'd risen from.

Frederico sat, waiting as Eduardo turned his attention back to the chess board for a moment, moving the black knight before looking again at Eduardo without introducing his companion. "You had only the one son?"

Eduardo would already know the answer of course, but the question served as the opening to negotiations. "Yes, he was my only son and also the only grandson."

"A tragedy. You believe perhaps it had something to do with the business conducted on my behalf?"

"No."

"Ah, then you wish a favor of me?"

"I want my son avenged."

Eduardo nodded. "Yes. Yes, I would see the same done were it my son. But how can I help you? My associates tell me there have been no arrests. No reason given in the news for this tragedy and no suspects named by the police."

"It's a personal matter. I know who ordered my son killed."

He had not been ignorant of Jordão's faults, faults worsened because his son did not fear the authorities in America. When the police had told him of the other boy's confession, and he'd heard the full extent of Jordáo's behavior, he'd been sickened. But even knowing his son held some of the blame for his own fate, it did not diminish the suffering or lessen the desire for revenge.

"Who do you wish me to strike against?" Eduardo asked.

"The Dunnes."

Frederico paused, torn between fear of being denied his request and fear of reprisal should he remain silent about the possibility of dangerous complications.

The greater fear prevailed. "One of the American agents told me the Dunnes are suspected of being mafia."

Eduardo nodded. "Irish mafia."

Relief at having released the secret trapped the breath in Frederico's chest. "Are the Irish a concern?"

Eduardo laughed. "They are hardly worth bothering with. Their glory days are long past, set in a different era."

He glanced at his silent companion, watched the movement of a white rook and countered it with the move of a black bishop. "A life for a life? Perhaps a son for a son? Is that the nature of the revenge you seek?"

He would have the entire family killed but . . . Let another father know the pain he knew. "Yes."

"Very well. The day will come, in turn, when I will require a large favor of you."

An icy chill swept through him. Silence filled the space between them for a heartbeat, and then a second before he responded, "I understand."

"Excellent." To the man he played chess with, Eduardo said, "Use the Mexicans for this."

* * *

Etaín couldn't remember a day ever having felt so endless. Dream and nightmare and dream again. This morning she'd woken up in Cathal's arms with nothing more to worry about than getting to the shelter fund-raiser and doing her part as both tattoo artist and organizer. And now . . .

She squeezed Cathal's hand as they approached the hospital entrance. "I don't think I could do this without you." An admission, coming from her, that was tantamount to another woman screaming *I love you* in a crowded room.

He halted, turning her to face him, a hand going to her waist, his lips covering hers in an all-too-brief kiss. "Let's get this done, then we can go back to my place."

She'd draw there. This wouldn't really be behind them until she'd handed off the results. Already she could feel the impending press of hospital walls.

They tightened when she stepped through the door into antiseptic-scented space. The captain stood next to a dark-suited Hispanic detective.

"Gustavo Ordoñes," the man said, giving a slight nod rather than offering a hand. "If you'll come with me, your friend can wait for you here."

"No. He stays with me." Maybe Eamon wouldn't have to worry about the police asking for her help after this.

Detective Ordoñes accepted her terms with a graceful shrug, turning and leading them into the bowels of the hospital.

"The surviving victim's wife is with him. We'll clear her out, but you'll be quick, right? I don't want her detained for long. He's gone code blue once and been revived. It was touch and go. I wouldn't bet on the doctors being able to do it a second time."

"His name?" Etaín asked, stumbling when Ordoñes answered, "Kelvin Hughes."

"What was he doing at the Curs hangout?"

This time it was Ordoñes whose footsteps faltered. He glanced over his shoulder. "You know him?"

"Yes." Grief clamped its fist around her heart. "I know him."

He'd turned his life around. He wore a tattoo meant to give him strength in the face of temptation. She'd inked it into his skin years ago, when he'd gotten out of prison and had nowhere to go but the homeless shelter.

She swallowed against the tightness in her throat, thinking about his coming by Stylin' Ink with his wife and a brand-new baby. *Just checking in with you,* he'd said, *to let you know your work's still good.*

They reached the intensive care unit. A uniformed officer stood nearby, as if there was concern a masked gunman would show up to finish the job started at the bar. He let them pass without asking questions, but his face held curiosity.

Melinda Hughes didn't turn her head when they entered the room. She sat, hunched forward, her husband's hand clasped in hers. A monotonous beep marked what remained of life, along with the forced respiration of equipment meant to sustain it.

Etaín squeezed Cathal's hand then allowed it to drop away as she approached, tears stinging her eyes at the remembered feel of a baby in her arms and the panic that had accompanied it, the laughter at her expense and merciless jibes by her coworkers as well as Kelvin.

"I'm sorry," she said, stopping next to Melinda.

"Etaín."

Melinda reached out and Etaín took the hand, the other woman's grief slamming into her, joining her own and driving her to a crouch. Voice thick with emotion, she asked, "Why was he there? Why?"

"Fool." Tears slid downward, dropping onto the white sheet. "I told him not to go around there. I told him to give up on Toney, that nothing he said was going to stop his brother from hanging with the Curs and selling dope with them. But he wouldn't listen and look where it got him! Now Ayana is going to grow up not knowing her daddy."

Wrong place, wrong time. But there was no comfort in that.

"Was this over drugs?"

Melinda jerked her hand from Etaín's, taking her grief but leaving the sting of anger and betrayal. "Is that the only reason you're here? To get answers for the police? I already told them what I knew. Kelvin was done with that kind of trouble. I thought you believed in him."

"I didn't know it was him until I got to the hospital. I would have come anyway. I'm sorry, Melinda. Sorry for you and him and Ayana. Sorry this happened." She braced herself against the bombardment of emotions but still reached out and covered Melinda's hand with hers. "I'm here to do what I can to help."

"How?" Melinda asked, hope, that traitorous emotion, sliding into Etaín where their skin touched. "He's already in the arms of the Almighty. The doctors say he's gone, only his body doesn't know it yet."

Etaín glanced at one of the monitors, saw the flat line of a brain with little activity and guessed that beneath the bandages covering most of Kelvin's head and face he'd taken a bullet to the brain. There was no good way to handle this, no good way to honor her promise to the captain without further exposing herself, something she hadn't wanted even *before* Eamon and his revelations.

"You know what they've been saying on the news about me?"

"That stuff about you being psychic? That same stuff the police have been denying?"

"Yeah. That stuff. That's why I'm here."

Hope dissolved into the raw hunger for justice. "I'm not leaving this room."

"You don't have to."

Etaín stood, grateful Melinda was predisposed to believe

because Kelvin had believed in the transformative power of the tattoo. She glanced at Cathal standing with the captain and Ordoñes.

She'd known by the lack of a handshake or a question about why she didn't have a sketch pad that the captain had clued Ordoñes in, giving him a ticket to the show. Right now she didn't have enough energy to get mad over it, and at least the three men served a purpose, blocking anyone else from seeing her use her gift.

She moved to the opposite side of the bed. Taking Kelvin's hand between hers, she felt an immediate connection, would have known blindfolded that he wore her ink.

Her forearms tingled. The eyes at the centers of her palms woke in a way they hadn't previously, sending her heart into a skittering near-panic.

Concentrate. Just concentrate and get this over with. Kelvin couldn't be harmed by her gift, not now.

"What happened at the Curs hangout?" she whispered, just once as she used the knowledge she'd gained from Eamon, her focus razor sharp, a camera zooming in on the relevant scene.

Cigarette smoke filled his mouth and lungs. Damn but it felt good, even if he was trying to quit on account of the baby.

He took another drag, savoring it the way Toney was savoring the weed. Melinda was gonna kill him if he came home smelling like reefer.

One more draw and he felt the heat against his fingertips, the burn of paper at having smoked all the way down to the filter. Man, what a pussy he'd become. Used to be he'd roll his own, not worrying about lung cancer. Not worrying about nothing. And now . . .

He had a wife and baby girl, a good job in times when a lot of folks couldn't find work. He dropped the butt, grinding it into the asphalt behind the bar with his foot. Smiling inside at what he had in his life. Not this and he didn't miss it. This was nothing compared to life with Melinda and Ayana.

"What the fuck!" Toney said, reaching for the gun he packed, body jerking and going down.

A glimpse of a masked figure. No! No!

Inky blackness served as transition from the memory, and across the screen of it, gold lines formed, taking the shape of script, *I shall overcome*, the words chosen by Kelvin but interlaced with the hidden symbols she'd dreamed before using the hand needle and tattooing them across his chest.

Wasssteful. The sound of the sibilant voice accompanied a burst of pain in Etaín's chest, followed by nothingness and then light so bright it was blinding.

Etaín opened her eyes, wondering if this was dream or afterlife.

She stood in sunshine filtered through ancient trees. It was like the forest she'd often imagined, never sure if it was forgotten childhood memory or something else altogether.

Magic. If it had a smell, it was in the air in this place. In the very soil she touched, bare feet against rich loam.

It took her a moment to notice the absolute silence, and with that silence came a nameless fear. She moved, afraid she couldn't, and felt only the tiniest of relief when she discovered she could.

Turning, she expected to find fire in the center of this forest, as she always had in the strange imaginings. Magic's primordial birthplace, Eamon had called it, though there were differences here, not the least of which was the milky green lake now in front of her.

It looked as if someone had ground up emeralds and saturated the water with them. But even as she thought that, what had been diffuse became an infinite number of particles coalescing in the center of the lake, freeing the dark blue of water until the surface was nothing but, and then that surface was broken by an emerald-green Dragon's head, and that head was followed by neck, by a winged torso, though the entirety of the creature didn't emerge from the water.

You arrive early.

This was the same voice she'd heard before.

A wassste if I allow you to remain.

As if she had any fucking intention of staying.

Disresspectful.

Nostrils flared and Etaín saw the fire she'd expected to find here. It burned across the water, its heat reaching her though the flames stopped just short of her feet, a warning, a lesson. She could suffer in this place, perhaps even die in it. Fear trickled in, making her aware of the silence again, the absence of a heartbeat.

Yesss. You understand now.

"What do you want?"

You will soon discover your purpose. Pupils narrowed. *Sooo your mother saw true about the need for the bond with a human.*

Old, old pain came to life with a vengeance, nearly smothering her in the questions of a child abandoned at eight. "And when was that?"

Before your birth. Even in paradise there are politics. Some pairings are a threat to those in power.

"Do you know where she is?"

I could find her if I desire. But the answer to your question will cost your human's life. Time passes and you are unaware of its consequences. You are still changeling, as easy to kill as he is, though the magic will sustain your physical body a little longer.

Fear almost started her heart. "Cathal's heart stopped too?"

Of course. Do you not understand what you did when you claimed him with your ink? Your bond is new enough that he can die and no harm will come to you. The same is not true of the reverse. Go. I will not hold you here any longer. But neither will I help you find your way back.

The Dragon opened its mouth, this time sending a burst of blue fire, the flames an ice-cold magic that slammed into Etaín, knocking her into the bright white of a nothingness followed by inky darkness.

Six

Liam appeared in the room, his inexplicable arrival unnoticed in the fury of activity. Medical alarms screamed. A doctor and several nurses worked to restart the heart of the human lying on the bed. They used electrical shock while the detective used manual compression on Cathal, and Etaín's father did the same to her.

Liam knelt next to his future Lady. The silence in her chest was deafening, like being immersed in deep water. He could start a heart with his magic, just as he could stop one.

Suppressing all fear of what a changeling *seidic's* touch might do if she grabbed him, he reached out to touch her, halting inches from contact at hearing Cathal's moan, followed by, "Shit," then a panicked, "Etaín."

She gasped, the hungry inhalation of one starved for breath. A heartbeat accompanied the sound, strong and steady, though unlike Cathal she did not regain consciousness.

Activity ceased at the bedside of the human. Liam heard the doctor call time of death but it held no relevance to him. Only the *seidic* changeling did.

Cathal lifted Etaín into his arms despite the angry protests of her father, voice urgent as he asked Liam, "Why isn't she waking up?"

"Take her, they will be able to do nothing for her here."

He turned the gaze of an assassin on the captain. "You understood this could be dangerous for her. Don't ask anything of her again."

It was the only warning he intended to give. It was enough to get them out of the room and then out of the hospital without hindrance.

Cathal stopped next to his car, torn as to what to do next. Go back to Eamon's, where the chance of escaping again seemed slim, or take her to his place.

He closed his eyes, pressing his cheek to hers, breathing in the scent of the shampoo he'd lathered in his hands as the three of them stood in the shower. "I can't lose you, Etaín."

Not to death. Not to Eamon. Not to this supernatural shit that had him fighting constantly not to give in to fear.

"Come back, Etaín," he whispered, because this time he couldn't follow her, he couldn't find her, not in the physical sense. "Come back," he repeated, unashamed of pouring desperation and longing and need into the bond he had proof existed between them.

He imagined himself grasping it, tugging as if the vines on her arms and the ink she'd put on his were connected and he could reel her in that way.

She stirred, a reward for his efforts.

He continued them.

Her eyelashes fluttered open after what seemed like an eternity.

"Fuck, Etaín, you scared me."

"Yeah, let's not do that again."

Her lips sought his and he loosened his grip, allowing her to slide from his arms and onto her feet so he could feel the press of her body to his as the kiss deepened, turning into a prelude to something they were in the wrong place for.

He pulled away, but only far enough so he could meet her eyes. "You okay?"

"I'm good. Kelvin?"

"No. They stopped trying to revive him right about the time your heart started beating again."

He leaned in, touching his forehead to hers. "You want to go to Eamon's place?"

"No. Nothing's changed."

"Etaín—"

"Do *you* want to go back there?"

"No."

"Then let's stick to the plan. I need to draw."

"You draw. I'll get the pictures to the police, deal?"

"Afraid of letting me go out in public?" She sounded more tired than defiant.

"And if I admit I am?"

She sighed. "At least for what's left of tonight, I wouldn't blame you. I'm surprised Eamon hasn't shown up."

"Liam did."

She shivered. "Did he do anything?"

"Other than warning your father not to ask anything else of you, no." Cathal kissed his way to her ear. "He's a killer, Etaín, and it was a threat. I've seen enough of them—hell, I grew up knowing that's what my father and uncle are—to recognize one. It just took a while to notice it in him."

"Understandable given the whole gorgeous Elf thing he's got going on. But you're not wrong about him."

Etaín shivered again. In Cathal's arms, surrounded by all the trappings of an ordinary world, the Dragon, the voice, even Eamon's revelation seemed more exotic dream than reality.

Cathal captured her earlobe, giving it a quick suck then releasing it. "You're cold. Let's get home. I think I can find a way to warm you up. How long will the drawing take?" *How much terror did you live?*

Sadness rushed in with the return of Kelvin's memories, a nearly overwhelming sense of loss. A life wasted because he was trying to help his brother get to the same place he was.

His death wasn't on her, if anything Kelvin had very nearly taken her with him. But Vontae's death . . . She couldn't shake the guilt, the sense of having been responsible, because her gift was changing.

"It won't take me long to draw." She wondered if she could get word to Melinda, that Kelvin's last thoughts were of his wife and daughter, then fisted the fabric of Cathal's shirt as it occurred to her that in the moment she'd brought Kelvin to the point of death in his memories, she'd caused his heart to stop.

"Did she blame me?"

"Who?"

"Melinda?"

Cathal sighed. She heard his regret at not being able to offer her the comfort she desperately wanted. "I don't know, Etaín. No one expected him to survive, not even her, given what she said when we walked in. Would he have wanted to, like that?"

"No."

"Let it go. There's no point in playing the blame game. All I can tell you is that one minute I was standing there watching you do your thing, the next it felt like my heart exploded in my chest. I don't know how long I was down and out, only that when I came to it was with Detective Ordoñes doing CPR."

"He's a good-looking man. Too bad I missed seeing the mouth-to-mouth part," she joked, escaping the serious.

He bit her earlobe. "Funny. Some of your fantasies I'm game for, not that one."

"And especially not with Eamon."

"He's not my favorite person at the moment."

With a final kiss he disengaged long enough to open the car door for her, closing it afterward to go around and get in the driver's seat. He took her hand as they headed toward San Francisco. She couldn't stop herself from saying, "I could ask Eamon to start looking for a way to break the bond. Free you from this . . . weirdness. You could have died back there, because of me."

"Leave it alone, Etaín." He carried her hand to his thigh. "How about we just pretend we're a normal couple for a little while?"

She hesitated, torn between an aversion to lying and the need she sensed in him, finally saying, "For a little while."

They made a quick stop at Stylin' Ink to collect her tattoo kit and a change of clothes. Then Cathal ushered her into his house, his hand warm against her back. "Where do you want to do this thing?"

"How about the TV room?" She didn't need total silence to draw.

"Sound's good. I've got some demos to listen to, including one Salina sent me of Lady Steel."

Etaín laughed, turning into him and wrapping her arms around his waist. "Are you mentioning that because you're hoping to get lucky in exchange for launching Salina's band into stardom?"

"I do seem to remember having some mind-blowing sex because of Lady Steel playing at Saoirse. I wouldn't mind an encore performance."

His eyes went hot and dark, creating a liquid pool of need low in her belly. She touched her mouth to his, teasing along the seam of his lips with her tongue, seeking comfort and escape.

He opened for her, his tongue tangling with hers, his hands sliding upward, cupping her head and holding her in place as he deepened the kiss, turning it into a carnal promise for later, because guilt and duty wouldn't allow for this until she was done keeping her promise.

He released her reluctantly and she stepped away from temptation, wheeling her kit over to the coffee table while he went to the sound system, electing to use headphones though he settled behind her on the couch, legs stretched on either side of her as she sat on the floor to draw.

It didn't take long, less than an album's worth of time for her to capture in detail the relevant images. Kelvin hadn't seen much, one man wearing a black ski mask and black clothing, firing bullets into Toney while another, unseen assailant went for a head shot, his death and his brother's probably the first two casualties of the invasion that followed.

She tore the pages from the sketchpad. Before Eamon, she would have rushed to the bathroom and puked her guts out after touching a victim and stealing their memories. She would have needed sleep for those same memories to surface in a nightmare that would once again send her running to hug the toilet bowl before she could draw. And afterward . . .

She understood now it was magic that helped her push those memories behind a mental barrier and keep them there, completely separate from her own life, though that barrier had become thin, fragile. Because she was changeling? Or because there were so many horrifying images behind it, years and years of touching the victims of violent crime, people left so damaged and traumatized they could barely function.

Those had been the only types of cases her father and brother had ever asked for her help on, because what she learned couldn't be used in court and once she had the memories, the victim was free of them.

Kelvin's memories weren't a burden she couldn't carry. Weren't a reality she intended to distance herself from. She wasn't absolutely sure she could, given everything else: the events she and Cathal had witnessed while locked in a dream, her heart stopping at the hospital, and Cathal's. The voice she'd started hearing. The primordial forest and emerald-green lake. The Dragon she wasn't positive had been real. Because what, in the end had she learned from the conversation?

Nothing. Nothing at all, except hope exposed, that one day she would find her mother and be able to ask, *Why did you abandon me?*

She leaned back, smiling when Cathal pulled off his headphones and leaned forward, arms draping over her shoulders, lips brushing against hers in an upside down kiss. "Taking a break?"

"Finished."

He was quiet for a long, very noticeable minute, no doubt wrestling with his own stated desire to pretend they were a normal couple. Finally he said, "What about the other scenes?"

In the past, she would have drawn what she and Cathal witnessed in the dream that wasn't a dream and handed it off to the captain. But not now, not when things were so unsettled with Eamon, not with Liam's threat.

"I'll pass them on to the captain after I've had a chance to do a little asking around, to give him a place to suggest the cops start looking."

Cathal understood the why of it immediately. "Fuck Eamon."

"Yeah, well, that's what got me into my current mess," she joked. And to be fair, "Maybe without him, maybe without you both, I'd be dead at the hands of the Harlequin Rapist, or wishing I was, and all this would be moot."

Cathal sighed. "I don't have to like this, right? You don't expect me to."

She shrugged, but doubt reached into her chest and grasped her heart, squeezing it just enough to make her vulnerable, so she asked, "Having regrets?"

"Ask that one more time and I'm not going to be responsible for what happens next." There was a distinct growl in his voice.

It chased away the doubt. "I need to get the drawings to Detective Ordoñes."

"I'll do it while you draw the rest of it."

"You could pass them off to the captain instead of going back to Oakland. He's on this side of the bay. I could call ahead."

"Works for me." He gave her another upside-down kiss then straightened.

She tore a sheet from her tablet and wrote down the address of a house she hadn't entered in years, though once she'd called it home. After taking Cathal's offered cellphone, she punched in the captain's number.

"Chevenier," he answered.

"Cathal's bringing the drawings over now. You can hand them off to Ordoñes."

"Bring them yourself. I want you to stay here for a while."

Oh yeah, that'd go over well with the captain's wife. The results of the paternity test Laura had insisted on all those years ago hadn't diminished the animosity. If anything, it'd increased it, because the captain refused to let it be known that he didn't have a bastard child after all.

"I'm good where I am." The traitorous part of her that still believed reconciliation was possible added, "But I appreciate the offer."

"Etaín—"

"Captain—"

"He was giving you CPR when I came to," Cathal said from above her, sidetracking her, stalling out an argument that was sure to come around to her choice of men and the captain's lack of approval.

"I guess I owe you thanks, for what you did at the hospital." She cringed at how that came out but forged ahead. "A lot has happened today. I just want to curl up on the couch and chill. Is it okay if Cathal brings the drawings over? I'm not sure they'll be useful, Kelvin was outside behind the bar, but I figure Ordoñes still wants them as soon as possible."

"I'll get them to him."

"Thanks, Captain."

There was a long silence. Her pain. His. It was there, shimmering between them, constricting her throat and turning her fingers white as they tightened on the phone and she fought against speaking again just to call him Dad.

He broke first. "You need to take a step away from your current situation, Etaín, so you can see it more clearly. Stay with Parker if you don't want to stay here, or better yet, get out of the city for a while."

She nearly laughed but she was afraid it'd sound hysterical rather than amused. Knowing the captain, he'd have her locked up for her own good if she started talking about magic and Elves and the gift she was losing control of.

"You've made your point. I'm hanging up now."

She handed the phone to Cathal, following it by gathering up the sketches and rolling them, using a rubber band to keep them that way. She rose to her feet and Cathal did the same behind her, his arms going around her waist, holding her to his body.

Wonderful lips found her neck, making pleasure shiver through her with soft kisses and small, sucking bites. "Think about me while I'm off being your errand boy?"

She tilted her head to give him better access. "Errand boy? I've got you starring in the role of well-hung cabana boy."

Heat coiled in her belly as she remembered the last time she'd been here, and just what he'd done to and for her during a late night session in the hot tub. Her nipples went hard and tight, ache spreading outward from those center points of desire when he pulled her shirt from the waistband of her jeans then pushed beneath it, firm possessive hands stroking her abdomen before moving upward, forcing her bra ahead of them so he could cup naked flesh.

She needed this. She wanted to lose herself in him, in what

they'd found together despite the reason for his first seeking her out.

She moaned and felt his smile against her neck. "I think I can do cabana boy to your sex goddess."

"Sex goddess. I like the sound of that. Bring on the worshipers."

That gained her the sharp, quick feel of teeth. "One worshiper, Etaín."

"At the risk of ruining the mood . . ."

"Don't say his name."

"We're still pretending we're a normal couple?"

Seven

Cathal grimaced at the irony of the pretense a short while later as he handed the drawings to Etaín's father, knowing he'd pay a visit to his own before returning home.

"She should see a doctor to make sure there's no damage," the captain said, both hands on the rolled sketches, as if keeping them there was necessary to his self-control.

"I'll mention it to her." And then, because he knew the estrangement hurt her, and her involvement with him only added to it he said, "I'm not my father or uncle."

"You made my daughter an accessory to murder."

It would always come back to that, though he wasn't foolish enough to respond and incriminate himself, his family, or her.

"Good night," he said, turning away.

"If you really love her, you'd get out of her life and stay out of it."

"That's not possible." He didn't slow or look back, and in his car, he called ahead, to let his father know he intended to visit.

When he arrived, they went to his father's office, the only place in the house where his father would speak freely.

"What brings you here? I'm surprised you're not with Etaín." His father poured himself a drink. Cathal declined the silent offer of one.

"She's at my place. You've heard about what happened in Oakland?"

"Hard not to. It's the only thing on the news."

"There was a survivor."

"Dead now, according to the news."

"I was in the ICU when it happened."

"The cops asked for Etaín's help?"

"Yes. I dropped the sketches off at her father's place a few minutes ago."

"Who'd have thought my son would be making nice with Captain Chevenier. We go back a ways, he and I. When he was still a green cop he thought he'd make his bones by catching me in a sting operation. It didn't go well for him, though I've got no hard feelings toward him, neither does your uncle."

Cathal felt sure the same couldn't be said for Etaín's father. "You know anything the cops don't about the hit in Oakland?"

"That my son, now interested in joining the family business asking? Or my son, who's involved with a cop's daughter?"

"Etaín knew some of the people who got killed. She intends to ask questions, to do what she can to find answers."

"Could be dangerous to her health."

"Any more dangerous than getting involved with the Dunnes?"

His father shrugged.

Cathal pressed, "You know anything about the bar invasion, Dad?"

His father took a long drink from the glass in his hand, finally saying, "Drugs would be my guess. I can't say more than that, Cathal."

Can't, or *won't*. Gut-sick and unable to stop himself, he asked, "Are you involved in what went down?"

His father's eyebrows lifted. "No. I'll even swear it if that'll make you feel better."

Cathal believed him. "One other thing, Dad, I'm going to marry her."

"I figured that might be in the cards. What about Eamon? I could have him taken out of the picture, permanently. Call it a wedding gift."

The offer chilled him, but not in the way it once would have. It'd be his father who ended up dead if he tried it, maybe his uncle as well.

"Stay out of it. The same way I stay out of your affairs."

He meant it literally, felt the anger rise on behalf of his mother, though for all he knew, she turned a blind eye to the existence of her husband's mistresses, women who came and went and didn't enjoy the same wealth or status she did.

His father lifted his glass in silent acknowledgement of the threat. Cathal rose. "I'll see myself out."

"No." His father set the drink down and accompanied Cathal to the door, surprising him by saying, "I'll make some inquiries. I've got a vested interest now, in keeping the mother of my future grandchildren from getting hurt."

A quick hug followed, and then he went home, walking in to find Etaín stretched out on the couch, vulnerable in sleep and stirring feelings of protectiveness as well as possessiveness, the depth of which he wouldn't have thought possible days ago.

He lifted her into his arms, catching sight of the drawing of a green Dragon rising from a dark blue lake, and smiling, until thoughts of one fantasy creature led to another. Elf. He forced it away, along with his fears for the future.

Etaín woke as he placed her on the bed, her eyes going from slumberous to dark molten pools of desire as he slowly unbuttoned her shirt, parting it, hands moving next to the front clasp of her bra.

"You're overdressed for a cabana boy."

He opened the bra, pushing it away to reveal hardened nipples. "Any decent cabana boy will tell you the best tips come from seeing to other's needs first."

He leaned down, licking the tight, rosy peak as he undid the front of her jeans.

Her hips lifted. He turned it into an invitation rather than a silent demand, a torment by sliding his hand beneath the waistband of panties meant to drive a man to his knees, wispy pieces of material that begged to be stripped away by hands or teeth.

She was wet for him. "Were you dreaming about me?" he asked, sucking her nipple into his mouth, his fingers stroking the underside of her clit, circling the tiny head.

"Maybe."

He punished her with a bite, followed by the rub of his tongue over her nipple, hiding his smile because she never ceased to challenge him, to intoxicate him with her provocative nature. "Not a good enough answer."

She laughed. "It's the only one you'll get unless you persuade me otherwise."

Her hands went to her jeans with the intention of pushing them lower, baring herself to him. He stopped his ministrations to her clit, drawing a moan of protest and then a small purr of approval when he captured her wrists, pinning them to the mattress above her head and holding them there with one hand.

Tonight he wanted something different from her, needed it. He stroked his tongue over her nipple, aware of the way her heart raced and her belly quivered where his hand rested, for a second time sliding beneath her waistband and eliciting a cry from her with the capture of her clit, with the filling of her channel.

He could spend hours touching her, looking at her, being enthralled and intoxicated. It would only get worse when she made the change from human into . . .

He blocked the thought, wanting to concentrate only on the

present. On this, maintaining the pretense they were a normal couple.

Lifting his head, he studied the nipple, turned on by the sight of it glistening, wet from his mouth, love abraded from his sucking.

"The other one wants the same attention," she said. "A good cabana boy would know that."

"A good cabana boy makes sure he's done a thorough job before moving on."

"So I'm a job to you?"

"More like an obsession." He kissed his way to her other breast, using the change of angle to fuck his fingers deep into her slit, to rub his palm over her engorged clit.

Her breath caught. Then caught again. Her sheath clamped down on him in demand. Her moans were praise and payment enough. Her whispered, "I want your cock inside me," very nearly derailed the slow pursuit of pleasure.

She liked it hard and fast and rough, probably because touching a lover had always posed a danger, before him. She could touch him with impunity, but at the moment he prevented that touch, knowing how quickly the feel of her hands on him stripped him of civility and reason.

"Promise to be good and I'll take off the jeans," he said.

"Define *good*."

"Hands above your head, or clenching the bedding, not on me."

"And if I cheat?"

"Don't. That'll be a game for another night, Etaín."

"Mmmm, that sounds like a threat of punishment. Are we talking spankings? A belt? How kinky can we get?"

He bit her nipple because her question reminded him that he shared her with another man. Because with her teasing words she'd flooded his mind with dark fantasies and unbridled curiosity.

He should know better. But then he'd already admitted that when it came to her, he was a slow learner.

"Do you want the jeans off?"

"I'll be good. Under protest. But it's your loss."

"You'll make it up to me."

He released her hands, straightening to look down at her. Clothed, with only her breasts bared, she was still a wanton temptress.

He shed his shirt. Watched her eyes fill with heat and nearly groaned as her tongue darted out to wet her lips.

He undid his pants, freeing his cock from the torment of confinement. There was no pretending he'd be able to hold out for much longer.

"Is this cheating?" she asked, hands going to her breasts, fingers toying with darkened nipples.

Fuck! She was trying to kill him.

He pushed his pants off his hips to drop to the floor, hand circling his cock, sliding up and down on his shaft. "I'll give you a pass."

Her smile mesmerized him. It beckoned to him, demanding the press of lips. Hell, her whole body did.

He released his cock in favor of stripping her out of jeans and panties. She splayed her thighs and he was riveted by the sight of her flushed cunt and erect clit. He caught himself leaning down, drawn by the scent of aroused woman, by the craving to taste, to stab his tongue into the hot wet place his fingers had been, an interim fuck before his cock filled and stretched her.

A feminine hand arrived, interrupting one view and giving him another. An artist's fingers stroking, parting, pleasuring.

"Borderline cheating, Etaín." He nearly panted. Jesus. What she did to him. But he didn't tell her to stop touching herself, didn't protest when her hips began jerking upward, the movements quickening with impending orgasm.

He waited until her sharp cry marked it, and then he lowered his face, unable to deny himself. Inhaling, lips pressed to flushed folds, sucking, tongue lapping, penetrating, consuming.

His hand returned to his cock, not to stroke but to clamp down on it in a vise-grip of restraint. Her fingers tangled in his hair, holding him to her, the promise of good behavior forgotten.

He brought her with his mouth, her second cry and the flood of hot arousal against his tongue very nearly causing him to come.

Once again he straightened, his voice husky when he said, "Definitely cheating."

"Maybe just a little. Cabana boys probably expect it. But I wouldn't want you to feel put out."

She slid from the bed and onto her knees with feline grace, her palms settling on his thighs, her glance sloe-eyed and sultry. "You still want me to be good?"

He guided his cock to her mouth. "Oh yeah, Etaín, I want you to be good."

Ecstasy. There was no other word to describe it. Tongue and lips working in concert. She took him shallow and deep. Shallow and deep. Swallowing on him, her hands on his thighs preventing him from taking control.

White noise filled his head. White heat filled his cock and he thought he might have begged but couldn't care as his world shrank to the searing pleasure of release.

They made it onto the bed, probably because they were right next to it. He gathered her close, felt her smile against his neck. "I think I'll keep you in my employ," she teased. "Maybe even buy some massage oil for you to work with."

"Mmmm, maybe I'll buy you a French maid's costume."

She laughed, the tightening of her arms an unconscious shift to things serious. "How'd it go with the captain?"

"About how you'd expect. Your father said if I really loved you I'd get out of your life and stay out."

"And you told him that wasn't going to happen."

His cock began to harden as though to emphasize the existence of the supernatural. He was more comfortable on some level with subtext, especially when it came to the risky. She dodged the question he was really asking, or didn't recognize it.

He hated the neediness that came out of nowhere. No. Not nowhere, but from seeing her on the hospital floor, dead because she was an Elf changeling who'd used her gift. From insecurity at what it might mean to be a human in the world Eamon had revealed to them.

"In fewer words, but yeah, that's what I told him. Etaín—"

"Yes," she whispered against his lips, the soft quality of it bathing him in liquid sunshine. "You're wondering if this is love. It is for me."

"Me too."

She laughed. Parted lips and the tease of her tongue allowed him to escape actually saying the words *I love you*, neither of them comfortable with them, by the promises they implied for the future.

He lost himself in kissing her, in the scent of her, conversational intentions sidetracked, his will further eroded by the scrape of her nails across his chest to zero in on his nipples.

He managed to leave her mouth but didn't go far. "I swung by to see my father afterward, to tell him I meant to marry you."

"How'd he take it?"

"He offered to get rid of Eamon as a wedding gift."

"I'll just assume you declined."

"I was tempted, for a split second."

"It wouldn't go well for your dad. Does this mean Eamon is no longer a banned topic?"

His mouth slammed down on hers in answer, his tongue thrusting, rubbing against hers in sensual prelude as he rolled her onto her back, his thighs parting hers, his cock entering her, Etaín's muffled laugh and eager willingness making his heart sing.

Eight

The dense fog was shades lighter than Eamon's mood after a sleepless night. He'd lost control of the situation with Etaín, *again*, and it had nearly cost her life for the second time in a single day. Perhaps now she'd begin to shun involvement in the human world.

Eamon grimaced. He was not a man to engage in whimsy or to purposely delude himself. When Liam had called to report Etaín's nearly dying at the hospital, it had taken everything in him not to rush to Cathal's home and demand entry. He'd refrained, barely, and only because there was wisdom in Etaín's so-called breathing room.

Today he intended no such restraint. He had no recourse other than to join Etaín in her folly, despite the risk to all of them if his presence caused her existence to be discovered by Elven spies or other supernaturals.

He'd given them a night together. A night to calm and consider the things he'd revealed though he harbored no illusions they'd return to his estate unless the situation were truly dire.

He closed his eyes against the pain that thought brought with it, stabbing him with the rejection implied by her actions. She was important, not just to him personally but to those he ruled.

The wet embrace of fog against his skin as the speedboat moved through the dense gray of seeming nothingness soothed him. Courtship was not a seamless dance even among Elves.

He would see to this task and then he would go to Etaín. He'd erred, numerous times, but there had also been hours of enjoyment in each other's company, unparalleled pleasure as well. He began hardening in anticipation of being with her, fantasy assuaging the ache in his chest caused by the emotional distance between Etaín and him.

The reprieve lasted until reality intruded with a deeply drawn breath, the scent of ocean and fish and diesel causing him to open his eyes. Seconds later voices sounded in the fog and the outline of a fishing vessel came into view.

In the driver's seat Heath adjusted their course, the deep red of his aura a strike of bold color against the unrelenting grayness. "It's a fifty-six-footer by the look of her. That'd make the captain Garret."

Familiar tension filled Eamon. Of all his duties, this one, monitoring and passing judgment on those who were changeling, was the one that left him feeling powerless despite having immense power.

Fear for Etaín clawed its way into his heart again and he fought against curling his fingers into fists, though he would gladly use them to strike out physically at any danger that couldn't be battled with knowledge or magic. Had she started hearing voices? Or would magic's will simply manifest as it had when she'd lost control of her limbs, the eyes on her palms seeking Parker's bare skin to feed on memories that would increase the appetite for them rather than sate it? Or would magic strike as it had done in that moment of weakness at orgasm, when she'd grabbed at his power without any awareness of it?

Thoughts of the damage she might do prior to his reaching her, and worse, the guilt she'd feel because of it, flooded his veins with ice, nearly paralyzing him with one of water's deadly aspects. He combatted it with fiery determination. He could do nothing until he saw to this responsibility, and then he would go to Etaín and remain with her.

He stood as Heath maneuvered the speedboat to the rear of the fishing vessel, easing alongside a ladder extending down to the water. When they were close enough, Myk, his fourth, standing guard in Liam's place, climbed upward, his waist-length hair the same dark color of ancient trees.

Impatient to get to Etaín, Eamon followed, though he knew Myk would have preferred him to wait until he could verify there was no threat. The boat's captain waited, offering a slight bow of his head when Eamon stepped onto the fishing vessel, murmuring, "Lord," in greeting.

"The ocean is treating you well today, Garret?"

"I believe it will be a satisfied group that'll step onto the dock when we get back."

"I'm glad to hear it."

Eamon scanned the deck. There were easily thirty men, women, and children onboard, no small number of them watching, curious about the arrival of visitors.

He needed no permission, but he asked anyway. "May I move about the vessel and speak to your guests and crew?"

Worry filtered into Garret's expression. He glanced toward the opposite end of the boat, where his changeling son, Farrell, worked at a bait bar.

"Of course, Lord," he said, knowing Eamon was there to judge how well Farrell was dealing with the magic.

Eamon didn't go directly to the changeling. Those brief moments at yesterday's fund-raising event notwithstanding, it was rare for him be out among humans who were ignorant of the supernatural world. While it was true that en masse he had no love for them, individually they weren't objectionable. Over the course of his life he had even found some of them to be interesting.

Amusement rippled through him. Cathal might yet fall into that category.

Eamon paused at a family group with five children, the youngest little more than six. "Did you catch anything?"

The girl ducked her head shyly. Her older sister answered, "She caught a striped bass but it was too small so we threw it back. I caught a halibut that's twenty-six inches long."

Their three brothers chimed in, bragging about their catches and softening Eamon's smile. It was hard not to react to the young. Among Elves, children weren't easily conceived, making each of them a treasure.

He felt a tug in the vicinity of his heart as one of the boys excitedly began reeling in a fish. It would please him to have a son—or a daughter. A small copy of Etaín—or completely differing in looks, it wouldn't matter.

He moved on, stopping next to an elderly couple. The woman was bundled up but shivering, the rod in her hand shaking.

"Can I have the captain get you a cup of tea or coffee?" he asked, placing his fingertips lightly on her shoulder and subtly tracing the sigils of a warming spell.

Her trembling stilled. She sighed in relief. "I'm fine, thank you. That's the trouble with getting old, the cold creeps up on you more often and bites harder."

Eamon looked at her age-lined face and suppressed a shiver of his own. Humans might breed easily, but their lives passed quickly and at the end they were often reduced to the helplessness of their first years.

He didn't envy them, despite their control of this world.

He continued on, aware Farrell watched his approach though he pretended not to. The boy was twelve, small for his age but wiry, and like all changelings at the beginning of the process, the aura surrounding him was more humanlike than Elf. Thin color instead of deep, rich tones, the predominant hues of blue and purple indicating a connection to water.

The bait bar was near a father with two boys who looked to be about fifteen or sixteen. Sullenness radiated from one boy, a surly demeanor that didn't change with the tug on his line.

He drew his line in as Eamon neared. A small silver body coming over the railing as Eamon was footsteps away.

With no warning the boy shouted, "This trip is fucking lame!" and swung the fish, slamming it down on the deck with a force that sent scales and fish guts flying.

Debris landed on Eamon's pant legs as magic pounded against his senses. A wild, raging mass of it possessing Farrell's form as the changeling leapt from his position and attacked the boy.

Against a changeling's strength and fury, the larger boy didn't have a chance. Fists and kicks drove him backward, knocking over coolers and sending ice and fish along the deck so both boys went down.

A toss into the ocean and the sullen teen would drown before any of them could reach him. That was the power of magic, the danger of water.

Eamon entered the fray along with the human boy's father, emerging a moment later with Farrell in his grip, though the changeling continued to thrash and kick, controlled by elemental magic until Eamon shielded him from the water's voice with a spell.

Farrell sagged like a puppet with cut strings. He kept his head bowed, trembling, the contact transferring more scales and guts and water to Eamon's clothing.

This was the hope Eamon believed Etaín might offer his people, that with her ink she could quiet the dangerous voice of magic, possibly even rechanneling it, making the relationship between it and the Elven in this world parallel to the one in Elfhome.

Garret arrived, fear on his face at how Eamon might judge his son.

"Lord," Garret said in a voice that wouldn't carry to the humans. "There was provocation and just cause."

The human boy's father said, "I apologize for my son. His behavior was inexcusable. Farrell can't be blamed for reacting to it."

"Not for reacting," Eamon agreed, "but for his actions he will be held accountable."

Eamon turned Farrell, hands locked on scrawny upper arms. He shook the boy so he looked up, fear in his expression where seconds earlier there'd been raw, unfettered, and unreasoning power.

Magic's voice was quiet. For now. But Eamon couldn't risk leaving the changeling, not surrounded by so much water, not when there was a strong likelihood the human teen would provoke another attack. "Gather anything of importance to you and get in the speedboat."

"Yes, Lord," Farrell whispered.

Eamon released him, turning toward Garret. "You and your wife may visit him at Aesirs when you bring clothing and whatever else you see fit to. He'll work and live there." Where the wards would keep him safe for a time, and where he would also remain close to his family.

"We'll come this evening, Lord."

Farrell cast a quick, shamed glance at his father then did as Eamon ordered. Eamon followed moments later, climbing down to the waiting speedboat, this time with Myk following him.

"You have all the fun," Heath said, straight-faced and yet still failing to suppress his amusement at the sight of Eamon's wet and fish-spackled clothing.

"It's a perk of being Lord," Myk said, dropping lightly into the boat, as irreverent in his way as Liam was.

"Aesirs," Eamon said, command and destination both. Rhys

could take charge of Farrell, leaving him free, in turn, to take charge of his future consort-wife.

Truth time," Etaín said, unlocking the spare helmet and offering it to Cathal.

He took it with a flashing smile. "I'm not afraid of letting you take me for a ride."

She laughed, moving in, pressing the front of her body against his. "Oh I know that. In fact, I'd say you're a big fan of woman on top."

"Definitely." His arm snaked around her waist. "Continue this conversation and we'll get an even later start."

"Tempting." She exhaled, the sound of it marking the end of levity. "Really tempting. I dread this."

Her skin felt stretched thin, her nerve-endings already jangling and her heart rushing in anticipation of visiting Vontae's family and being in the presence of so much raw emotion.

"I'm afraid," she added in a whisper. Afraid of losing control the way she had with Parker, of forcing answers and in the process stripping minds without Eamon there to stop her.

Cathal's arm tightened at her waist. He rubbed his cheek against hers. "You don't have to put yourself through this. I told you I'd cover the bill if we pull Sean McAllister in and give him a list of all the people you've tattooed who are likely suspects. He's good at what he does. It wouldn't take him long to locate them and see what they're up to. Someone will pop as a high probable and you can turn the name over to the police, let them handle it from there."

"Or I could be sure first, by getting close enough to take a memory that'll give Ordoñes something to work with."

The ease with which she accepted doing just that had her chest constricting as Cathal's emotional *no* slammed in her, though he refrained from saying the word out loud.

"Let's head to Sean's boat," he murmured, lips brushing her ear in an attempt to persuade her. "I'll even let you drive."

She accepted his attempt to lighten the mood. "Big of you, considering we're taking *my* bike."

Stepping away from him, she picked up her helmet, not completely able to shed the seriousness. "I need to get the hard part over with first. Then swing by the shelter to ask Justine what she remembers. There's a lot I don't." She met his gaze squarely. "I was high a lot of the time, early on, when the call to ink arrived and things became difficult at home."

Not that they'd ever been easy, thanks to the captain's wife and daughters. But stir in arguments with him and fights with Parker, along with the heavy, heavy weight of disapproval, and it had gotten easier and easier to blow off curfews, and the repercussions from that had, in turn, fostered greater rebellion.

"Vontae was early on, but I tattooed a shit-load of people back then, anybody willing to offer up a patch of fresh skin. Sometimes I did it stoned out of my mind, transferring the surreal things in my head onto various body parts."

She wasn't proud of it. But shame didn't cling to her either. There wasn't much point in it though she regretted the ink now, regretted other things from that time in her life, not the least of which was the inability to get beyond it when it came to the captain and Parker.

She couldn't change the past, even if it apparently was coming back to haunt her. The best she could do was damage control. Starting now.

"After Justine, then I'm game to involve Sean. Mmm mmm. He gives the eye candy at Aesirs a run for the money. Yummy, Johnny Depp in the role of pirate. If I didn't already have enough man trouble I'd be tempted."

"I'm glad that was man, singular, not plural."

"How do you know I'm not talking about you? Eamon hasn't joined us yet, therefore, no plural."

Cathal laughed, touching the garage door button. It rolled upward. She put on the helmet, afterward pushing the Harley out and straddling it.

He joined her on the bike and she liked the feel of him at her back. With a roar they took off, leaving luxury and blue skies for a small house smothered by the fog that still clung to the Bayview-Hunters Point district.

It didn't surprise her when Liam appeared, emerging from wet gloom to join them without speaking, as if he'd been waiting for their arrival. *Shadow walker.* Her voice, not the—

She shelved thoughts of the supernatural, or tried to. A glance down at the eyes on her palms and she was reluctantly glad for Liam's presence, though despite Cathal's desire for Eamon's continued absence, she wished it was Eamon who'd stepped out of the shadows instead of his assassin.

Cathal took her hand in his. "It doesn't have to go further than just paying your respects."

"I used to crash here sometimes, when I was fourteen. Me and about five other kids." Four would go on the list. The fifth had OD'd at sixteen, the same year the captain's version of scaring her straight had worked.

At the door she knocked. It was opened by a rawboned man in his fifties, light enough skinned that the tattoos on his neck and arms popped.

OG. Original gangster. Her palms buzzed, reminding her he wore a little bit of her ink. Tiny footsteps above his heart along with the word Janelle, the name of one of his kids born in the days she'd hung out with Vontae.

"Long time, Tyrone."

He glanced at Cathal, but his gaze lingered on Liam before returning to her. "You've traded up since last time I saw you."

"That's one way to look at it. Okay if we come in?"

He stepped out of the doorway. "Most everyone's either over at the funeral home or talking to the preacher about services. Mama's here though." Vontae's grandmother.

"You know why it happened?" Etaín asked as Tyrone led them down the hallway, toward a kitchen she remembered as being a place of warmth and laughter as well as stern lectures.

"Your daddy send you to ask? Cause we already had cops stopping by. Plenty of cops."

"I came on my own."

"If you say so."

"I was at the hospital last night with Kelvin. He didn't make it."

"You going to get out of the life, then you got to stay far away from it." She heard a warning in that message.

"You didn't answer my question."

"Not going to. What went down is the MC's business."

MC. Motorcycle Club. Meaning the Curs.

"You a member now?" He wasn't when she was a teen.

Tyrone didn't answer.

They entered the kitchen. "Mama, Etaín's here. You remember her?"

"Of course I remember her."

The old woman pushed up from her chair, the smoke from a cigarette on the edge of a saucer curling upward. She was rail-thin, the way Etaín remembered her, except now, with adult eyes, she saw the way age and the weight of kids and grandkids who'd ended up in gangs, in prison, and on drugs had shrunk her, bending height and hunching her back with it.

Her hands gripped Etaín's upper arms. "Look at you, all grown up."

"What passes for grown up anyway. Some people might argue it."

Momma Leeona smiled, as Etaín had meant her to. "I appreciate your coming by," she said, pulling Etaín into a hug.

Guilt slid into Etaín like a hot knife, coming with the memory of Vontae on the floor of the bar, reaching for a gun. "He was a friend." Once. Time hadn't changed that.

"Eat something?" Vontae's grandmother asked, the counter crowded with food.

"Cathal and I had something a little while ago."

Etaín paused to introduce her companions. Momma Lee said, "We can move into the living room."

"This room's fine. I always think of you sitting in here." She sent a glare at the cigarette, though god knew, she'd done a lot worse when she hung out here.

Momma Lee laughed and reclaimed her chair, sitting heavily despite her slight frame.

Etaín sat across from her, Cathal moving into place behind her, his hands on her shoulders as she said, "We can't stay for long. We're on our way to the shelter. I need to talk to Justine."

"She was by here last night." Momma Lee picked up the cigarette. It trembled as she carried it to her lips. "I can't even turn the TV on. Seems like every time I do, they show pictures of bodies being brought out in black bags. And I wonder if that one's got Vontae in it, or that one or that one. Or if maybe it's Lomas or Roddy or Ahman, or somebody else that used to come around here and sit at this table like you're sitting."

Shame crawled into Etaín, that she hadn't called Detective Ordoñes or any of the Oakland cops she knew and asked for the names of the victims. "The police will find out who did this."

"Maybe. But not before other people's babies get killed."

"Is this the start of a drug war?" she asked, drawing on what Melinda had said at the hospital.

Vontae's grandmother shrugged. "You ask me, this trouble has to do with Anton."

"Mama," Tyrone said at the same time Etaín asked, "Anton Charles?"

"Yes. How do you know him?"

"From the shop where I work. Stylin' Ink." She hesitated, adding, "I saw him a couple of days ago." Leaving it there, without mentioning being with him in the bar where Vontae and the others died.

"There's bad blood between him and some of the other Curs."

"Mama, you don't want to be messing with Anton's business. Or with the club's either."

"I'll say what I'm going to say, Tyrone, and pray to Jesus maybe it'll make a difference this time. Violence always begets more violence. I've been preaching it at the kitchen table since before you were born and I'm not going to stop now."

She took a draw on her cigarette, using it for fortification. Etaín could see the sheen of tears, see her fighting to hold them in. Smoke erupted from Momma Lee's nostrils, reminding Etaín of the Dragon's exhalation.

"Vontae." Momma Lee's voice cracked on the name. "Vontae and a couple of the other Curs, they were close to Anton. I heard them talking in this very room—"

"Mama—"

"They were excited about Anton being back, going on and on about him taking over the club and how he had big plans and they were going to be part of them. Got real quiet whenever they realized I was hearing them. I said my piece, and they said *yes ma'am* real polite then went off to do what they wanted to do anyway."

Etaín thought back to how the others had acted around Anton. Respectful, giving up the pool table when the two of them decided to play. One of the guys even hustling to rack the balls.

She glanced at Liam. He'd entered the bar and she'd known by the touch of his magic to hers he was part of the world her mother had been running from. And then all hell had broken loose, thanks to Eamon's arrival, and she'd learned that not only had Liam been sent to watch her, but that Anton's brother owned the place.

"You think this was Curs killing Curs?" she asked, pride and shame keeping her from asking if Anton and his brother were among the dead. She'd find out soon enough, with a call, then realized she already knew the answer when it came to Anton, given Tyrone's interruptions.

Momma Leeona seemed to fold in on herself more. "That's what I think. Same as I think other families are going to be affected like this one. Violence begets violence."

Etaín let the conversation drift to the past. There'd been good times mixed in with those she regretted. Not enough of them to fill hours of conversation, but enough so the visit didn't seem rushed, or dishonest.

"We should probably head to the shelter," she finally said. "Is there anything you need?"

Vontae's grandmother reached across the table, taking Etaín's hands in hers. Etaín jerked with the contact. Sweat broke out with the sharp burn of pain in her wrists where Momma Lee's fingertips rested, and with the unmistakable sensation of an alien awareness invading her reality.

Nine

❧

I'm going fucking nuts, she thought, bracing herself against the sibilant sound of a foreign voice in her head saying, *Look,* against a compulsion to turn her hands so her palms would be pressed to Momma Lee's.

Tension screamed through Cathal's grip on her shoulders. His touch lightened as he prepared to lunge for her wrists and jerk her clear of Momma Lee before she could do any damage, while Liam remained several feet away, a bored audience though she suspected he could move incredibly fast if he chose to act.

Yesss.

Etaín didn't flinch, but it was a near thing.

"I remember you doing beautiful work," Momma Lee said. "Fourteen and using homemade ink and a sewing needle to start with, and already people coming around here, looking for you in particular so they could get tattooed. What you can do for me, for all those like me, is don't do any work that supports gangs like the one Tyrone over there, trying to hush his mama, is so proud to be in, or clubs like the Curs, that only perpetuate the waste of a lot of lives."

"The only time I touch that kind of work is to cover it up."

Momma Lee squeezed Etaín's hands. "I'm glad."

They left a short time later, stepping from the house into thinning grayness as the sun burned through the fog. "Shelter still?" Cathal asked.

Etaín's hand went to her pocket, habit taking it there to retrieve her phone with Anton's number in it. The phone's absence was a reminder of having been abducted by the Harlequin Rapist. She shivered, hastily blocking further thought of him, or their time together.

"Yeah, the shelter."

Liam walked away, as if going to his car. Cathal grimaced. "I feel like my head could explode with all the weird shit."

"Now there's an image. I hope I'm not standing close to you when it happens."

He cut her a look. "You want to tell me how he not only found us but seemed to arrive out of nowhere? I'm pretty sure I didn't hear or see a car pulling in when we did."

She distanced herself with a step to the side. He reeled her back by grabbing her hand.

"I'm afraid if I answer I'm going to witness the whole head-exploding thing."

Cathal laughed, since meeting her he'd done a lot of it—that is, when he wasn't consumed by lust or jealousy or fear for her life. "Funny, Etaín."

"I get that a lot."

"Are you going to answer my question about Liam?"

"I think somehow he can travel between shadows."

Cathal felt an immediate tightness in his chest. "Okay. I think we can leave it at that."

She gave him a smile and he answered with a long, slow kiss before they pulled on helmets and made the trip to the shelter, parking in the back, to find Liam casually leaning next to the door.

Fuck, Cathal thought. It seemed like a lifetime had passed since yesterday, when he and Etaín had arrived at the shelter for the fund-raiser, him to manage the music, her to manage the tattoo artists as well as to work as one.

The fog hadn't come this far inland, and even if it had, it might not have mattered to the kids who now called this place home, along with their parents or in some cases, their grandparents—and were lucky to have a roof and beds rather than to be living in cars or split from their families and sent into foster care. There were some twenty boys and girls playing basketball or hopscotch or jumping rope on worn asphalt.

Many of those who sought shelter here were the working poor. That had been an eye-opener for him, this world so far away from the one he inhabited.

They entered the building, Liam a deadly shadow behind them. For a split second, Cathal considered asking him how he'd gotten there, to see if Etaín was right—only to remember Liam stepping into the room and having all illusion of being human melt away.

Why bother? He was a fucking Elf.

Uneasiness slid into Cathal with a glance to the side at Etaín. Because she was Elf too, already so fucking beautiful, and after the transition she would probably be more so, and able to do additional magic, or stronger magic. What if over time she became more and more like Eamon, and identified less and less with human concerns? Then what? Would she be the one with regrets, about him?

Fuck that. She needed him. And grudgingly, he could see she needed Eamon too.

He shook off doubts and dismissed Eamon from his mind. The shelter was crowded, because it was Sunday, he guessed, and the adults without childcare responsibilities weren't required to spend the day either at jobs or out looking for work.

Justine was in her office. She rose from her chair at the sight of Etaín, crossing the room with the brisk pace of a woman who could have been a drill sergeant.

Cigar smoke saturated the air around her. It made a bold statement about the woman who had to be in her sixties. It gave ad-
vance notice that she was more than capable of taking names and
kicking ass.

She pulled Etaín into a fierce hug and Cathal could swear he
heard the sound of ribs cracking. "Don't ever scare me like that
again."

Justine's command was as rough as her embrace. Etaín returned
the hug, Cathal seeing the way she kept her hands curled, as if she
feared even the contact of her palms with clothing.

Releasing Etaín to give Cathal a bone-crushing hug, Justine
said, "Your timing is perfect. I've been going over the numbers. The
fund-raiser was a huge success thanks in large part to the two of
you. If we do this again, maybe in six months, and have the same
or better results, I think we could add more bed space. Can I count
on you?"

"Etaín is not in a position to offer such a promise," Liam said,
startling Justine as if she hadn't been aware of him.

Cathal wondered if Liam could actually hide his presence altogether. It was not a pleasing thought.

Justine's eyes narrowed as she took in Liam, the look in them
making it obvious she didn't care for what she was seeing. A glance
at Etaín, and Etaín made the introduction, deflecting the confrontation his statement invited by saying, "Things are a little unsettled
in my life right now. Okay if we talk about another fund-raiser in
a week?"

A week, corresponding with Eamon's deadline. Aggravation
rushed into Cathal with the reminder, followed by amusement as
he imagined Etaín comparing him to one of Pavlov's dogs, where
thinking of Eamon or hearing his name took the place of ringing
bells. He couldn't believe Eamon had stayed away this long.

Etaín plopped down in a chair, guiding the conversation to
what had happened in Oakland with a mention of Kelvin. Justine

returned to her seat behind the desk, settling into it with a weariness that held decades of failure and disappointment, and worse, grief over lives lost after they'd been turned around to become shining examples of hope and accomplishment.

Like she'd done with Momma Leeona, Etaín worked back to her teen years, to the kids she hadn't seen in a long time and didn't know how they'd turned out. Not a request for a list as they'd set out to get when they left his place, but a subtle interrogation and collection of names because Liam's presence changed the equation, and Cathal understood that Etaín feared what might happen to those who wore her ink if Eamon were made aware of what they were up to and why.

Ultimately Etaín worked Vontae's name into the conversation as well as inquiring about those she'd tattooed at Justine's request. Cathal made mental notes, but other than that moment of recognition they'd experienced in the dream, there wasn't anything to identify the shooter.

He caught himself rubbing the back of his neck, anxious to come up with a list of names and turn that list over to Sean, to get back to some semblance of normalcy.

Right. And as if the lack of normal conjured him up, Eamon entered the room.

Cathal restrained himself from baring his teeth. Barely, and only because a glance from Etaín had a little bell going off in his head.

On yeah, very Pavlovian.

Time to go, Etaín thought, easing the conversation to a conclusion and saying goodbye to Justine with a hug, the mix of things she felt when she finally turned toward Eamon leaving her as jittery as a junkie in need of a fix.

How had she missed the brush of his magic against hers before today? She could probably get high just closing her eyes and soaking it in.

Yesss.

Not just high, totally hallucinogenic. She was *not* going there right now.

The draw of like to like and magic aside, desire pooled and spread through her, a hunger made sharper and fiercer by separation. Need solidified by visceral memories of what it was like to be with him. With them both.

She introduced Justine to Eamon and it occurred to her that maybe that's what he needed, more contact with humans outside his insulated world. That maybe if he spent time with her and Cathal, he'd come to understand the whole *Lord* thing worked against him when it came to them. And that Elf or changeling, this was still who she was and she had no intention of walking away from the important things in her life: the shelter, Stylin' Ink, the crime victims she could help, her friends, including Derrick, Bryce, and Jamaal, who were family in the way she wished Parker and the captain could be.

And the changes in her gift? The question sent her optimism plummeting.

Sssafe. The word came with a flash of fire through the inked bands at her wrists.

Hearing the Dragon's voice in her head suggested the opposite. But . . . A new day, a new start. It was what Justine preached here, making this the perfect time and place to reach out and take Eamon's hand.

His smile had need rippling through her, not just lust but a desire for peace, for a relationship that was fun instead of filled with anger and discord. "I want to give you a tour of the shelter.'"

A goodbye to Justine, and Etaín stepped from the office, her free hand capturing Cathal's when he might have walked ahead of them, consciously or subconsciously denying Eamon's presence with a turned back.

The hallway was empty, though sounds from the first floor filtered upward, several babies crying, an overlay to conversation and the laughter of children. The sound of pots and pans, of the cooking staff joking, the lingering scent of breakfast mingled with that of too many people in one building, not all of them freshly bathed.

"We lost our shadow," Etaín said, noting Liam's absence.

"He waits outside, along with Myk."

Eamon halted near the stairwell, his hand tightening on hers, forcing her to stop walking. Cathal choosing to do the same rather than release her hand.

It amused Eamon, and in truth he had no objection to it. The magic had chosen Cathal, and there was no denying that the human's presence heightened his own desire for Etaín. Lust and magic were inextricably tangled, as they had been from the first moment he'd looked down onto the terrace and seen the two together.

Turning to face her, Eamon cupped her cheek, the sultriness that slid into her eyes an indication she didn't intend to avoid the touch of his lips to hers. "It was a long night. Unbearable even."

"You brought it on yourself." Bold challenge, not words spoken in anger.

His thoughts flashed to deadly ocean waters and another changeling. "You can't know how important you are to me, to those who will call you Lady."

He claimed her mouth, wanting a response other than spoken words from her, needing it far more than he intended to admit, though his body didn't care if she knew his desperation.

A moan escaped in the first sharing of breath and taste and heat. Relief and satisfaction came with her tongue greeting his in a sensual, taunting slide.

Her pelvis pressed to his, the rub of her mound to his erection causing the fire that was his element to pool in his testicles and become a hot furious roar in his cock. Desperate for a deeper reassurance after the way things had ended the night before, he pushed her against the wall. His hand went to her breast, his pleasure doubled at encountering the hardened nipple, at having her whimper and arch her back.

He'd feared that Etaín would be greatly weakened after nearly dying at the hospital. Instead, raw, wild magic poured into him, changeling magic unfettered by any sense of control. And he, who understood well the danger of it, of her particular gift, allowed it to continue. Believing his protections would hold, he deepened the kiss until he forget where they were, his hand leaving her breast, but only to go to the front of her shirt and the buttons there.

A moaned protest and then the wrenching of her mouth from his stopped him, bringing grungy walls into focus along with the smell of hardship and despair, sweat and meals prepared in bulk, as well as the sound of a building crammed with humans.

"I won't spend this night away from you." The quick cooling of her eyes was a reminder that he needed to be cautious in his choice of words and tone.

"Careful, that sounds a lot like *Lord* Eamon talking."

He hadn't thought courtship would be such a tricky undertaking, but he was nothing if not a quick learner. He smiled, brushing his lips over hers, the slight turn of her head in denial only making it easier for him to nuzzle her ear, to caress the lobe and murmur, "If I'm not mistaken, Etaín, there have been times when you enjoyed going to your knees in my presence. Do you deny it?"

She laughed, his misstep forgotten, the husky, amused sound of her voice lightening his heart in a way only she was capable of. "I don't deny it," she said, rubbing subtly against his erection, fingertips brushing over the additional earrings he now wore and sending a spike of hunger through his shaft.

He rewarded the truth with the fuck of his tongue into her ear canal, with a quick suck to the lobe, and then another, at the tip still rounded, but an erogenous zone for her as it was for the majority of their kind. "Maybe Cathal would enjoy witnessing it." A small sexual taunt as he stepped back and away from her.

It took less than a second for his curiosity about Cathal's reaction to be satisfied. And Etaín the same amount of time before another man's lips captured hers in a possessive, raw demonstration of a more primal magic, one every bit as potent as that defining what the Elven were.

Eamon, for his part, enjoyed the show, enjoyed knowing he wasn't the only one who could be accused of a lack of control around her. His desire heightened in a wash of Elven pheromone and carnal heat, a dare forming, a challenge he might put to Cathal—which one of them could last the longest while pleasuring her.

The images accompanying the idea hardened him further, as did her husky, "Let's shelve the competition until we get back to your place and the clothes can come off."

Eamon caught the flash of Cathal's teeth, a quick baring that had his own lips curving upward as he followed her down the steps, content that when she took neither his hand nor Cathal's, it was simply to improve mobility.

He had not truly *seen* the humans he'd passed upon entering the shelter to find her. Now she forced him to as she stopped to chat with the workers, with the homeless she knew by name, asking questions about others who weren't there and lingering in rooms that shouldn't contain even one child, much less seem crowded by them.

If he had a weakness at all when it came to humans, it was the very young. But while there was no escape from this lesson Etaín seemed determined to teach him, and he understood it was a lesson, he wouldn't undo his earlier successful efforts at courtship by telling her this would change nothing.

She could hold him hostage here during this grace period of freedom. His focus on her, and those she spoke to, would remain unwavering because she was changeling, *seidic*, and he intended to keep her safe from magic and gift. But at the end of the week, he would set the terms.

If she's still alive.

He rejected the possibility she'd be otherwise though he couldn't prevent himself from sliding his hand beneath the thick fall of her hair so his palm rested on the smooth, warm skin of her neck.

"Where next?" he asked, given that they were now at the end of their tour of rooms. "Cathal's?"

The subtle tensing he felt beneath his hand was warning enough he probably wouldn't like her answer.

"No. We're going to visit a friend of his. We could hook up afterward though, at Cathal's place."

He elected to be amused rather than aggravated—or far more uncomfortable, hurt, giving her an easy smile and avoiding a reminder that her promise to spend a week with Cathal entitled him to be present too. "I think not, Etaín. So far I'm enjoying this outing among humans. It is proving enlightening, as you no doubt intended. Would you have me cut it short?"

"No."

He leaned forward, his lips claiming hers in an acknowledgement of just how thoroughly she enthralled him. It was a kiss interrupted by the sound of heavy footsteps.

Irritation flared when he lifted his mouth from hers and saw the muscled Cur he'd found Etaín dancing with days earlier, and that hostility was returned. "You still with this motherfucker, Etaín? That the reason you're not taking calls from your friends?"

Ten

It took effort for Eamon not to lash out with magic. No human who called him Lord would dare insult him in this manner or speak to Etaín in such a tone, nor would any Elf. A glance at Cathal and he saw that this man, Anton, had the same effect on him, though apparently the disrespect rolled off Etaín with ease.

"My phone went missing at the fund-raiser yesterday. Tyrone told you I was here?"

"Him and a shitload of other people after I put the word out I was looking for my friend Etaín."

"Happens I wanted to visit with you too."

Anton laughed, a quick burst of sound followed by the flat eyes of a man who could kill someone he called a friend. "I can guess what about. You already involved me in police business once in the past week. I'm giving you a pass on it 'cause it didn't blow back on me. Not going to happen a second time, not with something that involves the Curs."

Etaín had a bad feeling about why Anton had tracked her down. He confirmed it by saying, "You owe me a tattoo."

Eamon's sudden, complete stillness shouted *no*. A chill swept through her as it occurred to her that he might order Anton killed rather than let her honor the promise or become foresworn if she didn't.

"A memorial tattoo?" she asked, though not in defiance of Eamon. The prospect of adding more of her ink to Anton, especially now, with her gift changing, had ice settling into her core.

Touch him. Look for the answers you seek.

Cold sweat broke out on her skin. She couldn't be sure if that was her thought, her voice, or something else entirely.

"Yeah, a memorial," Anton said.

"Faces?" And once again she felt shame at not having learned the names of those who'd been slaughtered.

"My baby sister, she was working the bar, was saving the money to pay for nursing school."

Etaín shivered at the prospect of being bombarded by Anton's emotions. "I'll need pictures."

"Figured you might. I got a collection of them out front. Funeral for Taneshia is in two days. I want to be wearing the ink by then."

"My promise doesn't cover a rush job." It was an attempt to avert trouble *for* Anton. To make that more palatable, she added, "Where do you want the tat?"

He touched a place on the right side of his chest. In her mind's eye she saw his skin as a canvas already crowded with art, the ink she'd put on him as well as what others had done.

"Let's get the pictures."

Eamon's continued silence as they walked toward the shelter's public entrance concerned her far more than a voiced objection would have. She reached out, touching Cathal's arm. "You mind taking Anton's phone number for me?"

Cathal pulled his cell from his pocket. Anton snorted. "You got yourself a personal assistant now? Or he part of the boyfriend troubles you was having?"

"*Was.* Past tense." She hoped that didn't slide perilously close to a lie.

Anton rattled off his number. Cathal punched it into his phone's memory as they stepped out into bright sunshine.

A car backfired a couple of blocks away. Anton jerked and reached reflexively for a gun she couldn't see.

Adrenaline spiked through her, her heartbeat ratcheting up with something more than the fear of what might happen with skin-to-skin contact. "You expecting trouble?"

"Habit, that's all, baby."

Liam was absent, maybe lurking in back where the Harley was. But the unmet Myk lounged against Eamon's car, going instantly alert. He took a step toward them but stilled, probably at some signal from Eamon.

Anton's Harley was parked several spaces away. They stopped next to it. He opened a saddle bag, reaching in, eyes going wet. He blinked and gave her a hard look. "Tell them to back off, Etaín. Motherfuckers don't need to be all in my business."

She glanced from Cathal to Eamon, saying only, "Please."

They moved, giving Anton and her a little distance, not a lot.

Anton came around to stand next to her, spreading a collection of photographs on the bike seat. "Taneshia's three-year-old little girl," he said of the child in one of them. "My mama has her now."

An image started to form, despite all the reasons why honoring this promise was so dangerous—to him. "What did you have in mind?"

"I'm going to leave that to you. You come up with the art, I'll wear it. Take whatever pictures you want."

She pocketed a couple of them and was reaching for a third when she heard Myk yell, "Sire."

Magic rushed across the ink on her skin, a bomb detonation of it rather than a mild wind as she was slammed into Anton. The two of them hit the asphalt along with Cathal and Eamon, like human bowling pins taken down in a single strike by Myk.

Bullets ripped into Anton's bike, part of a spray from automatic weapons that pelted the ground all around them, deflected by a shield she thought had to be there. Otherwise they'd be bleeding. Dead.

A car sped away leaving a sudden hush. A silence that exploded in a rush, like the pop of a balloon.

Sirens could be heard in the distance. Those willing to have their names included in a police report clamored out of their cars, talking excitedly. The pile of masculine bodies on top of her lightened.

Eamon's eyes held ice. He didn't ask if she was okay, though Cathal did, hands roaming her body.

"I'm good," she said, feeling the glassy stare of cellphone cameras pointed in her direction and using him in a vain attempt to shield against having her picture taken.

Justine rushed from the shelter along with a swarm of workers and volunteers, and Etaín felt sickened by the possibility that someone inside might have been hit. "Everyone okay?"

"Yes."

Relief came with a shiver and the remembered feel of magic blasting over her. It had been no small expenditure of power, as if the shield she knew had to exist covered more than those on the ground behind Anton's bike.

Yesss. The Earth-bound Elf protects you. He protects what you care about despite the risk.

She could feel the burn of magic from inked wristbands into her forearms like a fiery leash attached directly to the Dragon. This time she confronted the surreal beast and the possibility she was going crazy by asking, *What risk?*

Such a large use of magic will draw attention where a simple shield would not have. It will be investigated.

By Elves?

By more than that. Peordh. Predestination. Predetermination.

Peordh?

But the ink on her wrists and arms went cool. "Peordh," she said, looking at Eamon. "Do you know that word?"

Justine heard and answered, "It's the name of a rune symbolizing fate." Adding, "I think it would be better if you waited inside, Etaín, out of sight."

"Good idea." Her chest tightened with the knowledge that at least one person had managed a picture of her; she'd felt it. She wondered if the early Native Americans had a similar awareness, if that's why they'd thought the white man's cameras stole pieces of their soul.

She didn't want more media attention. She was lucky the lid seemed to still be on when it came to her being taken by the Harlequin Rapist. But sending the Elves looking for whoever had managed the picture didn't seem wise.

In the gathered crowd Anton had slipped away, leaving his Harley pock-marked by bullets, its tires flat and seat lined with holes. The remaining pictures lay scattered on the asphalt like litter, but the steely clamp of Eamon's hand around her arm prevented her from picking them up.

She noticed his car as he guided her past it and into the shelter. It hadn't escaped the spray of bullets.

Blinds allowed them to see out but not be seen as the first patrol car arrived, lights flashing and siren screaming. There was no point in trying to make an escape, though she contemplated it. A second patrol car arrived, followed by a TV van.

"Peordh," Eamon said. "Where did you hear the word, Etaín? Why did you ask about it when you did?"

His voice was smooth, cool, water without a ripple in it, but she sensed the riptides beneath the surface and shrugged, preferring no answer than to struggle with a lie.

The hand on her arm tightened while his other cupped her cheek, the heat of it offset by the chill in his eyes and the frost in his voice. "You'll answer the question I've put to you, Etaín."

Lord once again, but given what he'd done she gave it a pass, turning her head to place a kiss in the center of his palm. "You shielded the people in here from stray bullets. Thank you."

He touched his forehead to hers. "It was not a rational decision, Etaín. In the end, it may well cost more than one Elf their lives."

"Your people?"

"Our people." He smiled slightly. "And no. If not for the fact that you didn't grow up among us, Liam would take offense at the question. As would Myk."

Mention of the unmet Elf gave her an excuse to continue avoiding talk of Peordh. She turned her attention to the dark-haired man—one as mouth-watering as all the other Elves she'd seen.

"Thanks for the save," she said.

He gave a small bow. "Lady."

"Peordh, Etaín," Eamon repeated.

"It popped into my head." True enough.

Through the window she saw Justine speak with a policeman, and that policeman speak into his shoulder mic before heading in the direction of the shelter door. Etaín had never been so glad at the prospect of being interrogated. "Looks like they're ready to talk to us."

He didn't say more about the rune. She hoped the reprieve wasn't temporary. He didn't protest when the uniformed policeman entered and led her away, but with Liam present, hidden in some obscure shadow, why would he.

Detectives joined the uniformed cop. What she had to say took only a few minutes. She'd seen nothing. She knew nothing. She could only offer a guess, that Anton was the target given what had happened at the Cur's hangout. But they kept her, making her repeat herself, a stalling tactic she understood as soon as the captain stepped into the room, dismissing the other cops.

She tensed at being alone with him, tried desperately to

blockade her heart against a rush of hope. But that hope crashed easily through the barrier she'd erected when he crossed to her with quick strides, hugging her fiercely.

"Christ, Etaín. Enough of this. Enough. You could have been killed."

Impossible with Eamon at her side but she couldn't give her father that reassurance. "I'm okay."

"For now. I'm putting you into protective custody."

"No." It wasn't even a remote possibility. "Eamon's got top-notch security. He'll keep me safe."

Her father pulled away. "For how long? Until it no longer suits the Dunnes?"

"Despite what you think, Eamon is not involved with Niall and Denis any more than Cathal is involved in their business."

"I'll cede you Eamon, but not Cathal. I'll believe you didn't knowingly become an accessory to murder, but he made you one regardless. Don't let the Dunnes destroy you. It's not too late, Etaín. I can help you out of this mess. The first step is going into protective custody."

The burst of warmth she'd felt at his greeting and hug faded. Ugly suspicion crept in.

If she was in protective custody, rumors could be circulated, making her bait, a target for Cathal's father and uncle, a trap set. Or the prospect of having those rumors circulated, and the possibility of an ordered hit, could be a threat used to get her to admit to having touched Brianna then drawn the scenes from her memories and given them to Denis.

Etaín couldn't forget those moments of fear and horror when the police had arrived at her doorstep, dropping her to the floor and cuffing her. Of being taken to a place that held remembered terror and locked in a small confined space, as if they'd known it could break her. As if they'd been told that by the man in front of her, or by Parker. The captain had never been shades of gray when it came to the law and his duty to it.

She jammed her hands into her pockets, because she couldn't risk touching him. "I don't want to argue with you. Am I free to go now?"

"Etaín." He swallowed, and her own throat tightened at the tears she thought she heard in his voice.

Reaching out, he gripped her upper arms, and though it wasn't skin-to-skin contact, it seemed as though his fear was real, pulsing into her, creating a fist around her heart that squeezed and released in time to the subtle tightening and release of his hands. "You're going to get yourself killed. It's a miracle you didn't die today. You can't count on surviving the next time."

"There won't be a next time. Today I was in the wrong place with the wrong person. I admit it. Okay. Satisfied?"

"No." He shook her to emphasize the point. "This drive-by may have had nothing to do with the slaughter in Oakland. The Dunnes killed four boys, one of them was a Brazilian diplomat's son. You can't know that boy's family didn't have ties to one of the South American cartels. You can't be certain this drive-by wasn't retribution. Accept the offer of protective custody. Please, Etaín. Right now. We leave immediately." *While she was separated from Cathal and Eamon. While there were plenty of cops on the scene.*

"I can't." She nearly added Dad, but knew that'd only make what she had to say next even worse. "I *am* going to marry Cathal Dunne. Disappearing isn't a possibility for him. He's got a club to run."

The hands on her arms fell away. "This is just the beginning of the trouble, Etaín."

He left the room first. She followed, searching the shelter and finding Eamon and Cathal together after passing the officer who'd apparently been making sure they remained at the far end of the building while she was taken into protective custody.

They came instantly toward her, emotions rising like a tidal wave and slamming through her at their approach. She wrapped her arms around their waists the instant they arrived, closing her eyes and savoring their heat and strength.

There hadn't been time for this after the shooting, with the rush of witnesses and the need to get out of sight of cameras and reporters. "My fault," she admitted. It seemed her past was coming back in a dark rush.

"Bullshit," Cathal said, slamming his mouth down on hers, tongue surging past quickly parted lips to rub and twine with hers. He didn't care who saw. Who knew he was sharing her with Eamon, because Eamon's kisses along her neck made it plain they were both her lovers.

Jesus. They'd all come close to dying.

Not the truth. Not today with Eamon and the other Elves present. Intellectually he understood there'd never been any possibility of it, but that didn't prevent his body from believing otherwise.

He wanted to take her back to his place and make love to her. More than that, he wanted to keep her there, safe from her own choices. And the fierceness of that desire, and that it was so similar to Eamon's, was enough to bring him up short.

His mouth left hers. "Let's get out of here."

Etaín laughed. "Guess that means group hug time is over."

Eamon's hand moved upward along her spine, slipping beneath her hair to gently stroke the back of her neck. "You and Cathal are more vulnerable on the motorcycle. It would be wiser for us to leave together in the sedan. Liam can ride your bike. If increased safety isn't incentive enough, I'll even make you the same offer I did the other night. If the Harley is damaged in any way I'll replace it with another of greater value."

It wasn't solely her decision. "Cathal?" she asked.

He nodded, and as if waiting for just that clue, Liam stepped into the doorway, a hand out, ready to take the bike key. "Myk is out back with a different vehicle. There are no obvious watchers."

"Excellent," Eamon said, eyes meeting hers then Cathal's. "Shall we?"

They left, Etaín pulling the Harley's key from her pocket and giving it to Liam as she passed him. In the car Myk asked, "Where to?"

"Sean's boat," Etaín said, the drive-by only making her more determined to do what she could to find those responsible for the bar invasion and slaughter.

Eleven

———

S weet," Ernesto *Jacko* Munoz said as Cyco opened the case to reveal the weapon inside.

"More than sweet. War on drugs means there's some pretty toys to be had. You're looking at a Milkor M32A1, nine grand of killing power."

Jacko lifted the grenade launcher. "I could have me a lot of fun with this."

"Yeah, that mother carries six rounds and I got four different types of load."

Cyco caressed the charges like they were a woman's titties. "One smoke. One flash-bang. Three standard high-explosive rounds. And one called a hell-HOUND. Know what that stands for?"

"No assholes left alive."

Cyco laughed, the sound of it and the way his eyes looked doing it the reason for the street name he'd lived up too. "You got it, homie. High Order Unbelievably Nasty Destruction. HOUND. Double the killing power of the standard round."

"They're showing you some major respect."

"Yeah. They know I'm the big dog when it comes to getting things done."

Cyco's cellphone rang. He checked the incoming number, answered by asking, "You finish it?"

A minute later the call ended. "The fucker survived. Two *cama-radas* emptied their guns and they didn't hit him."

"Where was he?"

"In front of some homeless shelter."

Jacko handed off the grenade launcher like it was a pacifier. "You want me to throw in some of my crew?"

"Na, man, I got it handled. Next time Anton shows up, there won't be any mistakes. Besides, you got your own thing to manage, killing the Irish dude."

Jacko hefted one of the grenade launcher rounds. "Should be easy enough to do."

The sight of Sean's boat coming on the heels of the encounter with the captain had an ache sweeping through Etaín like a small wave of salt water over an open wound.

Would it ever stop hurting?

No.

She'd only be lying to herself if she thought it would. He and Parker had once been her anchors in a world as foreign to her as the supernatural one Eamon had revealed.

Until she'd been left in San Francisco, the only permanent thing in her life had been her mother. They'd moved constantly, changing names with each move. She'd had dozens of them by the time she was presented to the captain as his illegitimate daughter.

He'd accepted the truth of it immediately, refusing to give in to his wife's demands for a paternity test, not that it'd stopped Laura from getting it done. Even now, Etaín didn't know exactly when he'd found out she wasn't actually his. She knew only that he had forbidden it from becoming public knowledge, despite intense pressure from Laura and her moneyed, politically powerful family.

Etaín remembered those first months, rushing to the door each time the bell rang or she heard a car in the driveway. Always certain it was her mother coming back for her. There'd been no warning, no preparation for the abandonment that had marked her life, the shadows of that pain haunting her still.

Run and keep running. See but don't be seen. Those were her mother's lessons. And yet she'd brought her to San Francisco, left her at an age when it was impossible to either run or remain unseen.

The smell of the bay was a reminder of the happier times that had come after she'd finally accepted that her mother wasn't coming back, when comfort offered had led to fierce love, for the man she believed was her father, for the older brother who was constant companion, best friend, and protector, two relationships that were now like a still smoldering and smoking ruin.

Etaín became aware of the heat in her tattoo-encircled wrists, the burn flowing through the ink her mother had put on her just prior to coming to this city. Looking down, she was reminded of those moments in the shower with Cathal when the water had washed away her blindness.

She'd seen and understood that her mother wore tattoos exactly like the binding ones she'd placed on him. Now, for the first time, it struck her that the emerald green woven throughout the design at her wrists was like a long strand of interconnected sigils, one that spread upward into the tattoos on her arms and was the exact color of the Dragon.

Yesss.

The voice jerked her gaze upward, the motion abrupt enough Cathal asked, "You okay?"

She shook off the effects of the voice, wondering if her throat would constrict and her jaw lock if she tried to ask Eamon about it, the same way she'd only barely been able to ask for his help in preventing her from harming Parker with the touch of skin to skin. "Just thinking about how things used to be, with Parker and the captain."

She shrugged. "There's nothing I can do to change it."

"You think like a human," Eamon said.

She smiled at hearing his tone and recognizing it was very carefully neutral. *Lord* Eamon just might be learning his lesson.

"I am human, in the ways that matter." But curiosity didn't allow her to leave it there. "What does thinking like a human have to do with my relationship with the captain and Parker? You weren't exactly putting out the welcome mat for them at your place."

"You didn't yet know what you are, Etaín. What I told Cathal applies to you as well. You will have a say as to whether those you are close to are brought into our household. Knowledge fosters understanding, and distance where there are strong emotional ties is hard to sustain when life is measured in centuries, not decades. If you make them part of our world, things can be made right again."

There was no denying the flare of hope fanned by his words, though her mind shied away from the full ramifications that came with having that kind of choice. Of what it would be like to keep living as those she knew died not from drugs or accidents or violence, but from the causes associated with old age. To know the cycle would be repeated over and over again wherever she lived.

Maybe that's why Eamon preferred to keep himself insulated from the human world. He avoided being touched by death, from having acquaintances become friends he would one day have to make a decision about—because the flip side of that was what happened if they declined.

Sean stepped out on the deck of his boat, dark hair pulled back in a ponytail and shirt opened to expose a gorgeous, tanned chest and tight abs above well-fitted jeans. She couldn't help herself, she sighed, because damn, he still had the whole *Johnny Depp playing a pirate* thing going on.

Her fingers twitched with the desire to touch that lovely skin, though in her defense it was a fantasy born in ink rather than a carnal one, not that she couldn't appreciate a nice looking man despite having two stellar specimens of masculinity on either side of her.

Cathal hooked her with an arm across her shoulders, pulling her against him so their heads touched. "You remember you're taken, right?"

She laughed. "*Taken*. I like the sound of that. It's shades of some kind of wicked erotic scene. Maybe we could act it out when we get back to your place."

"I'm up for it."

That had her attention dropping to the front of his pants. "So danger turns you on."

"You turn me on."

The huskiness of his voice changed the nature of the heat burning at her wrists and forearms, moving beyond the ink to settle in her nipples then sliding downward into her labia to become a liquid reflection of desire. Fierce need, not just for him, but for Eamon too, accompanied a hope that they'd overcome several hurdles in their relationship today.

Myk moved in front of them for the first time, with the clear intention of boarding first. Sean recognized him for what he was, a bodyguard, giving tacit permission with a quick upturn at one corner of his mouth, and a, "Knock yourself out, but don't expect either Quinn or me to let you pat us down."

Etaín smiled at the mention of the man she'd added ink to several days earlier, hiding the Arian Brotherhood tattoos he'd collected while working undercover. She could see the Dragon she'd put on him in her mind's eye.

Her smile widened, because satisfaction at a job well done wasn't the only thing she thought of with respect to Quinn. Days ago he'd not only been coming up from undercover, but stepping out of the closet about his sexual orientation.

In a stroke of pure genius—if she did say so herself—she'd set him up with Derrick—a total win-win, though thinking about one of her best friends brought an ache of a different kind. She'd been away from the shop for days and she missed it. More than that, she needed the connection to other people. She needed to create her art, to make it come to life on canvases of skin.

She opened and closed her hands, opened and closed them, the eyes flashing as though they winked. She couldn't return to Stylin' Ink to work now, she understood that, but at some point she'd get control of her gift again. And then she would. She had to. When she'd accepted Eamon and Cathal's importance in her life, she'd known it would necessitate change, but their relationship couldn't define the entirety of how she lived.

She glanced at Cathal then at Eamon, who turned his head as if he felt her attention, maybe even the nature of her thoughts. Their eyes met, held, his unreadable until he smiled.

She felt the impact of it shudder through her. He was both dangerous and desirable, an erotic combination that apparently enthralled rather than repelled her. It was more than just like to like, otherwise she'd feel drawn to Rhys or Liam or Myk.

Destiny. And she shivered again, this time at the clarity of a sibilant voice that was not hers, though only she heard it.

Myk reappeared on the boat's deck, a signal he was satisfied no supernatural enemies waited below. They boarded, amusement obvious in Sean's expression with the introduction of Eamon. To Cathal he said, "I'm glad to see you took my very expensive advice."

"Don't go there."

Sean grinned. "Still working out kinks?"

He waved them toward the cabin doorway, the one Myk now lounged next to, reminding Etaín of Liam. She moved toward it, heart rabbiting in her chest at the phantom sensation of coils tightening around her, as if the ink at her wrists and up her arms had become living vines expanding into some kind of protective cocoon—or a strangling one.

The imagery changed when she entered the cabin and saw Quinn. The ink she wore became the hot burn of fire, the smooth feel of Dragon scales accompanied by a flare of magic and purring satisfaction. Of triumph.

Quinn stood, and though he wore a shirt with the sleeves rolled up, the Dragon she'd inked onto his skin filled her vision. He took a step toward her and in that instant control deserted her.

Her throat locked, preventing her from issuing a warning or call for help. Her legs froze midstride. She pitched forward, unable to stop from reaching out.

Quinn grabbed her at the forearms and she watched helplessly as her hands clamped at his wrists, palms locked to his skin in what she knew would be an unbreakable grip.

It was her last flicker of awareness.

Eamon felt the surge of magic. If it had an analogy at all, he would liken it to a power line set free in a wild, whipping storm that smelled of primordial forests, of wind and water and fire that felt so old it could only be of Elfhome.

Cathal leapt forward, going immediately to his knees. And Eamon followed, fear like ice sliding through his veins at the violence of the seizure gripping Etaín. He'd seen changes marked this way, but not like this.

She lay on her back, her hands white against the human she grasped, her spine bowing to the point he imagined the sound of it cracking and splintering like a tree in a hurricane, as if she was caught in the eye of it, but rather than a calm center, magic poured into her, forcing its way into every cell with pounding fury.

He tried to counter it as he'd done with Farrell, by grabbing her arms and casting a spell that would insulate her, but he felt his own magic burn away as if having taken his measure the last time, the magic that was hers could now defend against him.

If he'd felt fear in that taste and pull in the aftermath of orgasm, he now felt something well beyond it, desperation bordering on the frantic, an unmitigated agony at the prospect he'd have to pass judgment this very day, and that judgment would be a death sentence.

He'd worried his use of magic at the shelter would draw the attention of any supernatural within miles, but this was like a continuous, jagged lightning strike, where each bolt of it landed in the same spot.

Close to so much water, he'd thought its origins lay there, but as her skin heated and grew slick beneath his hands, he recognized the pour of fire, his own element, though he found nothing of what burned in her that he could either grasp or cool.

"Do something," Cathal said, his body now partially covering hers, his weight across her ribs and abdomen, though even then her back arched, pressing him upward.

In the presence of the unknown humans, Eamon did not bother to respond, but pulled one spell after another from his vast repertoire of them, trying to find a chink in the armor surrounding her, some way of cutting off the flow of magic.

He found none. Perhaps if he wore her ink as Cathal did . . .

Maybe that's where his opening lay.

"She's burning up," Quinn said, drawing Eamon's attention to the press of Etaín's palms against Quinn's skin. She didn't seem to be doing him any obvious damage, to Cathal either for that matter.

It might have relieved some of Eamon's worry except another seizure gripped her, a violent heaving and twisting that created enough of a distraction so the humans didn't see him trace the glyphs of a sleep spell directed at Etaín over the tattoos on Cathal's forearm.

She continued to seize, to burn, ratcheting up his fear until it became a wild clawing inside him, a primal reminder of his own transition, though his battle had been unlike this one.

Her shirt clung to her, but instead of sweat he smelled fire and water and the scent of ancient forests not of this world. She thrashed, finally breaking the silence of her internal torment with a sharp, harsh cry, and with it, a release from the magic gripping her, though she tumbled immediately into a spell-induced sleep.

"Christ," Cathal said, gathering her up in his arms and holding her tightly to his body, his cheek touched to her forehead as he remained in a crouch, relief only barely winning out over continued fear. "She's cooling down."

"You need to get her to a hospital," Sean said. "The paramedics would already be here if this asshole hadn't stopped me from calling them. You want to explain what's going on?"

Cathal noticed Myk then but had no idea of how long he'd been in the cabin. He also noticed Quinn, rubbing wrists reddened where Etaín had gripped them.

Worry penetrated relief. The guilt would tear her apart if she'd stripped Quinn's mind of memories.

"You okay?" he asked, knowing the question was inadequate.

"Yeah. I feel fine. You need to get her to the hospital. Like now."

"We should call 911 first," Sean said. "See if we should try to revive her."

Cathal stood with her cradled his arms. "I've got it under control."

"You're a doctor these days?" There was censure in Sean's tone, anger that provided a glimpse into what his future held—chasms created because he was part of a world those around him didn't know existed—and he didn't like the look of it.

"Trust me to do what's right for her. You know how important she is to me." Important enough he'd been willing to risk dying for her if his father and uncle thought he'd betrayed the family.

Sean nodded. "You'll be in touch?"

"I'll be in touch."

When they were away from their audience, Cathal asked, "That had to do with her being a changeling?"

"Yes."

"It was normal then?"

"No."

"You put the sleeping spell on her?"

With Eamon's nod, Cathal's arms tightened on her involuntarily. It had taken all his strength to minimize her movement, and the entire time he'd been terrified it wouldn't be enough and she'd break her own bones as she seized.

"My heart stopped when hers did at the hospital. This time nothing happened. Why?"

"I don't know. The bond you have with her is unique to the *seidic*. And the *seidic* themselves are shrouded in mystery and secrecy. There have been so few of them born into this world, and all have been turned over as law requires to the royal family."

Eamon opened the car door, allowing Cathal to slide inside with Etaín, then he joined them in the back seat. "The seizure was magic related. It was not a small manifestation of it. This is why she needs to stay at my home, or if you prefer, Aesirs. You may choose our destination."

Big of you. But he understood the anger came from feeling helpless. "Can you guarantee she won't seizure again if she's at either place?"

A muscle spasmed in Eamon's cheek. "No."

"Then we go to my house." It was a concession of a different type. Though when they arrived, he carried her into the TV room rather than the bedroom, placing her on the couch because he wasn't yet ready for the three of them to be together in his bed.

Straightening, he noticed his hands shaking now that he was finally in the safety of his own home. Fuck, what a day. "Get you a drink?" He sure as hell needed one.

Cathal's question barely registered as Eamon stared at the drawing on the coffee table. A green Dragon breathed fire as it formed and climbed onto shore, emerging from an emerald lake, the center of it cloudy with magic not yet gathered into symbolic form.

There was no question as to origin. He'd seen similar drawings done by other changelings. In this visual representation, he recognized what he'd experienced through scent and touch in those last moments before she was free of magic—fire and water and ancient forests not of this world.

"Etaín did this?"

"Yes."

"When?"

At the bar Cathal poured himself a drink. "Last night, I think."

"I'll take one, whatever you're having." Not because he desired a drink but because he recognized the relationship between the two of them had shifted favorably and he wished to sustain it.

At the fund-raiser Etaín had made him laugh by suggesting he go bond with Cathal over some tunes. Apparently they were to do so over much more serious matters.

Eamon accepted the glass, pulling a chair close and allowing Cathal to claim the spot on the couch next to Etaín. An ache formed at watching Cathal's hand brush across her cheek, eliciting a murmur from her. Would his relationship with her ever be so uncomplicated? So natural?

"How long do you intend to keep her under?" Cathal asked.

"She sleeps naturally now."

"Meaning I could wake her."

"Yes." But he made no move to.

"Does she hear voices?" Eamon asked, and saw Cathal's fingers whiten on the glass he held.

Fuck! Cathal hated everything Eamon's question implied. He considered not even bothering to answer it, but . . .

Jesus. If his hands were free he'd scrub them over his face in case this entire day—or at least the part of it beginning after they left the house—was a nightmare he just needed to wake from.

Ignorance is deadly. Reluctantly he'd come to understand just how true those words were with respect to Etaín.

"As far as I know, she doesn't hear voices." He took a long drink. "Why?"

"Elves wield magic, and that magic has at its roots, the elements. Sometimes the wielding is more in line with a human knack or talent. An Elf with a tie to water, for instance, might become a fisherman, though gifts vary in strength as well as focus. One of us might be able to reliably navigate through violent storms while another is always able to locate sought after schools of fish."

"Handy talents to have."

"Yes."

"But . . ."

"We wield magic because we are also its vessel. In this world it is not a seamless joining of will and power—especially in the changeling years. Our young can become a destructive force, acting out the will of the elements where the elements themselves can't easily do so given the constraints of natural law. Most often these are spontaneous acts but not always."

"As in? Give me an example. I'm having a hard time wrapping my head around this." Fucking truth, it was making his head pound.

"If not monitored closely, and prevented from acting, they might come to be what the news calls eco-terrorists."

Cathal pressed the cold glass against his forehead. He doubted the things he'd seen Eamon do barely scratched the surface of what was possible. Hell, what Etaín could already do was pretty damn scary. "Are we talking all . . . Elves . . . being at risk of going off the rails at any given time, or just changelings?"

"The battle to maintain control is lifelong but very few slip after the physical change takes place. It is during that transition period we are most vulnerable. For us this can start at twelve or thirteen and last a dozen or more years."

Cathal's chest felt tight as they came full circle, back to the very word and idea he hated, but he forced himself to ask, "Changelings hear voices, like a schizophrenic does?"

"Yes. Sometimes magic has a voice." An elegant, lord-like wave of Eamon's hand indicated the drawing. "And sometimes it even appears in the mind as something best described as an avatar. Did she say anything about the Dragon?"

He closed his eyes, torn because he'd noticed her hesitation and nonanswer when he'd asked her about the picture as they'd grabbed a bite before heading out to visit Vontae's family. He wanted to deny the uneasiness he'd felt then, the fear he felt now, the icy cold of it having crept back in, deeper than it had been because of the seizure.

Could he trust her?

The question brought instant, gut-level protest. He refused to think he couldn't. But . . .

Fuck. Considering she'd slept through this conversation, she knew even less than he did now about what it meant to be Elf and changeling.

And as far as trusting Eamon went . . .

He understood that when it came to Etaín, Eamon was capable of the same level of ruthlessness his father and uncle were. Hell, he was too. He could still feel the weight of the gun he'd held and his intention to use it.

Opening his eyes, Cathal looked at the drawing, an earlier conversation playing out, Eamon saying, "Many would slaughter any human who wore your ink, with or without cause." And Etaín's response, "You say that as if there could be cause." Followed by Eamon's remaining silent, which was an answer in itself.

Would she forgive him if he turned that page over, revealing the next one and the ones after it, the horrifying scenes to the dream they shared, some part of their consciousness tied to a murderer wearing her ink? Would she forgive him if he told Eamon the reason for the stops they'd made today, so she could reconnect with her past? The why of their going to Sean's boat? Her hopes of identifying a killer, possibly even getting close enough to touch him?

Cathal shifted his attention to the woman who'd become not just important, but essential to him. He traced her eyebrows, followed the ridge of her nose down to her lips, smiling when she smiled.

He couldn't lose her. But he couldn't keep her safe by himself. He couldn't stop her from pursuing this, and didn't want to. The guilt over Vontae's death was too strong, the pain over Kelvin's too sharp. If she did nothing, it would destroy something inside her.

Maybe, *probably*, Eamon had answers that would help her. If he knew what was going on with her, if she would share it with him. If she *could* share it.

The thought gave Cathal pause. At least once she'd been unable to speak, to control her limbs.

Eamon leaned forward, tipping the balance, his voice that of a worried lover instead of an Elf lord making a demand when he asked, "Did she talk about the Dragon?"

"No. But there's something you need to know."

Cathal swallowed the last of his drink then set the glass down on the coffee table. He flipped the page, to an opening scene that soon became self-explanatory though he told Eamon everything.

Twelve

Etaín woke to the sound of pages being flipped, her reality sharpening as slowly Cathal's words came into focus. She opened her eyes and everything stopped. Then a rush of horror came as she remembered. "Is Quinn okay?"

"No harm, no foul," Cathal said.

She sat, the movement and the surroundings making her feel a little dizzy and disoriented. "You're sure?"

Cathal took her hands in his, turning them upward to reveal the eyes on her palms. "You held on to him for a long time, Etaín. A long, long time. There wasn't anything obvious, but I only met him the one time, in Derrick's apartment the other morning. He seemed normal." A glance at Eamon, unity instead of its opposite. "Eamon thought the damage would be very obvious."

Eamon moved from his chair to join them on the couch. He slid his hand beneath her hair to cup her neck. "What do you remember?"

The question alone was enough to have phantom coils tighten around her throat as if ready to choke off a revealing answer. "I went into the cabin. Quinn was there. I pitched forward. He reached out to catch me. I grabbed him. Then nothing."

She could count on one hand the number of times she willingly tried to breach the barrier between her reality and the alternate realities created by stolen memories. "I need to remember," she whispered. "I need to be sure. If I hurt him . . ."

She'd hate herself for not going back to Eamon's estate, maybe for ever having left it in the first place. Maybe she'd come to hate Cathal and Eamon too.

Eamon stroked her cheek with the back of his hand. "Access the memories if you can, but be warned, Etaín, you will sleep again if I perceive there is a problem."

A smile came and went. "Lord Eamon speaks." Gentle tease this time instead of a battle's opening salvo. "Any suggestions?"

"How well do you know Quinn?"

"Not well. I—"

Her throat closed, preventing her from saying she'd done cover-up work on him only days earlier. At the narrowing of Eamon's eyes in suspicion, she felt a flutter of panic and substituted a different truth. "I set him up with Derrick."

"So if you took nothing from him at the boat, there is no reason you would have Quinn's memories?"

She felt the prickle of sweat on her skin, remembered too well the visceral feel of a knife pushed through flesh and the image of a face in close proximity when she'd asked Quinn about the three red lightning bolts on his neck. "Only casual transfer," she answered, as close as she felt she could get to mentioning Quinn wore her ink, though Cathal knew it.

Eamon's expression became thoughtful. "I believe your best approach in trying to determine if you caused him harm would be to use your will as you do your gift, with razor sharp intention. Only instead of piercing flesh, imagine yourself slicing through the mental barrier you've erected against what you've taken, a precision cut with Quinn your sole focus."

"Makes sense." Though that didn't keep her heartbeat from

fluttering and skipping wildly at the prospect of pushing through the barrier protecting her from the horror-filled realities she'd made her own.

She closed her eyes, breathed in and out slowly, as if somehow that added to her control. The memories were like waves behind a storm wall, some lined-up, some overlapping, some stronger than others, capable of pushing more recent ones underneath in a surge of horror.

Focus on Quinn. Focus on Quinn. It became a mantra.

She concentrated on his face, but like ripples in a pond, that image slowly expanded until she saw the work she'd done on him, a sinuous water Dragon covering a vast amount of skin, its wings stretched and curved in flight, enfolding him as though man and beast were one.

She saw it then, the green snaking through the reds and blues and black that had been necessary to hide the AB tats. *Yesss. Your gift. My gift.*

From a seemingly long distance, she heard herself whimper and felt Eamon's fingers on the back of her neck in response to it, there to make good on his promise to trace the sigils of a sleep spell.

The voice whispered through her mind again. *Peordh.* And the barriers parted like a funnel, reality becoming warm, emerald green waters with none of Quinn's memories to be found there.

Peordh. The word lingered, resonating like a promise given.

She opened her eyes. "Nothing. I think it's all good." Though the fear that she'd harmed him still clung to her, and probably would until she saw for herself that he was okay.

"You seized, Etaín," Cathal said, his fear slamming into her. "It's not all good."

Eamon leaned in, touching his lips to her ear, beading her nipples and banishing the fear. "A great deal of magic poured into you."

"Changing me somehow?"

He hesitated. "Possibly."

"I don't remember any of it." She very carefully kept her gaze from going to the tablet, with its picture of an emerald green Dragon. She was more than willing to let the heat that came from Eamon's mouth and the apparent truce between the two men divert all conversation, at least for a little while.

She turned her head, lips seeking Eamon's, finding them. Her tongue greeting his, desire a molten fire pouring into her with his taste, with the feel of Cathal's gaze on them, his need untainted by jealousy.

He released her hands and she made good use of their freedom. Tangling one of them in the long strands of Eamon's hair while the other went to the front of Cathal's jeans.

Satisfaction purred through her at the feel of his hardened cock pushing aggressively against the zipper, that satisfaction deepening when his hands joined hers, making quick work of button and zipper, granting her access accompanied by a husky moan.

She loved the feel of him. Silk over hot steel. Loved finding the tip of his cock already wet in anticipation of being inside her. But more than anything, she loved the lack of tension and resistance, the sense of rightness at being together like this.

One of his hands covered hers, controlling the up and down slide of it while the other went to the front of her shirt.

Desire was a liquid heat in her belly, an ache centered in taut nipples. The promise of longing fulfilled.

Her back arched and it was Eamon who swallowed the soft moan that was agonized anticipation and a demand for Cathal to hurry with buttons and bra clasp, so she could feel his hands and lips on her bared breast.

Her cunt clenched at the imagined feel of hard tugs and sweet suction. Her stomach quivered, retreating from the waistband of her jeans, as if providing a gap between material and skin would summon touch, the slide and cup of a masculine hand. The torment and ecstasy of fingers on her clit, taking possession and returning pleasure, playing a game of dominance and submission as she grew wetter and wetter, her hips lifting and thighs splaying in a pleading for penetration and release.

She closed her eyes, taken over by the sensations bombarding her. The smooth satin of hair, and lips, and cock. The wet heat of an endless kiss. The rub and twine of tongues accompanied by the hot pulsing of a thick, fisted shaft.

Air caressed her breasts. And then Cathal did.

She cried out, pressing her nipple against his palm. Circled her thumb over the tip of his cock and was rewarded with the jerk of his hips, the slick flow of arousal—his, hers. She tore her mouth from Eamon's just long enough to say, "Touch me."

And he did, in the place that needed it most. His hand lingering only a moment on her belly, burning hot there then sliding lower to discover for himself just how ready she was to be loved.

This was magic enough for her. Having them both. Being able to enjoy them together like this. Deep relief and solidarity.

She lifted her pelvis in welcome. Her folds plump and swollen like well-kissed lips, her channel clenching with the proximity of Eamon's fingers to it, begging to be filled by them, stretched and plundered. Her clit was erect, a knotted bundle of nerves sending fiery streaks of ecstasy all the way down to her toes with each of his strokes to it.

More. Harder. She wanted—

Her channel clenched violently, repeatedly, as orgasm came shockingly fast, her cry making the cock she stroked pulse and swell and strain. But rather than being sated and content, release only left her needy for more, for a deeper connection, a physical joining, to give as well as to receive.

She chose Eamon because they'd been separated, because he'd saved their lives today, because he'd made further inroads into her heart, and because he'd issued a sexual taunt about having her on her knees, with Cathal serving as witness.

Her lips curved in feminine anticipation of answering that taunt now, in this moment of bliss, when there was harmony instead of dissention.

Her hand slid from beneath Cathal's, leaving his to continue the up and down stroke to his cock. She sent him a sultry glance, a challenge. "Your turn to watch."

His nostrils flared but he didn't deny her, didn't snarl or bare his teeth when she moved, one knee settling on the cushion between Eamon's open thighs, her hands going to the front of his shirt, freeing buttons as he placed his arms on the back of the couch, a lord waiting for his due, and she laughed against his mouth because even those who ruled could be made to beg.

She kissed him long and slow, captured and sucked his tongue in prelude to going to his ear, tongue exploring the new earrings he'd added along the shell, mouth settling on the tip, lingering there.

Victory was the catch of his breath. The arch of his back and the drop of his hand to his lap to free himself, to curl around his thick erection.

Elven pheromones. The scent of arousal. The feel of Cathal watching, all of it turned desire into a burning need, an inescapable destiny.

She captured tiny masculine nipples, tormented them with her fingers and then with her mouth, kissing downward until she was finally on her knees in front of him.

His expression was fierce demand. But she didn't answer in the way he wanted.

She nuzzled the head of his cock, tongue darting out to lick, to explore the slit in it, to lash the part of his shaft above his hand. Only when his hips jerked upward with each of her touches did she relent, replacing his grip with hers, a tight fist that allowed her to take only what she wanted in her mouth.

"Etaín." Growled, masculine command. Lord still.

Until she began sucking. Then the sound of her name became a pleading for pleasure and finally a shout of it as he came.

She swallowed him down, the taste of his release like molten magic. And even when liquid essence ceased pulsing into her mouth, she kept him there, worshipping him with tongue and lips as he hardened because of it, her movements allowing Cathal to see what it meant for the both of them, to be part of this world Eamon had revealed.

J esus, he was beyond denial now. He couldn't look away as Etaín continued to go down on Eamon. Couldn't stop the up and down sweep of his hand on his shaft.

All he could think about was how much he wanted her mouth on him. Fuck, want was too tame a word. He was desperate for it.

A moan escaped. A pant followed.

He was burning up despite having shed his shirt. He was seconds away from coming on his chest and abdomen. His buttocks clenched as he remembered the way she'd ground her cunt against him the day before, ready to let him mark her with semen on her belly.

She finally stopped treating Eamon like a lollipop and came to him, eyes hot as she straddled him, sultry gaze promising ecstasy if he could survive long enough to experience it. Her lips were swollen, making him want to drag them downward.

"You could have made a fortune as a porn star," he said, hand fisting in her hair.

She laughed. "Objectifying me now? Or offering to pass me on to one of your partners for representation?"

His lips pulled back. Instinctual baring. Possessiveness fully present even if jealousy had been submerged beneath an onslaught of lust the moment she'd put her hand on his dick. "Never."

She bent down, mouth going unerringly to his nipple. Tongue a hot caress, a lightning strike straight downward.

His hips jerked upward. He didn't even pretend control of them. "Put your mouth on me. Suck me off like you did Eamon."

Points for him for acknowledging they weren't just a couple. Instead of making him beg, she slid downward, taking him in hand, taking him between her lips.

"More."

Deeper. Harder.

And she gave him what he wanted.

Took him until there was only white noise and searing, addictive release. Ecstasy that ebbed into a sensual lethargy invading every cell until it was dissipated by the swirl of her tongue and pull of lips.

He began to harden again as Eamon had. Desire returning in a thick fog. "I want inside you."

Etaín wanted it too, but the screeching, trumpeted, fingernails-over-chalkboard rendition of *Here Comes the Bride* coming in through the window was a distraction she couldn't ignore. "We're about to have company."

"Derrick?" Cathal guessed.

"Derrick," she confirmed, a glance at the sketched Dragon and a splinter of fear for Quinn making her hurry to refasten bra and shirt then hustle to the front door.

She half expected Liam to step out of a shadow and prevent her from opening it. Let him try, she thought, stepping outside, the strike of sunshine and hit of fresh air a promise of intoxicating freedom.

Derrick was in the process of turning to make another pass in front of the house. He punched the horn and gave the bike a shot of gas at the sight of her.

Apparently she was allowed to be more than a leash-distance away from Eamon. He didn't join her or trail after her as two and three at a time she took the steps leading down to the wrought iron gate.

Temptation came when she stepped onto the sidewalk and Derrick pulled up next to her. It gripped her in a wild euphoric rush.

If she swung onto the seat behind him, he'd take off. *Run and keep running.*

Her mother's life. Not hers. But a flash of aggravation came when she realized Myk had moved in close enough to grab her if she attempted escape.

Derrick cut the engine and removed his helmet.

"Quinn?" she asked, his confusion over the question answer enough.

"I am not his keeper *yet.*"

"Your timing sucks then."

"And hello to you too."

He got off the bike, enfolding her in a hug, rocking them slightly as she hugged him back with the same intensity, inhaling his familiar scent and feeling a deep sense of peace.

She needed Cathal and Eamon. But she needed this too, this *normal* in her life.

"I've never been so scared," Derrick whispered, hot tears wetting the side of her face as he alluded to her being taken by the Harlequin Rapist.

"Yeah, well, the feeling is mutual." She rocked them harder, a ward against guilt. She should have done this first thing this morning, made a point of seeing her friends in person. In truth, she should have done it yesterday rather than settling for a call to let them know she was safe and that Cathal and Eamon had reached her in time.

She'd been injured and taken to a healer. And then there'd been time with her men, the enforced sleep, the captain and Parker, the hospital . . .

Excuses. Her arms tightened on him and she felt the burn of her own tears as fear spiked into her, at how easy it could be to lose touch with the people who mattered to her. "You know I love you."

He took a loud, shuddering breath, rubbing his wet cheek against hers. "Enough of this B-movie melodrama."

She laughed. "That's rich coming from you."

"We all have our skills, Etaín." He touched his forehead to hers. "I love you too. You're my best friend. Do you think maybe you could just stay out of trouble for a little while?"

"That's what I was trying to do but someone's obnoxious horn interrupted."

He leaned away from her and grinned. "Oops. Sorry." Though he absolutely didn't sound it.

His hands went to the front of her shirt, undoing the buttons all the way down to her navel and redoing them so they actually lined up properly with their correct slots. Her body hummed with an awareness of the ink she'd put on him.

"Not that I'm unhappy to see you, but did you come by just to act as the fashion police?"

"Your name is all in the news again because of the drive-by at the shelter. They're also saying you were seen at the hospital last night—with your father and another policeman—visiting a victim in that shooting over in Oakland." He touched his forehead to hers again. "Someone's been keeping secrets."

His voice was light, but it didn't mask the pain. Even with the leather of his jacket between her palms and his skin, the hurt he felt ran up her arms to fist and squeeze her heart.

"That part of my life is so strange and fucked. It's always just been easier to keep it separate." And maybe some of her mother's teachings had been too deeply ingrained to escape.

"If that's an apology Etaín, it's terrible."

"Yeah. I know."

"We'll just have to work on that aspect of *sharing* in our relationship."

"Says the man with a whole library of self-help books. How'd you know I was here?"

"I have my sources."

She considered just what Derrick had interrupted. And what the seizure had interrupted before it. The point of visiting Sean personally was because he was a private investigator and good at what he did. Letting Sean direct the conversation might pry loose additional names and faces and facts, adding to the list of possible killers wearing her ink. But she already had enough for him to start with, and though she could give him the names over the phone, it made better sense to do some sketches then have Derrick deliver them.

"Come on," she said, noting that Myk had retreated, his attention on their surroundings rather than on Derrick and her. "Let's go inside."

She stepped away from him, breaking the physical contact to reach for the gate and open it.

"Aren't you going to invite that delicious example of a bodyguard to come with?"

"Stick to one boyfriend, Derrick. Two is twice the work and twice the headache."

He laughed, following her into the TV room. Seeing both Cathal and Eamon, one with no shirt and the other with the buttons undone, Derrick stopped her with hands on her shoulders. "Oh you naughty, naughty girl, you."

Heat crept up her neck and into her face. "You're on the crotch rocket and wearing leather, usually that means you're channeling your inner man."

He lifted his hands, fingers clawing the air. "Meow, meow. Just how many secrets *are* you keeping?"

But at least this time Derrick emoted pure relish rather than hurt.

She made the official introductions then took a seat, grateful for an excuse to flip the sketch pad to a clean page and away from the picture of the Dragon waiting there like a storm warning now that the fun and games had been interrupted.

As she drew faces and the tattoos associated with them, she skirted the issue of magic and Elves and changes to her gift, though she shared some of the truth with Derrick. What she'd done in the past at the captain and Parker's request. Why she'd been at the hospital and how she'd come to owe Anton the favor that had her standing with him in front of the shelter. She hoped as she did it, and then later, when she handed Derrick the finished sketches, that she wouldn't come to regret involving him in this.

"Walk me back to my bike?"

"Definitely."

When they got to it he said falsetto-voiced, "I am sooo jealous."

"They are both gorgeous, aren't they? Lucky me."

He hugged her and his pain vibrated through her, sharp enough she felt the Dragon's awareness in the heat racing through her tattoos, and that made her nearly jerk from his embrace. "I'm sorry," she said.

His arms tightened. "We've been best friends for years, a lot longer than you've known them, but you trusted them—"

"Let's not do this, Derrick. Please. I've got problems enough waiting for me inside. There's more to all this than it's safe to tell you right now, okay?"

"But you will tell me?"

"I'll tell you what I can. When I can."

"Promise?"

"Yes."

He circled back. "What problems?"

"Two boyfriends. Twice the work when it comes to relation-ships."

He buried his face in her hair, whispered, "Mr. Edible isn't close enough to grab you this time. You could leave with me."

"I've got a better plan."

"Does it involve sex?"

"Yes."

"Yummy. I think I'll go see what Quinn is up to."

Giving her a final hug, he left.

Etaín turned, pausing to take in Myk with his ass-length brown hair and beautiful features. Oh yeah.

One side of his mouth kicked up, turning stunning into mes-merizing. "If it pleases the Lady, I'd appreciate it if she didn't men-tion the nickname."

"I'll think about it." Though steps later, as she passed him, she couldn't resist adding, "Mr. Edible."

She entered the house, kicking off her shoes, unbuttoning and ridding herself of her shirt as she traveled down the hallway. The bra she discarded just as she reached the TV room. The best de-fense was a good offense.

Thirteen

S tepping into the doorway, Etaín was suitably rewarded by very appreciative masculine glances. Her nipples beaded under their scrutiny. Her hands dropped to the front of her jeans, her labia instantly slick.

Eamon stood. Elegant, deadly grace and unmistakable power. She shivered at the prospect of taking him on while surrounded by one of the elements at his command. She licked her lips, wetting them. "In case either of you are interested, I'm going to relax in the hot tub. See you there—or not."

Cathal laughed. As if either of them could resist the sight of her naked body.

The hell with it. He followed her example, stripping out of his clothes and letting them lie where they dropped on the trip outside. Tall hedges and the house's position on the hill guaranteed privacy, at least from voyeurs.

A distinctive breeze kicked up when they neared the tub, smelling of tropical islands instead of the San Francisco bay. It swirled, gathering enough force to lift the pieces of the cover and carry them to the ground as though they were no more substantial than leaves.

"Useful," he said, giving Eamon credit where credit was due, though he couldn't take his eyes from Etaín as she slipped into the water, disappearing from sight then emerging, skin glistening and nipples puckered, wet and making him want to kiss and lick every inch of her.

He got into the hot tub, Etaín's smile beckoning so he reached for her, pulling her flush against his body for a kiss.

No regrets. Fuck, he could barely remember what life had been like without her in it.

The ink on his arms hummed. Magic. Desire. He didn't care.

"Jesus I can't get enough of you."

Her hands glided over his ass, up his back, then down again. "The feeling is mutual."

He claimed her mouth. Tongue thrusting and retreating, in sole possession as Eamon stripped, what they'd shared prior to Derrick's arrival making it seem perfectly natural to allow space for Eamon's hands on her breasts when he joined them in the water.

She moaned appreciatively. Rubbed against his cock, and by extension Eamon's, both of them already hard for her.

Bed would have been a better destination. Hell, the couch in his entertainment room would have been. But he knew her well enough now to understand what she was up to though she had to know Eamon well enough to understand this was just a temporary reprieve from discussing the drawing of the Dragon.

His arms tightened on her with thoughts of it and the conversation that had followed with Eamon, desire taking on the edge of desperation. Christ, he couldn't lose her.

And then he couldn't think as her hand found his cock, fingers wet and hot around it, her fist becoming a substitute for her slit, eroding his will to resist with each stroke until he was helpless against the searing need boiling in his testicles, the eruption of it in a jet of semen.

"Happy now?" he murmured against her lips.

"Very."

He released her to submerge himself in water, rising to find her turned to face Eamon, teasing him about his use of magic, challenging him to demonstrate what he could do in his own element.

Eamon's laugh promised pleasure. "Very well, Etaín. But it'll require that neither Cathal nor I be touching you."

He parted from her, taking a seat on the ledge beneath the water's surface. Cathal followed his example, curious.

"First something Cathal will find entertaining," Eamon said, enjoying the shedding of responsibility and worry.

A spell bound to air created a symphony of sound surrounding them, wind song accented by the chimes and bells in the yard, accompanied a moment later by the lift of water in a dance reminiscent of elegant fountains.

Etaín's laugh was pure delight. Cathal's easy smile a reward in and of itself.

"Next time I'll put on some tunes," Cathal said.

"I'd suggest doing it now but I don't believe you'll want to miss the next part of this."

He let the spells fall away, his will directed in a much more carnal pursuit.

Water became his hands stroking Etaín's body. His tongue swirling over nipples and clit, invading her channel in thickened pulses.

Her head went back on a moan, face flushed and eyes closed. She was the very picture of a woman in the throes of exquisite ecstasy. Accepting pleasure, uninhibited and uncaring at having them watch her climb toward orgasm then reach it, embrace it, lingering there and drawing every beat out until nothing was left other than lassitude.

She opened her eyes, sending him a provocative glance. "I won't need a man at all if I gain that ability with the change."

"Let me dissuade you of that particular notion."

She laughed with delight when he lifted her, removing her from the water and placing her on the padded deck at the edge of the hot tub. His forearms splayed her thighs, holding them open as he put his mouth on her cunt.

The hungry thrust and lap of his tongue dominated, commanded in a way that water couldn't. Cathal's claiming of her lips, her breasts reinforcing the lesson that neither of them could be replaced, though even with her cry of release, he couldn't stop himself from driving the message home by lifting and turning her to face Cathal.

Magic, another man, and his own arm across her abdomen held her into position as he slammed his cock home. The tight welcome and press of her buttocks into him made him surge against her with the relentless thunder of ocean against land, elements as wild and beautiful as the magic of their joined, perfectly synchronized bodies.

Pleasure was a riptide carrying him under at orgasm. Carrying them both under, though moments later, after he'd watched Cathal thrust inside and drive her to another heated release, he made no protest when she said, "I think I need to just drift for a little while."

Niall Dunne hit the remote, silencing the news reporter's voice. A cool rage spread through him as he contemplated what he'd heard. Someone had nearly killed his son over this business Etaín had dragged Cathal into.

Maybe. Probably.

She was trouble. He'd known that the moment he'd seen Cathal with her. He could look back now and understand by the time he met her, it was already too late to remove her from Cathal's life without it also costing him his son.

He had a vested interest in keeping Etaín alive. But his interest only went so far.

He'd take estrangement with a chance at reconciliation over a dead son. There was no reconciling from the grave.

He set the remote down in favor of picking up the gun he'd been cleaning, then the silencer, screwing it into place, the act relaxing him. The weight of the weapon was comforting, the feel of it in his hand like an extension of self.

For now he'd wait. He'd hold off acting, because if he was being totally honest with himself, he had to accept that there was a chance this didn't have anything to do with the violence in Oakland.

For as long as he lived, he would never forget the pictures Etaín had drawn. They'd known there was risk associated with the one boy, the possibility of ties to a South American cartel, but he'd accepted Denis's need to put this behind him.

As far as he—*they* were concerned, there was only one punishment for a rapist. Death.

Some crimes were too heinous to be tolerated. He'd never forget that night the two of them returned home to find their mother dead, her naked, lifeless body bound to the bed, panties stuffed in her mouth to prevent her screams.

He'd been fifteen. Denis fourteen. It had taken them two years to find the man responsible and kill him.

W hen's this asshole going to show up to work?" Jesus *Lucky* Fuentes asked as they drove past Saoirse for something like the fifth time.

He lifted the gun in his lap, aiming it at the picture taped to the dashboard of Sleepy Ruiz's car and pretended to shoot, same as he'd done every time they passed the club, his arm jerking with the imaginary recoil. "Rich *pendejo*."

"Yeah," Sleepy said. "Probably walking around with a Rolex on his arm and a grand of cash money in his wallet, maybe even some coke in his pocket."

Lucky pretended to pull the trigger again, wanting to get this done. "If I can't take him out riding shotgun, I'm going to get him walking from his car to his club. I do that, I'm going to take what he's got on him, get myself a little bonus for doing this job."

"Gotta look random, homie. You follow me? That was how you said Jacko wants it."

"I know man. I know."

He lowered the gun, loving the feel of it in his hand, the rush of power that came with knowing all he had to do was pull the trigger and the thing would be done. It was a hell of a lot better than walking around with a shank keistered in his ass and waiting for the right moment to pull it out and strike. A lot easier too. Killing someone with a shank was hard. He'd seen guys jumped and stabbed twenty times and live. You had to get lucky and hit the right spot, not easy to do when someone was fighting against you. And you had to get lucky not to get caught trying it, which was how he'd gotten his street name in juvie when he'd made his first kill.

He put the gun on his lap, giving a little salute to Puppy, one of the lookouts he'd put in place. "This is getting fucking old. You feel me?"

"I feel you."

He and his homeboys had been watching for this guy Cathal Dunne since yesterday, when Jacko had come around, pulling him aside and saying after he got this done, he was going to introduce him to another mafia member, and not just any member but Cyco Chalino.

No way was he going to fail Jacko. Prove himself enough times and he'd become a made member. Already he was a *camarada*, a trusted associate. Fuck, maybe he'd be put up for a vote after this kill. Who was going to say no if Cyco and Jacko said yes?

"You think it's true about Cyco being in town?" Sleepy asked, sounding all no-big-deal when Cyco was a fucking legend, a hardcore member in tight with a cartel down in Mexico.

The guy and his crew had invaded a rival's territory, stormed into a club selling drugs and prostitutes, killing twenty-five of the enemy and getting away with it until he got caught up in a raid by *Federales* in the pay of another cartel. He'd done a little over a year in a Mexican jail before busting out.

Lucky cut a look at Sleepy, dying to tell him that fuck yeah, Cyco was in town and he was going to get an intro after this, along with a little coke for doing the favor. Instead he said, "Probably just a rumor, man, because of that shit that went down in Oakland."

"Yeah. I guess." Lucky jerked upright in his seat. "Fuck man, the fuel gauge just dropped to empty from all this driving around."

"Time to steal us some gas, then maybe take a break and stop by Rosena's. What do you think?"

"I get her. You take Tracy."

"I was thinking we'd switch off, take a turn with each of them."

They laughed, turning the corner, though this time Sleepy sped up rather than slowing down as Saoirse came into sight.

Lucky picked up the gun, aiming it at the picture of Cathal Dunne, imagining the pull of the trigger, his arm going up in pretended recoil. "Let's go fuck us some homegirls. We got this place covered. The *pendejo* shows, Drooler or Puppy will call and we'll come back."

*T*his is ridiculous. Simply ridiculous.
　　Deep breaths. Deep calming breaths.

Derrick sucked them in.

They didn't help.

His heart stuttered and popped like a man facing a firing squad. His hands were wetter than a client dripping sweat and screwing his face up against the pain of getting a tattoo.

Ridiculous.

What he needed was a joint.

A small medicinal toke.

No. Absolutely not. That wouldn't do.

Quinn had *not* seen him at his best the other night. They'd gotten past it, and the sex . . .

Delicious.

Devine.

He'd never been anyone's first before. A shiver of pleasure moved through him, sweet and warm, like honey left out in the sun.

A spasm followed, longing and ache, the wild fluttering that was part of the rush of falling in love.

I am not rebounding. I am absolutely not.

Quinn was different. He wasn't like—

No! That name didn't bear thinking, not ever again and certainly not in proximity to Quinn's.

The connection with Quinn was real, totally unlike anything he'd ever experienced. It felt right. Magical even. He touched the spot on his right hip, just one of the places on his body Etaín had tattooed.

He and Quinn both wore one of her Dragons, though his was smaller. Much, much smaller, and that was *not* a reflection of penis size, where Quinn's . . .

She'd outdone herself there. Fabulous work. Exquisite.

Derrick dried his palms against his jeans for a second time. He should have called ahead instead of just dropping in like this without warning.

He and Quinn had talked on the phone since that glorious night Etaín had introduced them. But then between Quinn's reunion with a family he hadn't seen in five years and his needing to be there as his father underwent chemotherapy . . .

It'd only been days but if felt like months. What if the thing with Quinn was all in his imagination? What if it was only about sex?

The craving for a joint returned. He stifled it with an immediate *No!*

The last thing he wanted was to smell like reefer today. Quinn hadn't made an issue of it the other night, but he hardly thought an ex-cop who'd eventually need to get a PI license would want to risk having it all go down the toilet because his boyfriend liked to smoke a little weed from time to time.

Derrick took a sniff at each shoulder then bent his head forward to make sure nothing clung to the leather. Secondhand smoke was a killer.

Enough stalling. He patted his zippered pocket, a nervous gesture since there was no possibility the carefully folded sketches had escaped. *Do this for Etaín.*

Hah! He knew exactly why she'd sent him here.

Matchmaker! She'd given him this excuse to see Quinn again.

His heart took a dive, settling with a hard crash at the pit of his stomach as a reality bigger than the state of his love life gripped him. Twice in two days she'd nearly disappeared from his life permanently. First the Harlequin Rapist and now this brush with death in front of the shelter.

He hadn't been sure she'd be at Cathal's house, not until tall, delicious Mr. Edible made his presence known and tried to send him away. Well, bigger, nastier brutes had attempted it in the past but when something mattered, he had a spine of steel.

Not that Etaín had needed him to rush to her side. She had Cathal and Eamon. They were enough. She didn't need him—

No!

No! No! No!

That was negative thinking.

He was done with negative thinking. He'd had weeks of negativity. Months even, if he was being honest about the state of his life prior to Quinn.

Strength was his middle name now and because of it, he could face a hard truth. There was a reason Etaín hadn't fully shared. True, she'd always played things close. It was there in her apartment for everyone to see. No personal touches. Nothing. As if at a moment's notice she might pick up and leave.

Since he'd known her, she'd been the rock and he'd been just plain pathetic. Some of his choices when it came to men . . .

He shuddered. Bad. Worse. Horrible. Totally awful.

Well, as of now, that had changed. He was going to be her rock. He was going to help her get the police some information, whether it meant working with Quinn or not. He wasn't without contacts. He'd found her, hadn't he? He had access to the records at the tattoo shop and he'd been there when she'd tattooed a lot of her clients.

"Time to pull on the big girl panties," he said, striding purposely to the dock that would take him to Sean's boat—and Quinn.

Fourteen

Quinn rolled his shoulders. Christ, he'd forgotten how much he hated sitting at a desk and mentally grinding through mostly irrelevant data as a way of gathering intel.

The Internet search on the Curs MC was a slow, excruciating crawl that had landed him on Facebook more than once. Facebook! There was a reason the jails were full. Call it the stupidity of criminals, though unfortunately nothing had popped that had any relevance to the killing at the Curs hangout.

It'd be so much easier to tap into law enforcement files, even kiss someone's ass in a different agency, but one of Sean's sources had gotten back to them with a warning that one wrong move would trip plenty of red flags and cause a shitload of trouble for anyone who didn't have official cause to be looking into the club.

Didn't mean it couldn't be done, but their involvement in this didn't warrant trashing a contact or leaving anyone hanging out to dry. What they needed was the list of names from Etaín, a place to start, and truth be told, an excuse to *move*.

He was antsy. Itchy. As if at any moment he just might come right out of his skin.

He didn't like the feeling even if he understood the source of it. There'd been plenty of down time when he was undercover, but even then he'd been playing angles and pushing limits, living at the sharp edge between life and death.

He'd felt like a soldier in the trenches, especially during the stint in prison. He'd longed for freedom more fiercely than a lot of the inmates, because for him freedom was a call away.

And now, days into that freedom after making the call and having supposedly been shanked by another inmate and bled out, he struggled against the urge to escape the chair in favor of pacing as a swell of frustration and helplessness came. He wasn't used to not being able to take action, but other than being there for his family, his father's cancer wasn't an enemy he could fight. And he hated it. If not for Derrick—

He stopped himself because the only thing worse than the slow crawl of a worthless Internet search was doing that same search with a raging hard-on. Jesus, what a way to come out of the closet.

A muted tone sounded, announcing someone had just tripped the farthest of Sean's sensors. There was the tap of keys as Sean opened a camera's live feed.

Quinn used it as an excuse to leave his chair but the boner he'd been trying to avoid came on like a battering ram at seeing Derrick on Sean's screen. A few clicks later, and Sean had pulled up another image, Derrick at Stylin' Ink.

"I thought I recognized him," Sean said. "What's he doing here?" It was followed immediately by, "Fuck. Etaín's worse."

Sean reached for his cellphone as if to call Cathal. Quinn stopped him by saying, "Hold on, Derrick is probably just stopping in to see me."

"You know him?"

A throb of pure heat went through his dick at just how well he and Derrick knew each other. Unfortunately that heat also slid up his neck and into his face just as Sean glanced at him.

Sean laughed. "Like that, huh? Why don't you intercept him on the dock, blow off a little steam, because for the last hour I've felt like I was trapped in the cabin with a caged beast."

Quinn headed for the doorway. "Back in a few."

"Take it out of camera range unless you want me watching."

"Will do. I'm not into kink."

"Hey, don't knock it until you've tried it."

"Not going there," Quinn said, stepping out into the wet, silky caress of fog arriving in thin wisps.

The feel of it against his skin momentarily halted him, driving the heat of lust back with a desire equally intense and not totally foreign. He'd always enjoyed being on, in, or near the water, but not like this, at least not since he was a kid visiting his grandparents in the sweltering heat of the South, days so hot he'd wanted nothing more than to rip off his clothes and dive into the lake.

He shook his head, partially clearing it as he resumed walking. "Been cooped up too long," he muttered, gaze straying to the Bay and water cold enough to shrivel his dick and pull his balls up tight in protest if he jumped into it. Jesus, it might come to that if he and Derrick couldn't get somewhere private, though when his path finally intercepted Derrick's, thoughts of privacy, water, and Sean slid away like raindrops down a building to be replaced by fiery possessiveness and a growled *Mine*.

Fuck, where had that come from? But he didn't deny it, and he didn't care who witnessed the kiss as he pulled Derrick to him, locking their bodies together for the grind of hard cock against hard cock as he slammed his mouth down on Derrick's, plundering and claiming with the thrust of his tongue.

It didn't end with the one kiss. Or even a second, though he restrained himself from touching anything but Derrick's shirt-covered back even when his own shirt was pulled from his jeans and unbuttoned, then pushed open so talented fingers could stroke over taut nipples, sending hot streaks of fire straight to his dick.

God it felt so good. Better than good. Better than anything.

He'd gladly give up breath, but the need for it forced a momentary separation of his mouth from Derrick's, and in that instant Derrick seized control with the press of lips against Quinn's throat, a caress that had him fisting Derrick's shirt in his hands to keep himself from urging Derrick lower, and lower still.

"Let's take this private," he managed. Hell, if it had to be in his car he'd settle for that if it meant he could free his cock and feel Derrick's hands and mouth on it.

Derrick leaned back, satisfaction on his face though there was a hint of vulnerability in his eyes when he said, "Someone's anxious to do the nasty. It's a good thing I showed up when I did."

"Yeah, it is, considering my current state is because of you."

"Well, I'm not apologizing, you delicious man you. I intend to just eat you right up." Derrick radiated pleasure, practically preening with it until his eyebrows drew together in surprise.

He stepped out of the hug, making Quinn's cock scream in protest though the physical separation and the wet feel of the air against his heated flesh cleared his mind enough to remember Sean's cameras. With the reminder of their existence, he'd swear he felt someone watching with intense, focused interest. It was real enough he blushed when Derrick reached for him.

"Oh, don't turn into a prude *now*, you sexy man you. Take off your shirt, Quinn, so I can see the rest of the artwork."

"Derrick . . ." But a glance down at his own chest and with a start, Quinn complied, because instead of skin in its first week of recovering after taking on a massive amount of ink, his flesh was healed, and the colors of the Dragon vibrant and deep, richer and even more beautiful than they'd been that morning when he dressed.

"Amazing." Derrick whispered, awe in his voice as he moved around Quinn, taking in the full design. "Simply amazing. It almost looks alive. And your skin . . ."

Fingertips traveled down Quinn's spine, and his thoughts snapped back to the carnal. He turned, throwing his arm around Derrick's shoulder. "Let's go, Derrick."

Derrick allowed himself to be guided away from the dock, his conscience clear because Etaín had sent him there. She had to have suspected there might be a small delay in handing off the pictures. Certainly a shorter delay than if she'd meant to come herself considering she was with *two* men. Naughty naughty girl. One lover at a time was enough to handle, and a healed Quinn . . .

A shiver of anticipation went through him. He absolutely refused to think about the weirdness of it, or to dwell on how he'd also noticed the healed tats on Cathal's arm, tats he'd heard were absolutely fresh yesterday morning when Cathal and Etaín had shown up at the shelter fund-raiser. There were more secrets, but he *would* root them all out.

His arm tightened around Quinn's waist then tightened again when he noticed he wasn't the only one totally enthralled by Quinn. Tall, Dark, and Predatory stood on a yacht that screamed money. Worse, as they neared, the man jumped from the boat, radiating a subtle threat.

Sooo, Cage thought, landing lightly on the dock. He'd felt the singing call of one magic hidden in another and he'd come.

Lord Eamon would have left watchers to see who might investigate but he didn't trouble himself to look for them. The bargain made decades earlier allowed him to hunt in San Francisco.

His presence would be noted, but the Elves had long since ceased trying to follow him, though he tore his eyes from the approaching men in order to read the deep shadows. The Lord's Assassin and he had a history. Undoubtedly he would encounter Liam soon enough.

His attention returned to the man who was of greater interest, a man whose arm tightened on his companion, nostrils flaring and body tensing possessively. Understandable. No treasure was more valued than a mate, and the human morsel he'd heard called Derrick clung with a tenacity that deepened Cage's appreciation of him.

This was mystery wrapped in a clue impossible to miss, surprise already becoming dangerous curiosity. Stepping in front of them, he said, "The body work is exquisite. Who is the artist?"

It was Derrick who answered, "Etaín."

His shock was genuine. He had been in the area long enough to recognize the name and know how thoroughly it was enmeshed in human affairs. "She has been much talked about of late."

Derrick's chest puffed out. "She's my best friend. I also work with her."

"Is she at the tattoo shop today?"

"No."

Derrick nudged his companion to continue walking, not so subtly putting his body between them.

Cage allowed them to pass though he turned, following them with his eyes, mesmerized by the ink and what it had to imply in this Elven-controlled territory. *Seidic*. And yet he could not begin to fathom what game played out here, though that had never stopped him from joining the fun.

T̶ell us about the Dragon," Eamon murmured against her ear, returning to the abandoned conversation with the lazy trace of a nipple as Cathal's wicked hand stroked her belly while sensuous lips teased an ear lobe.

"Ganging up on me now?" she asked without heat.

"If that's what it takes to keep you safe," Eamon said.

Beneath the water her palms rubbed over muscled thighs, not

an effort to distract them but a delay as she battled the fear that her throat would close up, preventing speech and shattering the peace.

Cathal's teeth were a sharp nip to her lobe accompanied by a growled demand. "Answer the question, Etaín."

Reality or hallucinogenic effect? Science had an explanation for the whole bright light at death thing. But not for the rest of it.

She hadn't imagined the voice or the locking of her limbs. She licked her lips as if somehow the moisture would guarantee the smooth flow of words. "It started with the nightmare of the slaughter. Just a hissed voice before Cathal was with me."

Cathal's immediate tensing was a sharp thrust of terror. "Saying what, Etaín?"

"I see."

Eamon's expression gave nothing away. "Not surprising considering your gift, and the likelihood one of the killers wears your ink."

She licked her lips again. "Then the voice came a second time, calling Liam a shadow walker."

A nod indicated Eamon's lack of surprise and encouraged her to go on. But when she thought to tell him what had happened outside the shelter, to speak of Peordh, phantom coils encircled her throat in silent warning.

She said instead, "I didn't actually see the Dragon until the hospital. I caught the last of Kelvin's thoughts, just when he was shot from behind, I'm guessing. There was blackness, followed by golden script, the tattoo I'd done for him."

Her breath caught at the remembered pain. Guilt crept in, that she might have brought about his death rather than him causing her heart to stop, and because of the bond, Cathal's.

"I went from darkness to bright sunshine, to a place like the one you called magic's primordial birthplace for those like us. Meaning Elves?"

She was proud of herself for managing to say the "e" word without hesitation or a lingering hint of disbelief.

"For Elves," Eamon answered. "For other of the supernaturals."

Relief relaxed the pressure in her chest, though the lake hadn't been part of what appeared in the mirror. "So the Dragon is real?"

"I do not believe so." A cautious answer, because he didn't want to lie. "It's not uncommon for changelings to hear voices, to give magic a form in order to separate it from the self. I have seen drawings similar to the one you did."

"Of Dragons?"

"No. More often the avatars take the form of ancient, elemental deities. Phoenixes for those linked to fire. Merfolk for those with a tie to water."

He sounded sure, reasonable, making her doubt herself and believe him. Did it matter if the Dragon was real or imagined manifestation?

Gift and magic were inextricably entwined. She already knew the cost of denial.

When the call to ink had come, and with it, the need to touch others, to turn skin into canvases for her art, she'd answered it with a feeling of rightness, of absolute certainty that this was her purpose in life. Sometimes she'd placed images found in her dreams on those who wanted tattoos. Other times she'd drawn based on their preferences, content with the chance to hone her skills. But that heady time of happiness was short-lived by the start of conflict with the captain. And the trouble at home was compounded when the parents of her tattooed classmates threatened lawsuits and demanded reimbursement for the expense of removing the ink.

She'd tried to stop tattooing and failed. The need for a steady stream of canvasses became a natural gravitation toward rougher and rougher kids, and experimentation led to the discovery that drugs buffered the pain of being a disappointment and shielded against the captain and Parker's disapproval. It was a vicious circle whose shadow entangled her still, making the two men who'd once been the center of her world see darkness in her rather than light, failure rather than success.

Eamon's gentle pull and twist of her nipple returned her to the present. "Does the Dragon guide your actions?"

Yes. No. She couldn't deny there was a cause and effect, but it was easier, and more reassuring to say, "It doesn't tell me what to do."

"It will. Today only my presence prevented another changeling from killing a human boy."

"What happened?"

Fear slid into her veins and traveled down the ink in her arms to settle in the eyes on her palms like ice as he told her about his visit to the fishing boat and how Farrell had become the unreasoning vessel for wild, raging elemental magic. She balled her hands into fists against masculine thighs, chest so tight she could barely breathe. There had never been any real doubt that the killer had been aware of Vontae because they both wore her ink, but now she whispered, "What if I'm responsible for the slaughter. What if because of the ink—"

"Bullshit, Etaín," Cathal growled.

"Unlikely," Eamon said, abandoning her nipple to take her hand and straighten it from its tight fist. "Magic does flow through your ink. That is why many would kill any human wearing it. You empower humans with your art, giving it a specific focus. Doing it siphons away magic, which is perhaps another reason the barrier against the memories you've taken has grown thin. But I don't believe humans wearing your ink will hear magic's voice or be victim to it in the same way we are."

He carried her hand to his mouth, pressed a kiss to her palm. "There are sigils of shielding, of deflection and channeling, as well as one to produce the glamour that will become necessary to hide what you are after the change."

"Spells?"

"No, more like mental patterning taught from a young age because of the complexity of the sigils and the difficulty in memorizing their shapes."

"Do you know any of them?" Cathal asked her. "Did your mother hide them in a game maybe?"

She remembered all the times she'd traced the tattoos on the backs of her mother's hands and curling around her wrists, the sigils she now knew were hidden there, asking, *What do they mean?* Always getting the same answer. *See but remain unseen.*

"No."

"Start tonight," Cathal said. "I'll go to the club for a while and work. I can't lose you, Etaín. That seizure . . . Jesus."

He leaned in, kissing her. Lips and tongue working in sensual persuasion, the hand on her breast creating an ache for explorations of a different kind.

She murmured "Okay," when his mouth lifted from hers, standing when he did, pressing her mound to his rigid length, teasing him, the prospect of arduous, mental exercise making her say, "If I have to suffer, you do too."

Cathal's laugh verged on a pant. "And that's fair somehow?"

"Who said life was fair?"

Fifteen

$\sim$

Sean glanced up as Quinn ushered Derrick into the boat's cabin. "I hope you've got good news. I called Cathal but it went directly to voicemail. He hasn't gotten back to me yet."

"Good news and then some," Quinn said, heat creeping up his neck as he made the introductions even though he didn't use the word boyfriend, not that he needed to, considering the show on the dock and the cameras he hadn't been able to care about.

Fuck, better get used to people knowing.

His mind shied away from imagining what it was going to be like introducing his family to Derrick, and the conversation that had to precede the event.

Later. Put it away for later.

"Derrick stopped by Cathal's place. Etaín seemed fine to him, not that any of them mentioned the seizure. She brought him up to speed and sent him with some goodies."

"Excellent." Sean motioned toward a counter between the desk he was working at and the one he'd given Quinn. "Let's see what you've got, Derrick."

Derrick pulled the drawings from his jacket pocket, carefully unfolding six sketch-pad-sized pages and lining them up on the counter. Twelve faces in all. Some were identified by legal name, others by street name, all of them included at least one picture of a tattoo and a note about body placement.

Sean whistled in admiration. "Damn. I wish she worked for me. These are good enough to run through the facial recognition program."

Pride surged into Derrick on Etaín's behalf. "She's incredibly talented. These are nothing compared to what she can do on skin. Has Quinn showed you the artwork she put on him?"

"Not up close and personal, but I got a good look at it when he met up with you on the dock." Sean's smile was deliciously wicked, and totally at Quinn's expense.

The blush returned. Derrick couldn't resist saying, "So you watched?"

"Hey, I gave Quinn fair warning. Guess he forgot in the heat of the moment."

Derrick preened. "When you've got it, you've got it."

"True enough. Your friend Etaín definitely has it, enough for Cathal to be willing to risk his life for her, but more telling, enough for him to overcome his social conditioning and share her with Eamon."

Surprise had Derrick gaping. "You knew?"

"Not until earlier today." Sean moved over to his desk, swiveling the computer monitor toward the counter then picking up the keyboard and returning. "Let's see what shakes out by running the names first."

Within minutes they ruled out five of the men.

Sean cut a look in Derrick's direction. "All in prison. All gangbangers. She hung with some rough kids."

Derrick felt defensive on her behalf. "These aren't all people she was tight with. Some are known acquaintances of Vontae, one of the dead bikers. And others . . ." His chin went up. "She traded art for drugs. It's not something she's proud of, the acting out, the rebelling when things got rough at home. But you'd understand why it happened if you'd ever met the nasty stepmother and equally atrocious stepsisters."

Sean laughed. Quinn said, "I take it you have?"

Derrick shuddered dramatically. "A horrid accidental encounter at the de Young Museum and not one I'd like to repeat in this lifetime. You'd think Etaín and I were unwashed winos off the street from the looks we got and the whispered conversation that followed. Bitches, and I don't mean that in a friendly way. Not that Etaín will talk about any of them, her father and Parker included, but I think Bitchzilla and her demonic daughter spawn probably made Etaín's life a living hell while she lived with them. Oh, to be a fly on the wall when they find out she's snagged the owner of Aesirs."

Sean laughed again. "And Saoirse."

"True." There was immense satisfaction in imagining them seething with envy and fuming at her good fortune—until Derrick considered how they would no doubt do their best to make Etaín out to be a whore.

Not that it would matter to Etaín. She didn't travel in their social circles.

Right now.

That would change because of Cathal and Eamon.

Fear edged in, a milder form of the one he'd felt earlier, that he could lose her. He shook it off, going quiet as Sean typed another name into the law-enforcement database.

The results came a few moments later, Tony *Shank* Medeiros, suspected of having fled to Mexico after being implicated in a drug-related murder. The same was true of the seventh person Sean entered, Roberto *Spooky* Jimenez.

"Always possible they're back in town," Quinn said.

"Can't discount it." Sean typed in another name.

The results came back noting a sealed juvenile record for Torrey Baker. It was the same for Luis Galvez, while Jose Estrada,

LaQuann Terry, and Marc Ruiz had done time in jail as well as in juvie.

Derrick felt himself getting defensive on Etaín's behalf again. "They're not all friends or people she ran with. Some of these she met at the shelter and tattooed because Justine asked her to. They've gotten right and want to stay out of trouble."

Sean took a pair of scissors from the desk and separated the images so instead of six sketch pad pages there were twelve. "Etaín give you anything on the guy who was the target of the drive-by?"

"Anton Charles. No. But he's gotten a lot of work done at the shop." Derrick pursed his lips, deciding against sharing the delicious secret of how Anton had helped identify the Harlequin Rapist. That was need to know, and unless Etaín said otherwise, not something to blab.

"Is Anton affiliated with a prison gang?" Sean asked.

"Probably." Derrick hesitated. "I don't know for sure. He doesn't have gang tattoos, at least not that I've seen and noticed. Jamaal would know. Etaín too. Can't you just do a search?"

"The Curs are too hot right now." Sean gathered the pictures of the men currently in prison and set them on his desk along with the scissors. He reordered those remaining, leaving a wide space between the two groups, three pictures against four.

"Guys whose home turf is San Francisco on the left, those from Oakland on the right. I'd expect retribution by now if the Curs thought they knew who was behind the bar invasion."

"Unless this is Curs against Curs, like Vontae's grandmother thought it could be," Derrick said. "And those responsible are in hiding."

Sean nodded. "True. It doesn't track that way for me. But this hit makes zero sense. It's like something that would happen across the border, in the cities where the cartels are battling for territory."

He checked the time. "It's late. I'm good with wrapping things up for the night. Tomorrow I'll do some face-to-face time with cops on the Oakland side. See what I can learn, and if I'm lucky, find out if Baker, Estrada, and Terry are still in the area or if there's word that Jimenez has slipped back into the US. If you're not needed at home, Quinn, why don't you concentrate on the three from San Francisco?"

Derrick straightened, his shoulders going back. "I can help."

"No," Quinn said, a growly answer that sent a little thrill through Derrick.

He imagined his lips zipped because this wasn't the end of it, though there was nothing to be gained by arguing in front of Sean. And besides, he wanted to bask in Quinn's protectiveness.

Quinn made copies of the relevant drawings, adding notes before the two of them left the boat. Derrick's heart fluttered in his chest at having Quinn's muscled arm go around his waist as soon as they were on the dock.

"I'm leaving later than I intended," Quinn said. "I can't—"

"I understand." Derrick's heart sank momentarily then buoyed at remembering what they'd done earlier. "I'm partly to blame for your being late anyway."

Tall, Dark, and Predatory wasn't on his boat. There were no lights. No doubt Mr. TDP was on the prowl, and not in a gay bar. His loss. He didn't know what he was missing.

They reached the bike far too soon as far as Derrick was concerned, but despite Quinn's need to get home, the first goodbye kiss wasn't rushed. Nor was the second, or the third.

He was breathless by the fourth, aching for so much more than a good fuck by the fifth, though he'd welcome that too.

"I really can help you and Sean investigate," he said, nibbling along Quinn's jaw. "And it's not just an excuse to hang out with you. I know people, I can—"

"No."

Derrick pouted. "You don't think I have the cojones."

Quinn's laugh was husky. "Oh, I know you've got balls."

"That's not what I meant. I'm not just a pretty face."

"Definitely not."

Quinn's mouth covering his prevented further argument. The rub of tongues and press of cock to cock elicited a moan from Derrick, taking the fight out of him but not draining his determination.

"I'll call you," Quinn said, finally stepping back so their bodies no longer touched. "If you want to do something, keep tabs on Etaín. Okay? That seizure was really bad."

"I'll check on her tomorrow." He'd do more than that.

Quinn turned and walked away. And with Quinn's back to him, Derrick touched the pocket containing his copies of the drawings. It was time for him to step up. And thinking about the picture of Marc Ruiz, he knew just where to start. There was something in the eyes that reminded him of Emilio Delarosa, not that he'd ever imagined visiting that asshole or asking for a favor but . . .

Derrick tugged on his helmet. He'd do what he needed to do. Emilio no longer had the power to hurt him.

Cage approached Saoirse with caution, though that caution had little to do with the young human loitering up ahead. He kept expecting to feel the sting of Elven wards or perhaps even the cool edge of an assassin's blade against his skin, not that such a thing could easily penetrate his natural shields.

Few blades could, and many of them had already been found and made part of his hoard, including the one he wore at his back. Kestrel.

He smiled at what the elders of his race would call his foolishness. Or perhaps his arrogance, though even he had been tempted to find a way to destroy the blade when he'd finally located it.

Kestrel woke hungry half a block away from the boy. And as if sensing it, the teen turned, his gaze clashing with Cage's, the blade's judgment validated by what Cage saw in the boy's face. There was no innocence remaining. This child had already been consumed by a culture of violence and drugs and the power both offered him.

In centuries past, Cage had killed humans as young as this one. He would prefer not to do so tonight, though he played out the deadly game of chicken, his path taking him close to the boy.

The teen did not reach for the gun Cage smelled in passing. And the blade's hunger for blood was not met. Nor would it sleep again until it was sated.

He'd known the likelihood of it awakening. But he enjoyed not just collecting the arcane, but using the things in his possession rather than merely hoarding them.

His puzzlement returned as he crossed the street to Saoirse. The mystery of Etaín and whatever game was being played here had deepened after watching the news reports of a drive-by shooting at a homeless shelter.

Now that mystery was made even more tantalizing as he entered the club. There were no wards here either.

He moved through Saoirse, aware of the desire-filled glances given him by more than one beautiful woman, and they were exquisite creatures, though despite the long hair several of them wore, none of them were Elves. When it became clear that Cathal Dunne wasn't present, he found a spot affording him a good view and stopped.

A lovely brunette rose from her chair and approached. He smiled, prepared to amuse himself with a different type of hunt as he waited for his main quarry, Cathal, and through Cathal, Etaín.

L ucky took another drag on the joint then passed it to Tracy. He could hear Sleepy fucking Rosena in the bedroom next to the one he was in, grunting while she moaned and screamed.

"You want to do it again?" Tracy asked, her hand zeroing in on his dick.

He took the reefer back, thinking he wanted a blowjob more. Tracy was good at giving head. And besides, she wasn't nearly as nice to look at as Rosena.

His cellphone rang before she'd even gotten him half hard with her hand. "Yo," he answered.

Puppy said, "That guy showed up. He just walked out of the parking garage but Drooler and me didn't see him drive in. He must have come in from the side we weren't watching. You close?"

"No."

"He's gonna walk right past me on the way to his club. You want me to do him?"

"No, man. You did good. Time for you to get out of there. Sleepy will pick you up after he lets me out. Talk to you later."

He called Drooler.

"Come on, man, let me kill this *pendejo*," Drooler pleaded, dying to do something that'd earn him a new nickname. He hated the one he'd gotten when he'd first started hanging around and they saw him drooling after he got drunk and passed out on the couch.

"No. This one I have to do personally." He didn't mention Jacko's name. Only Sleepy knew that's where this job came from. "Get eyes on the club entrance. Text me at that number I gave you when this guy leaves then haul ass. I'll be waiting for him between the club and his car."

"Puppy tell you we don't know what he's driving? We didn't see him going into the parking garage."

"Yeah. Puppy told me. No problem. It's not going to matter what car he's got in a little while. The garage has cameras in it anyway. Stealing his ride is out. Later, homie."

He hung up and left the bed. "Hurry the fuck up!" he yelled to Sleepy. "We need to roll!"

"You gonna be back here later?" Tracy asked, the sheet falling away when she rose to her knees.

He got a boner looking at her tits and pussy, her acne-covered face out of the picture. "Sure." Why not? Maybe after he snagged the blow from Jacko, they'd invite some others and have themselves a party.

He dressed, pulling the burner phone from his pocket and muting it so he wouldn't have to remember later. Rosena let out an "I'm coming" scream as the bedsprings really cranked up their squeaking. He went to the car, stashing his personal cell under the seat.

A few minutes later Sleepy came out of the house, strutting after having done it with Rosena. She didn't give it up to just anybody. "I want me some more of that," he said.

"I hear you, man." Though now he was jonsing for a different kind of action.

He aimed the gun at Cathal Dunne's picture, pulling the trigger in his mind. "I hope I don't have to wait all night for this rich *pendejo* to come out of the club."

"As long as you get it done."

"No problem."

A couple blocks over, Sleepy did a double park long enough for Lucky to stuff the gun into the waistband of his jeans and get out. "Later *ese*. Soon as I off this guy and get to a good place, I'll call for a pick up."

"Later."

Lucky headed to his hiding place as Sleepy drove off. A day of waiting for this guy to show up had given him plenty of time to scope the area and notice where the cameras were.

If he missed some of them, he missed some of them. Ending up in prison didn't scare him. He knew he could handle himself there. He had before. He would again. And fuck, if things got hot here, maybe he'd end up heading south with Jacko or Cyco if they split.

Ducking into an alleyway on the route between Saoirse and the parking garage, he had a view of a Jag hugging the curb in front of a Tesla and behind a BMW. Fucking rich bastard with his fucking rich club crowd.

Come on. Come on.

Waiting was the hard part.

Lucky let his mind drift while staying aware of his surroundings, a lesson he'd learned doing time.

Jacko had chosen the right *camarada* for this job. It didn't matter why this guy needed killing. All that mattered was getting it done.

The Jag and the Tesla and the BMW had him dreaming about getting a crew together and going in, taking out a shit load of people the same as Cyco had down in Mexico. Fuck man, he did that, he'd be a legend too, and after becoming a made member, he'd get a territory to tax. He'd be rolling in the money, maybe even buy himself a bad-ass car, something better than the ones he was looking at.

He pulled the gun from his waistband.

Come on. Come on.

Sixteen

Eamon watched her sleep, his chest expanding with feelings of tenderness, and though he lay next to her, their bodies touched intimately together, it was not enough contact. He had begun to believe that state wouldn't be remedied until he wore the same tattoos Cathal did.

"You enthrall me," he whispered, a dangerous admission as he leaned down to whisper kisses along her neck. "In centuries I have not experienced a day like this one."

From harrowing fear to wild crests of ecstasy.

From distrust and alienation to the promising spread of harmony and unity.

Progress had been made with respect to their future as a cohesive family unit. But with respect to her gift, her magic . . .

Uncertainty remained. Grave uncertainty. And the chill of it made him give her more of his weight, the feel of breasts with their sweet-wine nipples against his chest fanning the flames of hunger, though the burn of it did not completely diminish the ice of his fear for her.

Her artistic ability had given her an advantage in learning the complex sigils, but it had still been grueling work. He'd taught her the bare minimum a changeling raised among them would know about channeling and containing magic, and about shielding herself to lessen its voice. But he wasn't sure it would be enough, not given the old, old feel of her magic and the violence of the seizure that had taken her. It had seemed to him that magic forced its way into every cell with pounding fury, while at the same time, created an impenetrable shield around her so that his spells burned away at contact.

He'd come to worry that he didn't grasp the full truth of her connection to the elements, and wouldn't begin to without wearing her ink. A dangerous prospect for the both of them, one that might well hasten the moment when duty would require him to render his judgment.

A fist closed around his heart, his mind locking out images of her death by his decree. There were answers to be had about the *seidic*, costly answers with no guarantee any of them would lead to her survival.

He looked away from her, gaze settling on the picture she'd drawn, the way magic presented itself to her, seeking control rather than to be controlled. The Dragon suggested a tie to water and fire, *his* elements, and yet on the boat, close to so much water, the power he drew from it hadn't made a difference, and though he'd recognized the pour of fire into her, he'd found nothing of what burned in her to redirect or cool.

The Dragon stood for other things as well. Chaos. Upheaval. Drastic change. That her magic presented itself in those terms . . .

His arms tightened on her. Need slammed into him, a desire transcending the physical. He took her ear lobe between his lips, pulled with tender sucks. Fierce satisfaction burned through him at having her hips cant immediately, her leg climbing over his so she could press her heated mound to his hardened cock, craving the joining of their bodies despite being submerged in sleep by utter exhaustion.

His smile dissipated as the barest disturbance in the wards surrounding the city reached him. It was a small, nearly imperceptible ripple. One he might not have noted at all if he hadn't strengthened the magical alarm system after she and Cathal left the estate, and one, even now, that gave nothing away as to what had passed through the barrier. The disturbance was so minute it might have taken hours to ripple its way through the wards until it reached him.

The chill returned. There were assassins, the queen's among them, who were said to be able to move through wards without triggering a warning.

Fierce protectiveness gripped him, and the spell to trap Etaín in sleep rather than risk her refusing his order hovered on his lips and tingled in the fingers touched to her skin. It was madness to continue allowing her any place other than the estate or Aesirs.

Cathal could be persuaded to his side and to his view. And yet . . .

Eamon hesitated. His will not sufficient enough to hold the spell or direct it. The trust brought by the events of the day was too precious a thing to risk. Not only Etaín's trust, but Cathal's, who'd left expecting to find her here when he returned, and who might well view with suspicion the claim she had to be moved.

The argument could be made that in allowing Etaín to remain, he demonstrated his care for her wishes as well as Cathal's. He had no real evidence she was in greater danger now that the rippled note of passage had reached him.

Eamon stroked the soft nape of her neck rather than trace a sigil onto it. His mouth returned to hers, swallowing sleep-murmured sounds of pleasured welcome.

His hand went to her breast, cupping its weight, her back arching with the brush of his thumb over a nipple drawn tight with the need to be suckled.

Forcing his lips from hers was a prelude to levering his body up and away from the paradise his cock sought. He caressed her lobe with his tongue, daring a shallow thrust into her ear canal then brushing his mouth against the still-rounded tip before finally managing to separate from her.

Etaín whimpered in protest at the loss of his attention but didn't wake. He left her alone only long enough to dress and retrieve the comforter from Cathal's bed. A kiss followed his covering her with it, the light touch of lips to lips because he couldn't bear to part from her without it.

Straightening, Eamon gathered a strand of her hair, the gold of it like captured sunshine twined around his fingers. Using words of magic, he summoned Liam, calling him through the shadows, this type of binding dangerous to his third because it could be used to trap him.

"Sire," Liam said.

"The city wards reacted to something passing through them. I need to pinpoint the place of the breach and see what can be learned there."

Liam glanced at the sleeping Etaín. "Given the presence of the other changeling at Aesirs, I assume you want her taken to the estate."

"She'll remain here."

"It's not a choice you would have made in the past."

Eamon heard increased concern beneath the none-too-subtle questioning of his decision, that he was being unduly influenced by his *seidic* intended, perhaps even altered by her uncontrolled magic. "You will better understand the desire to avoid unnecessary conflict when you meet your match."

"An unlikely event, Lord. Made more so by what I've witnessed of your courtship."

"Your time will come. For now I'll leave you to guard Etaín. In all likelihood, the ward was tripped by the arrival of a tourist possessing some small, native amount of magic, or by an artifact."

"And if you're wrong about what passed through the wards?"

"Do you question your ability to prevail should a would-be assassin or kidnapper come for Etaín?"

"Hardly. You'll take both Myk and Heath with you?"

"No. I'll leave Myk outside with orders that no one except Cathal is permitted entry."

Cathal shifted restlessly in his chair. He'd handled the most urgent items of business and prepared for the meetings he couldn't put off tomorrow morning.

Doing anything more required a level of concentration he couldn't find. And that lack of focus left room for scenes from the couch and the hot tub to flicker across his mental screen, heating his skin and sending molten blood to his cock.

Were they done with the lessons yet?

He grimaced, hearing in that question a kid's voice asking "Are we there yet?"

But it was no child's fantasy that came with a possible "yes." Thoughts of what Etaín and Eamon might be doing at the moment bombarded him. Images of them in his bed, their bodies joined.

A shaft of fire streaked through him, pooling in his balls. He clenched his fists to keep from reaching down and freeing himself, from jerking off. Jesus.

He'd rolled his sleeves up while he worked. Now he looked down at the tattoos she'd placed on his forearms. Honeysuckle and thorn she called them, an apt description encompassing sweet pleasure and sharp-tipped jealousy. The latter had abated, but in its stead had come the ambush bleeding away of confidence, the worry it would one day matter that he was *only* human.

He wanted to go back home. He refused to.

It stung his pride to admit that Saoirse, the club that had been his dream and sole focus for so long, couldn't hold his interest against the craving to be with Etaín.

It'll fade into something manageable, he told himself. Not for the first time. *It's just the newness of the bond and a natural reaction to nearly losing her.*

Christ. He'd nearly died himself at the shelter. If not for Eamon . . .

Only it wasn't Eamon's acts at the shelter playing out vividly in his mind. It was Eamon thrusting into Etaín's body, her back arched and breasts flushed. It was her midnight-colored eyes drawing him to her, making it impossible to care she was wet for another man, wet *because* of another man as he shoved into her seconds after Eamon had spent himself following the erotic display of magic.

The clench of Cathal's buttocks drew him out of the memory, a curse escaping when he saw his hand in his lap, circling his cloth-covered erection. "Fuck." Then *fuck* again, this one silent as remembering the sensation of being inside her sent a pulse of sheer need through him, forcing his hand up and down on his length.

He broke the hold of lust when pre-cum escaped, more of it leaking at remembering the way she'd made him come like someone getting his first hand job. "Jesus."

To distract himself, he checked in with his father.

"You at home?" his father asked.

"I'm at the club."

"I don't like it. Whoever nearly killed you is still out there, unidentified and on the loose." Meaning none of his father's sources had come through with a likely suspect in the drive-by.

"Wrong place at the wrong time with the wrong person. Had to be connected to what happened in Oakland."

"Probably. I'd feel better if you let me arrange for a couple of bodyguards."

"No." The last thing he wanted was to give the authorities additional reasons to believe he was involved in his father's business.

Etaín's brother and father had already convicted him. Having mafia soldiers as bodyguards would be a piece of incontrovertible evidence to them.

For Etaín's sake he didn't want to do anything to make the situation worse than it already was. She might be willing to sever her relationship with the captain and Parker over him, but *he* didn't want to carry that load of guilt, not when he knew how much the estrangement hurt her.

You think like a human.

That's because I am one. Will always be one, he argued in his head with Eamon.

Distance where there are strong emotional ties is hard to sustain when life is measured in centuries, not decades.

He didn't want to contemplate the kind of lifespan ahead of him, ahead of *them*, or the choices that would come with it.

"I better get back to club business," he told his father, and pocketed the phone, the restlessness returning, the heat that came with carnal images of Etaín.

"Ten minutes," he said out loud as a way of firming his resolve. *Pathetic* an internal voice chided, but he couldn't make himself care.

He rose and moved to stand in front of the screens monitoring what was going on inside Saoirse as well as at the entrance and exit. The place was packed with no shortage of attractive, available women.

It wasn't arrogance to know he could have his pick of them. Until Etaín, he'd never had to work at gaining female companionship, never struggled with jealousy or possessiveness. The one and only time she'd come to Saoirse, he'd hustled her to the office and taken her on the desk, then needed to stay close afterward, alarm bells going off in his head at the uncharacteristic behavior, but he'd ignored them.

No regrets. Though he grimaced at the effort it took not to check the time to see how many moments remained in the self-imposed wait. He was hard and horny, his club full of gorgeous, available women, but they held zero temptation for him against the hot flame of desire he felt for Etaín.

A flash of red caught his attention, causing him to focus on one particular woman. Her black hair tumbled down her back in a mass of thick curls. Elf? None of the views captured her face, but on every screen the ring she wore on her thumb glowed in an unnatural way, a deep red captured by cameras that had never enhanced a piece of jewelry.

He studied those patrons standing near her, but there was no evidence any of them saw what he saw. Magic? He rubbed his forearms, palms gliding over the tattoos, curiosity compelling him to investigate.

S hock rippled through Cage at seeing Cathal Dunne step from what he assumed was an office. There was no mistaking the ink on Cathal's arms as anything other than a binding of a human to an Elven *seidic*.

What game played out here? What part belonged to Lord Eamon?

Since arriving at Saoirse he'd seen no Elves nor felt a hint of their magic, and given the wealth of shadow, he couldn't imagine the lord's assassin wouldn't have used the opportunity to make his presence known.

The only whisper of magic at all had come from the dark-haired beauty who'd entered a short time earlier, though what magic she bore emanated from the ring she wore. An artifact he didn't immediately recognize, though he'd already made the decision to examine it more closely and at his leisure while her naked body lay beneath his.

He glanced in her direction, frowning when he didn't see her. Cathal too was on the move, but so much in demand by the patrons of his club, that every few steps he was halted. Cage settled against the bar, following Cathal's progress.

The music segued into a slow, sultry song. Verses ripe with heated imagery that drew couples to the dance floor, their mouths seeking and finding as bodies melded in grinding, steamy embrace.

He was not unaffected by the flood of human pheromones or the evocative music. Nor, apparently, was Cathal.

Cathal headed toward the club entrance, firm strides signaling an intention to leave, or to at least step out into the cold, ocean-wet air.

Cage abandoned his place at the bar, timing his pace to intercept the *seidic's* mate just as he reached the door. In close proximity, heat radiated from the human, magic flaring along the marks on his arm, both familiar and strange.

"Am I correct in thinking you're Cathal Dunne?" he asked, stepping out into the night behind his quarry.

"Yes." A smooth, courteous answer as befitting a club owner.

"I am Cristo Cajeilas. Cage." He offered his hand, both curious and wary as to what the brush of magic against magic would produce, his interest in the *seidic* deepening at the seemingly sentient stroke and taste, as if in the distance she took his measure, though the human showed no reaction.

"You are much talked about, as is your mate, Etaín."

Suspicion hardened Cathal's expression. Cage shrugged it off, making a show of glancing downward at Cathal's exposed forearms. "I am a collector of the arcane. I recognize what's been written in ink. Are you curious to learn more?"

Lips firmed and body tensed in response, but Cage had sought treasure for the entirety of his existence and easily recognized the flare and gleam of temptation in another's eyes. A glance toward the club, the barest hesitation marked with a flicker of concern, preceded Cathal's saying, "I'll listen to what you have to say on the way to my car."

* * *

In the alley, the burner phone vibrated, flooding Lucky with adrenaline. *This is it.* Time to show Jacko he was a man of his word, a man who got the job done without trouble.

He angled to the left, wanting to take this rich bastard out quick. He thought he could make out the sound of approaching footsteps but couldn't be sure. The city was too loud, the club casting off the muted sounds of the band inside it.

He stroked the trigger. Jacked, wanting to pull it.

Come on. Come on.

Cage's strides easily matched Cathal's. This was not quite the chat he'd envisioned, but he found he enjoyed the intrigue, the added challenge, and in truth, he was hampered by ignorance when it came to how much Cathal knew of the supernatural.

The ink suggested intimate familiarity with it, but the lack of any type of protection served as a sharp contradiction and a warning against making assumptions. It left him to pick through possible openings until finally choosing to say, "Are you familiar with Aesirs?"

Cathal's pace slowed though not dramatically. "Yes."

"And the man who calls it his?"

"Eamon."

Not Lord Eamon. Interesting.

The blade sheathed at his back drew Cage's attention with a hungry wave of anticipation before he could tease out an interpretation.

Kestrel's focus was on an alleyway ahead, and so that became Cage's as well.

Ah, there it was, the rabbit beat of a prey's heart, the smell of adrenaline and drugs. A human with dark intentions, a killer whose death would be enough to satisfy Kestrel—for now.

He could easily halt Cathal with a low indication of trouble ahead but allowing the attack was far more advantageous. A step closer and Cage raised his natural shield, expanding it to include Cathal, the ability an evolutionary adaptation arrived at over millennia.

A murmured spell gained in a bargain with Lord Eamon hid them from cameras. The disappearance from view could, in itself, be dangerously revealing in this technology-addicted world. But it was a necessary risk as he drew Kestrel and sent the blade flying in the instant darkness became the form of a man with a gun.

Seventeen

⁓

Fuck! Shock surged through Cathal along with adrenaline, his reality twisting and altering further as the ink along his forearms flared in connection to a seamless, eye-blink-fast sequence of events.

A punk with a gun held sideways gangster-style becoming visible, aiming unmistakably at him.

The flight of a knife on a whispered cry that sounded like the call of a hawk.

The unerring slide of that blade through cloth and skin, flaring blue as it pierced an assassin's heart, that bright color fading to black in a graduated slide.

"We are safe from the prying eye of camera lens," Cage said, startling Cathal, suspicion slamming into him, though it didn't stop him from getting a closer look at the body.

Gangbanger. Hired gun. Hispanic. And it was no stretch to believe this attempt was payback for what his father and uncle had done to the boys who had drugged and raped Brianna and Caitlyn.

Justice. Revenge. Sometimes the two were so close as to be nearly inseparable, nothing more than shades of intention.

Having seen Etaín's drawings of what his cousin and her friend had endured . . . He didn't know whether it was hope or dread that had him asking, "Is he human?"

"Ah, so you know the possibility exists that he might not be."

Cage knelt next to the corpse, his eyes flaring red as he pulled the blade from the body.

Primal fear urged Cathal to bolt. He stood firm.

White teeth flashed in a darkness made less so by distant street lamps and a bright moon. "Yes, this killer is human. He is no loss to your race. The same could not be said of you. I've answered your question. In exchange, I'll ask. Do you know what Eamon is?"

"Yes."

"And Etaín?"

"Yes."

"Name it."

"Changeling."

There was a fleeting expression of surprise on Cage's face. "And *seidic*."

"Yes."

"She recognizes Eamon as her lord?"

Despite the détente of earlier, Cathal felt a twisting in his gut, a tightening at the prospect of being a human living among the supernatural. "Neither of us do."

"You don't call him Lord, *yet*. It surprises me that he hasn't claimed her for his own."

Cathal glanced away, images filling his mind, of Eamon between Etaín's thighs. The sound of her cries of pleasure accompanying the replay of reality, reminding him of why he'd left the club, so he could join them, jealousy submerged under new-found ecstasy.

Cage read him. Or guessed. "So they're lovers already."

Cathal forced himself to answer. This was the truth of his life unless something changed. "Yes. They're lovers."

Cage understood then the lack of Elven wards or presence, a large piece of the puzzle sliding into place. Among the supernatural, be it territory or jewels or in this case, a mate, you possessed only what you could hold against challengers or thieves or any

manner of other predator, though death was not generally a consequence of failure when it came to the long-lived.

He would not have thought Eamon ruthless enough to play
such a game with this bound mortal, but to gain full control of a
seidic, a truly powerful one . . .

Cage felt no compunction in pointing out the obvious, in using
it to his advantage. Indicating the body he said, "Eamon has apparently chosen not to protect you by assigning a guard. It suggests
to me that blame wouldn't have fallen on him if this human had
been successful in taking your life. It's an easy way to get rid of a
rival, wouldn't you agree? An easy way to free his lover of one
choice in order to make a more advantageous one should he wish
to share her at all."

Suspicion returned with a hot burn, though not directed at
Eamon. "Yes," Cathal said, crouching next to Cage and wondering
again if this was a setup to gain his confidence. Familiar paranoia
gripped him, a side effect of being a mafia don's son and one only
heightened by the presence of a corpse.

"The *seidic* could be yours alone, unless it's you who prefers an
arrangement that includes another man. I have books in my possession, knowledge to ensure she survives the change. It would require a move to Seattle. I can keep you both safe there from Lord
Eamon as well as other Elven threats."

Cathal rolled his phone in his hand, for the first time becoming
aware of having pulled it from his pocket. He'd instinctively meant
to call 911 but hesitated because he was in the presence of the supernatural, because it was easy to anticipate Eamon's reaction. It
was easier still to envision Eamon attributing the reason for the
attack to the Dunnes and using it as an excuse to remove Etaín
from harm's reach, his power one Cathal couldn't hope to either
challenge or defeat.

Noting the phone, Cage said, "The spell I cast hides us from
cameras only, not from prying eyes. If you intend to call your

human authorities, I'll be on my way and leave you to explain what happened here. Or say the word and I will ensure the corpse is not discovered. In exchange, I ask only that you consider what I've said and arrange for an introduction to Etaín."

"No demand for secrecy?"

Cage shrugged. "What do you think will occur if Eamon knows of either my interest in your mate or my offer to help you escape his control?"

Incarceration.

Cathal pocketed his phone in answer, going through the dead killer's clothing and finding a cellphone, but nothing else of interest. He removed it, asking, "How would I get in touch with you?"

"I believe you were at the marina earlier in the day, or if not, then your mate was, visiting Quinn and possibly his lover. Am I correct?"

"We were there."

Suspicion and paranoia faded beneath the memory of Eamon's warning that the magic causing Etaín to seize would draw the supernatural like a beacon. "What are you?"

Cage's eyes flashed red. "That's an answer to be gained in a meeting other than this one. Time is running out. Do you wish me to take care of the corpse?"

"Handle it," Cathal said, standing and walking away, misgiving filling him with each step, bordering on regret.

The dead man's phone was heavy in his hand. Choice and consequence. Innocence and guilt and the ominous weight of what was right and what was wrong. This was why he'd never wanted to take that first slippery step into his father's world . . . and yet doing it had led to Etaín.

He managed to get home before the shakes started and he had to battle a wave of nausea. Christ. Christ. He'd nearly died. He'd watched another man get killed and he'd walked away. But those weren't the only reasons for the twist in his guts, the uneasiness.

Hard to miss Myk outside the house and Liam inside it. Body-guards because Etaín was important.

Suspicion gnawed at him as he climbed the steps to his bedroom. He braced himself, and didn't bother denying the relief he felt when he saw Etaín alone.

I could have her to myself. He liked Seattle. He could open another club, have someone else manage the one in San Francisco. It'd put distance between him and his father and uncle. He could have Brianna come to stay with him, away from the truth she'd eventually piece together.

Temptation rode him, made fiercer when Etaín kicked off the covers as if sensing his arrival. Jesus she was beautiful.

He stripped, gaze roaming her body, dark pink nipples and splayed thighs, woman's folds and a small triangle of golden hair pointing to her clit and opening, though he didn't need anything to guide him to heaven.

His cock was already hard and insistent. He could lose himself in her.

Hell, he already had. He'd been out of control from the moment he stood outside Stylin' Ink and saw her through the window.

"Maybe it'll be simple," his father had said after leaving Caitlyn's gravesite, that day his involvement with her had begun.

Simple? Cathal's silent laugh was a rough, sharp scrape over raw nerve endings.

He got on the bed next to her, the jostle enough to have thick eyelashes fluttering to reveal eyes so dark they seemed black.

"Eamon?" she murmured, and his lips pulled back, a baring of teeth because her greeting ripped away the barrier that jealousy and possessiveness had been secured behind since her seizure on the boat.

"I don't know where the fuck he is." He didn't care. Eamon was probably getting an update on the events at the club.

Wouldn't *Lord* Eamon know Cage was in his territory? Wouldn't he have had Elves stationed outside the shelter and at the marina to see who showed up, given all the dire warnings about magic drawing others to investigate? Wouldn't he have had Cage followed?

Fuck it. He didn't want to think about Eamon, though suspicion crawled deeper into his gut.

"He doesn't matter. Not right now." A growl to match the baring of teeth, his mouth slamming down on hers, his body covering hers, vibrating with the need to dominate, to drive any thought of another man out of her with the pounding thrust of his cock.

Her legs went around his waist. He surged into her.

Not deep enough.

Not deep enough.

Everything inside him demanded more.

He pulled out, experiencing a primal satisfaction at her whimpered *no.*

Wrenching himself upward, breaking the lock of her legs, he slid his arms under them, the position rendering her more vulnerable, allowing him to have what he wanted. Needed.

He pushed into her again. It didn't matter how many times he had her, she stayed tight and hot, internal muscles clinging even as they resisted, making him work for it, making him feel like a well-hung stallion.

She'd probably call him a bull.

And still she met him thrust for thrust. His equal in this because despite how her body might soften, or the whimpers and cries he could draw from her, she wasn't submissive at her core.

It didn't matter. All that mattered was this.

She was his.

His.

His.

The word reverberated with each thrust.

Again and again and again. Becoming a primal scream when her channel clamped down on him, release and demand at the same time, her orgasm triggering his own.

He came in a scorching blast only to discover when his head cleared that it wasn't enough. Might never be enough.

Adrenaline. Elven pheromones. Nearly dying. He'd already hardened again inside her, the sultry expression on her face a claim of female victory, a challenge that had his nostrils flaring.

He pulled from her sheath, the exodus creating a flood of semen and arousal. He followed it to the tight rosette, watched smoldering eyes flash with a hint of erotic fear.

"Have you ever let a man take your ass?"

"No."

His cock thickened in anticipation, as something primitive and dark took hold of him at being the first. He'd promised her this, though he took the time to prepare her. And then he claimed her, fingers working her clit, making sure she came before he did.

Eighteen

 Sleepy Ruiz was too amped up to worry about being pulled over by the cops or getting caught cruising through territory that belonged to other gangs. Where the fuck was Lucky? He should have called by now, should have called a long time ago.

Something bad had gone down in that alley. Something real bad.

"We gonna keep cruising all night?" Puppy asked, passing a beer up to Drooler who was riding shotgun.

"Pull the phone out from under the seat," Sleepy said.

Drooler did it, handing off Lucky's cell.

"Tell me again," Sleepy said.

"It's like the tenth time already. The guy left his club with another dude and headed toward the parking garage. They were talking, totally into their conversation and not paying attention to what was going down around them, which was nothing, man. Nothing. I texted Lucky and split, like he told me to do. He should have let me take the guy. I could have done it no problem."

Sleepy wanted to tell him to shut the fuck up. What mattered was Lucky. No way Lucky cut and ran. No way. This was nothing, an easy hit compared to taking someone out behind bars.

He stomped on the gas pedal, leaving rubber behind. This was personal now. He didn't have the in with Jacko, not the same way

Lucky did, but he wasn't going to let this go, not without a direct order.

Scanning through Lucky's phone numbers, he found Jacko's and pulled over. He got out of the car, not wanting Puppy and Drooler to hear. A few steps away, he made the call.

Jacko gave his companion a thumbs-ups. He was the man here, getting things done.

"Yo, Lucky. Tell me something good, *camarada*."

"It's Sleepy."

His high deserted him. "Where's Lucky?"

"We don't know. It was all set up. He was in place, only needed the Irish *pendejo* to walk past him. He was supposed to call for a pick-up. That was like hours ago."

"The police involved?"

"No. We've been cruising. It's like nothing went down."

"He shows, he calls me."

Jacko hung up. Lucky had vouched for Sleepy, but he didn't know him well enough to trust him right away.

"Your *camarada* fail you?" Cyco asked.

"Cathal Dunne must have taken him out."

"You sure he didn't run?"

"Positive."

Cyco leaned over, lifting the grenade launcher. "Say the word, I'll do you a favor."

Etaín woke, or would have said she did except for the lake in front of her and the thrum of magic against her senses, the beat of it pulsing through the soles of her feet. It took her a second to recognize the cadence, to compare it to the absence of sound that had been testament to a heart silenced.

Relief filled her. This was no post-death visitation. Though as the water rippled toward the center, green condensing and yielding to blue, solidifying in a precursor to the Dragon's forming, she understood that if not a visitation, then this was a summoning, and she, the one summoned.

The beat against the bottom of her feet quickened. Involuntary reaction rather than panic or fear, there was no point in either. She'd be dead if the manifestation now rising from the lake wanted it so.

Sunlight caught on emerald green scales and turned droplets of water into glistening rainbows of color. It was hard not to be awed by the sight, harder still not to take a step backward as the Dragon approached.

In its presence, she couldn't accept that this was an avatar. The Dragon's laughter was a snorted puff through her mind. *I exist as you do.*

"Where am I?" Etaín asked, hoping to learn something though doubting she'd been summoned to satisfy *her* curiosity.

The beast cocked its head. *The place of your birth.*

"Figuratively speaking or literally?"

Clever changeling. Your mother found her way to my lake already heavy with child. She and I made a bargain, and on these shores you were born. In these waters you were bathed after taking your first breath, and for a time you both remained here.

"This is Elfhome?"

Fire came in answer, exhaled in a snort, though its flame parted when it reached her, making her aware of bare skin and her own nakedness. Fuck. Not that she was self-conscious about her body, but she'd prefer to choose who got to see it.

Another blast of flame reminded her that in this place—at least for now—her thoughts weren't hidden from the being who'd summoned her.

She considered drawing the glyph of containment Eamon had taught her but discarded the idea.

The Dragon was real. This place was real.

Yesss.

Not Elfhome. But somehow connecting.

Yesss. See for yourself.

She turned to view the primordial forest behind her, heartbeat skittering as if in preprogrammed joy at its proximity.

It was a dark place, trees tall and wide, close-set like border sentinels. But enough light snaked through to hint at a trail. She understood instinctively it would lead to a fissure between realities, to a gate, like the one Eamon had spoken of during their lesson, only this would take her into the world his ancestors had been banished from.

A few steps and she could be on the trail. It would almost be like walking into the past, into shrouded memory.

Yesss. But to retrace your mother's path is to travel to your death.

Etaín turned to face the Dragon, the magic pulsing against the soles of her feet becoming liquid fire. It surged upward to the vines inked in her arms, concentrated there in near agony before sliding to the bands at her wrists, the burn there seeming to waken the eyes on her palms, so she opened clenched fists to release hundreds of streaks of gold, as if Dragon fire had been converted to captured sunshine.

Choose one.

There was nothing to make one stand out from another so she chose the closest of those shooting upward from her left hand.

The others winked out like the golden highways had the night she'd piggybacked on a murderer's reality. Only this time she knew immediately who wore her ink, her vision filling with the sight of DaWanda above her, generous breasts cupped by hands she recognized as Jamaal's.

Shit! Etaín jerked away mentally, slamming the door on the scene, unwilling to invade a friend's privacy.

Sometimes invasion is warranted. Sometimes it is necessary.

Her thought? Or the Dragon's?

She couldn't be sure and because of it, she felt a creeping uncertainty, a worry that maybe Eamon was right, and none of this was real.

A snort buffeted her with smoke and surrounded her in flame. *Earth-bound Elf. What does he know of a* seidic *born in a realm forbidden to him because of his ancestors' acts?*

Heat and haze faded and her palms were alight again with rays of gold. Each representing a person? Or a tattoo?

I could teach you to use this. With it you could identify the killer you seek. Yesss?

The sibilant sound of it made her think of a serpent in a tree of knowledge, a metaphorical image for temptation, and she was tempted. But the remembered feel of coils around her neck, choking off choice, had her asking, "At what cost?"

Fire came on a controlled breath, the Dragon creating a sigil burning in the air between them, taking up the entirety of consciousness and continuing to flame against her eyelids even when she woke.

In her mind's eye she saw where the sigil would interlock on the insides of her wrists with the tattoos there. Understood it was ink that couldn't be applied by others, that would require Cathal or Eamon to stretch the skin while she used the hand tool on herself.

Slowly the immediacy of it faded. She tried to put off confronting what it meant by snuggling in a cocoon of masculine warmth, but couldn't. Finally giving up to sit and reach across Cathal's naked chest to snag the tablet and colored pencils on the night stand.

He sat as well, distracting her with thoughts of sex when the sheet fell away, enough moonlight remaining to reveal the erection against a taut stomach. A tug on the comforter by Eamon hid it from view, refocusing her on the tablet in hand as Cathal muttered, "Asshole."

"That's Lord Asshole to you," Eamon said. The twitch of very kissable lips would have derailed her for a second time if not for the tension running through Cathal and his lack of response.

"How long have you been back?" she asked Eamon.

"Only a few hours."

"Before I came up to bed, Liam told me you'd gone to investigate a disturbance in the wards around the city. Did you find anything?"

"Nothing definitive."

Cathal turned the bedside lamp on, her uneasiness growing at the increased tension in him. She stopped herself from reaching out, from touching him, afraid, very, very afraid she wouldn't be able to control her gift. That she'd rifle through his mind to find the answer to what was bothering him.

Something must have happened. Not here, unless she'd slept through it.

At the club seemed more likely. When he'd arrived home . . .

Delight shivered through her despite a sudden surge of insecurity. Maybe being totally immersed in his own world, in everything normal, had led to him having regrets about this, about them. It would explain the fierce lovemaking. The underlying violence and desperation.

She bit her lip, the small pain clearing her head. Later, when she and Cathal had a moment alone, she'd ask him what was going on, why the change from when the three of them were together in the hot tub.

Selecting an emerald-green pencil from the box, she drew the sigil without commenting on its origins. When it was done, Eamon leaned forward, his chest touched to her shoulder as he traced the intricate design with an elegant finger. "It represents servitude. You saw this on one of the humans who are part of our world?"

He meant the ones who'd been in her line at the shelter fund-raiser, the very same humans they'd fought about before she was taken by the Harlequin Rapist.

"I saw it in a dream." Truth? Lie? What could she call it other than a dream? "How is it used?"

"At its core, it signifies an oath-bond. For you, most sigils are things to be applied in ink. That is what makes the *seidic* unique, and why Elves typically wear no tattoos. The *seidic* are rare and few have access to them when they exist at all. In this world, at the whim of the queen, the *seidic* are used to punish or reward."

"But for some reason, you immediately thought I'd seen this sigil on a human. Why?"

"An aside first, Etaín. Because we don't typically have access to the *seidic*, whose gifts include the ability to enhance magic or deny it, and even to gift it with the application of their ink, we compensate with magical focal points, things usually crafted for a single purpose. The earrings I wear are such items."

Etaín touched a fingertip to the stud Eamon wore in his left ear, moved on to the ones above it, along the rim, smiling at the way his gaze heated as if remembering the feel of her tongue and lips on them. "You made them?"

"Not the base pieces of jewelry. Metal work and stone craft aren't my gifts, but the specifications, yes. They're bound personally to me and useless to anyone else. The majority of Elves who are able to claim and hold territory are spell-casters. It's because of that ability, humans can be made part of our world, and their lives extended."

"Hundreds of years added just by wearing a spelled piece of jewelry?"

"It's a little more complicated than that. It requires a blood-oath given in a witnessed ceremony. It entails an acceptance of responsibility matched to a pledge of obedience."

"Why servitude?" Cathal asked, a growl in his voice, and she didn't blame him, not when the word *obedience* set her teeth on edge.

Eamon shrugged, a gesture almost guaranteed to end the peace if Cathal's behavior hadn't already announced a change to it. "Few humans are touched by magic." Meaning, in essence, they'd never be considered equal.

Not a thought for relationship harmony. She glanced down at the pad in her lap, the emerald green a reminder of the Dragon. "What about between Elves, or between Elves and something not human? Would the sigil be used?"

"It could be." His tone said it wouldn't often be.

Her mother wore no jewelry, nor did she wear the mark in ink, but Etaín shivered, realizing she couldn't be certain her mother didn't bear the Dragon's sigil of servitude. Like the emerald green she wore, until the ordeal of the Harlequin Rapist was behind her, she'd been blinded to the truth of the marks she'd put on Cathal.

She hadn't seen truly until she stood in the shower with him, the rivulets of water streaming down his arms turning the design into a circle in her mind's eye, so she recognized that her mother wore the same pattern around her wrists, hidden by the entwining of other sigils—and even then she hadn't made the connection as she did now.

Her father was *seidic*. Her mother had the gift of sight, she was now positive of it.

Even in paradise there are politics, and some pairings are viewed as a threat by those in power. Your mother found her way to my lake already heavy with child. She and I made a bargain, and on these shores you were born.

"What has you frowning so fiercely," Eamon asked.

"I was thinking about my mother and the sigil."

"You believe she wears it?"

"I think it's possible she might be bound to the Dragon."

"For your mother's sake, I hope you're mistaken. It would mean the magic controls her rather than the other way around."

"*If* the Dragon isn't real," Etaín said, though sitting in Cathal's bed, surrounded by the everyday things of a normal world, the absolute certainty she'd felt faded as she thought about the emerald-green water rippling toward the center, like dissolved magic condensing and solidifying into an avatar that never completely emerged from the lake.

Given the stakes, she tried to tell Eamon in detail about the dream, but the tightening of her throat and freezing of her hand when she might have drawn what she couldn't say, was warning enough, and struggle would only make her lack of control obvious.

She applied the magic lessons that had left her an exhausted lump on the couch. Imagined the sigil that would divert and channel magic away from her in a harmless loop, but freedom to speak was returned to her only when she changed the subject completely. "I need to go to Stylin' Ink in the morning."

"I'll accompany you. Cathal?"

Was there command in Eamon's voice? Cathal couldn't be certain.

His gaze strayed to the clothing he'd been wearing, eyes lingering on the pocket where the dead gangbanger's phone was. What the fuck should he do with it?

Taking it to the police was out, given the dead body and his failure to call them. Taking it to his father could lead to a blood bath, though he realized he'd have to visit his father too, because guilt would chew him up if Brianna was targeted for revenge and someone got to her.

Hand it off to Eamon? Like a good little obedient human would?

He suppressed a snarl. That left Sean, and a lot of dancing around the truth about where the phone came from and why it might be important.

"No. I've got some meetings I couldn't reschedule. Afterward I'm going to meet up with Sean to see if he and Quinn have gotten anywhere on the drawings Derrick delivered.

"Heath, my fifth, will accompany you as bodyguard," Eamon said, yanking the string of paranoia that existed in Cathal because of his father and uncle.

The suspicion in his gut burned hotter. Why now and not before? Because Eamon knew about the gangbanger? Because he knew Cage's boat was moored near Sean's?

The magic chose him. I accept the choice though I wouldn't have made the same one. Eamon's words, spoken to Etaín. Only now Cathal considered that with him out of the way, Eamon's options expanded.

Regardless, she'd be safe with Eamon and the guards. Safer still away from him now that it seemed just as likely the drive-by in front of the shelter was meant to take him out, not Anton.

The wrap of Etaín's arms and press of feminine curves allowed him to escape the darkness of his thoughts. What he needed was some breathing room and he'd have it in a few hours.

For now . . .

He captured her mouth, content to lose himself in her.

Nineteen

~⚬~

Derrick stood at the garage entrance. The smell of grease and oil, the blast of Mexican music and the sound of power tools along with shouts in Spanish all bringing back memories. The earlier ones were almost sweet, but the later ones, painful, though he straightened his spine, not allowing them to be more than just a scratch against his toughened emotional fortitude.

Never again! I refuse to be that needy again!

He steadfastly refused to look at the workbench where a particularly horrifying example of neediness had happened on his last visit here, when he'd tracked Emilio down after he'd been a no-show for their date.

I'm not that weak person anymore.

He touched the drawing in his pocket as proof of it. Etaín needed him and here he was.

Emilio looked up just as Derrick found him among the overall-clad mechanics. His smile was cocky, as though he'd known it was only a matter of time before Derrick came around again.

Oh please! Derrick nearly rolled his eyes. Emilio was such a *boy* compared to Quinn.

He strutted forward, hips swaying to let Emilio get a good look at just what he was missing. This was the new Derrick, confident, strong, *loved*.

Now *that* caused a crazy fluttering in his chest because Quinn hadn't spoken the words yet. But it was there. He absolutely knew it was.

And if Quinn hadn't said them, Etaín *had*. If anything, she was a much harder case than Quinn. Much, much more guarded emotionally.

"Miss me?" he asked when he reached Emilio.

"Looking good, Derrick, looking good." Emilio's eyes dropped in a once-over that lingered at the crotch of very tight jeans.

Derrick preened. Not that he was interested of course. But he'd dressed to get answers and answers he'd get if there were any. Now for the flattery.

"You're looking divine, absolutely delicious yourself." There was a modicum of truth to be found in the compliment, though really, baggy grease-stained overalls did nothing for anyone. The boots on the other hand . . .

Heavy, rugged, manly. He might personally prefer heels when he wanted to look good, but he appreciated other footwear and what it said about the wearer. Put a naked Quinn in those same boots, polished to look like a soldier on leave or a policeman ready for some off-duty action . . .

Oops, there *was* a downside to tight pants but . . .

Use it baby. Use it.

He gave his jeans a tug and nearly laughed at the way Emilio's chest puffed out. Cocky rooster thought the hard-on was for him.

"So what brings you around?" Emilio said.

This was the tricky part. This was where experience or having a taste for books with private investigator heroes would have come in handy. He bit his bottom lip, worried that maybe this was a mistake, one that would lead to Quinn being pissed or getting in trouble with Sean.

Emilio glanced over Derrick's left shoulder, at the spot where a window allowed people in the office and waiting area to see into the garage. "Look. Whatever gives, my boss is going to come in and cap my ass for not working in about thirty seconds."

"Okay. Okay." Deep breath. "You know a guy named Marc Ruiz?"

"I know a couple of them."

Derrick pulled the picture out of his jacket, unfolding it and showing it to Emilio. "This Marc Ruiz."

"Why are you asking?" Was that a yes?

"I'm helping a friend. She's trying to track down some guys she put art on. It's for a book project, but it's all hush-hush right now."

Emilio looked down at the picture. "No. Don't know him."

How much to say without making this sound like a police investigation? Mentioning the rap sheep was *definitely* a no-no, but LA seemed safe enough. "My friend said he was a gang member in LA, it was the same one I thought you told me you had cousins in."

"Like I said, I don't know him."

"Okay, okay." Emilio sounded defensive, it might mean he *did* know but it might also be because the teen who'd been sweeping the floor at the other end of the garage was now a couple of steps away, the broom abandoned for a cellphone, and Emilio didn't want anyone thinking he'd give out information about a gang member.

The teen fired off a burst of Spanish at Emilio. Derrick understood the gist of it, something along the lines of, "Boss just noticed you got company. Better send your boyfriend away."

"Thanks, Drooler."

Derrick shuddered. Drooler. What a street name. Pathetic. And the art visible on his hands and neck practically screamed gangbanger, or wannabe.

Derrick folded the sketch and returned it to his pocket. "See you around."

Emilio stopped him from turning with a hand on his arm. Once there would have been a little zing but now, nothing. No tingles. No regret. No *heat*.

"You with someone?"

"Definitely taken."

A delicious shiver went through him. *Taken*, that word embodied sex with Quinn.

The hand fell away. "Too bad. We had some good times together."

It didn't stop you from breaking my heart and tossing me away like trash.

No! Said and done. Over with.

The new Derrick did not dwell on past mistakes or past hurts. The new Derrick left without a backward glance, though he felt eyes drilling into his back.

Sheer joy, there was no other way to describe it. It exploded in Etaín's chest and spread outward the moment they pulled to a stop in front of Stylin' Ink.

Bryce was visible through the glass, standing behind the counter, hand twirling in a hurry-up motion that whoever he was talking to on the phone couldn't see. He smiled when he caught sight of her, and she returned it, feeling it all the way to her soul.

The men in the car with her were forgotten until Eamon stopped her with firm fingers around her wrist and a softly spoken command. "Wait. Allow Liam and Myk to exit the car first."

Even that brief delay was almost more than she could stand. She couldn't give this part of her life up. She'd slowly wither and die inside.

Back doors opened by beautifully lethal guards indicated a lack of danger. Eamon released her to get out of the car, Myk only barely managing to precede her into Stylin' Ink.

"We've got ourselves a princess in the house," Bryce called out, coming around to enfold her in a tight hug.

Her arms snaked around his lean waist, her grip as fierce as his.

"Princess? You trying to ruin my kickass reputation by tagging me with that prissy nickname?"

"Kickass, yeah, if that means somehow managing to walk away after terrible shit has gone down." He trembled despite the tough talk, whispering, "Fuck, Etaín! Fuck!"

Guilt grabbed her by the throat, choking her words off as effectively as the Dragon did. She closed her eyes, cheek pressed to his until she was able to speak. "I should have come back to the fund-raiser, at least for a few minutes."

"Forget that shit. You had busted up ribs." His arms loosened immediately, a small jolt going through him. "You good?"

She hugged him tighter in demonstration. "I'm good."

As good as she was going to be considering she was a freaking near-Elf who visited with a Dragon that may or may not be real.

Jamaal joined them, hands covered by blue latex, his arms bare, showing off muscles and art and making her face heat with the remembered image of DaWanda above him, her breasts in his hands.

There was a buzz against her senses, the nearly overwhelming awareness that he wore more than one of her tattoos. When he grabbed her up in a fierce hug, she balled her hands into tight fists against the thin material of his shirt, shivering not just at the prospect of invading his privacy, but at stealing his memories.

Fire slid through the ink on her arms and into her wrists. She would have wrenched herself away had she not been frozen in place, at least long enough to hear the Dragon's sibilant voice. *Sssafe. My gift.*

As fast as the searing heat had come, it winked out. She tightened her grip on Jamaal, heart thundering. There had to be a way to prevent the hijacking of her body, though true anger and fear at the loss of control was obliterated beneath relief.

Jamaal was safe from her. She half expected the sigil representing servitude to blaze across her retinas.

He released her. Bryce said, "I cleared your schedule for the week."

She gave Eamon props for not immediately telling Bryce she wasn't coming back to work. Her throat clogged when reality settled in, that losing this might not happen by Eamon's decree but by her own choice.

How could she continue to come here if it put those she loved at risk? How could she continue to apply ink when loss of privacy might be the least of the danger her tattoos presented?

Bryce interrupted the painful introspection with hands on her shoulders. "Thought you said you were good."

She blinked away unshed tears. "It just feels like forever since things were normal."

He moved behind the counter. "Speaking of normal, one of the shelter workers came around with your phone."

Fishing it out of a drawer, he handed it to her as Jamaal went back to his workstation. Longing swelling with the hum of his machine, creating a hollow emptiness at the prospect of losing this. Somehow she had to find a way to keep this as part of her life and make it safe for everyone.

Even if it meant servitude?

A glance down at inked wrists, and the sigil shimmered in her mind as if already on her skin and entwined with the bands her mother had done. She blinked, clearing the mark from her sight before powering up the cellphone.

See but remain unseen.

Her mother's mantra. Her mother's life.

No longer applicable.

It would take hours to return all the calls from people who'd heard about the drive-by in front of the shelter. The concern humbled her. It firmed her resolve to stay part of this human world in a way that mattered.

Slipping the phone into her pocket she turned just as Derrick breezed in. "Yummy! You've got Mr. Edible with you along with that luscious, tasty morsel you call a boyfriend."

"A permanent mate," Eamon murmured, his amusement making her smile.

"You don't know the half of it," she told Derrick.

He grinned, hugging her and whispering, "I can hardly wait for a blow-by-blow description."

With emphasis on *blow*. "Not happening."

His mouth formed a pout against her cheek. "Spoilsport."

She felt carefree despite the slide of fire down her arms and with it the sharp awareness of the connection between her and the Dragon. "The details would make you green with envy."

"Maybe in the past, but not now. I *do* have Quinn."

She couldn't stop herself from asking, "He's okay?"

"Better than okay." The purr said it all, but as the moment stretched, her easy happiness fled when there was no sibilant offering of *sssafe, my gift*.

Worry tightened her chest, and though she suspected Eamon would consider her foolish for attempting it, she reached out mentally, seeking the Dragon, seeking reassurance and gaining nothing except a penetrating dread, a dark foreboding that Derrick might be used against her, or worse, that she might cause him harm.

She eased out of the hug, feeling both haunted and hunted, not daring to risk more touch of skin to skin.

Eamon watched the play of emotions over Etaín's face, from happiness and joy to something that tugged at his heart, opening a crack in his resolve to separate her completely from the human world. For the first time since standing on the other side of the window and being horrified by the reality of how she used her gift, he considered that there might be room for compromise, that if he cut her off from this place and these people, ripping her away from what she loved, bitterness would find its way into their relationship.

Eventually they would all have to leave San Francisco, including those humans made part of their world because of ties to Cathal and Etaín. Glamour only went so far when it came to hiding the lack of aging. Nor was it easy for those who no longer measured their lives in decades to remain in a place where the people they had interacted with for years grew old and died while they didn't.

The door to the shop opened and a well-dressed man of Hispanic descent rushed toward Etaín and was immediately blocked by Myk.

The human laughed, leaning to the side to see Etaín. "Bodyguards or cops in plainclothes?"

"Bodyguards." She gave a small sigh. "Francisco is a client, Myk. Please let him pass."

Eamon didn't counter the command.

Francisco hugged her as all of them had. "I caught a glimpse of you from my office. Do you have time to add the name to my tat?"

"Kiss of death to the relationship," Jamaal called from the work area. "Unless you're putting family on your skin."

Derrick sniffed. "Ridiculous superstition. Don't listen to him."

Jamaal shook his head. "You so sure about that? Last I counted, Bryce has covered three names since he hired you, and I'm betting any day now you're going to be begging either me or Etaín to hide that last loser's name."

"Those where bad choices. I'm a different man now."

"Uh-huh." Jamaal leaned forward to concentrate on detail work along his client's shoulder.

"You have time?" Francisco asked Etaín again.

"Okay if Derrick does it instead? His lettering is better than mine."

"Sure. That's okay if he's willing."

Derrick motioned toward one of the workstations. "Come on back. Let me see what you've already got on you and hear what you're thinking."

Pleasure flooded Eamon at the choice she'd made. He pulled her into his arms, the sense of completeness he felt when he held her growing stronger.

He claimed her lips in tenderness, his tongue a slow glide and thrust, a sensuous taking reminiscent of lovemaking rather than the carnal pounding of heated sex. When she moaned softly, pelvis grinding to his, their surroundings forgotten, he left her mouth in favor of her ear, marking his effect on her by the race of her heartbeat against his chest.

Her hands burned through his shirt where they played at the base of his spine, her touch and nearness enough to keep him hard and anxious to be inside her.

"You restrained yourself," she murmured, acknowledging his lack of interference with the flick of her tongue against his earlobe.

She might as well have captured his cock in a welcoming fist.

"I'm restraining myself now."

She laughed, the heat of it across his ear sending a shiver of pleasure through him.

"When you're like this, instead of doing your lord-of-all-you-see thing, it makes me believe this will work."

He cupped her cheek, tenderness welling up inside him. "Tattoo me as you have Cathal."

Without needing to glance at them, he sensed Liam and Myk's immediate resistance to the idea, though it was Liam who voiced it. "Is that wise, Lord?"

Was it wise? The question could only be answered honestly in retrospect.

Taking her ink was a calculated risk, but he believed he could keep himself safe. She didn't yet know how to push magic into the ink, to forge the bond as he'd done in her stead when it came to

Cathal. And his protections had held. There'd been no sense of threat since that first violent plundering and pull of magic.

"Tattoo me as you have Cathal," he repeated, ducking his head to nuzzle along the length of her neck.

The design was there in Etaín's mind, identical to Cathal's except in color and location, and she shivered, unsure whether the emotion surging through her was anticipation or trepidation. "Are you asking me? Or calling in the promise Cathal made on my behalf?"

His lips returned to hers in a slow trail of kisses that had her head tilting backward in order to give him greater, deeper access. "I'm asking." Though the thrust of his tongue and hard press of his lips were hungry and demanding, pouring liquid fire into her belly to sink lower and become the slick evidence of desire.

"Somebody open the damn door, it's getting to be a sauna in here," Jamaal yelled, making Etaín laugh and end the kiss.

"Oh no, no, no," Derrick said, and she could see him fanning himself at his workstation. "I for one am enjoying myself."

Bryce made a motion toward the privacy screens. "The shop isn't licensed for porn. You want to take this out of sight?"

Jamaal snorted. "Better crank up the music so we won't be hearing what's going on back there. Imagining it is bad enough."

"Shall I send Myk for your kit? Or do you have what you need here?" Eamon asked, smiling at the banter around them.

"You're serious about doing this?"

"Absolutely. I thought you might prefer to do it here, but if I'm mistaken . . ."

She wavered, torn, fear nearly getting the upper hand. Her surety about the design and it's placement, the same confidence she'd always felt and what had turned out to be foresight when it came to Cathal, slammed hard and fast against the possibility she was somehow being influenced by the Dragon.

This is what it feels like to be mind-fucked. And with sudden insight she understood it would never end if she didn't take control. Didn't decide and move on, learning through trial and error and consequence rather than being paralyzed by doubt.

Doubt had never been a problem for her before. She wouldn't let it continue to plague her.

"No. Send Myk for my kit."

She guided Eamon to the area set aside for tattoos and piercings done on breasts, buttocks, and genitals, or that risked flashing those body parts.

Seconds later Adele blasted through the room speakers a couple of decibels louder than usual, Jamaal's laughter saying he was making good on his comment to block out sounds coming from behind the screen.

She laughed too. It worked for her. It meant they could talk more freely.

With a grim expression, Liam took up a position leaning against the screen while she had Eamon sit on the massage table rather than the client chair. "I didn't hear you offer him any assurances," she said, reintroducing the assassin's unanswered question.

Eamon shrugged, producing a ripple of muscles beneath his very expensive shirt. "I am lord here."

"Careful," she said, touching a fingertip to his lips, a flutter going through her belly when he pulled the finger into his mouth for a quick suck as his gaze dipped to nipples that ached to have him do the same to them.

Two could play this game.

Her hands went to the front of his shirt. "This needs to come off."

He made no move to help or hurry her as button by button she exposed smooth golden skin. He trembled when she circled pebbled nipples, inhaled sharply when she covered them with the eyes at the center of her palms though she didn't need them to see what they had between them. Like to like, the call of it was an ever-increasing compulsion she had no will to resist.

He spread his legs and she stepped into the space he'd created. Her hands moved upward, sliding across his collarbones and then down to his biceps, closing around them to the extent she could. "This is where the tattoos will go, like something a Viking would wear, except instead of fashioned gold it'll be my ink."

"A fitting analogy. Truth has been distorted over the centuries and with the merging of one culture into another. The Vikings once called those of us they glimpsed gods. The Aesir. Though the name was a broad label encompassing a number of the supernatural."

Aesirs. She didn't want to delve into the reasons he'd named his place what he did. But she couldn't resist saying, "A god, huh? Don't expect me to worship you except like this."

She kissed him, teasing him with lips and tongue and hands that had already learned how and where he liked to be touched, his desire rebounding, ratcheting up her own until they were both breathing hard, the craving for more heightened by the impossibility of having it, given the Elven guard.

Eamon's smile was pure masculine satisfaction. "As humans are fond of saying, this works for me."

It took a moment for the haze of need to clear. She laughed. "You mean as worship goes?"

"Yes." His eyes darkened as he fisted her hair with enough strength to be both threat and turn-on. "Though I also enjoy having you on your knees in front of me."

Taking his cock in her mouth. Pleasuring him.

Her cunt clenched at the imagery. At the remembered feel and scent and taste of him. With the knowledge that he gave as good as he got, and then some. Always.

We could forget about the tattoo and go home. But the words remained unspoken, held back by premonition or instinct or something other than the Dragon, and then Myk arrived with her kit, locking the future in place.

She shook the weird thoughts and sensations off, the routine of setting up tools and ink reducing the burn of desire until it simmered in the background even when her hand circled Eamon's arm. She held it steady as she used an antiseptic wipe then picked up the disposable razor and stroked it over skin that looked as though it didn't need it.

"Last chance," she said after a second hit with the wipe and the application of a small amount of Vaseline.

"Proceed, Etaín."

The corners of her mouth kicked up at the lordly answer. "Go ahead and lie down then."

If she were using her machine, she'd put him in a different position, but the handheld needles required intense concentration and strength of will, along with physical stamina and control to push them through skin and put the ink in at a consistent depth.

She closed her eyes and took a deep breath as a final step. The design was there in her mind with crystal clarity, the muscle memory of it already in her hand from putting it on Cathal.

A second deep breath and she picked up a thin needle, dipping it in black ink. "If you need a break from the pain, tell me."

Lord Eamon didn't deem the instruction worthy of comment, and she felt his utter confidence as she placed her left hand on his right biceps and stretched the skin.

Outline first. The change in position required by it allowing him relief from the sting of the needle even if he didn't ask for it.

Then shading, though unlike the all-black art she'd put on Cathal, she threaded red and blue and gold into Eamon's tattoo, the same shades found in the vines and band she wore. The electric hum of connection and awareness snapped into place, stronger than what she'd experienced hugging Jamaal and Derrick, and not yet what she had with Cathal.

Eamon took her hands as she rested after finishing the work on his right biceps. He brushed his thumbs over the eyes on her palms, and immediately Liam was there, stepping into her consciousness like the dark promise of death. "You tempt fate, Lord."

Because of the magic. Because of the Dragon he believed was only an avatar.

"Come with me to Aesirs," Eamon said, thighs widening as he pulled her forward until she stood close enough to feel the heat always radiating from him. "Meet more of those who will call you Lady. Spend time in the world that's your birthright."

She couldn't deny him. "I'll need to detour to my apartment for a change of clothes."

"The dress of the other night wasn't the only clothing I purchased with you in mind. An entire wardrobe of outfits suitable for Aesirs is in our suite there."

She balked at hearing *suitable,* the word still capable, after all these years, of scraping off the thin scab covering old wounds of rejection. She couldn't prevent the instant stiffening, but she did manage to keep from pulling away and taking the first steps toward escape.

He touched his forehead to hers. "If you like none of the outfits then wear what you have on. I bought them for your pleasure and my own, though personally I prefer you with nothing on at all."

"I bet you do," she said on a laugh, kissing him before stepping back, her gaze going to the broad, bold band announcing her claim on him. "I'll go with you to Aesirs after we're done here."

Twenty

"P ass it," Sleepy Ruiz ordered, mood shifting from generous to pissed as Puppy kept sucking on the pipe.

That's how Puppy had gotten tagged with the street name. Beer, meth, didn't matter what was being offered, he was like a *cachorro* on its *madre's* tit.

Puppy gave up the pipe. Sleepy took a long draw. "Motherfuck, this is good stuff," he said, getting the flash that made his dick go instantly hard.

He took a second hit before passing the dope to Puppy then picking up the cellphone and looking at the picture Drooler sent from the shop. It was making him crazy not knowing who this guy was and why he was asking around about him.

The only thing he could think of was that it had something to do with Lucky. Fucking Cathal Dunne must have made Lucky talk. Using drugs maybe. Or torture. Lucky would never have given up a homie otherwise.

Lucky wasn't a coward. An order came down and he'd take care of business. The only way he wouldn't, especially when Jacko did the asking, was if something bad happened.

Sleepy speed-dialed Drooler. "Come on, man, answer your fucking phone."

But he knew Drooler wouldn't if his uncle was out in the shop.

Drooler wouldn't even text; he wouldn't risk his *tio's* temper. The man wouldn't use his fists there, but he'd sure as fuck use the heel of his boot on any phone he caught being used while someone was on the clock.

He got voicemail. "I'm dying here, *ese*. Call me!"

He put the phone on the couch and held out his hand for the pipe.

Puppy made a little whimpering sound, like they were litter-mates and he was getting knocked off the teat. Motherfucker might already have been blooded a couple of times, but he wasn't going to lose the nickname anytime soon.

Sleepy sucked the last of the meth into his lungs, feeling energized, ready to hunt down the guy asking around about him and beat out some answers.

The cell chimed. Drooler.

"Yo, homie," Sleepy said.

"Emilio didn't want to give anything up. He said he wanted to stay uninvolved."

Sleepy lunged to his feet. "He's going to change his mind when I get there."

"Chill. Chill. I worked it. You're going to love this. Might even get some money out of it. Guy was just doing a favor for some tattoo artist friend of his. Supposedly got a book deal going down and needs pictures of the guys she's put art on."

"She?"

"Yeah. Yeah. I think Emilio said she. I'm outside on break. I go in to ask, I won't get back to you for a while."

"Don't bother man." *She.* There was only one she who'd ever put ink on him, and he felt the burn of those places like they'd suddenly come alive and were trying to drag him down and make him feel like a loser.

Bitch. But his eyes skittered to the crystal pipe on the table.

He'd shaken the habit off once. Even come up to San Francisco to stay with an older sister to get clear of the gang scene. Homies down in LA didn't appreciate him covering those tats. Fuck him for letting Justine talk him around to it. But hanging with Lucky who was in tight with Jacko and on his way to being made had smoothed that shit over and now he was sporting new art showing the tie to his boys.

Etaín. That was who covered up his old gang tats. "Emilio give you the guy's name?"

"No. But somebody else said Derrick something. Said he was a tattoo artist, too, worked at a place called Stylin' Ink."

Stylin' Ink. Yeah, seems that was the place Etaín worked too.

"Thanks, homie." He took off his shirt and made the muscles ripple, picturing himself in a book.

Cathal pulled to a stop behind Sean's Hummer, tension like a vise grip squeezing him, and not eased by the constant presence of the ominously silent Heath. Guard? Or bodyguard? The distinction was important.

He'd made himself go by Saoirse earlier, made himself walk past the alley where he'd left Cage to deal with the body. He'd subtly watched his newly acquired companion for a sign Heath knew what had happened but had gotten no hint as to what the Elf thought. Why now and not last night?

A stab of guilt came and went for not swinging by Stylin' Ink after his meetings. And then a sharper stab because it was a relief to be away from the supernatural.

Yeah right. He caught himself rubbing the tattoo on his left arm. When he concentrated on it, he could feel a low hum. Confirmation Etaín was alive? Or warning he was in the presence of someone not human?

He got out of the car, pulling his cellphone from his pocket and dropping it onto his seat. Probably overkill given Sean's electronics, and the high probability of there being a powerful jammer in the Hummer. Heath also left the car but didn't make a move to follow him.

"What have you got for me?" Sean asked.

Christ. Now the dancing began. "How about an update first." In case Sean decided he wanted no part in this when presented with the would-be killer's phone.

"Derrick give you anything on last night's meet?"

"If he's at Stylin' Ink, he might have told Etaín something, but I haven't seen or talked with him since he left with the sketches."

"Okay. Long things made short. We narrowed it down to seven persons of interest, including two that are possible but not probable given they've supposedly fled the country. Today I scratched another three off the list."

"That from your police meets?"

"More like from my superior skills of investigation, and the reason you pay top dollar and are damn lucky I'm willing to work for a Dunne."

Cathal managed to suppress a grimace but apparently he had another *tell* given how quickly Sean said, "You want to go ahead and just spit it out? Or are we going to play dodge ball here?"

He pulled the cellphone, now wrapped in a bar towel, out of his jacket pocket and placed it on the console between them. "It'd be better if you don't know how I came by this. Plausible deniability and all that. Best guess, it's a burn phone. Only been used once." This time he did grimace. "There may or may not be any recoverable prints besides mine."

Sean made no move to either pick up or uncover the phone. "This tied into your father's business?"

Cathal felt like scrubbing his hands over his face. But a lifetime of experience told him it wouldn't make any of this go away. It never had. It never would.

"How do I answer that?" Part stall. Part frustration.

"What about, 'Why, yes, Sean, it certainly does. In fact it's con-nected to that last matter you involved me in. And yes, it comes as a surprise to me too that instead of being cunning and patient, my father and uncle are apparently batshit crazy.' Does that work for you?"

"Yeah, yeah it does."

"And how do you fit into this equation?"

There was only one place an honest answer would lead. Fuck. He'd known it would go down like this, but he needed a neutral party. More than that, he needed a friend he could trust, not that he'd break from his lifelong conditioning to communicate through subtext rather than laying the truth out in cold light. "Violence breeds more violence."

"And sometimes violence is the only way to end things."

It startled him to hear Sean say it, though it shouldn't have. Sean had known what would happen to Brianna and Caitlyn's rap-ists. He'd been a cop with an up close-and-personal look at how well criminals worked the legal system.

"They go after you?" Sean asked.

"Seems like it."

"Hence the phone?"

"Yes."

"If I get prints and a name associated with them, any point in trying to locate the owner?"

Moment of truth.

"Probably be better to concentrate on his associates."

Sean sighed. "Do you know what you're doing here? Ever watch CSI? Hear of a thing called forensics? Despite what you read in the papers or watch on the news, a lot of crimes *do* get solved."

"Any blood on my hands came *only* from retrieving the phone."

Sean flipped the bar towel open to reveal the cellphone. "Who's the guy with you? One of your father's goons?"

Cathal laughed at the thought of applying that word to an Elf. "One of Eamon's men."

"He clean?"

"Seems to have his personal hygiene under control."

"You want to joke around, hey, it's your dime. Far as I'm concerned, I'm still on the clock here and if you'll remember, my rates go up based on an aggravation factor. So I repeat, is he clean?"

Meaning Eamon. "Do I know this for certain? No. But gut read, yes." When you have centuries to accumulate wealth, and magic to make it even easier, why dirty yourself by dealing with *human* criminals? Hell, Eamon had probably purchased the Renoirs and Van Goghs from the artists themselves if he hadn't gotten them as gifts for patronage.

Silence filled the car. Sean coming to a decision.

Cathal had an answer when Sean opened the console and pulled out a Ziploc bag, dropping the cellphone in it then sealing it and putting both back in the console. "No promises."

Of results. Or that he'd pass those results on to Cathal if he did get them.

"Fair enough. Anything else on the killing in Oakland?"

"And by extension, the drive-by, though I guess we can no longer be certain who the actual target was there."

"True enough."

"Other than narrowing down the list of people Etaín thinks could have been involved, the only thing to come of my meets is some off-the-record speculation by more than one cop. Some of the Curs definitely have ties to the Black Guerilla Family. No surprise. And Anton Charles apparently seemed pretty tight with the BGF in prison. There have been some raids on pot-growing operations in Sureño territory, your basic bad guys stealing dope and money from other bad guys. It has been suggested to me that the bar hit and drive-by are payback but there are greater implications. As in, the Bay Area becomes a line drawn in the sand, and this escalates into a well-armed gang war pitting the Mexican Mafia and their Sureño soldiers against BGF and any of their allies, which would pull in the Norteños and La Familia."

"The raids happen before or after Anton got out of prison?"

"There's the rub. Both. Meaning who the hell knows if he's the catalyst for this. It's really all speculation. For all we know, a bunch of guys juiced on drugs decided to make a name for themselves and one of them said, 'Hey, let's hit the Curs.' But the heat is on and I felt the burn of it hot enough I was tempted to pass on the names. I didn't because I'm *assuming* here that Etaín's going to take anything I come up with directly to her old man or brother, and that would give it a hell of a lot more weight."

"That's the plan." Mostly. Except for the step in-between, where Etaín used her gift to find something the police could use.

Christ. He tilted his head back and closed his eyes, torn between fantasizing about taking Cage's offer of escape to Seattle and wishing Eamon would just take Etaín to his estate and force her to remain there until after the change and until *all* danger had passed. And the truth was, the boner he got every time images came of watching her with Eamon had the lock-down edging out sole possession of her. How was that for fucked-up given that Eamon might be just as happy to have one less *human* complication to deal with?

"Why am I getting the vibe that all is not rosy on lover's lane?"

One of Sean's damn hunches.

Cathal grimaced.

Sean laughed. "Hey, I never said doing the threesome thing was easy."

"Tell me about it."

"I'm going to take that to mean, not in a personal way but in an advice from Sean kind of way."

"Time for the Doctor Phil impersonation?"

"There are those who actually seek my input."

Cathal opened his eyes, paranoia striking when he checked the side view mirror and saw Heath leaning against the sports car's passenger door. He didn't have a clue what the Elf was capable of. For all he knew, magic could trump whatever high tech Sean used to combat the possibility of law enforcement eavesdropping. "I'm listening."

Catching where Cathal's attention was directed, Sean said, "Eamon have him watching *over you*, or just watching you?"

Sean and his damn hunches. "There's the million dollar question."

"And let me guess, you haven't asked it." Sean shook his head. "My total surprise at having you show up yesterday with Eamon and Etaín has been validated. You do know it's hard for a guy to defend himself if he doesn't know he's been charged with something. Right?"

Sean tapped the console where he'd put the phone. "I take it you didn't share this either? Honesty is the only way it works. Secrets are a relationship killer."

Guilty of a lack when it came to the first. Guilty at keeping the second.

Anger crawled through Cathal. At Sean for pointing out the obvious, at himself because he could see the place when what was starting to work had derailed, when fear, the presence of the supernatural and a dead body had collided with ego and gut-twisting insecurity because he was a fucking *human* and Cage had so casually said *You don't call Eamon Lord, yet.*

Until that, he'd been on his way home hard and hot and ready for a replay of what they'd done before he'd left for the club so Etaín could have her magic lesson. Yeah, the uneasiness had been there, something to deal with, but he had been dealing with it.

"You might as well walk away from the relationship right now."

He closed his eyes and tipped his head back.

"Are you signaling me to shut up?" Sean asked.

"No. Just admitting to myself I might have fucked up."

"Yeah, it happens," Sean said on a sigh that made Cathal wonder why Sean was living alone on a boat. "It happens even after you've been together for a while. One last piece of advice then I'll take down the Doctor Phil shingle you keep hanging out there for me. Beyond honesty and trust, the biggest pitfall to avoid is the two against one scenario, even when two people are in agreement and the third needs to either be brought around to the same point of view or accept being outvoted this time, which is highly dependent on knowing it won't necessarily happen next time."

Except in *Lord* Eamon's world, his was the vote *and* the veto that mattered.

Only Cathal realized he didn't entirely believe that anymore. It wasn't so cut and dried as that. Didn't it make sense for one person's will to prevail sometimes, depending on the situation? Cage for example? Eamon knew what he was, had apparently even had dealings with him, while he . . . pretty easy to see Cage had an agenda, access to Etaín, but apparently one that didn't require kidnap or extortion or he wouldn't be sitting here with Sean right now given the freaky knife in Cage's possession.

He'd been played perfectly, his weaknesses apparently obvious. Cage had planted the suspicion Eamon might want him dead and he'd glommed onto it though he'd declined his father's offer of bodyguards minutes earlier.

He hadn't considered himself in danger despite the drive-by or his family's actions. Hadn't thought it when he left Etaín and Eamon.

And then Cage had dangled the ultimate prize, Etaín, without having to share her. When he'd been rushing home to do just that, when he'd barely been able to concentrate at the club because of it.

He opened his eyes. Easy to blame Cage. Easy to parade out the discussion of servitude, and what he read into it every time Eamon made a reference to *humans*, but this was really on him. He'd told Etaín no regrets, but then lost track of what that meant. Keeping the attack and Cage a secret from Etaín and Eamon was like an open door to distrust and paranoia.

A quick visit with his father, then time to come clean. And afterward . . . hopefully kiss and make up.

Or make out. Etaín's words after Eamon's apology.

Cathal smiled. Feeling more light-hearted than when he'd climbed into the Hummer.

Sean reached out, turning up the volume of the police scanner that had been going in the background. Several blasts of conversation later he turned the sound down. "Drive-by shooting in Sureño gang territory here in Oakland. Victim status unknown. Shooter was African American. Second hit today. The victim of the first one is still alive. Time to get back to work and hope Etaín's leads go somewhere and some arrests will keep this from erupting into shades of LA."

"You'll run with the phone later tonight?"

"As soon as I can. No promises remember? Quinn didn't make it in today so I'm going to check out the names I handed off to him."

Cathal froze in the act of reaching for the door handle. "Quinn okay?"

The question earned him a look, Sean picking up on vibes again. "Yeah. Why wouldn't he be? He's with his family. His dad had a chemo treatment this morning, apparently a rough one. I told Quinn not to sweat this, it's easy enough for me to handle."

Quinn's gut burned. He hated feeling helpless. He hated the sense of waiting, the uncertainty of the outcome.

He snuck another look at his father sitting eyes closed, swallowed up by the recliner in front of the TV, his once muscular body now thin and gaunt. His strength depleted so he slept and woke, one History Channel program ending and another beginning as Quinn checked to make sure he still breathed.

"I can still kick your ass when you need it," his father said, sensing the sneaked glance and the worry.

"You can try."

His father opened his eyes and looked at Quinn, the love in them making his throat go tight. "Some treatment days are rougher than others. I'm going to change the locks if you're going to hover every time there's a bad one. Go bother your sister. I'm not going to throw in the towel today."

Quinn pushed himself off the sofa. *I love you, Dad.* He said it with a touch to his father's shoulder in passing, neither of them wanting things to descend into maudlin. "I'll see what she's up to."

He detoured into the kitchen, drawn by the smell. His stepmother picked up a long spoon, brandishing it. "Don't even think about touching anything on the counter."

He grinned. "First Dad threatening bodily harm, now you."

He closed the distance to get a better look at what Jada had going in the skillet. "How long until we eat?"

"Half hour. Longer if you get in my way."

"Is that Hamburger Helper?"

She popped him on the shoulder, hard enough he was damn glad the tats were healed even if his mind shied away from exactly how impossible that was.

"It's a secret recipe that's been handed down in my family for generations I'll have you know."

No surprise considering her family owned several restaurants, including the one where she and his father had met. He gave her a hug. "I'm glad he's got you."

He'd been just shy of eighteen when his father married Jada, but he'd wholeheartedly approved, the race issue a nonissue for him. And then Jahna, his baby sister had come along, making going undercover so much harder. There'd been no way in hell he was coming back home wearing Aryan Brotherhood tats.

Jada slid her arm around his waist. "Your being back is good. He worried about you, not that he ever let on just how much. It scared him, the idea of one day having some stranger show up at the door delivering bad news. I hope this job with your friend Sean works out and you enjoy doing it. You don't hear about private investigators getting shot or disappearing and turning up dead."

"True enough." Quinn hugged her, tempting fate by reaching for a slice of pear.

The spoon struck his hand with laser precision. "Hey!" he yelped.

"Out of my kitchen!"

"I'm going. I'm going."

He jogged up the stairs, halting in the open doorway to Jahna's bedroom. She said "Enter" without turning from her desk to look at him or pausing the flow of her pencil on a sketch pad.

Quick strides took him to where she worked and then he stood transfixed. Gaze traveling hungrily from magazine spread to the open pages of a book, to magazine, to book, to magazine, his attention captured and held in the grip of glittering bracelets with the commonality of gold.

Slender fingers waggled in front of his face. He growled and snapped with enough force his teeth clacked.

Jahna's peals of laughter did what her gesturing couldn't, released him to focus on her.

"Finally!" she said. "You totally spaced."

"Inspiration for your next project?" He risked a quick glance at her reference material, pride in his talented sister keeping him from becoming ensnared again.

"I'm making something for Mom's birthday."

He'd been deep undercover for five long years. But some of the memories he cherished were ones of taking her to the craft store to buy beads and string so she could do up jewelry to give to her friends. Now she had a workbench next to their father's, complete with machinery to grind and polish rocks, and he was betting not much about her jewelry-making was cheap anymore.

He leaned over her but she snagged the tablet and held it to her chest, hiding the design she was working on. "Sorry. Top secret. You know all about that."

"What if I cover some of the cost? Could I see it then?"

"No can do. The work has already been commissioned by someone else."

"Commissioned?" The word made him grin. "How old are you?"

She scowled. "Old enough to know you're dissin' me with that question."

"Oh man. Home only a few days and already on my way to the dog house."

"Like you could fit. Besides, Versace doesn't even have a dog-house."

Versace, hearing his name, got off the bed and pranced over to Jahna. She pushed her chair back and the Chinese Crested jumped onto her lap.

Gray skin with a smattering of pink patches, bald except for hair on his head, feet, and tail, he was a little king sitting on his throne. Cute, Quinn'd give him that, though petting him felt like touching a hot worm.

"I do have some availability," Jada said, taking on an accent to go with a *jewelry designer to the stars* persona, "if you're interested in commissioning me, for say, an engagement ring or something."

Quinn's pulse sped up in a rush of anxiety over the conversation he hadn't yet had, the big reveal that the *special* someone they would meet, soon, was male. He needed to do it. Hell, in his heart, he knew they'd accept it and move on, but finding the right time . . . Hard to do with the worry over his dad's health.

"Let's just stick with *or something*. A piece for your mom, say, for Christmas. I'll talk to Dad and see if he'll throw in with me."

Quinn's throat tightened, an ache spreading through his chest with the possibility his dad wouldn't be there for Christmas.

No! No! No! Positive thoughts only!

Derrick's imagined voice cut through the fear and worry, bringing with it a surge of possessiveness and a whole lot of discomfort at not having line of sight on him. Not new feelings, but he was coping and it helped knowing Derrick was at work and safe at Stylin' Ink.

"Got any suggestions about what she might like?" Quinn asked.

"Come with me."

He followed Jahna to the stairwell. She freed Versace when he struggled in her arms, indicating his desire to see what was happening downstairs.

"Mom, can I show Quinn your jewelry?"

"Make it quick. The table needs to be set."

"Okay." She turned to Quinn. "There is a price for this consultation, you know."

"My sister the shark."

She touched the side of her head. "I will be working up here while you set the table."

"Ever heard of multitasking?"

"Ever hear of prioritizing? Christmas is not that far away."

He put his hands up in surrender. "Okay, okay. I'll do the heavy lifting while you *think*."

"*So* not funny."

He laughed and followed her to the master bedroom. There were several old-fashioned jewelry boxes on the dresser, yard sale finds his father had restored.

Jahna went to the one at the far right, lifting the lid and filling the room with the sound of music. "These are her best rings. If you're looking for the cheapest option, we could go with turquoise and silver. She doesn't have anything like that."

"Say money is no object."

"As if."

"So young. So cynical."

Jahna shot him a scowl, ruined by a giggle an instant later. "I *am* trying to help you."

She dropped the lid, silencing the music. "Okay. Real deal here. While you were gone Mom inherited an amazing necklace. I'm thinking a companion piece to it, probably a bracelet and definitely some earrings."

Instead of opening a second jewelry box, she pulled the top dresser drawer out and stepped away. The sparkle and glitter grabbed his attention and held it. But it was only a short burst of infatuation lasting until she said, "Guess which one." Causing his eyes to seek and find, and the moment he did, he caught himself wanting to steal it.

Jesus! Where did that come from?

"This one," Jahna said, exasperation in her voice as she picked it up. He retreated when she held it out to him, sweat breaking out on his skin at just how loud, *Mine, Mine, Mine* pounded through his head like it'd become his heartbeat

What the hell was wrong with him?

"A companion piece sounds great," he said, backing away another couple of steps. "I better get those dishes out."

He turned and fled.

"You got any shit left?" Puppy asked.

Sleepy glanced at the empty baggie next to the pipe. "Not right now. Maybe later. Let's go over to Rosena's place. I tell her you're with me, maybe you'll get a little pussy."

Puppy bounded out of his chair like a starving mutt, then slouched, pretending it was no big deal to fuck Rosena. Sleepy laughed, feeling good.

His cell rang just as he got to his car. Drooler. "Yo, homie!"

"Can't talk man, my uncle's on the warpath. I'm sending you a picture from the newspaper in the office. If something is going down, text me. I'll say I forgot I'm supposed to meet up with my probation officer. Later, *ese*."

The buzz deserted Sleepy when he saw the picture. The guy they were supposed to off was standing next to Etaín. A *mamacita* like that wasn't one to forget, and the two of them were in front of the shelter where Justine worked.

Motherfuck. There was no tattoo book. That was bullshit.

Sleepy slammed his hand on the car roof. Then hit it again, putting a dent in it.

He'd been right. That Irish *pendejo* had made Lucky rat before killing him. Now he was going to return the favor.

"Change of plans. You're going to check out a place called Stylin' Ink and see who's there." He tilted the phone so Puppy could look at the picture Drooler had just sent then flicked it back to the photo of Derrick. "One of these three people is going to talk. They're going to tell us what went down with Lucky and where his body is. Then they're going to die."

Twenty-one

Etaín stood naked in front of the mirror that could be so much more than a mirror. The outfit she'd selected was tossed carelessly over the back of a chair despite its being every bit as expensive as the dress Eamon had produced the last time she was in his suite at Aesirs.

"You're sure a do-over is necessary?" she asked, her heart imitating surf pounding against the shore.

Eamon stepped behind her, bare-chested and barefoot, the ink on his arms drawing her attention and banishing trepidation with a fierce surge of satisfaction.

"A do-over is definitely required," he murmured, hands cupping her breasts so they filled instantly with heat and need. "What is that saying you're so fond of?"

Tormenting lips captured an earlobe and sucked as fingers took possession of her nipples to tug and twist and squeeze, rendering her incapable of considering his question under the onslaught of pleasure.

She closed her eyes on a moan of surrender. His hands stilled. He released her earlobe.

"Watch or I won't continue. Isn't that what I was forced to do when we were here last?"

"Payback is hell," she said on a husky laugh. "Is that the phrase you're looking for?"

She lifted her arms and reached behind her to entwine her fingers in his hair, the gesture thrusting her breasts harder against his hands, a spellbinding erotic scene caught in the mirror. "I'm not sure this qualifies as hell. And you were the one playing hard to get that night."

Her channel clenched as she remembered his hunger and the heat of his gaze as she touched herself in the shower, as she made herself come while he watched.

She ground bare buttocks against his trouser-covered erection and watched his face go taut. She was already flushed and swollen and slick, her cunt lips parted in invitation. She lowered her lashes in defiance and challenge, rubbing against the hard ridge of his erection. "Apparently playing hard to get is a game you enjoy. It's a good thing you favor dark pants."

Eamon's fingers tightened on her nipples as need pooled in his testicles and became a burning, pulsing demand in his cock. His mistake, in starting this, when he knew just how easily her actions created a fire in him that would only be temporarily quenched by the thrust and retreat and mindless release that came with taking her.

She was as powerful as any of the multitude of sirens who'd once called this world home, before technology made it more difficult to lure sailors to their deaths in a great sacrifice of bodies to the sea. He wondered just what he might sacrifice to keep her, what he might do if magic got the upper hand and killing her became the wiser action.

He abandoned a breast, his hand descending in a slow glide over smooth flesh and sleek muscle. Her lips parted on a low moan, tongue darting out to moisten them in carnal invitation and a command that nearly rushed him to his destination. He resisted, measuring this moment against the memory of her in the shower, tormenting him with the caress of feminine hands to a feminine body, with the slick plunge of fingers into sultry depths and the swirl of them over her clit.

Her hips jerked when he reached the engorged nub, and then his did when he found her wet, ready for him, her lower lips plump and parted. He abandoned the other breast in favor of freeing his cock, saw the flash of feminine triumph in her expression and nearly answered with a predatory smile of his own.

"Put your hands on the mirror, Etaín."

She complied, far enough away from it so her upper body now angled forward and gave him an advantage she hadn't counted on. Rather than sheath himself, he slid his cock between her thighs, stroking over swollen flesh and erect clit without allowing her the release of orgasm or the satisfaction of having him inside her.

It wasn't without cost.

Each stroke was as much an agony of denial as it was a sensual victory. Each clamping of her thighs and spasming of her labia against him was a heated reminder of the ecstasy he was denying them both.

Arousal beaded at the tip of his penis, pre-cum lubrication no longer needed given how thoroughly prepared Etaín's readiness had made him. On a groan he surrendered, nearly coming as she tightened in a merciless demand for a fierce taking.

Now their position worked to her advantage, giving her leverage to thrust backward and force him deeper, then deeper still. Until the ocean roared in his head, a powerful surge that left him helpless as his body followed suit in a hot rush of ecstasy.

He placed a hand next to Etaín's, the other one sliding around to her abdomen to keep her from moving so he could remain inside her. As the fog of satisfaction lingered, he triggered the spell bound in the mirror covering the wall, yielding to the desire to see what wearing her ink might mean for him.

Color exploded beneath their palms and spread across the

expanse in a swirling capture of power, a mix of elements that told him nothing about himself though the wild, unbound nature of the movements vibrated like a precursor to violence and made him want to take Etaín to the estate, willing or not.

"Hoping to see the Dragon?" she joked.

"Hardly." He let the spell go and reluctantly pulled from her sheath, guiding her to the shower.

A hand on his chest prevented him from joining her beneath the spray of water. "The tattoos shouldn't get wet."

"Easy enough to prevent." He modified a defensive spell so a shield formed to cover skin and ink. "One of the many benefits of magic."

"And this is another one?" she asked moments later, when water and the rub of her slick skin, the touch of her hand had him hard again, ready again.

"A delay tactic, Etaín?"

Her husky laugh might be acknowledgement or invitation. "And if it is one?"

With strength unaided by magic, he lifted her and felt the ever-present thrill at her responsiveness when sleek legs wrapped around his waist, wet opening and hot female flesh made available for him. If he allowed it, she'd tease and torment before ultimately satisfying the fierce craving her presence in his life had created in him.

"Put me inside you," he ordered, voice a harsh whipping wind. "Or we'll go downstairs without finishing this."

Desire was a flash of fire in her eyes, the promise of sexual retaliation in the future and one he looked forward to. She gripped his cock, obeyed, but on her own terms, allowing only inches into her slit, her hand a warden preventing him from escaping into complete ecstasy.

He slammed his mouth down on hers, demanded she take him all the way in with the thrust of his tongue, with a hand going to her breast as he held her pinned to the shower wall. His fingers captured a nipple, pain in the pursuit of pleasure.

The jerk of her hips and grind of her pelvis signaled her need for deeper penetration. It was a prelude that moments later had her freeing him, legs a tight clamp, holding all of him inside her as she clung, writhed, and finally came, the ripple and squeeze of her sheath a demand he answered with head thrown back and near violent release.

"Delay it is," he murmured, lingering in the shower, the strike of water against his skin a sensual refilling, the intimacy between them pouring into the wellspring of his soul. Desire reawakened when finally they left the shower, and she took her time dressing, making him envious of the clothing he'd purchased for her, making him fantasize about removing it in a fire-flash of magic.

"Ready?" he asked.

Etaín took his offered hand, remaining silent rather than lie. Ready? No. She wasn't sure she'd ever be, but that didn't change a damn thing.

They rode the elevator to a lower floor. "A little detour," he said, guiding her into what was clearly his office given the quality of the artwork. Extensive windows along one wall were a summons she couldn't ignore. When she stopped in front of them, it wasn't the view of San Francisco that drew her attention, but the private terrace below, every table occupied by the wealthy and powerful, with some of the famous thrown in for good measure.

Not her world. Even when she'd lived with the captain, she hadn't been a part of it. Physically present, yes, when she was young there hadn't been a way to avoid it, but mentally, she'd learned at eight it was better to retreat. No knife was sharper than words wielded by jealous girls or hate-filled stepsisters, and for a time, she'd been vulnerable.

Perhaps if she'd been a boy, or homely, but she'd been neither.

And then the call to ink had come, and with it, unknown then to her, Elven allure, and that had only made things harder at school and at home.

Eamon came up behind her, enfolding her in a hug and chasing away thoughts of the past. "You stepped through my wards on that first visit, interrupting my work and drawing me to the window. The moment I looked down and saw you, I knew you'd be mine."

"Despite the fact I was with Cathal."

"A minor complication."

"Fighting words if he heard you say them."

"Perhaps." He touched his lips to her neck and she felt him smile as he added, "Probably."

A sucking bite followed, then another, and a third, before he sighed, murmuring, "You have a disastrous effect on my intentions."

She laughed. "And that's a bad thing?"

"Those who know me best would say yes."

"The bodyguards?"

"And my second in command, Rhys."

Warm lips were replaced by the cool touch of a collar-like necklace.

The switch didn't go unnoticed.

Like a heated charge of electricity down her arms and around her wrists, the alien awareness of the Dragon came, there long enough to determine no threat existed but even that was long enough to make her pulse beat against the collar like a prisoner against a cell door.

Eamon's mouth brushed her ear. "Relax, Etaín. It's merely a piece of jewelry, something enhanced by your beauty, an item to complement the outfit, nothing more."

"You didn't sense the flare of magic just then?"

"I am always aware of your magic. It constantly twines with mine." He kissed her neck. "But it was the rush of your heartbeat that gave your nervousness away. For you, perhaps it was accompanied by a different sensation. For changelings especially, emotion and magic are often experienced together."

A hand at her elbow guided her to an attached bathroom. Her breath caught at the sight of opals inlaid into an intricate twist of gold, dark stones that reminded her of the mirror with its captured fire and water.

"And here I was worried about it being a studded dog collar," she said to mask a sudden nervousness at seeing a woman who looked like she belonged among the restaurant patrons, instead of one who enjoyed talking trash with clients and fellow artists.

His tender smile made her heart flutter. "A studded dog collar? I'd worry your friend Bryce might decide to claim my gift if you happened to take it off at the shop."

Her eyes jerked upward to meet his, happiness spreading through her at what his words implied. "He does have his moments when he goes full punk. And his girlfriends almost always have the look."

"Then no studded dog collars for you."

Eamon touched his cheek to hers. "I'm tempted to return to the bedroom and strip you out of everything except for the necklace."

"I could be convinced that's an excellent idea."

"If we return to the suite, you won't meet anyone until tomorrow, especially if Cathal joins us." He gave a small, teasing suck to her neck then stepped backward and snagged her hand.

On the first floor the elevator door opened in a discreetly placed alcove between public area and private, as if occasionally humans were allowed deeper into Elven territory.

Eamon guided her toward the back, the kitchen, she presumed, given the deepening scent of food and the cadence of called-out orders interspersed with status updates. A waiter passed, as enticing as the food he'd collected from the counter where it waited to be taken to diners.

It occurred to her that all the Elves she'd seen at Aesirs were men. "Do you allow females to work here?"

"Some."

"Why only some?"

The question held an edge of militancy. She'd been lucky in her chosen profession. Her talent, her looks, and though she hadn't been aware of it at the time, magic and Elven allure, meant she'd never experienced discrimination in the same way other female tattoo artists had. She'd brushed up against assholes, and men with a boy's club mindset, but they'd held no power over either her advancement or her earning a good living.

"Peace, Etaín, peace," he said with a laugh. "I'm glad you so readily champion our females. Those who wish to serve here do so at one time or another."

He opened the door to the kitchen, allowing her to precede him. The moment she did, all motion and conversation ceased. Their wariness slammed into her, unmitigated by the smiles that quickly followed because of Eamon's presence, tentative on several faces and forced on others.

In a rush, the desire to escape into comfortable reality returned. Her gaze went to the outside world visible because of a service door propped open for a delivery.

A boy stepped through the doorway, carrying a crate. Lost in thought, he didn't immediately notice them, but when he did, his attention was solely on her and stark terror filled his features.

"No!" he cried, dropping the crate. Fish spilled across the floor as he turned and fled.

"Farrell! Stop!" Eamon ordered, and she felt magic across her senses.

The boy—the changeling he'd told her about—only barely got outside before the door slammed shut.

"I'll go after him, Lord," one of the kitchen workers volunteered.

"No." Eamon grabbed Etaín's arm, turning her to face him. "Do not leave Aesirs."

Denial was her kneejerk response to his command, to the autocratic ruler who had replaced teasing lover. She remained silent, offering neither promise nor protest as the door he'd closed with magic flew open and then he was gone.

As if summoned by Eamon's absence, Liam was suddenly at her side, his arrival releasing those in the kitchen to go back to their tasks, though with fierce concentration instead of the easy glide and cadence they'd had moments earlier.

The urge to bolt through the open door was nearly impossible to resist. She didn't belong here any more than she did in the elegant dining area serving men and women she had nothing in common with—not even being human.

Ignoring the Elves who were steadfastly ignoring her, she turned to Liam. "Why was he terrified?"

Terrified enough to ignore Lord Eamon's order, and she couldn't imagine those he ruled often did. Scratch the surface and Eamon was more like Cathal's family than Cathal was. She had only to look at Liam to know Eamon was capable of ruthlessness. Why else would he have an assassin serving him?

"That's for Lord Eamon to answer."

Liam's response was a scrape over raw nerve-endings. *I'm out of here.*

The compelling need to run and keep running increased with the first step, done in fuck-me heels that suddenly seemed meant to hobble her as thoroughly as the tight skirt and the lack of transportation. Panic swelled with the sense of being out of control.

Until she'd been taken by the Harlequin Rapist, and then rescued from him, she'd lived life completely on her own terms, trusting in herself and her gift and confident in her ability to survive. Could she even leave, given Eamon's command to stay?

Her skin felt unbearably tight. It occurred to her that she hadn't been back to her apartment in days, and as quickly as the realization came, she craved being alone in her own space, at least for a little while.

Without a word to Liam, she headed for the public area, strategy rather than any desire to see and be seen. It'd be harder to stop her from escaping where there were witnesses—that is, if she could pass through the wards at all.

Only those guarding the terrace could contain you if triggered, the Dragon's voice whispered through her mind, the sound of it increasing her urgency to leave.

Maybe once outside she'd consider herself a coward for not forcing herself to stroll through the restaurant as if it were hers, to imagine herself at Eamon's side, or Cathal's. She wasn't foolish enough to think this was anything more than a temporary reprieve.

The maître d' stand came into view. Seeing the three women who'd just entered Aesirs only solidified her determination to leave this place she didn't belong in. It'd been a year and a half since she'd had the misfortune of encountering the captain's wife and daughters.

Like piranhas zeroing in on some hapless living creature dropped into the water, they noticed her. Lips painted bright red tightened and eyes narrowed to accompany expressions of disdain that were really only polite masks for a voracious hate.

Turning tail and heading in the opposite direction wasn't an option. She'd never give them that much power over her.

Liam moved ahead of her. Protection? Or merely to position himself to prevent her from leaving?

She'd fight that battle after she dealt with the one in front of her, because there was definitely one brewing given the way the three women had moved to block her exit, forcing her to stop and interact.

Twenty-two

"Still trading on your looks, I see," Portia, Parker's older sister, said, eyes making a sweep over the outfit then returning to stare at the necklace.

Etaín touched the cool stone. "It's beautiful, isn't it?"

The maître d' came out from behind his stand. "If you'll follow me, ladies," he said firmly enough to imply that patrons involved in unpleasantness would be escorted out rather than escorted to a table.

The captain's wife stepped into Etaín's personal space, her voice a whispered hiss. "You're dragging my husband and son through the mud with your antics and your association with gutter trash. I want you gone from their lives."

Etaín shrugged, refraining from pointing out that Parker and the captain were the ones who called her, who involved her in their cases. "Nothing new there."

"Oh but there is something new. If I tell you where your whore of a mother is, will you leave my family alone?"

Anger and loathing poured off Laura. Visceral. Rabid. Fresh enough to give birth to hope. "Where is she?"

"Agree to have nothing to do with my husband and son. No calls. No contact."

It wasn't a promise Etaín was willing to give. It wasn't an oath she could make without becoming foresworn.

Her hands lifted, will and gift not entirely in accord. Inherent magic was nothing but a shimmering possibility in a span of time measured in heartbeats, a hush and stillness that disappeared in harsh, ruthless decision before either Liam or the maître d' could stop her—if they dared.

She shackled Laura's wrists, inked eyes pressed to skin. Demand a sharp knife sliding through flesh and cutting into Laura's mind. "What do you know about my mother? Where is she?"

Bitterness engulfed Etaín. Fury and pain that weren't hers and yet they became a part of her.

What do you know about my mother? Where is she? This time a compulsion, a mental demand, and Laura had no protection against it.

Standing in the memory, her hands trembled at receiving the text message. *I've got something for you. Check email for the link.*

She rose from the chair where she'd been enjoying a cup of tea, pain splintering through her chest, sickening dread and a sense of betrayal battering against the walls of her heart. It grew with each step toward her private office, feeding a hate so intense and directed that it jarred Etaín, driving her out of the memory in self-defense against having the swell of it trapped inside her when she was its target.

She was vaguely aware of Portia and her sister screeching, demanding she let go of their mother, their nails digging into her arms through the fabric of her blouse as the Elves allowed it, too wary to touch her themselves and no doubt hoping the humans would manage to break the contact and stop the use of magic in the process.

Focus. Control. Eamon had taught her the rune for channeling magic away from her, but with a leap of intuition, she shunted Laura's emotions into an imagined sigil and forced the memory forward, pulling back mentally as if she was a camerawoman capturing a scene instead of an actress living it.

It was very like the slaughter she and Cathal had witnessed in the shared dream, except this time, as Laura sat down at the desk and logged into a Yahoo mail account using a made-up name, Etaín's own emotions buffeted her, hope and happiness and anticipation.

The sender hadn't disguised what he was. The return address was a detective agency.

A click opened the email. There was no explanatory text, only the link.

Surprise rippled through Etaín. It came with the whispered sense of destiny at seeing the date. The email had been sent on the very day she'd met Cathal and Eamon.

Foresight. Her mother's gift.

For a long moment the curser hovered over the link, the hand that wasn't her own leaving the mouse and returning, leaving and returning until finally opening the link. Shock came first, at seeing the captain with her mother in a time-stamped recording made a little over a week ago, and then came a hungry longing. The camera lens cut through glamour so there was no sign of aging. Her mother looked just as Etaín remembered.

A heartbeat, a second one, and Etaín realized she'd paused the memory, freezing it outside of time, isolating it like a movie frame, like the sketches she'd always drawn upon waking from someone else's stolen reality. Reluctantly she let go and moved forward, becoming aware of the backdrop against which her mother and the captain stood facing each other, hands clasped but bodies separated.

This time the pain invading Etaín was her own. A fist of it around her heart as she recognized the shabby motel in Seattle, even the room number was the same, everything about it etched firmly in her mind and replayed over and over again, especially in those early years. She could still remember the vivid beauty of the scenery, and the excitement of traveling by rail instead of by bus, and the way her eight-year-old world had expanded in a burst of joy at meeting the man she was told was her father, only to be shattered when what she'd believed was a short visit became abandonment.

At sixteen, she'd gone back to Seattle. She'd stolen a car for part of the journey and hitched the rest of it, sure there'd be clues, answers. Believing her mother must have left something for her to find because this shabby motel was the last place they'd stayed before boarding the train and coming to San Francisco.

In Laura's memory, her mother turned her head to look directly into the camera, jolting Etaín as though there'd been a shouted scream to pay attention. *See but remain unseen.* This was no accident. She and her mother had the same sixth sense about cameras pointed directly at them.

An expression came and went, a dare Etaín thought. Her mother looked away, closing the distance between herself and the captain with a laugh, something that put a smile on his face as he enfolded her in a hug, the act triggering a rage in Laura that took her back to the day Etaín and her mother had shown up on the doorstep, humiliating her with the existence of a bastard child fathered by her husband.

Curses flowed through Etaín's mind as her ability to maintain the sigil funneling away Laura's emotions failed, her reality submerged under another's as she dressed for the function Isaac had bowed out of in order to spend time with his bastard, the spawn of a whore he'd probably picked up at a cop bar.

It didn't matter that they'd been separated at the time—or so he claimed. He'd shamed her by accepting the child. He'd angered her, disrespected her family by not demanding a paternity test, by refusing to even consider it.

Hours late and the bitch hadn't returned. Isaac hadn't seen the obvious yet. Or hadn't dared broach the topic but she knew what was happening. That slut wasn't coming back for the child.

If it were up to her, she'd call Social Services and have the girl taken to the shelter. But he wouldn't stand for it.

He'd pay for that. Not directly. She cared too much about their children to drive him away after they'd reconciled—even if he didn't. But his little by-blow would understand she wasn't welcome here, that she didn't belong in their lives.

At least Parker and the girls were visiting their grandparents, grandparents who were seething at learning of the child's existence. Measures were being taken to put this behind them. Private detectives had already been hired to locate the girl's mother and offer a monetary incentive to make this all go away.

Stomping over to the bedroom safe she opened it only to remember the necklace she wanted was in the downstairs safe. Isaac had picked it up from the jeweler on his way home and put it there rather than make the trip upstairs with it.

Spine stiffening she left the bedroom. The sound of the child's laughter had her silently screaming with indignation.

Her husband didn't acknowledge her as she passed the entertainment room on the way to the den. She went to the safe and opened it.

A manila envelope lay on top of the jewelry case. Her lips thinned, suspicion coming on a wave of hostility.

Taking the envelope she opened it, nostrils flaring at the picture she pulled from it. Bitch. Whore. Slut.

Whether it was the venom of the diatribe or the emerald green of the lake in the photograph, Etaín's reality diverged from Laura's. Her mother stood as if caught in sunrise or sunset, luminescent, heart-stoppingly beautiful in the same way Eamon had been when he let the glamour fall away as proof he wasn't human.

She stared directly into the camera, the fingers of her right hand touched the base of her throat, making Etaín aware of the collar-like necklace she wore. A message given the color of the water matched that of the Dragon? She couldn't be sure of anything except that she was meant to find this memory.

In a furious rip the picture was torn, then torn again and again and again until suddenly the destruction was halted by the captain's presence. Angry words were like leaves caught in wind for Etaín, swept away without examination as the pieces of the picture scattered to the floor and she stared hungrily at them, seeing by the way they fell that there had been a second picture on the back of the first.

Laura's angry exit from that long ago scene forced Etaín's attention away, drawing her fully into the memory again, the necklace she'd come downstairs for forgotten until she reached the doorway, then abandoned altogether in disgust at the sight of Isaac kneeling and gathering the pieces, bitter hurt filling her at knowing he meant to put them together and keep the picture.

Etaín ceased using her gift, the need to see the second picture dominating her thoughts.

"Take your hands off me," Laura hissed, no less venomous for having some of her past erased, or at least Etaín assumed she'd stolen those memories with her gift. There was no way to know for sure without asking, and she was as ready to end the contact as Laura was.

Freeing the captain's wife, Etaín stepped to the side, noting the wall of Elven servers who'd kept what was happening hidden from casual view. Their expressions were carefully blank though she could sense their fear, not quite the stark terror she'd seen on Farrell's face, but she suspected it would appear if she were to reach for them.

They fled back to their duties the instant Laura and her daughters moved past Etaín, leaving a tight-lipped Rhys with his distinctive red-sun earring standing next to Liam.

"Shall I escort you upstairs?" Liam asked, his voice the chilled dark of icy rain on a deserted road.

"No." She took a step toward the door and saw the Elves stationed there blanch. "I'm leaving."

"I don't advise it. This is a perilous time for you."

"So I've been told. And don't bother playing the *Lord Eamon wants* card."

He blocked her exit and immediately the eyes on her palms flared, becoming a weapon. His gaze flicked downward and back, cold ruthlessness the only thing in them. "You're allowing magic to get the upper hand."

"I'm in control."

His smile was a merciless flash of white. "Openly stripping a human of their memories?"

His gaze dropped to her hands, remaining there for a heartbeat before meeting hers again. "Threatening violence you have no true understanding of? These are the actions of someone in control?"

Her skin dampened. Doubt crowded in.

She dispersed it with the stiffening of her spine and a step forward, into Liam's personal space. "Unless you intend to keep me prisoner here, move out of my way."

"The price you pay for this may be your life."

"Yeah, yeah." That particular threat was losing impact. Or maybe it couldn't stand against the conviction her mother had left the memory for her, and more than that, a clue meant to help her survive the change.

She'd never believe the captain was involved in an affair. Never. He was a man of too much principle.

Her mother's making contact with him on the very day Cathal and Eamon had come into *her* life was no coincidence.

Peordh. Predestination. Her thought. Not the Dragon's.

"Move," Etaín said, a direct order.

"The consequences are yours to suffer." But he stepped to the side and his yielding signaled the Elves stationed at the door to open it for her.

She escaped, breathing deeply of air that smelled of freedom and possibility. Lifting her face to the sky, the caress of muted sunshine was soothing balm and sharp contrast to the wild hammering of her heart and the flood of riotous emotion that surged into her as she relived the stolen memory.

The desire to see her mother again was a tidal-wave swell she couldn't hold back. Why? Always why? Why did you leave me? Little girl pain at the core of a woman grown.

This time, there was an answer. Sibilant Dragon's voice validating what she believed to be true, expanding on it. *Peordh. Destiny preordained. The righting of a wrong.*

The sigil representing servitude appeared, banishing stolen memory. Etaín rebelled against the thought of accepting it. And that rebellion brought renewed focus and determination, enough to hold back the trepidation and deeply engrained fear, a kneejerk reaction to her ultimate destination—the police station where twice she'd been held, and twice the barriers separating her reality from that of all the victims she'd touched had fallen away.

Longing swept into her with the temptation to call Cathal. She wanted to hear his voice, wanted him with her, but reason dictated she go alone to see the captain. Or as alone as someone accompanied by a shadow-walking assassin could be, even if he'd apparently elected to watch her from a distance given his absence at her side.

She headed toward Stylin' Ink, cursing the fuck-me heels and tight skirt by the time she stepped off the first curb. Finally removing the tortuous shoes and walking barefoot until she reached the front door.

Cat calls greeted her as soon as she entered the shop. She laughed, because obviously the expensive clothes meant to make her fit into Eamon's world didn't separate her from this one. Derrick left his station, striding rather than flouncing, his movements telling her the man lying facedown on the massage table was a homophobe, probably gay and in extreme denial of it. Derrick was a magnet for them.

Hugging her, Derrick whispered, "I must have a pair of those shoes. Simply must!"

"Eamon's choice. They'd probably cost a month's rent."

"Knock-offs, darling. They're god's gift to the working man."

"More like organized crime's."

She ruthlessly suppressed all curiosity about Niall and Denis Dunne's activities.

"Whatever," Derrick said, drawing away. "You look exquisite. That man *does* have an eye for clothing and jewelry."

"I'll let Eamon know he's got your seal of approval. In the meantime I'm just going to hobble on back to Bryce's office and change into something I can actually cover some distance in."

"You planning on running?" Jamaal called from his work-station. "I figured it was about that time. You've been with the same guy, maybe the same two for what? A week now? Got to be some kind of a record for you."

"I'm reformed," she said, going around the counter.

"Sex must be mighty fine then."

She wasn't quick enough to block the image of DaWanda above him, though she got rid of it by asking, "Where's Bryce?"

"Back anytime."

She went into Bryce's office, opening the cabinet where the last shirt and pair of jeans plus an old pair of tennis shoes were stashed to save her from having to cross the bay. "I am definitely going back to my apartment today," she muttered, shimmying out of elegant and expensive, except for the necklace, then pulling on worn and comfortable.

Bryce was steps away from the office door when she emerged. "Shit, Etaín, couldn't you have stayed in the fancy clothes for an-other couple of minutes? I missed the show."

"Take a look at that necklace and you'll get an idea of what it was like," Jamaal said.

Bryce whistled then rubbed his thumb and forefinger together. "Nothing says sexual satisfaction like expensive jewelry."

Jamaal laughed. "No surprise there, not the way we nearly had ourselves a peep show earlier today."

"Eamon know you don't give a shit about being decked out in bling?" Bryce said, capturing her in a hug and touching his nose to her neck. He inhaled loudly. "Yeah, smells like money all right. Lots and lots of money."

"Plebeians," Derrick muttered.

Bryce laughed. "Never claimed to be a class act."

He let Etaín go. "Where are you going that you decided to ditch both your men?"

"I need to take care of some things on my own. Mind giving me a lift somewhere? It's not far."

No point in doubling back for her bike or taking somebody else's ride. She was guessing Eamon would arrive shortly, or send Cathal to collect her.

"Ohhhh," Derrick said, "now she's being secretive. Well, we have our ways of making her talk."

"Hell," Jamaal said, "we don't need to make her talk. Bryce'll give us the lowdown when he gets back."

Bryce dangled his cars keys. "Ready? This has to be quick. I've got a piercing coming in."

It was quick. Too quick as far as Etaín was concerned. And Bryce was too perceptive, zeroing in on a fear she couldn't completely swallow and cutting the engine to signal she didn't have to immediately get out of the car and enter police headquarters.

"Are you in trouble? Shop bullshit aside, if you want to talk, whatever you say stays with me."

"No trouble." She managed a smile. "Except maybe with Eamon for bailing on Aesirs. Bad memories of this place, that's all."

She opened the door and slid from the car. "Thanks for the lift."

He waited, making sure she didn't have second thoughts before starting the car and driving away.

Liam appeared at her side. She didn't even flinch.

"Lord Eamon will not be pleased."

"Probably not."

She wiped damp palms against her jeans, the chill of remembered panic and terror pebbling her skin as her heart thundered like waves against a cliff. She wasn't absolutely certain the captain wouldn't hold her in the building in some kind of protective custody. Or worse, allow the feds to swoop in for another round of interrogation, a closed-room session to break her so she'd give them cause to arrest Niall and Denis Dunne for murder.

Her pulse throbbed in her neck. When she became aware of it, she also heard the shortness of her breath.

I have to do this. Of that she was certain.

Fighting for calm, she headed toward the front door. Reaching it she said, "You're not going in with me." Though of course he would, unseen, death hiding in shadow.

"Enter this building and you risk one of the humans you supposedly care about."

Promise and threat combined. She shivered. "Harm him and there will be consequences."

"His death wouldn't create even a ripple in our world."

"And your death?" she asked in defiance of the icy chill that settled in her core.

Liam laughed, the sound of his amusement like the scrape of barren branches against glass on a windy night. "I hope you survive, Lady."

Twenty-three

"Shit!" Sleepy said, banging his hands on the steering wheel. "Shit, shit, shit!"

"Sorry, *ese*."

He took a deep breath, cutting Puppy a look. "It's okay. No problem. Would have been nice, that's all."

A few minutes sooner and maybe he could have tailed Etaín to Cathal Dunne, or used her to get to him. "The dude inside will talk."

"And then I get to finish him, right?" Puppy lifted his arm, tilting it sideways and holding a pretend gun. "After that, everybody starts calling me Trigger."

"I don't know, man. Drooler hasn't spilled as much blood as you have. I'm thinking maybe this hit should be his, feel me?"

"Yeah. I feel you. Guess it's fair since he's the one that put us on to this dude. I thought you were going to get Drooler when you went to talk to Emilio."

"Wanted to, but his uncle got busy and Drooler didn't spin the bullshit about needing to meet up with his parole officer in time. No way was his uncle going to buy it with me there. I talked to Emilio, that's all. Then I left. Drooler's going to hook up with us here as soon as he can."

"Emilio give you this guy's address?"

"Yeah. I checked it out. Old one. Some neighbor told me she thought he was taking care of his sister's place. So we'll have to hang here. Walk past the shop, see if he looks like he's getting done tattooing."

Puppy climbed out of the car. Soon as the door was closed, Sleepy tugged Lucky's phone out of his pocket, going to Jacko's number, thumb hovering over it. He didn't want to let on that somehow he'd been made, but this was his chance to get in with Jacko and prove himself.

When Jacko answered, Sleepy said, "I've been asking around. I got a connection between Cathal Dunne and a tattoo artist who might know what happened to Lucky. We're grabbing him."

"Good. That Irish asshole isn't going to be talking to nobody."

"He's dead?"

"As good as. A friend of mine is waiting with a little surprise for him. Asshole won't survive this time."

Sleepy wanted in on it. But it sounded like Jacko was letting it ride too. Best he could do was try to pull Jacko in to his action.

"One of my crew is begging to earn his bones. I'm going to have him cap the guy we're snagging. You good with showing up? Be our guest of honor. Afterward we could celebrate. I can get my hands on some good shit."

"Call me when it's ready to go down."

Etaín stepped into the office, hands stuffed in the pockets of her jeans, fisted against possible use and to hide the trembling that had taken them when windowless hallways telescoped inward and sweat poured down her sides each time they passed a waiting interrogation room. The captain closed the door. Quietly, and somehow that was far more threatening than if he'd slammed it.

She couldn't stop herself from noting the shadows in his office, and shivering with the question of how large an opening Liam needed in order to pass through it.

The captain moved around the desk, separating himself as though he realized the unseen menace she brought with her. Or maybe Laura or one of their daughters had already called him about what happened at Aesirs.

Yeah. That was probably it.

"Are you here to talk about your involvement with the Dunnes?" he asked.

"No."

"Your choice in boys, and now men, hasn't improved."

And your choice of a wife is any better?

But she didn't say it. She was tired of this dance, tired of being judged and found wanting even if that judgment had its roots in love.

"Did you know Eamon has forbidden your brother or me from asking you to help us?"

Her expression was answer enough.

"I believe his exact words were something to the effect that we wouldn't be allowed access to you."

Aggravation flared but faded quickly, because the encounter with the captain and Parker could only have happened days ago, before Eamon took her ink, before he'd eased up on the whole Lord of Elves thing. "Yeah, that sounds like something he'd say."

Her flippant answer didn't set well with the captain. His face tightened into austere and disapproving, a look she'd seen often enough since she'd first used needle and homemade ink to mark skin.

"You've moved in with him I take it? Or Cathal Dunne?"

"I've still got my apartment." A place she was determined to go to next.

The captain's expression altered. Pity? Victory?

"Parker said you'd cleared out of your apartment."

"What?" The stuttered question matched the uneven beat of her heart.

"Parker got called back to DC after we left you the other night. He stopped by to leave a note when he realized your phone hadn't been recovered."

"I've got it back," she said, rote response as the panic that had swelled into existence at Aesirs, along with the sense of having lost control of her life, returned in a wild rush.

"Let me put you into protective custody," he said, voice gentled as if sensing weakness.

"There's no place you could put me where I'd be safe. I need Cathal and Eamon for that."

It was a mistake to admit as much. She knew it the instant the words left her mouth, but some little girl part of her wanted him to understand, to stop pushing for something impossible.

"They're going to destroy you, Etaín. If you're lucky, you'll just end up in jail."

"Nothing I say will make you believe they're not criminals."

"Look what you're involved in because of them! The murder of four boys!"

Who drugged, raped, and tried to cover what they'd done by overdosing two girls, succeeding in killing one of them.

Even though the federal agents had told her as much, any argument she made would only confirm for him what the surveillance pictures hinted at, that she'd touched Brianna Dunne and afterward drawn her memories.

"I can't say what you want me to say. Just like I can't be who you want me to be." She pulled her hands from their hiding place, turning them and opening the fists to reveal the stylized eyes, the ink that marked the beginning of their estrangement. Though for *his* brand of justice, he'd been willing to keep her in his life. "This is who I am."

He sat heavily in his chair. "Why are you here, Etaín?"

"You've got a two-sided picture of my mother. I need to see it."

She spared him the knowledge that his wife apparently had him watched by a PI when he went out of town.

Or she meant to.

His lack of surprise had additional questions tumbling out of her mouth. "Did she tell you I'd come looking for it? Did she give you a message for me?"

Dread sunk into her at his expression. It arrived in a heart clawing instant before he asked, "How do you know I saw her?"

She shrugged, hoping casual would deflect. "I just know."

His attention lingered on the necklace that clearly didn't go with the jeans and shirt then dropped to her hands, a detective's mind sorting possibilities. Hurt came, clouding his eyes. Resignation followed, deep-seated and painful for her to witness.

His gaze lifted, meeting hers, and there was only condemnation, an accusation that echoed Liam's insinuation that she was out of control. "You assaulted Laura."

Further evidence no doubt of her spiral downward into full criminality thanks to the Dunnes. It was childish. Etaín knew it was but she couldn't stop herself from saying, "Laura started it. And she was on my turf."

The ridiculousness of that last bit nearly made her laugh. "I'm surprised you haven't forbidden her from Aesirs."

He rose from his seat and turned away, a fist squeezed her heart at the weight of his movement, the age and weariness he'd gained since meeting her downstairs and escorting her to his office. Was this what happened when humans got tangled in Elven affairs? Had her mother even cared about him? Or had she slept with him only so he'd believe later that he'd fathered the child presented to him?

The questions stung her, filling her eyes with tears she wiped away while his back was to her. And yet still her hands tingled with the desire to use her gift to capture his recent memories of her mother. She imagined herself reaching out, touching. Taking.

No! No! She refused to be controlled by gift or magic or Dragon.

With ferocious concentration she envisioned one of the complex sigils Eamon had taught her. She imagined herself completely surrounded by the glyph meant to become a personal ward, a shield against more than physical danger.

It was enough to deaden temptation, though she wasn't entirely certain whether she'd actually created a barrier or if the captain's opening a cabinet drawer beneath the window refocused her desire.

Her mouth became dry. And in her heart, hurt and longing and hope clashed like tumultuous cymbals in the hands of a manic-depressive.

"We spoke briefly," he said. "About inconsequential things. I'm not sure why she asked to see me at all."

But Etaín knew. And her eyes grew wet again on his behalf.

She took the picture when he offered it, noting the way he'd carefully patched the torn pieces back together, her mother standing in front of an emerald green lake. And on the other side, the image she'd come here for.

Her mother stood in the doorway of a bookstore specializing in the occult, one hand resting on the jamb, the other at her side. Etaín recognized the store immediately, remembered the day they'd gone there because the shop was so out of the ordinary, so unlike the bookstores they'd haunted in each of the cities they'd temporarily called home.

It'd scared and thrilled her, going to this place specializing in things occult, though with adult eyes the exterior of the store was worn and dusty and faded, entirely nondescript and unworthy of even a first glance except for the woman about to enter it.

What do you think? Is this a good place to find answers? her mother had asked, and those long-ago questions were a beautiful, wrenching melody in Etaín's mind.

Was it? It hadn't been then, not to an eight-year-old, though she'd loved looking at all the tarot cards and had re-created some of them from memory when her mother refused to purchase a deck for her.

But now? Did her mother mean for her to go to New York? To this store they'd visited shortly before Seattle?

Etaín tensed at the prospect, causing the necklace to feel like a choke chain against her throat. Her gaze traveled down her mother's arm to the doorjamb in a search for glyphs, some tangible proof of magic or a connection to the Elven world.

Not finding it in old wood and cracked paint, she moved to the tomes visible in the front window, and a jolt went through her at discovering a Dragon among the images there. Not a book, but a tarot-sized card seemingly dropped haphazardly in the back corner and not retrieved.

A hooded woman stood in front of a great dark beast with its wings spread. Only the gold trim on her cape kept her from merging into the Dragon and becoming indistinguishable from it. In the upper left corner, there was a sigil rather than a card name.

"Take it and go, Etaín," the captain said, his tone full of weariness, making her regret.

"I'm sorry—"

His raised hand stopped her. "My offer of protective custody stands."

"No."

"Then enough has been said today."

She couldn't let it go. "Laura wanted me to promise I'd stay completely out of Parker's life. And yours. No calls. No contact."

"Let it go, Etaín. Just let it go."

But hand on the doorknob she hesitated, fighting the urge to look back, to admit that it hurt, to have this relationship based only on her using her gift, on his accepting just a sliver of who she was, that the ache for more couldn't fade when hope existed.

Maybe it'd be better to let Eamon win this argument. To stop touching victims when asked, to not see either Parker or the captain unless it was a social visit.

Words her heart didn't believe. She cared about justice for the innocent even if her vision of it was closer to the Dunnes'. But then she'd lived the memory of every victim she'd touched. She left the office with focus, a purpose, calling Anton as soon as she stood beneath open skies.

"You got a tattoo for me?"

"I need to see you in person. Can we meet up?"

"Where you at?"

She gave him the name of a café a couple of blocks away.

"I'll send someone to get you." And a short time later a sports car pulled to the curb ahead of where she stood waiting, sipping a mocha that went down smooth but churned in her stomach.

She took a step toward the car as the door opened and a lean, attractive black man got out far enough to flash a smile and say, "Your chauffeur has arrived."

The voice kicked her memory. He was one of Jamaal's clients. He had devotional ink from shoulder to wrist on his left arm. Jesus. Mary. A cross that was beautiful.

"Greg, right?"

"Good memory."

"Haven't seen you in a while."

He laughed. "Wife says I'm sporting enough ink. Besides that, I've got a new kid on the way. Got to be thinking about college funds. Hop in and I'll take you to see my cousin."

"Cousin? Small world."

"True enough." She didn't miss the way the smile left his eyes and lips.

Getting into the car, she inhaled the scent of leather and care. "New?"

"Had it a couple of years. Writing is on the wall though."

"College fund?"

"Yeah."

"You'll look good driving a soccer mom van."

"You mean the coach's wheels, doubling as the team equipment vehicle."

He got on 101, heading out of the city. She experienced a brush of fear, wondering where Eamon's territory ended, her gaze flicking to the rearview mirror and pulse skittering when she could almost believe she saw Liam about to materialize there.

"How far are we going?" she asked.

"Foster City."

Not too far then.

She caught Greg staring at her, as if he'd picked up on her fear. Saw his hands tighten on the steering wheel like he was arguing with himself. Finally he said, "Anton did me favor years back, a life-changing one. I owe him. Otherwise he wouldn't be staying with me."

"I owe him a favor too." Truth, but not the purpose of this visit.

Twenty-four

Home sweet home, Cathal thought. It'd been that when he was growing up, despite where the money came from, despite the presence of his father's mobbed-up soldiers and his mother's fixation with society and her place in it.

He couldn't shake the family loyalty, couldn't shake the lessons learned here. Scratch the surface and he could be what his father and uncle were, a stone-cold killer. He'd almost become that very thing in the presence of the Harlequin Rapist.

He parked across from his parents' house rather than having the gate opened so he could pull around back. He couldn't remember the last time he'd actually seen his mother or father enter or exit through the front door, though given his father's security, the chance of being attacked here was slim. He doubted the neighbors had as much of a handle on their own schedules and routines as the Dunne personnel did.

Paranoia? Deterrent? Or necessity? Because he didn't know the details of his father's business, he couldn't be certain which it was.

"Hold," Heath said, getting out as down the street a car door opened and a woman emerged, long, curling black hair shielding her face.

A glint of sunlight drew Cathal's attention to the ring she wore, the red flare of it as unnatural today as it had been at Saoirse. She twisted it on her thumb, hiding it in a fist as she turned toward him, steps faltering at seeing Heath approaching with rapid, smoothly menacing strides.

Her chin lifted in defiant courage and surprise hit Cathal at how much she resembled Brianna from a distance. Remaining in the car became impossible.

He got out and jogged forward, unsure what Heath was capable of if he determined the woman was a threat. He was there seconds after Heath intercepted her.

Jesus. Up close and personal it was more than something as tame as a resemblance. With her blue eyes and thick, black lashes, she could pass for a female version of Brian, the cousin who'd died less than a year ago in a car wreck, not a twin, but a sister one of his uncle's affairs had resulted in.

Christ. What was she doing here?

There was only one possible reason. She'd come to find out where her father was.

Did Denis even know she existed?

Heath grabbed her wrist. She tensed, shooting a look at Cathal, fear and defiance combined in blue eyes that were far too familiar.

"Let her go," he ordered.

"It would be best if I see the ring first."

Magic. It didn't even surprise him.

"Do you mind?" he asked this stranger who was probably his cousin.

She remained stiff but turned her wrist in Heath's grip, opening her fingers to reveal the ring.

Heath's eyebrows went up. He released her. "An interesting artifact," he said and walked away after having apparently decided there was nothing to worry about.

Fuck, if only that were true. "I'm Cathal."

"I know. My name is Mirela."

"Denis is out of the country."

"I'd still like to meet your father."

That answered Cathal's question about whether or not Denis knew about her. If his uncle did, then his father would.

Shit. This was bad timing given everything Brianna had gone through in the last year. Then again, when would the time ever be good?

Brianna could do the math. She'd know her father cheated on her mother.

Cathal glanced toward the house. His arrival had been noted. One of his father's bodyguards now stood in front of the door to usher him in.

"Your mother left about an hour ago." Meaning there'd be no witnesses.

Did Mirela know his mother preferred to remain blissfully ignorant of anything that might dirty her world or impinge on her enjoyment of it?

It was probably safe to take Mirela inside. Probably. No guarantee.

"You sure you want to do this?"

"I know what he is. I know what *they* are. My mother told me."

There was a slight accent, Eastern European maybe. The careful way she spoke nearly masked it.

A nod said he believed her. It was far too easy to imagine his father and uncle away from the United States, where there were plenty of beautiful women willing to consort with men seen in the company of powerful, dangerous, known criminals.

"Let's go then," he said.

They wouldn't take his father by surprise. Mirela's car would have been noted. Whoever was monitoring the security feed had probably written her off as a cop stationed outside the house. But the minute they got a good look at her, they'd have summoned the boss.

"You vouching for her?" the guard asked when they reached him.

Fuck.

"That is unnecessary," she said, holding her arms out in an invitation to be patted down for weapons.

Not a thing to bluff about here despite their being in plain sight.

The bodyguard was thorough and totally professional. A search outside, then just inside the front door a wand looking for listening devices, and still a misunderstood move or too quick gesture would land anyone, even him, on the floor in a heartbeat.

"He's in the sitting area attached to the formal living room," the guard said, motioning for Cathal to lead while he covered the rear.

The position meant Cathal couldn't witness Mirela's expression as they traveled through his mother's domain, a testament to taste and what could be done when a top-of-the-line interior decorator was not limited by budget. Then again, maybe she'd look around her and compare this house with its limited history to places in Europe.

The sitting room was done in whites and browns and beiges, the furniture a luxurious cluster positioned in the center of a room whose sole purpose, other than to impress, was to take in the view of the bay through windows that stretched the twelve feet from floor to ceiling, the strips of wall necessary to support them always making him think of an ancient Roman coliseum. Like the rest of this part of the house, the smell of flowers dominated, drifting upward from an arrangement delivered fresh earlier in the day.

His father rose from the sofa as they neared. Cathal said, "This is Mirela."

"My mother was Jaelle Dvorak," Mirela said, causing a flash of surprise in his father's eyes, and then the shock was his when she added, "On her deathbed she finally gave me the name of my father. You."

She thrust her hand out, the ring appearing ordinary against the backdrop of the San Francisco Bay. "In case you doubt me, here is your proof. You gave this to her in Prague."

Fuck. Not Brianna's sister. *His*.

Niall motioned to the furniture in a gesture to sit. When they had, he looked at Mirela and said, "Why did you come here? What do you want?" His voice was cool, his eyes assessing, in that moment, the mafia don Cathal knew him to be.

Mirela's chin lifted, and if her hands tightened marginally on the material of her pants, he still gave her props for bravery, and he admired her for it. "I came to satisfy my curiosity."

"Not always a smart move."

"Dad—"

A glance in his direction said this was between his father and, *Jesus*, his sister.

She sent him a glance too. "I wanted to meet Cathal. I have no other family now that my mother is dead."

Bad timing, Cathal thought for the second time since getting a look at Mirela. "We need to take this into your office, Dad." Code for *I have something to tell you and it's not something for the authorities to overhear.*

"It have anything to do with why you're traveling with a bodyguard now? From the look of him, one of Eamon's?" Proof his father had been called to watch what was going on outside.

"Yes."

Niall's focus shifted to Mirela. "Coincidences make me itchy. Now more than ever since I have a son who's hooked up with a policeman's daughter." Meaning he wasn't convinced she wasn't working for the authorities.

Cathal's own paranoia allowed for the possibility, ratcheted up a notch because she'd been at the club. Icy sensation swept over him. What if last night *was* some kind of a setup? What if the authorities had caught him walking away from a body, even if the death would be ruled self-defense in any court. What if—

He shook it off. For once magic and the existence of the supernatural actually provided some relief. Cage wasn't human. The blade wasn't simply a knife. And the ring Mirela wore as a keepsake was something more than that, he'd known last night and Heath's reaction confirmed it.

Careful subtext, he'd spent a lifetime communicating with his father that way, but in that moment he was tired of it. He took out his phone, typed in a text message he'd never send. *Someone came after me. Warn Denis in case Brianna is also a target.*

The cold in his father's expression deepened at reading it. "Your woman has some dangerous friends and acquaintances. You nearly got killed yesterday because of her."

Cathal laughed at the rich irony of that, coming from his father. "She's the one who would have been collateral damage. Fallout from seeing that justice is done." *Your brand of justice. Her father's and her brother's.*

The slightest tilt of Niall's head acknowledged the point and message. "I'll tell Denis that because of your association with her, you now feel the need for a bodyguard."

"Good enough." Which left Mirela, unprotected, a complication.

Another irony there. He could hear Eamon's voice in his head, calling him the same thing.

He wasn't sure whether his father would offer her protection. He couldn't be positive she'd be smart to accept the offer if made.

Mirela wasn't to blame for the circumstances of her birth. Acknowledging her existence wasn't a moral dilemma for him though his mind shied away from thinking about the impact of this on his mother.

"You interested in following me home and meeting my fiancé, Etaín?" he asked her, making his position clear to his father and also creating the possibility that Eamon would assign an Elf to guard her.

She seemed surprised by the offer, genuinely pleased. "I'd love to."

"Your mother's due home in a few minutes," Niall said, not that he couldn't easily have her delayed.

Cathal took the hint. "I need to get going anyway."

Niall escorted them as far as the front door. When it was closed behind them, he turned to Orin. "You get a tracker on her car?"

"Yes."

"Follow them. Then follow her after she leaves my son's house."

I expected you to hate me," Mirela said as they reached her car.

He shrugged. "Doesn't make sense to. I've always known what my father and uncle are. You want the address?"

Her smile reminded him of Etaín's, without the sexual jolt of awareness. "I already have it."

Of course she did. "You were at Saoirse last night. Why didn't you approach me then?"

She started to answer. Hesitated. Finally said, "You'll think me crazy."

He laughed at that. "Trust me, there's plenty I could say that would make me sound it."

"I felt it wasn't safe. A premonition. I've learned to listen to them."

He stepped back to allow her to get in the car. It was a rental.

Heath waited for him in his. "A sister? A cousin?" It was the first curiosity the Elf had revealed since accompanying him.

"Sister. Will Eamon offer her protection?"

"In the interim, I'm sure he will do so."

"What do you mean by that, in the interim?"

Auburn eyebrows lifted. "When the Lady becomes his consort, it will be in her power to assign bodyguards, and by extension, yours."

Cathal didn't have time to determine how he felt about that. His cellphone rang as he pulled away from the curb, the tone indicating Sean.

"You got a hit on the prints," he said.

"Always in a rush to get to the climax. I hope sex isn't that way for you."

"If I respond you'll be covering your ears and complaining about too much information."

Sean laughed. "Doubtful. I admit to my kink. Secondhand works for me when the parties are visually attractive."

"Ever been accused of being shallow?"

"Not recently."

"What have you got for me?"

"The prints belong to a banger who just happens to be in the same gang Marc Ruiz, street name Sleepy, is now part of. How's that for a coincidence?"

Cathal glanced in the rearview mirror, seeing Mirela's car tucked behind his, his thoughts echoing his father's. "I don't believe in coincidences. You don't either."

"No, but I've got a working theory that'd explain it."

"Want to share?"

"The gang Ruiz is in is Sureño. Individual gangs can be at war with each other over turf, but they all answer to the Mexican Mafia. As long as you have Sureños, some of them aspiring to be made members, *carnales*, of La Eme, you've got a steady stream of soldiers to carry out murder, extortion, whatever, you name it, including contracted hits."

"Meaning Ruiz and associates could also be a strong possibility for what happened in Oakland?"

"If the order came from a Mexican Mafia member, yeah, though their going across the bay bothers me. I'd have assumed an Oakland Sureño gang would have been used. But that's how assumptions go, they can leave you screwed and rushing to cover your ass for a bad call. I need more intel. I get it, I can take a stab at who ordered what."

"Find Ruiz. That might be enough."

"Find him and what? Make him talk? Hand him over to someone who will? And I don't think this guy is likely to spill his guts to the police."

Cathal tensed, shooting a glance at Heath, then thinking, what the fuck. Eamon knew Etaín intended this. He had to know by now he wasn't going to stop her. "A few minutes with Etaín, before the police show up."

The silence was complete, breath held in a shifting of belief, a full acceptance of what the evidence had suggested to Sean. "It doesn't matter whether they're willing or not? Whether they're heavily sedated or totally aware?"

"No."

"That explains your unnatural concern for Quinn earlier today."

"Yeah." He left it at that. "Call me when you have something?"

Sean sighed. "Remind me to revise my rates the next time you bring me work."

"Not in my best interests," Cathal said, smiling until he caught sight of a car pulling onto the street a little more than a block behind them.

His heart raced at seeing a Hispanic behind the wheel despite it being a Jag. Jesus, not every person of Mexican descent was a gangbanger or mafia member. He knew that, had friends encompassing a lot of different ethnic and cultural backgrounds, as well as employees and the musicians he'd discovered.

"Talk to you later," he said, forcing himself not to slow down so he could get the Jag's license plate number, though he couldn't stop himself from hitting the garage remote at the exact spot when he got in range.

Paranoid. Call him paranoid, but he cursed himself for not having gotten Mirela's cell number, assuming she had one. He rolled down the window, waving a message that she should follow him up the driveway and into the garage. The tightness in his chest eased when she pulled up beside him, the door already rolling downward.

Heath was out of the car in a flash. Cathal followed. Mirela emerged from the rental.

The ring flared, a blinding pulse that had Heath rushing toward them, hands gripping their arms in the instant they were hit with an incendiary concussion and fierce heat. The blast so powerful it nearly knocked him to the ground.

A wall of flame encased them, trapping Mirela's scream and his own shout of surprise. Chaos followed in a pound of debris and the choke of black smoke visible through a shimmer of red and yellow.

Sweat coursed down his neck and face. And though he wore clothes, he felt naked, exposed, as if flame touched every inch of skin except where Etaín's ink was. Cool ocean countered fire, like a buffer against the living flame they stood in.

Magic, Heath's, though this felt a hell of a lot different than what Eamon had done in front of the shelter.

Where Eamon's shield was a bubble deflecting whatever struck it, this was flame burning hot enough on the outside to melt the shrapnel the cars had become and counter the explosion and rage of gasoline.

Mirela's ring dimmed. How he could tell in the maelstrom he didn't know, but he did and that knowledge was confirmed when Heath said, "Through the house. Your survival can't be explained out here," his grip tightening in a message that they must remain connected. A message Cathal understood when minutes later they staggered out of the house through the front door.

Heath released them, urging them to keep moving, toward neighbors he'd had little contact with but who now rushed forward, shocked that somehow he'd made it out of the inferno his house had become.

He heard a fire engine already racing toward them. From the other direction a police car's siren was a slashing noise that only invigorated the conversation going on around him. Discordant snippets.

Car slowing.

A Jag.

Fired something.

It sounded like an explosion.

Two of them.

Grenade launcher.

Jesus. There'd be no escaping the scene, not immediately anyway. If Heath hadn't been there and known to act . . . If Mirela's ring hadn't reacted . . .

He noticed her absence then and paranoia returned, that she'd set him up. He dismissed it. The wisdom of tracking down her father aside, he didn't believe she had a death wish.

The sweat on his skin chilled. He'd asked her back to the house thinking to protect her, but if she hadn't been with him he would have died.

A premonition. I've learned to listen to them, she'd said when he asked her about leaving Saoirse instead of introducing herself there. And he'd seen the glint of her ring on screens that didn't usually capture glittering jewelry, then again when Heath hurried to intercept her.

Firemen jumped from their rig, a second engine was close by. The police arrived, ordering everyone farther back. Beyond them Cathal saw his father's soldier, the man who'd let them into the house, talking on the phone. Catching Cathal's gaze, he hung up. An instant later Cathal's cell rang.

"Dad." More a croak than anything else.

"I'm handling this. Come home when the police cut you free. Bring Etaín. The two of you can stay here until it's safe."

"We'll go to Eamon's."

"I'll be in touch."

* * *

Niall hung up, only the iron will of self-discipline keeping his hand steady. *Enough. Enough.* He refused to lose his son.

Or his daughter?

The jury was still out on that one.

Going to the bedroom he opened the gun safe there, reaching in deep to retrieve the burn phone. There was only one number programmed in, one whose use he felt certain wasn't being monitored by authorities or the calls recorded.

He hit speed dial. A man answered immediately, a hawk swooping on prey. Better that than a vulture on road kill.

"I'm a little surprised I didn't hear from you yesterday," Niall's contact said. "You're calling to request an intervention?"

"Yes."

"Your son is keeping interesting company these days. How's your niece, by the way? Well on the way to recovery?"

"Miracles happen."

"You're at home?"

"Yes."

"We need to meet face-to-face to handle this. Do you have plans to visit your lady friend?"

"I could have."

"I can be there shortly."

"So can I."

"Is Denis going to accompany you?"

Bastard probably knew Denis had gotten Brianna out of the country, away from news of her dead classmates and their associates. There was no way he was going to confirm it.

"I'll be alone. My word is good with Denis."

"Accepted."

The call dropped. He placed the cellphone back in the safe then moved to the house phone and punched in an extension. When Brendan answered, he said, "Bring the car around."

He slipped on his suit jacket as he stepped outside. The Mercedes slid to a halt next to him. Brendan got out, opening the back passenger door.

"Marla's," Niall said when Brendan returned to the driver's seat.

He let himself in when he got to the place he'd bought for her and maintained the security on. She immediately rose from the couch and came to him, pressing her well-formed body to his.

He cupped her ass, enjoying the grind of her cunt against his cock, despite the business that'd brought him here. "I'm expecting company." He didn't need to say more.

"I'll wait for you in the bedroom."

"You do that."

She sauntered away, hips swaying for his benefit, knowing he watched her. She was a beautiful woman, an accomplished lover who knew what the score was. It made his thoughts stray to Mirela's mother. He couldn't guess what'd made her have his kid, then keep quiet about it.

A dark-suited man arrived minutes later, intense, looking exactly like what he was, a Fed, of the Homeland Security variety. He wasn't alone, though the guy who accompanied him had a whole different vibe. With the muscles and buzz cut he could pass for former military, the flat, hard eyes said Special Forces or mercenary.

Niall felt the first, sharp stab of foreboding, at just how expensive this call was going to be. "Didn't know you were bringing a friend."

"This is Desmond."

Irish. The sharp blade of foreboding sliced deeper into Niall's gut. He moved to the bar, pouring drinks before they claimed their seats.

The burn of the liquor met the cool of rage and determination.

He would do what it took to protect his family. "You wanted the face-to-face."

"You've got a mess that needs cleaning up. We can bring the necessary pressure to bear and you can deliver a personal warning to complement our actions. Unless you've left evidence around, then the best we can do is get you out of the country ahead of an arrest."

"We're not worried about evidence." The guns Denis had used were long gone and he'd personally watched as Cathal burned the only evidence that proved they'd known who the guilty were. "What do you want?"

"Desmond, inside your organization, pursuing our interests, starting now."

Niall glanced at the cold-eyed man who'd accompanied the Homeland Security handler. "Done."

Twenty-five

Derrick was too restless to remain at the shop, though he needed to catch up on his drawing. He'd planned on spending the rest of the day doing just that, but this environment just wasn't conducive to concentration. Or maybe it was the gnawing suspicion that Emilio hadn't told him the truth. That he was giving up too easily.

He didn't want to go home. Home was where his sheets smelled like Quinn. It was gaping emptiness.

And the bong.

Mustn't forget the bong and the little stash of weed.

Well, he wasn't throwing it away.

Derrick shuddered at the very thought. Waste not. Want not. He'd ration it out and then when it was gone. No more.

He brushed his hands together for emphasis.

"You okay over there?" Bryce asked. "You're talking to yourself more than usual."

"I think better when I verbalize."

Jamaal laughed. "Maybe he's falling out of love this time. Rosy glow he's had going the last couple of days says he's met someone."

"Shit," Bryce muttered. "Be better all-around if he stuck to sex and forgot about relationships."

"Says the man who likes to see his girlfriends wearing dog collars," Derrick said. "Probably so the tags identify them, requiring less strain on the brain."

Jamaal snorted. "He might have you there, Bryce."

Derrick shrugged into his jacket. "And on that note, I'm gone. Behave yourselves."

"Stay out of trouble," Bryce called after him, making him smile. Oh, they had their run-ins, but now that he was on the other side of that disastrous thing with—no, no, no, the man didn't even deserve to have his name acknowledged—Derrick felt guilty for letting Bryce down.

Well, that Derrick was no more. He brushed his hands together again for emphasis.

The new Derrick could be relied on. He swung a leg over the bike, thinking about Emilio. There was more than one way to get an answer.

His heart fluttered in his chest as he thought about the family albums and photographs on the wall of Emilio's parents' house. Did he dare?

Of course he did. Emilio's mother had always been very nice to him. No sleepovers of course. No public displays of affection. Her acceptance of her son's sexuality was the *don't ask, don't tell* variety of a flexible Catholic. But she was a law-abiding woman, and besides, he had no intention of even mentioning the law.

He'd tell her the same thing he'd told Emilio, that this was for a book. He'd ask if she'd seen Marc Ruiz around. And if the answer was yes, he'd find out what Marc was up to, who he hung out with and where he might be found. Simple. And if it gave him a reason to call Quinn . . .

Devine. Superb.

He pulled the bike out into traffic and gunned it.

* * *

Sleepy shouted with glee when the asshole who'd been asking about him crossed turf lines into *his* hood.

Next to him, Puppy turned in his seat, high-fiving Drooler in the back. "He's ours now."

Oh yeah. He was theirs.

Sleepy risked getting closer. "Gotta make this quick." Not everybody on the street could be trusted not to snitch, though they wouldn't do it openly.

He passed his gun to Puppy. "Soon as he parks the bike, you two get out, convince him to get in the car."

His hands were sweating against the steering wheel. Everybody knew his car. Couldn't be helped. He'd told Jacko this was going down. He'd lose respect if he didn't do it now. Besides, he owed this to Lucky.

The bike slid into a tight spot. He hit the gas, pulling alongside with enough room for his crew to get out.

A punch to the gut bent Derrick over with a cry, muffled by the helmet. Drooler shoved him into the backseat, holding him down with a body slam while Puppy got in the front seat and turned around to help.

Sleepy accelerated, leaving rubber on the road and slamming the doors shut with Derrick fighting in the back and Puppy using the gun to hit whatever he could. Nobody bothered to tell the motherfucker to stop struggling. It wouldn't matter whether he did or not.

A glance over his shoulder and Sleepy smiled. He knew just where to take this loser, and when they got done, they could leave the body where it dropped.

Eamon fought to remain impassive as he eased the vessel the changeling had stolen into its berth while a couple of slips away, Myk did the same with the boat they'd used in their search.

It had to be bad if his second had come personally with the news.

"Tell me," Eamon said, tossing Rhys the boat line.

"There was an incident at Aesirs."

"Etaín."

"Yes. She encountered Laura Chevenier and her daughters. By all accounts the woman provoked what happened with mention of Etaín's mother, and hints that she knew where she could be found. It escalated to the point of violence."

"Etaín stripped her mind of the information?"

"Yes."

"You witnessed it?"

"Yes."

Farrell began whimpering on the floor of the small boat where he lay bound by magic, dry now because of that same magic, after throwing himself into the ocean when Eamon finally caught up to him. Fear had driven the changeling to the act. Farrell's own tie to the elements whispering sweet seduction, offering a watery embrace along with visions of gills and tail, if only he shed his humanity.

Worry gripped Eamon at wondering what promises had whispered through Etaín's mind. He caught Rhys's glance at where Etaín's ink was hidden by clothing, though his second didn't say what all of those close to him were thinking, that it might not be safe to allow Etaín to live.

"Where is she?"

"She's on her way to speak with the Cur, Anton."

He could guess her intentions, but Rhys's expression said this wasn't the last of what had brought him here.

"Cathal?"

"There was an attack at his home by someone armed with a grenade launcher. Thankfully the garage door had closed far enough to make it plausible to witnesses that he'd gotten into the house and far enough away from the blast to survive it. He'll be at the estate shortly."

"Take Farrell. Confine him. Call me or have Liam do it when Etaín arrives at her destination. It's time I collect my intended." Before she forced him to render judgment.

The order was given in the cool tones of a lord, though there was no hiding the truth of his emotions from his second. Pain blurred into anger, a deep hurt that made it feel as though his heart had been cleaved in two because apparently she still did not feel enough for him to care how her choices affected him, about the message that he might read into them, that his needs as man and lord weren't important.

Pity and compassion warred in Rhys's eyes. Efficiency, and the desire to let Eamon retain his pride, won out. "Yes, Lord."

Quinn couldn't shake the panic. For the first time since leaving law enforcement, he wished he'd made a sideways move instead of getting out, a move that would give him a light and a siren to cut through traffic and make San Francisco pedestrians get the hell out of the crosswalks.

He called Derrick's cell again. Repeating the action a block later.

Something was wrong. One minute he'd been laughing, playing Uno with his family, working his way toward the big reveal, and the next . . .

He'd felt like his world was about to go dark. He couldn't get out of the house quickly enough, couldn't get back to the city as fast as his gut screamed for him to do it.

"Answer, damn it. Answer."

Another call went straight to voicemail.

Close to Derrick's apartment his instincts screamed *Hurry. Hurry. Hurry.* Except this didn't feel like where he needed to be and that made no fucking sense. Neither did Derrick's leaving work after being adamant when they'd talked on the phone earlier that he was staying late at Stylin' Ink so he could catch up on his artwork. Unless . . .

A low growl emanated without conscious thought. *Mine!*

Shit, not more of this. He tried to shake the weirdness off, the same way he'd finally managed to do about what had happened with the jewelry.

Just some kind of post-traumatic-stress thing going on. Five years undercover with the Aryan Brotherhood had been five years of living hell.

A parking place opened up and he claimed it, screeching to a halt, hand going to the ignition key. Stalling out there because everything inside him said going up to Derrick's place was time he couldn't afford to waste.

I'm going fucking nuts. He scrubbed his hands over his face before checking for traffic and jerking the steering wheel sideways to pull back onto the street. He headed in the direction his gut told him to go.

For a split second he thought about calling Sean as backup. Then dismissed it.

He rubbed the back of his neck, hating the truth that cut into his thoughts like a sharp knife. If this was about work, he'd call Sean in a heartbeat, no hesitation. He'd lived on his instincts for a lot of years. That's what being behind bars reduced a man to, especially a cop undercover. And the times he wasn't in prison, he'd been living a lie twenty-four seven, which was just another kind of incarceration.

All day long he'd had those flashes of possessiveness and battled the need to check in, see Derrick for himself, like some kind of school girl with a crush. They hadn't made plans to see one another. Hadn't made promises.

For all he knew Derrick was out with someone else. Maybe bar hopping. And that was a big part of why he didn't call Sean.

Just go with it, he told himself, putting himself on autopilot, a part of him absolutely positive his instincts would lead him to Derrick.

N ice," Etaín said when they arrived at Greg's place.
It was a tri-level town house. An end unit in a neighborhood where it was easy to imagine parents feeling safe as they walked with their kids to the park a block away, or the library a little bit farther, or to the lake down the road.

High ceilings gave the place an open, airy feeling. At the nursery room doorway, Greg stopped to introduce his obviously pregnant wife, Monique, and, DeAngelo, the toddler-aged boy she was reading to.

"You're Captain Chevenier's daughter," Monique said.

The question produced the hollow twang of pulled heart strings. "You know him?"

"No. I've just been following the news about the Harlequin Rapist. I recognized your name."

She shot her husband a look, momma bear not wanting any threat in her home. "I hope this means Anton is intending to do the right thing."

"This way," Greg said without offering a response, leading Etaín into a living room with a built-in fireplace and a wall taken up by a big-screen TV.

Anton sat on the couch. He didn't stand as Etaín approached.

"I'm not seeing no drawing tablet. I ain't seeing your kit either, the one I know for sure you have with you when you're planning to lay down some ink."

"I said when I called it was to talk." She was close enough to extend her hand for the shake they usually exchanged.

He reached into the crevice between couch cushions and pulled a gun out instead.

The eyes on her palms blazed.

Greg threw his hands up. "Whoa, whoa, Anton. This is crazy. What are you doing, man?"

"I went by the funeral home," Anton said, directing his answer at her. "Paid my respects to Kelvin's mamma and heard about you visiting him at the hospital."

His eyes flicked to her hands then back up to meet hers. His expression hardened. "Now you're here, and I'm thinking it's because you're working for the cops, seeing as how my cousin picked you up not too far from where your daddy works."

"Leave," Greg said, muscling his way between her and Anton.

She didn't know whether it was directed at her or his cousin, but sweat rolled down her back because she could now feel a hint of magic, as though Liam was about to emerge from shadow. She shivered at where that would lead.

"It's okay," she said, fingertips touching Greg's back. "Anton and I understand each other. Maybe it'd be better if you weren't in the room for this."

"You sure?" Disbelief. Respect. Fear.

"I'm sure."

Still he hesitated, as if torn between doing what felt right and what was important for his own family, his survival.

"I'm sure," she repeated, demonstrating it by moving out from behind him to sit in a chair far enough away from Anton that he wouldn't feel threatened.

Greg left. Liam slid into view, forming like a genie escaping through a sliver-thin shadow in a corner of the room, shimmering there then blinking away when Anton glanced over his shoulder. "Cops outside waiting for me?"

"Not that I know of." She leaned forward, forearms on her knees, hands in a loose clasp. "For the record, coming here was my choice. What the cops asked me to do, I've already done."

"Seeing what was in Kelvin's head." He shoved the gun into his waistband at the middle of his back and sat on the couch, a couple of places and a coffee table's distance away.

"You don't seem freaked."

He shrugged. "Had a great grandmother came over from Haiti. Used to tell us kids about voodoo and shit, kept us in line because she was a true believer and we was afraid she'd put a spell on us."

He matched his pose to hers, leaning forward also meaning an easy draw if he pulled the gun again. Given the blazing heat in the centers of her palms, she wondered idly who could do the most damage if they went for their respective weapons.

"What's going down, Etaín? Why you here?"

"Because I care what happened to Kelvin and the others. Especially Vontae. I used to run with him, way back when."

"Yeah, I heard about you being a wild child."

She shrugged. "More rebellious than wild. While you were paying your respects did you hear that Kelvin brought his wife and his baby around to the shop a couple months ago? It hurts to think of him dead because he was trying to do something good and ended up in the wrong place at the wrong time. There's a chance of the same thing happening with any drive-by."

"You thinking I had something to do with the shootings in Oakland today?"

"Did you?"

"You don't have no fear, do you?"

"You baited that hook, not me. I was only making a point. Rumor has it you're trying to take over the Curs and you've got big plans."

He laughed. "Vontae's granny ain't never liked me. You know how the Curs started out? Just a bunch of brothers who liked to ride and wanted to make their own rules."

"And now?"

"Time will tell. You wondering if what happened at the bar is on me? All that killing payback for something I did or ordered done?"

"You baiting the hook again?"

He scrubbed his hands over his face. "Naw. Just trying to figure you out."

"That's easy enough." She turned her wrists, the stylized eyes becoming visible. "All I want is to find out who was behind the slaughter and pass the information on to Detective Ordoñes, so the guilty will hopefully be arrested and that'll keep the street violence from escalating."

His gaze settled on her palms. "Kelvin didn't see anything?"

"Nothing that identifies the shooters."

"How many were there?"

"Five." The police hadn't offered a number to the public.

"That a solid number?"

"If there were more, I can't know it."

"The only way this ends is when those responsible have paid for it."

"And jail time isn't good enough?"

"It could be."

"I'm listening."

"I know who ordered it done."

"But you can't find him."

Anton smiled. "That's right. I can't. But I'm betting you can."

"Who's responsible?"

"He ain't local so it's going to take you a little digging to find out which gang he most likely pulled his crew from. Maybe that's where daddy or big brother comes in, or maybe you play that detective for information." His eyes flicked down to her hands. "Then you pay some folks a little visit, same as you intended for me, and see what's inside their heads. Find his crew, find him."

"Give me the name."

"We in this together or we ain't in it at all. I'm no snitch. But I'm willing to cut a deal with my friend Etaín, who says she cares about Kelvin and Vontae and the others, meaning my sister too, who wasn't guilty of anything but trying to earn some money so she could make a better life for herself. You want to give the crew over to the cops, I can go with that. But I want the guy who ordered it."

"So you get vengeance and the other families have to settle for jail time?"

"That's the way it plays. And I call in some of what's owed to me and let it be known that the score has been completely settled. The drive-bys over what went down stop or there will be consequences."

"You have that kind of juice?"

He laughed. "You're sitting here."

"Owing you a tattoo. Nothing more."

"That's right, though considering everything, I'll take a pass on calling in that favor, at least for now."

She straightened and he tensed, ready to go for his gun. "You really going to shoot me?"

"Don't want to, and that's for real. Got two strikes and not looking for a third. Especially don't want one over nothing."

"Taking a bullet doesn't seem like nothing to me."

He flashed a smile. "See, that's what I always liked about you, Etaín. You cool. Wasn't no shit you laid down for Greg. You and me understand each other. Always have. Wouldn't have spent so much time trying to get in your pants if I was just looking for a good time."

His eyes chilled to the same icy nothingness she'd see in Liam's. "We deal or you leave not knowing what I know. I give you the name. You give him back to me. Or give me his body if that's the way you'd rather see this go down. Ain't no other options on the table. What's it going to be?"

She could walk away from this. Eamon would say she *should* walk away. Only she couldn't forget the burn, couldn't shake the guilt that because he wore her ink, Vontae was dead instead of his killer.

"What if I give the police the crew but the guy you want gets swept up when they are?"

"Then it gets handled on the inside. He goes to prison he's a dead man walking."

"So avoid a third strike. Let the guys already doing time take care of it."

"Your answer a no then?"

She closed her eyes and mental barriers fell, brought down in a juxtaposing of scenes, her own memories of Kelvin coming to the shop with his wife and new baby against what she'd taken from him at the hospital, running parallel to slaughter from a murderer's point of view, a quick montage blocked by an emerald green curtain and fire-emblazoned sigil. *There is another choice. I can give you the killer you seek.*

Escaping the voice, she opened her eyes to see Liam, ethereal, but no less deadly because he hadn't quite left the shadows. She stood, holding out her hand, eyes meeting Anton's. Dare and challenge and demand for a show of trust if they were going to deal. "Give me the name."

Anton laughed, the flash of it reaching his eyes. He stood and took the step that brought him within arm's reach. "*Cyco* Chalino," he said, his palm warm and dry against hers as they performed the combination of moves that served as a handshake.

The apparition that was Liam disappeared, only to reappear in the flesh moments later at Eamon's side as they both entered the room behind Greg.

"This guy have a fucking tracking device on you?" Anton asked, standing, ready to draw his gun.

"Don't," Etaín said, putting herself between Anton and the Elves to prevent violence from erupting in Greg's home.

Eamon's demeanor was ice but the anger she sensed in him was as hot as the fire he commanded. He wouldn't tolerate a threat or insult, not in his current mood and especially not from a human.

"Let's go," he said, extending his hand, imperious command in gesture and tone.

He was every bit the *Lord* and she bit back the flash of her own anger. Took a step toward him, undecided on how far she was willing to acquiesce until he tipped the scales by saying, "Cathal is waiting at the estate. There was an attempt on his life."

Her throat clogged with sudden emotion then. She took the offered hand, not turning to acknowledge Anton as he called after them, "Be hearing from you soon, Etaín."

Twenty-six

Eamon had too much pride to rage at her in front of Myk and Liam in the sedan's front seat. The hand he'd taken inside he'd released the instant she slipped into the car and perversely she felt its loss like a gaping wound, her anger fading. She'd never been good at holding on to it.

No surprise there, she thought, looking out the window and remembering the times she'd done the same, sitting next to her mother. The prospect of a new city, a new, temporary life, no longer an adventure but an ache she rarely put into words because she already knew the impossibility of staying in one place long enough to make permanent friends. Anger had been pointless when her mother was all she had.

She could call that anger now, using the captain's revelation about Eamon's having her apartment cleared out and the threat of denied access to her, but her stomach roiled at the prospect. She didn't want to cloak herself in that emotion, to use something she no longer cared about to strike out at Eamon with.

Guilt crept in as the icy silence continued, as the distance separating his taut body from hers seemed to grow larger despite the finite length of the seat. Regret came, intensified by memories of those moments preceding their stepping into the kitchen at Aesirs, by the joy of their time at Stylin' Ink, the closeness, the satisfaction at having him wear her ink.

Her hand crept to the necklace, fingers rubbing over smooth stones. It'd be a lie to say she was sorry for anything she'd done after he'd left to chase Farrell, but she was sorry for this. Another estrangement.

Tears came, the ache of what had happened with the captain joining this one. She blinked them away, mind scrambling for something to say that would breach the gap, not finding it, not with an audience.

She moved away from the window as they got closer to the estate, stopping in the middle of the seat rather than crowding close, reaching out, hating the tentativeness she felt, the vulnerability, scabs still thin over old wounds caused by rejection, loss, and fear of it.

She placed her hand on his thigh, the weight of it there like a feather easily brushed aside. Her chest tightened, nerves stretching taut, urging her to snatch her hand back and resume her study of the passing scenery.

His hand covered hers before she lost her nerve, and with it came hope fiercely embraced instead of warily circled.

"The encounter with the Cur couldn't wait until I was available to accompany you?"

"I wanted to get it behind me. Behind us. You caught up to Farrell?"

"Yes."

"He was terrified of me. All your Elves were."

His hand tightened on hers. *Ours.* But it'd be a lie to say she felt that way so she merely amended. "All of them except for the bodyguards and Rhys."

"You're *seidic*, Etaín, capable of stripping memories and gifts, reason enough for fear. But a changeling out of control is cause for terror."

His anger bit her, the calm icy waters parting to reveal it in his voice. She jerked reflexively, a tug to free her hand from beneath his.

"I wasn't out of control."

"You used your gift in full view of others. You stripped a human's memory without regard to consequences."

"Don't tell me you've never been ruthless."

He grabbed her wrist. "Ruthless, yes. But foolish? Not until I met you. Time and time again I've allowed—"

"Don't go there, Eamon. I thought we'd gotten beyond that."

His fingers tightened on her wrist. "I've allowed myself to believe that you could separate the man from the lord, yet understand I am both. I've been foolish enough to hope you might consider how your actions reflect on me, and what they mean for all those who've bound themselves to me, who could find their lives a lot worse because I've tied their future to yours."

I didn't ask you do it. I don't want the responsibility.

A defensive reaction to the pain threading through his voice, to her own guilt at having fled Aesirs, reacting to an order she'd known even then was given out of concern for her, but using it as an excuse to run. To keep running and in the process, add to his worries and put others in danger. The captain. Greg and his family. Anton.

Gifts came with responsibilities, of that she was certain, though the refrain was the captain's influence, not her mother's. And the *want*, the *need*, they weren't one-sided.

How Eamon had come into her life didn't matter. Peordh. Predestination. She wouldn't change it if she could. She'd change only this, the misunderstanding, the hurt.

"What happened with the captain's wife, my mother set that in motion. She foresaw the encounter and what would happen because of it. There was a clue for me in Laura's mind. The Dragon is real, Eamon. It's real."

His leaned in, eyes stormy. "The changeling you asked about threw himself into the ocean, the magic a siren song promising him gills and tail if he surrendered to it rather than allow me to catch him and help him gain control of it. He'd be dead now if I hadn't been close enough, strong enough to reach out with a spell, with my own command of the elements."

She tugged at her wrist to free her hand and retrieve the picture showing Dragon and woman and sigil. He tightened his grip, reading denial. She stopped, seeing the flash of pain in his expression and it hurt her.

Leaning forward she brushed her mouth against his. "I see the man and the lord, Eamon. I'll work harder at meeting you halfway. Halfway. I won't lose the part of myself that's human. I don't think I'm meant to, otherwise why would the magic have chosen Cathal?"

His free hand lifted, fingers sliding through her hair. He caressed her cheek, cupping it, the soft touch a blossom of pleasure and hope, an acknowledgement of her point.

"You've told me not much is known about the *seidic*," she said. "You've told me that my magic feels old to you. When I look at the bands my mother tattooed on my wrists, I see the Dragon's green. When I face it, that green travels up my arm as though the sigils making up its name are written there like inked destiny."

"Etaín." Her name held his doubt, his worry, the wealth of his desire as the estate gate slid back as it had the first night she'd come here, revealing Cathal waiting there instead of Eamon.

Eamon released her so she could get to Cathal, but sudden imperative held her. "Trust me to do the right thing," she said, before taking the freedom he offered. Her arms were around Cathal an instant later, her mouth fused to his.

Cathal couldn't get enough of her. He was as desperate for her as he'd been after the encounter with the gangbanger, except this was honest, with no agenda other than to celebrate life and love.

His mouth ate hungrily at hers, his cock about to tear through the front of his jeans to get to the place it considered home. His arms tightened on her at Eamon's approach.

Not jealously. Not possessiveness. But a grab for sanity to keep from stripping her out of her clothing.

Talk would have to wait. Confessions. Neither of them was as important as the touch of skin to skin, the urgent need to be inside her, to share her.

Pulling his mouth from hers, he said, "Let's take this to the bedroom," thoughts flashing to his fire and smoke and water-damaged house. Not Eamon's bedroom but *their* bedroom. For a while. Maybe permanently. And he found that the thought of living here, where she'd be safer—hell, where *he'd* be safer—didn't bother him.

His lips returned to hers, hands settling on her hips, though the will to stop the grind of her cunt against his cock deserted him.

In his mind he said, *we need to stop now*, but his body refused to yield, relishing the rub and press, the heat and scent of Etaín and the joy of being alive.

Quinn pulled to a stop near the chain-link fence, cutting the engine steps away from an opening in the fence to the right of a No Trespassing sign. Again he contemplated calling Sean. Again he dismissed it.

He pulled his gun from its holster and got out of the car. He'd just take a quick look around, enough to either confirm he was nuts or . . .

Hurry. Hurry. Hurry.

The refrain pounded through him with each heartbeat. Racing until there was no break between utterances.

The twist in his gut got tighter with each step, until caution was a struggle.

He heard voices speaking Spanish. Harsh-edged, ugly laughter

followed by the sound of someone being hit. A cry of pain, a pit-
eous whimper.

Derrick's cry. Derrick's whimper.

Rage poured into Quinn. The red of furious fire burning away
years of training, eradicating any thought of stealth.

He raced forward, driven by fierce possessiveness past abandoned buildings covered in graffiti, the sound of violence and
agony, the scent of blood reaching him, feeding his urgency and
providing a trail. He led with his gun, finger steady on the trigger
despite the adrenaline rushing through him and the pounding beat
of his heart.

"Please, no!" Derrick screamed, terror peaking, and Quinn
promised himself Derrick would never beg again, unless it was in
bed with him, and the words would be "Please. Yes!"

"Do it, Drooler," someone said as Quinn rounded the corner
and saw Derrick held between two teens, struggling as a third
raised a gun.

Pop. Pop. Pop The rounds left Quinn's gun in staccato beats,
taking the immediate threat to Derrick down, before eliminating
the others.

Shoot to kill.

Instinct. Training.

He was rushing forward when something slammed into him.

He took two additional steps before his brain interpreted what
his body knew. He'd been shot. Realization came with the delayed
impression of a man ducking behind a stripped, abandoned car.

Quinn hit the ground. His hand went to his chest in a feeble
attempt to stop the escape of blood, his consciousness wavering.
His vision was wet and blurry as Derrick dragged himself toward
him on his belly, using one arm while the other trailed.

"No, no, no," Derrick sobbed, his face was bloody and swollen.

Quinn wanted to scream *Run! Get out of here!* But a bubble of
blood gurgled up his throat and prevented it.

The shooter stepped out from behind the car.

A roar of denial blasted from Quinn's core. A determination to protect Derrick that held him to life and lent him enough strength to angle the gun upward and get off two shots.

Hits, both of them.

The man went down and didn't get back up.

Satisfaction tempered the pain of having lost a future with Derrick. *He'll use my cellphone. He'll make it out of here.* Comforting thoughts as Quinn slid into the oblivion that was death.

Etaín seized without warning, the violence of it tearing her out of Cathal's arms and throwing her to the driveway to flail and thrash, limbs wild and back bowing as though it would snap. He dropped immediately, grabbing an arm, pinning it to the cool concrete as his other hand pressed against her chest in an effort to hold her down.

Eamon was instantly there, kneeling opposite her. Etaín's hand flashed out, grabbing Eamon's wrist, her palm pressed to his flesh. Concern for her went to fear of her, a glimmer of expression quickly smoothed to hide its turbulence, but not quickly enough.

"Sire?" Liam said, stepping forward, Heath and Myk immediately flanking him.

"What's going on?" Cathal managed, and yet he could feel it in the tattoos along his forearms. Magic.

Eamon stiffened, head snapping back, the muscles of his throat taut, his face reflecting struggle, as if he tried to break away from Etaín's grip but couldn't.

Terror crawled into Cathal's throat. Survival instinct screaming for him to break contact with Etaín now, while he still could, demanding he flee because he was only human.

He held tight, denying everything, willing to sacrifice everything, believing in that instant that she needed him now more than ever, that magic, something intrinsically a part of her, had chosen him for more than a save from the Harlequin Rapist.

"She consumes you, Lord," Liam said, voice urgent, determined. "Order me to kill her!"

The magic blazed a trail for Cage though he didn't need one, given his close proximity to Quinn. He pushed through the opening in the chain link fence, urgent now with the scent of blood, Kestrel awake and hungry, the sound of a man crying, a body dragging chilling him to his core.

He did not limit himself to human speed in order to reach Quinn. Knew by the soaked front of Quinn's clothing and pool of blood spreading next to him that only the magic held him to this life and this body.

Cage scooped Quinn up, taking in the three dead, one of whom Kestrel had hungered for outside Saoirse. Pity moved through him when he recognized Derrick, beaten and broken but dragging his body forward in an effort to get to his lover.

There was no time to offer comfort. And reassurance was premature even this close to water.

Cage raced forward, hurling Quinn into the bay.

Behind him Derrick screamed. A heart-wrenching, primal sound of such anguish that it silenced even Kestrel's demands.

A wordless scream left Eamon and this time Cathal's head snapped back as pain ripped through him as though he were being eviscerated from the inside out.

"Eamon. Lord. Order me to kill her!"

"No." Cathal gasped. "Trust her."

"No!" Liam urged, tensed and coiled like a panther ready to spring. "No! Today's events demonstrated that the magic controls her, not the other way around. Accept her loss for the good of those who call you Lord."

Another wave of pain clawed through Cathal. Pulsing simultaneously to what was happening to Eamon. Building, building, then suddenly condensing, shattering in his chest.

Cage watched as the bubbles rising to the surfaced ceased, the body disappearing, sinking.

He caught himself holding his breath and forced an exhale, guilt settling into his chest with the next inhalation.

Brother. The sense of it was stronger now.

He had not been his brother's keeper here.

It wasn't too late. Not yet, though he could guess what the magical channeling was doing to the *seidic* changeling who'd made this possible with her ink. In the end, this might cause her death.

Jacko tried to use the car to get to his feet, but left only a smear of blood against metal next to concrete blocks and rusted axel. His thoughts drifted, sliding into the past with the memory of stabbing a shank into the last guy he'd killed in prison.

What was the motherfucker's name? His thoughts blurred. He could remember the blood wet on his hand and wrist.

Reality blurred, he looked down and blood gushed out faster, his heart pumping hard at seeing the gut shots, his fingers splayed across his stomach though his intestines were leaking out.

Motherfuck. He dug into his pocket for his phone, hearing Cyco say, "I'm about finished my business. You done?

"Jacko! Jacko!" The shout brought him back. He shivered. Fear coming when he realized he was shaking, so cold now he couldn't feel his legs anymore. Couldn't actually feel much of anything.

Motherfuck, they weren't going to find him curled up in a ball.

They weren't going to say he went out like a pussy. When they talked about him, they were going to say he was a man.

"Dead. Guy showed up." The words were slurred but he kept going, forcing more of them out. "I took him out. Need you to finish Cathal Dunne." Couldn't believe the asshole had survived the launcher attack.

"Him. His woman. Anybody else who's with him."

"Good," Jacko said, the phone dropping away as the numbness spread and all awareness ceased.

Etaín opened her eyes to tranquility, if facing a Dragon could be tranquil. It rose from the water, creating a ripple, and in that ripple Etaín saw Eamon on his knees, body bowed, rigid, his image thin, appearing more apparition than solid man while Cathal—

Agony engulfed her at seeing him prone, still, sightless eyes staring at nothing.

There is always a price to pay. He is human, mortal born, not created to be conduit or vessel for magic.

"No!" she screamed, the sound of it reverberating, making her aware of the ebb and flow, the serration of her own heart, still beating while Cathal's was silenced.

Clever changeling. The sigil of servitude appeared, writ in the air like a fiery brand. *It's what I can offer you now. There's still time for your human. Take it and return to him, transformed into what you were meant to be.*

Trust me to do the right thing, the words spoken before racing to Cathal mocked her now, everything inside her saying no price was too high to pay for Cathal's life. But those moments when she'd lost control of her limbs, when the ability to speak had been choked off at the Dragon's will, were too visceral.

This servitude was another name for slavery. And that slavery would extend to him.

Not slavery. The honoring of a promise. The righting of a wrong.

At what ultimate cost? In the water Eamon continued to fade, as if her touch was draining him of magic and gift, his accusation ringing in her ears that the lives of those who depended on him as Lord would worsen because he'd tied their future to hers.

"No," she said, concentrating on the complex shapes Eamon had painstakingly taught her, building the sigil segment by segment in the hopes it would allow him to get free of her.

S ire!" Liam urged again, enough control finally returning that Eamon was able to speak.

"No." The answer came from his heart, more gasp than word.

Liam's face reflected understanding and grief even as he moved to disobey, willing to give his life for his lord's. But Myk and Heath reacted as well, as if anticipating it, grabbing Liam, risking his gift, struggling though that struggle lasted only moments before Etaín's body stilled in human death and the flow of magic abruptly stopped.

Eamon felt as though his own heart had been ripped out of his chest. Searing pain spread through him, growing in intensity as moments passed instead of the barely perceptible seconds that had marked his own change, the tattoos on his arms inert, nothing more than ink, giving him no way to call her back.

"Fight, Etaín, fight."

T he lake, the Dragon, the burning sigil and the complex one she'd been building disappeared in a white burst and an echo of pain. Nothingness followed, an inky blackness that drained into the vines on her arms, and in its wake she again faced the Dragon— except this time there was silence. So she was dead now too.

*   *   *

Cage smiled when the water began churning violently, smoke rising from its depths along with bubbles and blackened debris. The thrashing continuing, creating a whirlpool that sucked them back in. A light show of color only he could see as a Dragon battled to regain a human shape, to make sense of facts and divergent realities, though those born in this rare, rare manner were born old.

Behind him Derrick sobbed, the slow scrape of his body marking his determination to reach his lover even now. Quinn had chosen well. Or the *seidic* had with her ink.

Cage turned away from the water, using his true speed to reach Derrick, offering comfort with a whispered, "He lives, and so will you," before offering merciful oblivion with a spelled charm he'd gained from Eamon.

In front of Etaín, the water rippled again. Only instead of images of Cathal and Eamon, the slaughter at the bar was replayed and she felt the phantom flare of heat at her wrists and along her arms, burning hot and fierce as Vontae and his killer became aware of each other. *I woke and you shared in my awakening. Not your gift to see the endpoint of magic. Mine.*

The sigil representing servitude flared between them again. *Take it and you can find the killer you seek.*

Even to find justice for the innocent, she couldn't. "No."

Eamon couldn't accept that he'd lost her. Physical survival from the change itself wasn't what he'd feared. Not for her. Not for any changeling. Death came by his judgment.

Too much time had passed. Transformation was marked in seconds, not minutes.

He pressed her palm to his heart as if he could will magic into her, could use it to summon her back, praying in that moment that the Dragon did indeed exist, and that Etaín merely visited at the shore of the lake she'd drawn.

Liam knelt next to him, freed now that the danger to Eamon was past. "Let me attempt it, Lord," and despite the wild struggle and intended disobedience, Eamon trusted his third, but said instead, "Cathal first," in the hopes it wasn't already too late.

Liam reached out and placed his hand above Cathal's heart. Once, centuries earlier, Eamon had felt the punch of magic that was Liam's gift.

An explosive gasp signaled Cathal's regained consciousness.

Etaín staggered and went to her knees as if she were an insubstantial piece of wood suddenly tethered by an anchor tossed into the ocean.

The scene in front of her wavered. The Dragon roared, the sigil of servitude melting into flames encircling her.

So your Elven lord has chosen to save the human. For another of the seidic *it would be enough. But not for you. I can hold you here. You were born on the shores of my lake and bathed in its water. You aren't only of Elfhome and Earth.*

Trust. There hadn't been time to show Eamon the picture. Hadn't been time to discuss the sigil at the corner of the playing card.

Etaín's feelings about her mother were as complicated as those she felt for the captain, but in that instant, remembering the feel of the collar-like necklace still adorning her physical body and the way her mother's hand rested at her throat in the first picture but not in the second, Etaín took a leap of faith.

She drew the sigil she'd seen on the card in the sand. "This binding I'm willing to accept."

Clever, clever changeling.

Fire rushed toward her, fully engulfing her, though the force of it was met by other magic that tasted of forests and smelled of spring air and sunshine, that danced and entwined, primordial and new, Elfhome. But also the place she called home, a blending of worlds that turned into sunshine traveling down a pathway and illuminating everything around it, becoming the liquid pour of ink into her own arms.

Twenty-seven

Etaín opened her eyes to find Cathal and Eamon hovering above her. "Jesus, Etaín, Jesus," Cathal said, hands shaking as he pulled her into a sitting position and then into his arms, not all-encompassing but angled so Eamon could embrace her too.

"Let's take this private," she whispered, the clothing she wore an irritant to her skin, and their clothing, an unacceptable separation.

"Let's," Cathal said, nearly a pant, and Etaín became aware of the hard ridge of his cock against her, the minute tremors coursing through him.

"A lesson first," Eamon said on a husky laugh, easing away and making her aware of the glow coming off her skin. Like sunshine. Thick and golden like the rush of it she'd been caught up in, returning her to life.

Her heart skipped a beat then knocked in rapid succession when Cathal's mouth found her ear, lips capturing the pointed tip. Desire streaking downward, causing the violent clenching of her channel.

Eamon traced a quick sigil on the back of her hand. It was a dousing spell he'd mentioned the night before but hadn't taught her because there'd been no need then and she'd been exhausted.

Her magic blocked his until she mentally made the sigil her own. Elven luminescence faded, but not Cathal's desire. Nor Eamon's.

Her need matched theirs though curiosity had her rolling up her sleeve. The visual change to her tattoo turned Eamon's face into a smooth mask.

He caught her hand, examining vibrant entwined strands of gold and emerald green anchored in the ink on her wrist then traveling up her arm, the sigil she'd drawn in the sand writ now on her skin. "Alliance," he said. "An irreversible magical bond."

Peordh. Predestination. Possibility fulfilled. A promise kept.

Cathal rolled up his sleeves to reveal the changes to the tattoos. The bond forged by Eamon's magic had locked shades of red and blue and gold in them. Now emerald green streaked through the center of every black line, glittering like Dragon scales caught in the sun's rays.

"Sire?" Myk said, question in his voice, concern, a reminder that they still had an audience.

Eamon shook his head. "The ink remains inert."

His tone was cool, unconcerned, but Etaín's throat closed, tightened by the pain of what his answer meant.

He didn't resist when she unbuttoned his shirt, parting it and pulling it off one shoulder. The band encircling his upper arm was ink and unhealed skin. Unchanged, though because it was hers, because of her gift, she felt the low hum of magic, a connection she shared with hundreds of others, not the same as the one she shared with Cathal.

"Why didn't it . . ." The answer came before the question could be fully formed. Because of the sigil she'd offered the Dragon, the bond created in that surreal time between human death and Elven birth had taken the place of what she might have had with Eamon.

She met Eamon's eyes, hers damp with sorrow, with loss, her heart aching for him, for her, for them. "I'm—"

He silenced her with a kiss, lips tender against hers, vibrating with echoes of pain. His tongue a soft stroke against hers, eloquent strength in the face of disappointment, exclusion, the poignancy of it freeing her tears.

"Stop, Etaín," he said, brushing them away. "The meaning of the tattoos is unchanged by the lack of a magical bond. This is a time for celebration, not sadness or regret."

His hand cupped her side. His mouth went to her ear, tongue darting into the canal, before lips captured the tip. Desire returned in a molten rush. Streaking downward so her cunt clenched and she reached for Cathal, pulling him into the embrace.

His phone rang.

He ignored it.

Hers rang until it went to voicemail.

His rang immediately afterward.

"It's a conspiracy," Cathal said, but icy foreboding had already gripped her.

She answered when hers rang again, desire chilled at hearing Quinn say, "We're ten minutes out and on our way there. Derrick's hurt. It's bad. Really bad. External and internal. Tell Eamon he needs a healer. Tell him Cage will arrive with us."

He hung up before she could ask more. "I heard," Eamon said, and Myk was already making the call on his lord's behalf.

"Fuck," Cathal whispered, tension running through his voice and his body where it still touched hers. "Fuck."

Guilt nearly bore Etaín to the ground. This was her fault. She'd known, she'd feared for Derrick when there'd been no sibilant promise of *safe, my gift* as there had been when she hugged Jamaal.

Why! She screamed at the Dragon. *Why!*

But there was no response despite the waiting quality that resonated through the bond, signifying awareness.

*   *   *

Cathal stepped away from Etaín, not willing to use the physical contact to mitigate the admissions he needed to make. "I've met Cage. Today's attack wasn't the first one."

Eamon's focus sharpened while added tension tightened Etaín's already strained features. "This is because of the drawings?" she asked, her oblique way of alluding to the boys who'd drugged and raped Brianna and Caitlyn, and his father and uncle's response to it.

"Yes. There was a gangbanger waiting for me outside the club last night. Hispanic. It was meant to be a hit. They used a grenade launcher on my house before the garage door could get all the way down. I think we can be fairly sure this doesn't have anything to do with what happened in Oakland."

He'd tell her about Mirela later. Considering he might never see his sister again after what she'd seen and experienced made it an unimportant detour compared to getting this said and out of the way.

"My father was here before you arrived. He said this business is done. He made some calls. He's gotten assurances. The last of it will be wrapped up at Aesirs tomorrow."

"It had better be, or I will see it handled," Eamon said.

"Understood."

"Cajeilas," Eamon prompted. "Cage."

"He approached me as I was leaving the club. If not for him I'd have died."

Eamon grimaced. "A debt he'll no doubt present me with. Or more likely, Etaín."

The reaction brought confusion along with a spike of familiar frustration and anger, because obviously things weren't what they seemed, but then he was only—

Bullshit. He was not going to revisit that cesspit of self-pity. Maybe he was going to have to buy himself a T-shirt with *I am human, hear me roar.*

The thought kicked one corner of his mouth up. Not imagining himself in it, but Etaín wearing it.

Since Etaín's survival was no longer in question, he spat out the most relevant part of his interaction with Cage, without placing blame. "He offered sanctuary for Etaín and me in Seattle and I was tempted not just by the prospect of having her to myself. It seemed reasonable to think you might want me dead."

"The result of a human-on-human crime. The origins of it unattributable to me, so Etaín would not hold me responsible," Eamon said, filling in the blanks with uncanny accuracy. "A reasonable assumption for Cajeilas given the lack of a bodyguard accompanying you. My failure. It didn't occur to me to offer one at your departure."

Relief was a warm spread through Cathal's chest. "You were kind of busy at the time." His eyes met Eamon's, both of them looking at a memory, a naked Etaín in desperate need of the magical lessons that might well be the reason she was with them now.

"So I was," Eamon said. "Cajeilas is neither my enemy nor my ally."

It was only when Quinn's car pulled into the estate that it occurred to Etaín to wonder how he had known where she was, or that such a thing as a healer existed, and seeking one out would be preferable to going to the hospital. But the moment he emerged from it, she knew he'd become what the ink she'd put on him to cover the AB tats foretold, the Dragon's *yesss* little more than a ripple preceding the soul-deep anguish at seeing Derrick.

Minutes became a crawl of agony encompassing the hurried trip to the bedroom where the healer waited, the horror of Derrick's clothes being cut away and the damage beyond what had been done to his face exposed.

Tears escaped unchecked, her sense of helplessness intensified at seeing the shattered bones in his arm and leg. But when she would have offered comfort with a touch, the healer gently denied her saying, "No, Lady, your magic might interfere with my ability to help him."

Cathal and Eamon took her hands, smoothing out the fists they'd become, nails digging ruthlessly into the eyes at the centers of her palms, while on the opposite side of the bed, Quinn hovered and Cage stood at his back, an unnecessary guard. Dragon.

He noted her regard, and amusement lurked in his expression, eyes flicking quickly at Liam then downward to her exposed arms, and she sensed Eamon's shadowy assassin was the true target of the barb when Cage said, "You've been my dam's pretty bauble all along."

Eamon's free hand flashed in instant command for Liam to go no farther than the step he'd already managed. "You're here at my sufferance," he told the Dragon.

Cage merely opened his arms to encompass the scene in front of him, including Quinn and Derrick. "The ink your new Elf wears suggests I might be hard to get rid of. The affection she holds for the mate of my *new* brother surely means you'll be seeing more of me."

"Sire," Liam growled, eliciting a wide smile in Cage.

"Who did this to Derrick?" Etaín asked, the need to understand allowing her to push aside grief and guilt.

Derrick whimpered and moaned, eyelashes fluttering as though he tried to fight through pain and unconsciousness in order to answer. "Lie still," Quinn murmured, allowed to touch Derrick where she hadn't been.

Her throat closed even though she knew from experience with the healer, that in the end, Derrick would be made whole. She braved the damage done to him, gaze going to the small Dragon she'd put on him years earlier. Not her gift to see the endpoint of magic according to . . . Cage's dam if he was to be believed, and yet . . .

Seer's daughter. Seidic's daughter. Some pairings are a threat to those in power. It was followed by urging instead of a hijacking of body, her focus shifted to Quinn. *The first righting of old wrongs.*

Oh shit, she thought, snagged on the word *first* until finally the conversation around her burst the bubble of her inattention with Eamon's asking, "And the bodies?"

"All four incinerated," Cage said, with no small measure of satisfaction. "I had to occupy myself while *my brother* Quinn rediscovered his human form."

"You searched them first?"

Cage snorted, emphasizing the reaction with flame and smoke. "No. They possessed no treasure of interest to me."

"We would have valued their identities," Eamon said, projecting the smooth of a calm ocean though inwardly he raged. He wanted this human business done, behind them.

"They are dead," Cage said, slanting a glance at Cathal. "They are of no concern though I recognized one of them from outside of Saoirse."

Both Cathal and Etaín went rigid, taking the blame for this upon themselves, but if there was blame at all, it was equally shared. He'd allowed the events set in motion by the Dunnes to play out. He had believed that, in the end, they would serve him, driving Etaín more fully into his arms.

"Derrick will be able to tell us what we need to know," he said, a subtle reminder that this would be set to rights.

His hand tightened on Etaín's, a gesture of reassurance for her and a battling of the sorrow that threatened to well up inside him. The unhealed tattoos on his arms were a raw wound piercing heart and reaching soul.

It changes nothing, he told himself as he'd told her. She would still be his consort-wife, her gift used for their people.

Her ink, visible on the bare-chested Quinn, a man who'd been human days earlier, served as harbinger to a great deal of change. If this was one of the abilities of the *seidic* then it added another cause for assassination. Dragons had always symbolized chaos for the Elven, and threat, because they were magical beings his kind couldn't sense.

Twenty-eight

Etaín watched the miracle of Derrick's body being knitted back together and smoothed into its correct shape by the glide of hands and concentrated magic. It awed her to witness this gift and be part of a world where wielding it was natural.

A laugh bubbled up with her radical shift in perspective, escaping when Quinn jerked the covers up to Derrick's hips, the instant the healer moved above them. "He'd enjoy the ogling," she joked.

"Well I don't." Dragon growl present in his voice, the exchange a tension relief for all of them, levity to carry them until Derrick whispered, "I fucked up. I just wanted to help."

A thick stream of smoke erupted from Quinn's nostrils, unseen by Derrick whose eyes were still closed. "I told you no."

"Well sue me." Little more than a mutter, but hearing the Derrick she loved had Etaín kneeling next to the bed, asking, "Who were they?"

"Marc *Sleepy* Ruiz and friends Drooler and Puppy." Beneath closed lids, Derrick's eyes rolled at the street names.

"Why you?" Etaín asked.

He turned his head, struggled until finally his gaze met hers. "I had a lead on Ruiz. I pursued it."

"Instead of just turning it over to Quinn and Sean?"

"Strength is my new middle name."

"That self-help book is going in the trash the next time I'm at your place."

His laugh turned into a whimper and gained her a stern look from the healer and a growl from Quinn.

"They kept asking me what happened to Lucky. What Cathal did with Lucky."

"Fuck," Cathal said. "Fuck."

"I'd love to," Derrick said in a prim voice. "But Etaín and I never share lovers."

"There was a fourth guy," Quinn said. "Older. Did you get a name?"

"Jacko." Derrick lifted his arm, his hand settling on Quinn's chest but not remaining still. "I think I was hallucinating at the end. You got shot. You were dying." His voice hitched and tears shimmered in his eyes. "And then Tall Dark and Predatory picked you up and threw you into the bay."

"I think that's our cue to leave," Eamon said, tugging Etaín to her feet.

Outside the bedroom, she said, "Anton gave me a name. It'd be better to ask Sean to run with it."

"You're done with this, Etaín," Eamon said.

It'd be easy to play the promise card. To point out she'd be foresworn. Instead she moved in to him, tracing lips firmed into an arrogant, lordly line.

"I have to see this through. I have to finish it. That's who I am. Becoming Elf didn't make me any more or less than what I was as a human. It didn't suddenly separate me from the world I've lived in all my life."

"Etaín—"

She pressed firmly. "Together. We do this together, with a little help from our friends."

"Sounds like a rock song," Cathal said at her back. "But I'm in. And afterward maybe we can stay in bed for the next week."

Eamon resisted. His will silently battling theirs. More form than substance given Etaín's determination and the respect that had grown along with his love for her.

It very nearly amused him, how simple he'd thought their courtship would be. How easily he'd thought to bend her while not bending himself. "Your plan?"

"Unchanged since this began, except now we go at it from a different direction, from the top down to a crewmember I can touch just long enough to get something useful for Detective Ordoñes."

She hesitated, old habits clinging until she shed them, giving him the full truth. "The Dragon can follow my ink. It . . . she . . . can see through the killer's eyes, enough to get a location but not necessarily an identification. I'd rather have that going in."

And he knew what she meant by going in. "It'll require a concession."

"Yes."

A muscle spasmed in his cheek, resistance radiating off him like the rays of a dark sun, but he said, "I trust you to handle it."

She brushed her lips against his, heart singing. Eamon's hand tangling in her hair held her as he deepened the kiss in a promise of what they'd share after this was behind them. When they parted, she gave Cathal the name Anton had given her.

He made the call.

"What's up?" Sean asked.

"There's a name for you to run, specifically to see if there's a connection to any of the guys wearing Etaín's art."

"Hold on."

Cathal heard Sean crossing the deck, then the sound of a computer waking up. Key taps followed, Sean logging in to a law enforcement database in all likelihood. "Let me have it."

"Street name Cyco. Last name Chalino."

Sean's low whistle seconds later said there'd been an immediate hit. "This is one bad dude. I'm shooting you a picture now."

"Shit," Cathal said. "This is the guy in the Jag."

"Responsible for the excitement at your place after I talked to you last?"

"Yes."

"Says here he's wanted in the United States for murder, a home invasion with a body count of three. Escaped to Mexico where he's believed to have done work for one of the cartels. Got caught there and tossed into jail but Mexico wouldn't extradite since he's facing the death penalty in Texas and the Texans don't back down. Escaped prison five months ago, but here's cause to tie him to the slaughter in Oakland. He's suspected of doing the same in Mexico. Twenty-five dead when he and his crew raided a whorehouse and drug distribution house run by a rival cartel."

"Known associates?"

"Getting there." Keystrokes followed, then a, "Damn. His cousin in Roberto *Spooky* Jimenez, wanted by the Oakland PD on suspicion of murder. Fled to LA, possibly Mexico."

"Looks like he's back, with a traveling buddy."

"Then I'd say they've got a pretty tight support network. I ran Spooky's name past my snitches as well as the cops I reached out to. No hint of him being back in the area. Not going to be easy finding him or his cousin."

"I think we have what we need. Go ahead and send the bill." Better all the way around if Sean didn't discover Lucky's associates were now missing too.

"You're passing the information on to the cops?"

"Yes."

"Consider me done then."

Cathal hung up. Etaín said, "Roberto was a friend, not just someone I knew. We used to hang out at Vontae's house together. He wasn't a gangbanger then, didn't have a street name, but there was a certain inevitability. I can see it now. He was obsessed with cred and respect."

She touched a place above her heart. "He idolized his uncle. I did a memorial tat of him. Later someone told me the guy was involved with one of the cartels and was killed during an ambush of newly sworn-in Mexican police officers."

Eamon's tight expression mirrored the hard knot in Cathal's gut. Even knowing Liam would shadow her, he didn't like the thought of her being around guys who had so little regard for human life.

He voiced what Eamon was no doubt thinking, "Spooky's wanted. Give Ordoñes his location, it might be enough. There's a good chance they'd get Cyco too. Your obligation to Anton would be met."

"Even if that's true, Spooky and Cyco won't give up the others, and without the guns, there'd be no hard evidence linking any of them to the bar hit. That's assuming the police act immediately. And if Cyco isn't with them when the police swoop, he'll be in the wind and probably out of Eamon's territory, making it a lot harder to put the deal I made with Anton behind us."

He knew she was right, had known it when he proposed the easy, less risky course of action. Christ, he just wanted this done. "Eamon?"

"She's correct. My territory doesn't extend into Southern California nor beyond the Northern borders of this state, and even then it's not all inclusive."

"Let's get it over with then." It should be safe enough, though he caught himself rubbing his forearm when he saw the quicksilver flash of pain in Eamon's eyes.

Fuck. Maybe when this was done they could approach Cage and bargain for access to the information he claimed to have about the *seidic*. There had to be a way for Etaín to shove magic into the ink on Eamon's arms.

"Ready?" he asked Etaín.

"As I'll ever be." She sat in the hallway, back to the wall, and closed her eyes.

Before Eamon, she hadn't spent much time contemplating magic, though if she had, she would have drawn from the stories she'd read and assumed practicing it required some type of circle, possibly with salt, and probably with candles.

It seemed anticlimactic, lacking in ceremony to simply reach out mentally, to imagine herself walking the path of the sigil starting from the point where it touched the ink on her wrists then moving forward, twined gold and green beneath her feet becoming less prominent as sunshine filtered through the dark, ancient trees of a primordial forest smelling of rich loam and magic.

She followed the trail to the lake and the emerald green Dragon waiting there. "You expected me."

Yesss.

"You know what I want."

The killer.

"And the cost?"

Flame accompanied amusement, a fiery snort. *Seidic born. Elf who is bound to a human, the magic at my command is not the only magic to touch you. What cost? I cannot know other than my price.*

"And that is?"

Your ink on one of my choosing.

She'd assumed that would be the cost. But a hard shiver went through her at not knowing the *full* cost. Her heart raced, aching with the remembered images of Cathal's sightless eyes and Eamon's fading image, the sundering of his magic and gift.

Trust yourself. Trust your gift. It took several repetitions because the fear of losing either Cathal or Eamon overshadowed and over-whelmed the confidence forged during the years when she didn't know about Elves or Dragons or magic, and had still managed to find her way after answering the call to ink.

"Not your gift to see the endpoint of magic. Mine," the Dragon had told her during the struggle to determine the bond they would share. Etaín looked down at her hands, wondering if she dared, deciding yes she did. "You can watch the killer?"

Yesss.

"You could call me here if you saw him with another man?" She held the picture Sean had sent of Cyco Chalino in her mind. "Of this man?"

Yesss. My price is tripled for such a task. I am no dog to set to watch.

Amusement in the voice, a purr of satisfaction. Enough to ease some of Etaín's worry about surviving the payment.

"If there's a danger of more people dying, you'll summon me even if it's only the first killer."

Yesss. But the bargain stands. Three of my choosing.

"Agreed," she said, needing only to open her eyes to leave mystical place for a real one.

"Got it?" Cathal asked.

"Not yet." She accepted Eamon's hand and the tug to her feet. Her arms went around both men, pulling them to her, the desire delayed earlier returning in a rush. "It may be awhile."

"You'll tattoo someone of the Dragon's choosing?" Eamon asked.

"Three people. In exchange for being able to snag Cyco Chalino along with Roberto."

Eamon's smile of approval warmed her though it didn't fully dissipate the chill of concern. "It might be dangerous to you and Cathal."

He stroked his thumb across the back of her hand. "I believe we will survive it. Peordh. Predestination. I have come to accept it where you are concerned. I believe that's why the magic chose Cathal, because he is of this world. A true anchor to it."

Her throat closed. She squeezed Eamon's hand but there was no promise she could make, that her magic would choose him as her heart had.

"Let's go upstairs," she said. *To the bedroom,* they heard, dark heat in their eyes as they accompanied her there.

No worries, she told herself. Embrace the moment. Embrace these two men who were more than she'd dreamed possible.

Clothes fell to the floor, shed in an impatient rush next to the bed. Then skin touched skin, fevered need reflecting a deeper one as masculine lips touched her neck, Eamon in front of her this time, with Cathal at her back.

"Together," she said. "I want you both inside me at the same time."

Skin didn't lie to her. Neither did the hard cocks pressed against her. A pulse went through rigid heat that thickened, swelling with the desire for that ultimate expression of how their lives were joined together.

Cathal's lips brushed across her ear. "Eamon's magic might make it possible to do this standing, but I'd personally prefer the comfort of bed." Husky amusement rather than the growled possessiveness that had sounded the first time she'd teased him with the possibility of this.

"Comfort it is, then," Eamon said, he and Cathal maneuvering Etaín onto the mattress with the physical contact unbroken, each of them with a leg draped over her open thighs, hands roaming, lips alternating the claiming of hers.

Perfect. *Or nearly so,* Eamon thought, disappointment and pain there to dim this celebration of life and love if he allowed it.

He ruthlessly suppressed thoughts of the unhealed, inert tattoos. He'd spoken the truth, lack of a bond through them didn't change what they signified, didn't change the shape of their future.

With each kiss, each swallowed moan he felt the twine of his magic to Etaín's. It was enough. She would always be enough, and Cathal, no longer a complication but a necessary partner.

His hand stroked downward, leaving a tightly furled nipple to rub across her clit, satisfaction surging through him at the instant lift of her hips in a feminine demand to give that pleasure center his attention.

She was wet, always wet for him. For Cathal.

His cock spasmed, liquid arousal escaping, making him laugh softly because she so easily made him ready for her as well.

Her breath came fast as he stroked slick fingers over her clit, took it between his fingers, pumped, and Cathal's hand joined his between her thighs, plunging into her slit before moving to her back entrance, preparing her. Heat and need built until it became impossible to remain separate.

"Now," Cathal said, hand circling his cock, a fist necessary to maintain control, masculine pride nonexistent when it came to Etaín.

A touch of her hand to his chest, a little bit of pressure and he was on his back. His hips lifted and his cock went unerringly to her opening when she straddled him. The hot slide into tight heat accompanied the press of luscious breasts to his chest.

Her mouth covered his. Their tongues twined as fingers interlocked, palm to palm and he didn't fear what she might see with her gift.

Then Eamon was there, and the squeeze of her channel became tighter, pheromones or the brush with death or magic turning the awareness of another man's cock against his, separated only by a thin feminine barrier, into something erotic, compelling, necessary. Natural. And they found their rhythm as if they'd always shared her this way.

There was no holding back. No possibility of it. Desire and need were raging fire and howling storm and crashing ocean. And release was a volcanic eruption, a lava-hot pour of molten semen and the awareness that Eamon spilled himself inside Etaín at the same time.

Rapture came as Eamon did. Physical. Emotional. A soul-deep, irrevocable joining of all that he was to Etaín, and through her, because of her ink, to Cathal.

Ecstasy was the fierce burn of the sun, golden rays piercing him with Etaín's cry of pleasure, pouring the magic of Elfhome and Dragon and this world into him. Magic not constrained by physics, magic demanding closure, completeness, traveling into the tattoos she'd placed on him in a surge of joy and irrevocable joining. The barrier between their minds thinning with the shimmering promise that they'd be able to communicate telepathically in the future.

Tears welled in Etaín's eyes at seeing the spread of color and the healing of Eamon's tats. Emotion pounded into her with the fast beats of their hearts, the touch of skin to skin. Satisfaction. Pleasure. Intimacy. Permanence.

"I love you," she whispered against Cathal's lips and had the words returned to her, repeating it with Eamon after he rolled to his side, freeing her to slide off Cathal.

They sat to view the changes in the tattoos. Purple had been added to the ones she and Cathal wore, as well as to the bands on Eamon's biceps.

"The color of Cathal's aura," Eamon murmured. The glittering green of Dragon scales now manifested in a sinuous line at the center of the design she'd put on him, the other colors were made more vibrant with the bond.

Pleasure suffused her, a bright glow needing expression. Connection. She touched her palms to the ink on masculine skin. "It doesn't get any better than this. The worst is behind us now."

Eamon leaned forward, lips heated velvet against her ear. Tongue a brush of carnal temptation to keep the chill of ominous prediction from settling in. "For the moment, Etaín. For *this* moment. There will be challenges to come. Never doubt it."

*   *   *

Cyco Chalino turned onto the street, the sound of Jacko dying still in his head.

A whole load of motherfuckers were going to die tonight. A gift for Jacko, a tribute.

And when the fire burned out and the building was razed, if Cathal Dunne was still alive, he'd come back and do him. Or he'd have Spooky take care of it.

But tonight, once that *rich pendejo's* fancy-named club was full, he was going to put a hell-HOUND into it. Maybe he'd hit the place with the flash bangs first, for maximum kill.

Oh yeah. He liked that. Or maybe when he got to Spooky's hide-out, they'd decide to send his crew in, two minutes blasting away with the AKs for fun before using the launcher. He laughed imagining it. Loved the message of fear it sent. As long as he was alive, no one was safe. Not here. Not down in Mexico.

The driveway was blocked and only a couple of feet were open along the curve. With a shout he gunned the car he'd replaced the stolen Jag with through the space, doing a tight donut on the dirt-patch and dead-grass front yard.

Beneath the tires, brittle plastic exploded and metal flattened as he took out toys and a bike on its side. He stopped with a slam of brakes.

Inside the house kids went quiet as he passed them. Their mother was smart enough not to ask him what the fuck was going on when he was in a mood like this.

He knocked open the bedroom door with enough force to send it crashing against the wall and bouncing back. He did the same to the closet door, tossing the shit he'd used to cover the grenade launcher onto the floor.

He pulled the case from the shelf above the clothes bar. Motherfucker was heavy.

The weight told him the weapon was there. He knelt, opening the case anyway to make sure, stroking the remaining rounds. Oh yeah, he was going to use them tonight, maybe fire off all of them. In honor of Jacko. Like a fifty-gun salute with more killing power.

There were more rounds where these came from and he was connected to men who could buy and sell the people who'd be dying tonight. Long as drugs were illegal and there were plenty of people wanting them, it was like riding the money train.

Twenty-nine

⟿

Fire summoned Etaín as the three of them stood beneath the shower, a burn of it where the Dragon's name lay camouflaged in the ink on her skin. "Get ready to move," she murmured, closing her eyes and mentally traveling the path of the alliance bond.

Sssoo the Earth-bound Elf is yours as well. Your mother told me it would be so.

Another day perhaps she'd bargain to learn more about her mother, about her birth father, but there was already enough debt between them.

Yesss.

The Dragon moved and a scene unfolded at the edge of the shore, scrolling out in the wake of a ripple to become a pool table with a masculine arm lining up a shot. Movement sent the white cue ball forward to strike the blue-striped ten but it didn't sink into the hole.

Turn lost. Roberto's head lifted, providing Etaín with a panorama of the room.

Anticipated victory rushed into her at seeing his cousin Cyco and four others, at recognizing this place belonging to an uncle. She'd been in this room, played pool on this table. Only once or twice, but she recognized the furniture, the curtains, the old shag carpet. She could find this house.

"Got it," she said, opening her eyes.

They left the shower, drying and dressing quickly.

Liam and Heath and Myk joined them at the sedan, informing them that Cage had taken Derrick and Quinn to his boat.

Myk straddled her Harley, an image straight out of an erotic fantasy with his long dark hair and masculine features. She gave both him and Heath general directions then got in the car.

A couple miles away from their destination she said, "Much closer and someone will tip them off and they might spook. I should get out here."

Heath pulled to the curb. Behind them Myk rolled to a stop. Eamon's hand tangled in her hair, forcing her mouth to his. "Take no foolish chances."

"I doubt I'll have the opportunity." She welcomed his lips and tongue, lost herself in scent and heat and the promise of a future together, doing the same with Cathal before making herself leave the car.

Liam had already disappeared into shadow by the time she took the offered helmet from Myk and put it on.

She straddled the bike then rode around the sedan, the kisses like liquid sunshine in her belly, blending in with adrenaline and a little kick of fear to make getting this handled and behind them urgent.

She took a corner, turning into an alley almost immediately, glad it wasn't cluttered with trashed furniture and bald tires abandoned there. The sedan followed and she felt the spell working like a bubble bursting against her back as the car disappeared from sight in her mirror.

Warmth spread through her in a rush of love. This was Lord Eamon bending, stretching, involving himself in human affairs.

She slowed at the end of the alley, waited for a car to pass in order to allow the sedan to stay right behind her. It was a clear shot to their destination.

She hadn't known the address, but memory got her to the house. A subtle hand signal noted it for Heath though she passed it, doing a U-turn in front of a neighbor's house then another U-turn before stopping, the delay giving the men time to park and leave the car.

She took off the helmet, making a show of shaking out her hair. She kept her face hidden to hinder recognition, bought time by giving the appearance of a woman wanting to look good before going to the front door.

Liam would be inside now, getting the lay of the land, counting, positioning himself to stop hearts if necessary.

That made her own skitter.

She got off the bike and headed toward the front door, a confident amble rather than a hurried approach. The whole point of this was to make it appear as if she went in alone, and make the tip she was a few minutes away from giving Ordoñes hot enough to act on immediately with a fugitive apprehension team.

She had someone's attention, inside the house and from across the street. She felt eyes on her, as well as the unseen caress of a masculine hand along her spine.

A hard knock on the door brought a guy in his early twenties. "Yo, *mamacita*, who you looking for?"

All good humor until she answered "Roberto Jimenez."

"Nobody by that name here."

"Roberto!" she yelled. "Roberto Jimenez."

He stepped out of the room that had the pool table in it. "Let her in, Cricket."

Cricket complied, making a point to look up and down the street before shutting the door.

She walked toward Roberto, experiencing a shimmer of déjà vu with Cricket next to her. It was like stepping back into the dream of the slaughter, the two of them approaching the bar together. There was no mistaking the intangibles that made up a person's presence.

"How'd you know I was here?" Roberto asked when she reached him. The boy she'd known wasn't present in this man's eyes.

"I've been asking around, trying to look up some of the people I used to hang out with. You know Vontae's dead? He was killed in that shooting at the Curs hangout."

"Yeah. I know."

"You have time for a visit?

"Sure."

"Check her for weapons and a wire?" Cricket asked.

"I'll do it." Roberto leaned the pool cue against the wall.

"Without an audience?" She made her voice husky and could have sworn she heard Cathal growl.

"Yeah, why not." A jerk of his head sent Cricket down the hall-way toward the room with the pool table in it. She strained to hear the clack of ball against ball but didn't.

Roberto crowded closer. Like a lover until he grabbed her, slamming her against the wall, hand locked on her throat, gun jammed hard against her chest.

The space around her took on a deadly, waiting quality. The eyes on the palms of her hands blazed, a weapon she didn't want to use if it meant the entirety of his memories would become hers, his life swallowed and made part of hers by a weapon she didn't understand.

"Talk," he said, putting weight behind the gun already digging into her. "Who else knows I'm here?"

Choices spun through her mind like a roulette wheel. An instant when the gun wasn't pointed at her, when the accidental pull of a trigger wouldn't kill her, was all her unseen companions needed.

She spat in Roberto's face.

He reacted with violence, meaning to strike her with the gun but finding his arms held by men who seemed to appear out of nowhere. And then he sagged between Cathal and Heath, forced into sleep by Eamon, the gun dropping to the floor.

"Get it done, Etaín," Eamon said, the heat in his voice and expression in his eyes making it clear she'd failed to follow his take-no-unnecessary-chances edict.

"The others?"

"Myk is capable of making someone lose consciousness. He and Liam have done what was required of them."

"Might as well make this easier for the police," Cathal said. "Let's put this guy in the room with the others."

He and Heath hauled Roberto down the hall, dropping him into a chair. Eamon allowed the air-cradled gun to fall onto the cushion.

"Moment of truth," Etaín said, crouching, pressing her palms to bared skin. "Where is the gun you used to kill Vontae?"

His guilt touched her, the barest flicker of remorse, the hesitation caught in the nightmare. *Where is the gun you used to kill Vontae?*

And she saw it, had felt it pressed below her breast. He hadn't even bothered to get rid of it.

Ballistics could do what her gift couldn't do for the police, provide evidence admissible in a court of law. "Where's the other gun you used at the Cur's hangout? Where are the silencers?"

The answers came easily, including who had accompanied him, though she posed those questions so only a sliver of memory would be lost, and felt satisfied the guilty and their the guns were all here.

"The sedan won't remain hidden for much longer," Eamon warned.

She acknowledged it with a nod, but delayed to ask a final question, because she couldn't leave without knowing. "Why kill so many people? Why did you invade the Cur's handout?" *Why?*

She slid into his memory. Cyco was across the table from him, the two of them eating burgers. "The three Curs die," Cyco said, "it sends a message that the rest of them don't want to be moving stolen weed for the Norteños."

Which three? she asked, delving deeper for the targets, recognizing the men by sight though she didn't know them. And never would. They'd all been at the bar.

Time flowed again. Roberto said, "I got a better idea, let me get a crew together. Let me take a shitload of Curs out."

Cyco laughed and she understood why he'd gotten the street name. "Trying to be like me?"

"Fuck no. I'm my own man." But his desires weren't hidden from her. He wanted what Cyco had, the name, the respect. He wanted to be a legend, like his cousin.

"You hit their hangout, you better make sure you kill Anton Charles and his brother, otherwise shit will go down."

"It'll be a clean sweep. Me and my crew might even top what you did in Mexico."

"Going to take twenty-six bodies then."

"When we get done at the bar, you'll see them bringing out at least that many."

It sickened her, made her burn with the need for justice. Vengeance. Sometimes there was little separating the two.

"Etaín," Eamon said, a warning they needed to leave.

She used her gift like a knife, this time entering Roberto's memories and excising the stretch of them from her arrival until the instant he fell to Eamon's spell. She shivered doing it, remembered Farrell's terror of her, the blanched fear she'd seen on other Elven faces at Aesirs.

When she stood, Eamon indicated Cricket with the flash of his hand. "Remove anything that will identify you."

It bothered her that she felt no guilt doing it. But only because for an instant, she imagined herself back in the captain's office, heard his condemnation, his accusation, calling the use of her gift an assault.

Mental rape. It could be.

The ends justified the means here, though she rubbed damp

palms against her jeans. Felt the fluttering of her heart until Eamon's hand at her back, joined by Cathal's, served as a reminder she wasn't alone in this, that she had two anchors to keep her from becoming a monster.

The inked bond was unique to the *seidic*, Eamon had told her. Maybe this was the reason for it.

L iam moved to where the man named Cyco lay in a half sprawl on the armrest of the couch. A case was open on the cushion next to him, revealing the weapon that might have killed any of their kind other than Heath. And Heath's survival had been made possible by the chance warning of a magical artifact.

Time to test Eamon's intended, to see if she was a Lady he would ultimately give his oath to. The choice was his in a way that didn't exist for most who called Eamon *Lord*.

Liam placed his hand on the human's chest, eyes meeting and holding the *seidic*'s.

Stop.

And the heart obeyed without protest, the exhalation of one final breath marking death.

"You're Lady now," he said in challenge. "Only by your command will I reverse what's done."

T here will be challenges to come. Never doubt it.

Had Eamon known Liam's intent? Guessed what he might do?

She glanced at Eamon and found his expression unreadable, though he said, "This is the price that comes of being involved in human affairs. You'll face it repeatedly if you continue as you have in the past."

"Meaning you're not going to stop me?"

"Oh, I'll try."

Violence led to more violence.

And yet sometimes it ended it.

This was where the captain's justice failed. Jailing men like Cyco didn't eliminate their influence. Wouldn't end the pain and suffering they were responsible for or stop them from creating more of it.

Her eyes met Cathal's in a wordless reliving of the past, the moment she'd stayed his hand because she'd known what killing the Harlequin Rapist would do to him. "Maybe I'm too much like your father and uncle."

He stroked her cheek. "Make your choice. It won't diminish what I feel for you."

"Let the police find him dead then."

"Liam will remain here as a safeguard," Eamon said, and the assassin moved forward, lifting his arm and pulling his shirtsleeve back to reveal a thin braid of gold. Her hair. And she understood how Liam could find her.

"Tricky," Cathal said, admiration in his voice.

A spoken word accompanied by the touch of Eamon's fingertip and the tether between her and the assassin burned in a flash of fire. "Let's go, Etaín."

She made the call to Detective Ordoñes in the alley after surrendering the bike to Myk, Cathal and Eamon at her side as if they couldn't bear the separation.

"You're sure?" Ordoñes asked.

"Positive."

He thanked her and she pocketed the phone. Getting into the car, she said, "If we're going to do much of this, we need some different vehicles. The sedan practically screams Feds!"

"Not happening," Cathal growled.

She laughed at that. "Never say never."

His lips curved as he pressed them to her neck. "I'm still a slow learner when it comes to you."

"You've got hundreds of years now to master the subject," Eamon said, a trickle of amusement in his voice.

Joy was a flower opening up in her chest. "Master the subject? In your dreams."

"Surely a Lord is allowed them." Eamon's mouth brushed her ear. "Home, Myk."

Home. It rang in her soul and heart like the chimes she'd heard before entering Aesirs that first time. Her hands curled around masculine thighs, desire returning, need both tidal wave and raging fire, what she had with Cathal and Eamon, pure magic.

Epilogue

⁓

Niall Dunne felt only a coldness of purpose as the man who'd tried to have his son killed sat down across from him. What was done was done. Rage had no purpose here.

Frederico Perera waved away the menu and ignored the glass of water set in front of him, though he had the look of a man whose fear had left his mouth dry and his bowels loose. And why not? Pressure had been brought to bear and he understood power, and how little of it he held, that he could be forced back to San Francisco before the earth had settled over his son's grave.

Let him fear.

"There are men who would threaten to have done to your daughters what was done to my niece and her friend," Niall said. "I am not that type of man. Nor is my brother. We abhor rapists. This ends now, in a truce. Or your wife becomes a widow and your children fatherless."

Bile rose in Frederico's throat, a festering rage with nowhere to go. No safe target except one. "And the boy who still lives?"

"Would it make your loss more bearable to imagine him in prison? Are you asking that he be spared the death awaiting him behind bars?"

"No."

"Then there is nothing more to discuss. Are we in agreement about a truce?"

"Yes."

Frederico pulled the phone from his pocket. He dialed the number he had been given by the American who'd driven him here, and was not truly surprised to have it answered by Eduardo Faioli.

"You wish something of me?"

"That matter we spoke of earlier. It is no longer something I wish to pursue."

"It has brought trouble into both of our lives."

His bowels became watery. "My apologies. It was not my intent."

He did not dare remind the man he spoke to that he himself had dismissed the Irish as no threat. He did not voice his suspicion, that Eduardo Faioli had already called a halt to further attempts on Cathal Dunne's life.

The silence stretched, a menacing threat that had sweat gathering under his arms. Eduardo Faioli wouldn't hesitate to target wives and daughters and parents should he desire to send a message of his displeasure.

Finally, Eduardo said, "I will stop my efforts on your behalf though they have not led to success. But I have expended political capital. Because of it, your debt to me remains."

"I understand."

He hung up, hand shaking as he returned the phone to his pocket. "It is done," he said, standing, leaving Aesirs, a place he couldn't have otherwise entered.

His bitterness grew in the presence of the dark-suited American who drove him back to the embassy. It was made sharper as he went to his small office to wait until he would leave for the airport and a long commercial flight home rather than the military jet that had brought him here.

He remembered the touch of his lips to his dead son's cold skin, the promise of vengeance he must forsake unless he was willing to get his own hands dirty. Looking down at them, he considered how easy it would become to kill at least one of the Dunnes if they believed the threat was over. He wondered if the sacrifice of his life might be better for Margarita and their daughters, might free them of the threat from Eduardo Faioli.

Or perhaps he could arrange for an assassin, someone who could make it look like an accident or suicide. His pulse quickened, fantasy born in grief but cut short with the sudden awareness that he was not alone.

He turned to find a stranger where it should be impossible for one to be unannounced and unescorted, a dark-skinned man with long braids, his appearance too similar to those who'd been serving at Aesirs to be a coincidence.

If he courted death, it was here in this stranger's eyes. In a voice that calmly said, "The man who holds my oath has some interest in the Dunnes. Remain a threat and there is no place you can go I cannot find you, nor will I wait for you to act first."

ABOUT THE AUTHOR

Jory Strong has been writing since childhood and has never outgrown being a daydreamer. When she's not hunched over her computer, lost in the muse and conjuring up new heroes and heroines, she can usually be found reading, riding horses, or walking dogs.

She has won numerous awards for her writing. She lives in California with her husband and a menagerie of pets. Visit her website at www.jorystrong.com.